PHILIPPA CARR

The Black Swan

Fontana
An Imprint of HarperCollins Publishers

First published in 1990 by Collins

This edition first issued in 1991 by Fontana,
an imprint of HarperCollins Publishers,
77–85 Fulham Palace Road,
Hammersmith, London W6 8JB

9   8   7   6   5   4   3

Photoset in Times Roman at The Spartan Press Ltd,
Lymington, Hampshire
Printed and bound in Great Britain by
HarperCollins Book Manufacturing, Glasgow

CONTENTS

Murder in the Street

We were at breakfast, my stepmother and I, when the letter came. Briggs, the butler, brought it in with the usual ceremony. It lay on the shining silver tray in which Belinda and I used to watch our grotesquely distorted faces leering back at us, while we grew hysterical with laughter.

My stepmother looked at the letter nervously. She was a very nervous woman. It was due I always thought to living with my father, who was rather a terrifying man to some people. I could understand her feelings, although his relationship with me was quite different from that which he had with anyone else.

For a few seconds the letter lay on the table unopened while I waited expectantly.

Celeste, my stepmother, looked at me fearfully. She said: 'It's from Australia.'

I had realized that.

'It looks like Leah's writing.'

I could see that, too.

'I wonder what . . .'

I was very fond of Celeste. She had been a good, kind stepmother to me, but she did exasperate me sometimes.

'Why don't you open it and see?' I suggested.

She picked it up gingerly. Celeste was one of those people who spend their lives in fear that something awful is going to happen. It had on occasions, but that was no reason for living in perpetual fear. She started to read, and as she did so, her face grew pink.

'Tom Marner is dead,' she said.

Tom Marner! The big hearty Australian who years ago had taken over the goldmine from my father, who had come to this very house and carried off Leah, our nurse, and Belinda with her, making it necessary to uncover long-buried secrets which could have remained hidden for ever, and so changed the entire course of our lives. And now Tom Marner was dead.

'What else?' I asked.

'Leah herself is ailing. She is clearly worried about Belinda. If anything should happen to her . . .'

'You mean if she died. Is she going to die, too?'

'She hints that it's possible. There's clearly something wrong with her health. The goldmine has been failing for some years. Tom lost a lot of money bolstering it up. I can see what she wants. She reminds me that I am Belinda's aunt.'

'She wants Belinda to come back here, then?'

'I shall have to speak to your father. Tom Marner had a heart attack. It was sudden. She is a widow now. She thinks the attack was brought on by anxiety.'

'How sad! She was so happy when she married him. I had never seen Leah happy before. And at the same time she was very worried about Belinda . . . and all that. But once it was settled, she was quite different, wasn't she? And now he's dead. Poor Leah!'

'*And* she is ill.'

Celeste picked up the letter and read it out to me:

'"What will happen to Belinda? If I could get her back to England, I'd be so relieved. You see, here there are no relations. You, Mrs Lansdon, are her nearest, I suppose. There is her father, of course . . . but I don't know about him. But you . . . you were always so kind to her . . . to

8

both of the children . . . even before you knew the truth. Belinda is impulsive . . ."'

Celeste stopped reading and looked at me helplessly.

'She will have to come back,' I said.

I felt excited, but I was not sure whether I was pleased or dismayed. Belinda had been so much a part of my childhood and she had had a great influence on my life. She had tormented me persistently, but when she had gone I had missed her very much. But that was more than six years ago . . . nearer seven, I supposed.

'I will speak to your father when he comes home,' said Celeste.

'It was a late sitting last night,' I said. 'He would have stayed at the Greenhams'.'

She nodded. 'Perhaps you could mention it,' she said.

'I will.'

She passed the letter to me and I read it.

What memories it brought back! I could clearly recall dear patient Leah, our good nurse, who had been kind and gentle to me, the outsider, as everyone – except Leah – had thought then, though it had always been obvious that I came second to Belinda with Leah. She could not help her feelings for her own child; and when the truth was revealed that all became clear.

And now there was a possibility that Belinda would return. What was she like now, I wondered? I knew exactly how old she would be because we had been born on the same day. We were now nearly seventeen years old. I had changed a lot since our last meeting. What of Belinda after those years in an Australian mining township? Something told me that whatever way of life had been hers, nothing would change the old Belinda.

During the morning I kept thinking of all that had happened.

Ours was a strange story and difficult to believe unless one knew all the people concerned in it.

Right at the centre of it was the scheming Cornish midwife, who had brought both Belinda and me into the world. Mrs Polhenny, self-righteous and fanatically religious, had had a daughter Leah, and Leah, while working for the family of French émigrés to which Celeste and her brother Jean Pascal belonged, had become pregnant . . . as it turned out later by Jean Pascal. Mrs Polhenny was understandably horrified that, after all her preaching in the neighbourhood, this should happen to her own daughter. So she made a devious plan. There was in the neighbourhood a crazy woman named Jenny Stubbs who had once had a child who had died and ever after Jenny suffered from the delusion of thinking she was about to have another. Mrs Polhenny planned to take Jenny into her home at the time of Leah's confinement and when Leah's child was born pretend that it was Jenny's.

She was greatly aided in this by circumstances. Indeed, she would not have been able to carry it out, nor would it have occurred to her to do so, if the scene had not been set for her.

Meanwhile my mother was about to give birth to me at Cador, the big house of the neighbourhood, and Mrs Polhenny was to act as midwife.

My mother died and, as I was not expected to live, it then occurred to Mrs Polhenny that it would be sensible to put me with Jenny and have Leah's child take my place at Cador, thus giving Leah's daughter opportunities which she would not otherwise have.

This she managed successfully to achieve; and Leah, wanting to be with her child, became nurse to Belinda, while I spent my first years in Jenny Stubbs's cottage.

My sister Rebecca came into the story here. Rebecca

always had a strong feeling for me. She used to say that it was our dead mother guiding her. I do not know about that but I was aware that, from the beginning, there was a strong bond of affection between us, and it was almost as though some strange influence was watching over me, for when Jenny died, Rebecca insisted on bringing me into the Cador nurseries to be brought up there. The circumstances of Jenny's death and the insistence of Rebecca, and the indulgence of her family, made this possible.

Rebecca keeps a diary, as the women of our family often do. It is a tradition. Rebecca says when I am older she will let me read it and I shall understand more fully how this all came about.

What I already knew was that Tom Marner wanted to marry Leah and take her to Australia and, as she could not be parted from her daughter, Belinda, she confessed to what had happened.

What a turmoil that made! Especially to my father and to me. From that time the relationship between us had changed. I had a feeling that he wanted to make up for all the years that he had been unaware that he was my father.

We seemed to have become indispensable to each other. Celeste never showed any resentment towards me and, with a rather sad resignation, she accepted his devotion to me which far exceeded his feelings for her. He had loved my mother singlemindedly and obsessively even though she was long since dead, and he had never recovered from the loss. No one could replace her. Over the years I had come closer than anyone to doing that. I suppose because I was part of her – her daughter and his.

His feelings towards my half-sister Rebecca had mellowed in time, but I was sure that he always remembered that, though she was my mother's daughter, she was not

11

his; and he could not bear the thought of my mother's first marriage. So I was the one he turned to.

He was a forceful man, distinguished in appearance; his entire being emanated power. Ambition had been the driving force of his life. There was a ruthless streak in his nature and a recklessness which at times had led him into dangerous situations. Such men rarely pass through life untouched by scandal. I sometimes wondered whether my mother, if she had lived, would have managed to subdue that side of his nature.

She had been his second wife and he her second husband. Although they had known each other from childhood, circumstances had separated them and then brought them together, idyllically but briefly. He was always deeply regretful for the years they had wasted and that when they found each other there should have been so little time together.

He had married his first wife for a goldmine; he had married my mother for love; and Celeste? I think he had been vainly trying to find consolation, someone to care for him and soothe that aching longing for my mother. Poor Celeste! She had failed to do this. I supposed it would have been small consolation to her to know that nobody could.

But because he had found a daughter, because he had always felt drawn towards her – as he told me afterwards – even when she had appeared to be a waif brought into the house by an eccentric whim of Rebecca's, he had decided that I could become a substitute for my mother; and because I was attracted and fascinated by this powerful man with the unhappy eyes, and because the fact that he was my father never ceased to fill me with wonder, I was only too ready to play my part; and so the strong bond between us was forged.

Once my father said to me: 'I am glad it was you. I could never accept Belinda as mine. I told myself that it was because in the beginning I had believed her coming had been responsible for her mother's death, but it was not that, for I feel very differently towards you. It seems to me that your mother has given you to me . . . to comfort me.'

I missed Belinda very much after she had gone. She had been part of my life, and although she had not always been easy to get along with, I felt a craving for her presence. There was, of course, my dear Rebecca; but soon after those startling revelations, she went off to live in Cornwall as Mrs Pedrek Cartwright. I visited her often and it was always wonderful to be with her. She was only eleven years older than I but she had been as a mother to me ever since she had brought me into the house.

I was not sent away to school. My father did not wish me to go. I had a governess and when I needed higher tuition, Miss Jarrett came. She was a middle-aged, very erudite woman, a little stern, but we worked well together and I do believe that she gave me as good an education as I could have received in any school.

I spent a good deal of time with my father in the London house and in Manorleigh where he had his constituency. Celeste always accompanied us wherever we went, as did Miss Jarrett.

Rebecca was delighted with the way everything had worked out, and but for this feeling between my father and me, she would have taken me to Cornwall to be with her. She often told me how she had promised my mother before I was born that she would always look after me.

'It was almost as though she had a foreknowledge of what was to come,' she said. 'I feel sure she did. Strange things can happen. I told her I would look after you, and I did . . . even when we did not know who you really were. At any time you want me you must come to Cornwall. Just arrive . . . at any moment. But I think your father needs you. I am glad of this love between you two. He is a very sad man at times.'

It was comforting to think that Rebecca would always be there if I needed her.

I had built up new interests. As the daughter of the house I had found greater confidence, something until that time I had lacked. It was probably because of Belinda, who had reminded me so often of my status in the house. No one else ever did – but Belinda had been a force in my life. I often thought nostalgically of her disturbing presence. Perhaps it was because we had grown up together, because we had been bound together by the dark secret of our births, and we had become a part of each other before we had had any say in the matter.

But I had quickly become absorbed in the new relationship with my father. Before, he had been a godlike presence in the house. I had thought he was scarcely aware of us children, although it was true that at times I had caught his eyes on me, and I fancied that if he ever spoke to me – which he did not very often do at that time – his voice was gentle and kindly.

Belinda used to say she hated him. 'It is because he hates me,' she explained. 'I killed my mother by getting born. He thinks it's my fault. I don't remember anything about it.'

Right from the beginning of our new relationship my father used to talk to me about politics. I found it hard to understand at first but gradually I began to get an inkling. I became familiar with names like William Ewart Gladstone, Lord Salisbury, Joseph Chamberlain. Because I wanted to please him, I used to ask Miss Jarrett questions and I learned a good deal from her; and she, being in a political household, as she said, found her interest aroused by what was happening in parliamentary circles.

As I grew older my father used to discuss his work with me; he even read his speeches to me and watched their effect on me. Sometimes I would applaud them, and I even dared to make suggestions. He encouraged this and always listened.

As I emerged into my teens I was able to talk with a certain knowledge and his pleasure in my company was intensified. He would open his heart to me. The man he most looked up to was William Ewart Gladstone, who, according to my father, should have been in power.

The Liberal Party had not been the government since 1886 – which at that time was some four years previously – and then only for a brief spell.

My father had explained this to me then. He said: 'It is the Old Man's obsession with Home Rule for Ireland which is the greatest obstacle. It is not popular in the country. It's splitting the party right down the middle. Joseph Chamberlain and Lord Hartingdon are breaking away. So is John Bright. It is the worst thing for a party when prominent men decide to break away.'

I listened avidly. I had a glimmer of understanding and I remember that night some years ago when he came home dispirited.

'The voting went against the Bill,' he said. 'Three hundred and thirteen for and three hundred and forty-three against; and ninety-three Liberals went into the lobby against the Bill.'

'What does it mean?' I asked him.

'Resignation! Parliament will be dissolved. This will be a defeat for the Party.'

And it was, of course; and Mr Gladstone was no longer Prime Minister. Lord Salisbury had taken his place. That had happened in 1886 when I was beginning to know something of the ways of politicians.

I realized how disappointed my father was because he had never achieved Cabinet rank. There were whispers about him, concerning past scandals, but I could not get anyone to tell me what they were. Rebecca would tell me one day, I was sure, with more details of my mysterious childhood.

My father was not a man to give up easily. He was no longer young, but in politics shrewdness and experience were greater assets than youth.

Mrs Emery, the housekeeper at Manorleigh, once said: 'You're the apple of his eye, Miss Lucie, that's what you are, and what a good thing it is that he is so pleased with you. I feel sorry for Madam, though.'

Poor Celeste! I am afraid I did not think very much about her in those days, and it did not occur to me that I might be usurping the place which she should occupy. She should have been the one he liked to return to, the one he talked to.

Now I knew that she was aware that he would not be pleased at the prospect of Belinda's return and she wanted me to broach the matter to him.

It was the least I could do.

On those evenings when he was late home from the House I made a habit of waiting up for him and, with the connivance of the cook, had a little supper waiting for him in his study. There might be some soup which I would heat up on a little stove, and a leg of chicken or something like that. I had heard that Benjamin Disraeli's wife used to do this for her husband, and I had always thought what a loving gesture it was.

It amused my father very much. He had scolded me at first and said I should not be allowed to stay up so late, but I could see how pleased he was; and I knew how much he looked forward to talking to me about the events of the evening, and we would chat together while he ate.

There was an understanding between us that if he did not arrive by eleven-thirty it meant he would be staying the night at the house of a colleague, Sir John Greenham, who lived in Westminster, not far from the Houses of Parliament.

On the evening of the day when the letter arrived he was late, so I made the usual arrangements to wait in his study for him. He came home about ten o'clock to find me there with his supper.

'I know these are busy days,' I said, 'but I guessed you'd be here some time.'

'There's a lot going on just now.'

'Working up to the next election. Do you think you'll get back?'

'We've a good chance, I think. But it will be some little time before we go to the country.'

'What a pity! But Lord Salisbury does seem to be quite popular.'

'He's a good man. The people don't forget the Jubilee. They seem to give him credit for that. Bread and circuses, you know.'

'I thought it was the Queen they were all admiring. Fifty years on the throne and all that.'

'Yes, the Queen and her Prime Minister with her. Oh, he's quite good, Salisbury. Bringing in free education is a mark in his favour. The Queen likes him, too. He doesn't toady to her as Disraeli did, and she is clever enough to respect him for that, although she loved the flattery Dizzy laid on . . . with a trowel, as he himself admitted.'

'The Queen doesn't have the same admiration for Mr Gladstone.'

'Good Heavens, no. She really has taken against him. Very wilful of Her Majesty. But there it is.'

'But you have high hopes . . . when the election comes.'

'Oh yes. People always want change. Never mind if it is for the better. Though we should be that, of course. But change . . . change . . . they all cry for change.'

He was in a mellow mood and I thought it would be an appropriate moment to introduce the subject of Belinda.

I said: 'By the way, there was a letter from Australia. Tom Marner is dead.'

'Dead!'

'Yes. It was a heart attack. Apparently the mine was not doing so well . . .'

'It has run out, I dare say. It has to be expected. Poor fellow! Who would have thought it?'

'Apparently it was a great shock, and Leah herself is not in the best of health.'

'What's wrong with her?'

'She didn't say. She has hinted at something . . . rather bad. And she has written to Celeste because she is worried about Belinda.'

'I see.' He was staring down at the chicken bones on his plate. 'So . . . she wrote to Celeste.'

'Well, Celeste *is* Belinda's aunt. The letter came this morning.'

'What does she want?'

'She wants Belinda to come back here.'

He did not speak for some time.

I went on: 'I think Celeste feels some responsibility.'

'That girl made trouble,' he replied.

'She was only young.'

'She might have ruined Rebecca's life.'

I was silent.

'I have to admit I was relieved when she went,' he said.

'I know, but . . .'

Silence again.

I went on: 'What will become of her? She will be out there . . . and if there isn't any money and Tom is dead . . . and Leah is so ill . .'

'I suppose you think we should invite her to come back here?'

'A lot of what happened was not her fault.'

'Ask Rebecca if she feels that. That wicked story of hers, pretending that Pedrek had assaulted her, trying to break up everything between them just because she did not want them to marry . . .'

'She thought it was best for Rebecca.'

'She thought it was best for Belinda.'

'Well,' I insisted, 'she was only young then. Only a child. She's older now.'

'And capable of greater mischief.'

'Oh, I dare say she has settled down. From the letters we've had they all seem to be happy out there.'

'Do you want her back?'

I nodded.

'Well, if she did come back we would not have any nonsense.'

'You mean she may come?'

'I expect Celeste feels she must have her, and you want it.' He shrugged his shoulders.

'Oh, I'm glad. I'll tell Celeste. I think she was afraid you might say no.'

'Good Heavens! This is her home.'

'She wouldn't dream of asking anyone you didn't want.'

'No, I suppose she wouldn't. Well, you have decided, have you, you and Celeste between you? So Belinda and Leah had better come here.'

I felt excited. Belinda was coming home!

He looked at me quizzically and said: 'I believe she was not exactly charming towards you.'

'Oh . . . she was Belinda.'

'That is just it – Belinda!' he retorted. 'Well, we shall see. But we shall have no nonsense. If she does not behave well here, she will go.'

'She will be different. She's grown up. She is my age.'

'Ah. The age of great wisdom! By the way, I've asked the

Greenhams for tomorrow night . . . dinner. That will please you, won't it?'

'Of course. I suppose there will be lots of speculation about the next election.'

'That,' he replied, 'is something you can be sure of.'

Then he went on to talk of the recent debate, but I fancied he was still thinking about Belinda.

I was always pleased when the Greenhams visited us or when we went to them – and the main reason was Joel Greenham. Joel and I were very great friends and always had been. He was about twenty-five, and although I was catching up on him now, I must have seemed like a child to him for some time, but he had always been attentive to me even before I entered my teens.

He had all the qualities I admired most in a man. He was not exactly good-looking – his features were too irregular for that – but he had a most charming smile; he had a musical voice to which I loved to listen; he was tall and looked even taller because he was rather slender. He was a Member of Parliament – one of the youngest, I believe – and I heard that in the House he spoke forcefully, with an air of strength; yet there was a certain gentleness about him which was rare in a man and which I found particularly endearing. He had never treated me as anything but an intelligent person. My father was interested in him and often said he had the making of a good politician. He was popular with his constituents, who had elected him with a good majority.

In his turn he had a great admiration for my father. Perhaps that was why my father liked him. One has to be very self-critical not to like people who admire one – and my father was certainly not that. Joel had always been interested in me, and was pleased when I contributed to the conversation and would take up the points I made as though they were well worth considering.

I would sit listening to them as they talked over dinner – my father, Sir John and Joel. Lady Greenham would try to engage me and Celeste in conversation, and I would make a great effort not to be drawn in, so that I could hear the men talk.

My father was always fiercely authoritative, Sir John amused and a little half-hearted. Joel would take up the points made by my father and when he did not agree with them he would put forward his views in what I considered to be a concise and clever way. I could see that my father thought so, too. I enjoyed listening to them; and I loved them both dearly.

It had been a century-old tradition with the Greenhams that there must be one politician in the family. Sir John had held the seat at Marchlands for many years and gave it up when Joel was ready to step into his shoes. Since taking it, Joel had increased the already sizeable majority.

There was an ancestral home at Marchlands in Essex, close to Epping Forest, so not very far from London, which was convenient, but they had the house in Westminster. Although Sir John was no longer an active member of the House, his life had been politics and he spent a great deal of time in London. He said he liked to be under the shadow of Big Ben.

There was another son, Gerald, who was in the Army. I saw him from time to time; he was amusing and charming, but it was Joel whom I loved.

Lady Greenham was one of those women who manage their families with skill and are inclined to hold anything outside family affairs as of no real importance. I fancied she thought that masculine pursuits which aroused such fierce

interest in her menfolk were some game, such as they
had played in their childhood, and she would watch them
with pursed lips and a mildly contemptuous indulgence
that implied she was perfectly agreeable that they should
play their little games, as long as they remembered that
she was the custodian of the family laws laid down for
them.

I looked forward to a little conversation with Joel.
Celeste always put me beside him at table and my father
clearly thought that was a good idea.

In fact, I think there was between him and Celeste – and
perhaps Sir John and Lady Greenham shared in this – a
belief that it might be a good idea, if in due course Joel and I
married and united the two families.

As the daughter of Benedict Lansdon I would be
acceptable to the Greenhams and Joel would be so to my
family. It was a cosy implication, and in the meantime I
continued to enjoy my friendship with Joel.

I think the two families looked forward to being together. Celeste was happy in the company of Lady Greenham. They would talk of matters of which Celeste was very
knowledgeable; and she seemed to find confidence in Lady
Greenham's approval.

Joel was talking of the possibilities of our spending a
week or so at Marchlands when Parliament was in recess. I
looked forward to that. The Greenhams sometimes stayed
with us at Manorleigh, so we saw a good deal of each other
both in London and in the country.

My father was saying something about an African
project and even Lady Greenham paused in her conversation with Celeste to listen.

'It's coming up for discussion,' my father said. 'It seems a
good idea to send out a few members. They'll be chosen
with care from both parties. The government will want an

unbiased view. Well, it is not really a matter of party politics.'

'What part of Africa is this?' asked Sir John.

'Buganda. There has been some trouble since Mwanga took over. When Mutesa was Kabaka things ran more smoothly. With Mwanga it's quite a different case. There were the martyrs, you remember. And now, of course, we are extending our sphere of influence.'

'Were the Germans in on this?' asked Sir John.

'There was the Anglo–German agreement, of course, but this was revoked recently, and that area embracing Buganda is to be under our influence. Hence the interest.'

'Are they going to send some Members of Parliament out there, then?' I asked.

'It's the usual procedure. To spy out the land and see how they are received . . . what impression they get. It's a rich country. We want to make sure that the best is made of it.'

'Who are the martyrs of Buganda?' I wanted to know.

'They were African Roman Catholics,' Joel explained. 'There were twenty-three of them. It happened a few years back, round about 'eighty-seven . . . and a little before that, too. The first mission was accepted by Mutesa. It was when Mwanga came to power that the trouble started. He organized a massacre of missionaries. An English Bishop, James Hannington, with his band of missionaries was murdered. So you see, we have to step in because it looks as though before long Buganda will become a British Protectorate.'

'And when is the jaunt going to take place?' Sir John asked my father.

'Fairly soon, I should think,' he replied. 'It is very important that the right people should go. The situation will require a certain tact.' He was looking at Joel. 'I think it would be very good for one's reputation to be a member of the party.'

'Are you going?' I asked.

He shook his head. 'No, most definitely not. It's a job for younger men. I've got too many irons in the fire here. So have others. It's for a strong and healthy young man. The climate needs a bit of withstanding. It needs a man with a little prestige . . . he'll have something to show his party and the people that he is capable of action.'

'You are looking at me,' said Joel.

'Well, it might be an idea.'

'It sounds exciting,' I said.

'Yes,' replied Joel slowly.

'Well, who knows?' went on my father. 'No one has been chosen yet, but I should say you have a very good chance, Joel . . . with a nod in the right direction.'

'It would be a great experience.'

'As long as you don't get eaten by the cannibals,' put in Lady Greenham. 'I believe they have them in those outlandish places. And there are fevers and all sorts of unpleasant animals.'

Everyone laughed.

'It's true,' added Lady Greenham. 'And I think it's about time to let these natives get on with their killing. Let them kill each other and that will be an end of them.'

'It was an English bishop whom they killed, Lady Greenham,' I said.

'Well, he should have stayed at home in England.'

'My dear,' said Sir John mildly, 'where should we be today if everyone had followed your advice?'

'*We* should be sitting at this table!' she retorted. 'And those who went would be massacred or eaten or die of fever.'

It was always Lady Greenham who had the last word. But I could see that Joel was rather excited by the prospect of going with the mission to Africa.

Then the talk turned to the burning question of the next election and speculation as to when it could be expected to take place. There seemed to be no doubt that Gladstone would be returned to power. The important point was with how big a majority.

Joel and I walked along by the Serpentine. We sometimes rode in Rotten Row while we were in London, but not very often. It was when we were at Marchlands or Manorleigh that we indulged our passion for the horses. But we did enjoy walking in the parks – Green Park, St James's, Hyde Park and Kensington Gardens. One could walk through one to the other and almost feel that one was in the country, only occasionally coming out into the traffic, which was considerably muted when one was under the trees or strolling along the sylvan paths.

We sat by the Serpentine and watched the ducks.

I said to him: 'Do you really think that you will go to Africa?'

'I don't know,' he replied. 'If I were chosen I suppose I would.'

'My father thinks it would be good for your career.'

'He's right. He always is.'

'I imagine he is putting your name forward.'

'His influence could count considerably.'

'Oh, Joel, how exciting it would be for you!'

'H'm. Your father has talked to me about it . . . and other things. He is very anxious that I should make a name in the House. It's absurd that he himself has never had Cabinet rank.'

'There is so much chance in politics. Everything has to be right at a certain moment. Time and place . . . they matter tremendously. Opportunity comes and if a man can't take it

25

he probably won't get another chance . . . and a politician has to wait for his party to be in power.'

'How right you are!'

'I don't know the whole story but I do know he came near to having a high post in the Cabinet. There was even some talk of his following Mr Gladstone as Prime Minister.'

'He might do that yet.'

'Who can say? Life is full of surprises.'

'He's been good to me.'

'I'm glad of that, Joel. I know he's fond of you.'

'And my family are fond of him and Celeste . . . and you.'

'It's a wonderful friendship between the two families.'

'Lucie, you are very young yet.'

'You're not exactly old.'

'I'm twenty-five. It's quite a bit older than you.'

'It seems so at this stage, but when we get older it will seem less so.'

'That's just it. I . . . I think they have plans in mind for us.'

'The families, you mean?'

He nodded. 'They think it would be a good idea if you and I . . . one day . . . when you're older . . . well, if we married.'

'Do you think it would be a good idea?'

'I can't think of anything better. What of you?'

'It seems a good idea to me, too. I'm not seventeen yet, you know.'

'I thought . . . when you were eighteen . . .'

'Is this a sort of proposal? I never thought a proposal would be quite like this.'

'It doesn't matter how it is . . . as long as it is acceptable to both parties.'

'There's one thing, Joel. I haven't lived yet.' That sounded so trite that I began to laugh. But I went on: 'It's true. Have you *lived*, Joel?' He did not speak, so I went on: 'I

26

don't know much about people . . . about men, I mean. It's as though we have been chosen for each other by our families. Is that the best way to choose a wife or a husband?'

'We have known each other for such a long time. There wouldn't be any unpleasant surprises such as come to some people.'

'There wouldn't be *any* surprises, pleasant or unpleasant.'

'Well, I think it's a good idea.'

'So do I,' I said.

He turned to me suddenly and kissed me on the cheek.

'Shall we say we're engaged?'

'Unofficially . . . tentatively. And, Joel, if you fall in love with someone else, you mustn't hesitate to say so.'

'As if I would!'

'You never know. Passion strikes like lightning, so I've heard it said. You never know what direction it's coming from.'

'I know I shall never love anyone as I do you.'

'How can you know yet? You haven't been struck so far. Some exciting female may come along . . . someone you meet for the first time in your life . . . someone mysterious . . . irresistible.'

'You're talking nonsense, Lucie.'

'Do you know, I rather hope I am.'

He took my arm and we snuggled close together.

Then he said: 'We're engaged.'

'Secretly,' I reminded him. 'We don't want the families to start planning yet. I have to grow up a little more and you've got to go to Buganda or whatever it is.'

'If I go . . . when I come back . . .'

'That would be a dramatic moment to announce it. You . . . the hero covered in glory.'

'Oh, Lucie! It's only a little mission. Half a dozen members going out on a fact-finding expedition. There's nothing glorious about it.'   'You'll come back on the way to becoming Prime Minister in the next twenty or thirty years. Prime Ministers are usually rather ancient, aren't they? We'll announce it then. That will be great fun. I know my father will be enormously pleased.'

'I hope he will.'

'You *know* he will. You're his protégé. He likes to watch your progress. I believe he thinks that if he can't be Prime Minister he'll make you one in his place. He'll surely do it for his daughter's husband, so you had better make sure that you marry me.'

'I'm always hoping that I come up to his expectations.'

'In future there will be only one person whose expectations have to concern you . . . and I am to be that one. All the same, I know how you feel about my father. He is a wonderful man and although he and I are the greatest friends, I often feel I don't fully understand him. That makes him exciting.'

'I think he is a wonderful man too,' said Joel.

We walked home rather soberly.

We were engaged. Our marriage was predestined. It would undoubtedly have the approval of the families.

Events were moving along in a very comfortable manner.

There was news from Australia. Leah wrote to Celeste and Belinda to me. The letters arrived at breakfast as usual and Celeste showed me what Leah had written.

It was a very sad letter. She believed she was dying. There was nothing that could be done for her. She was very frail and weak now, too much so to be able to undertake a long voyage.

28

Celeste's letter had given her great comfort and she had made all the arrangements. She was greately relieved to know that when she had gone there would be a home for Belinda in England, and was glad that God had given her a little time to arrange this and had not struck her down too suddenly.

The last years of her life had been the happiest she had ever known. Tom had been good to her and to Belinda and they had had a wonderful life together. Although he had lost the bulk of his fortune he had been able to leave them a little money. That would go to Belinda, so she would not be penniless.

'It is just that I want her to have a home,' she wrote. 'And I am happy now that I know she can come back to that of her childhood. Life has been strange for me. I suppose it is, when one does unconventional things. But now that I know she can come I feel at peace.'

There were tears in Celeste's eyes when she read this letter.

'I am so pleased that Benedict agreed to her coming,' she said. 'Poor Leah. She was always such a good soul. What a pity she could not have gone on being happy for longer.'

Belinda's letter brought memories of her back to me.

> Dear Lucie, [she wrote],
> I know my mother has written to you and that she is very ill. In time I am to come to England. I remember so much of my life there . . . and particularly you. Do you remember me?

Oh yes, Belinda, I thought, I shall never forget you.

> The terrible things I used to do! I wonder you didn't hate me. I believe you did sometimes . . but not really, Lucie. We were like sisters in a way,

weren't we? I remember so much. The time I dressed up in your mother's clothes and pretended I'd come back from the grave. I really frightened you as well as Celeste. But don't hold it against me. I may not be entirely a reformed character now, but at least I am now old enough not to do such senseless things.

I'm very sad about my mother. It was awful when Tom died. It was so sudden. He was well and then he had this heart attack. It was hard to believe . . . and then he wasn't there any more.

That was when everything changed here and my mother became ill. She is really very ill. I feel a little scared. I'm here in this country and somehow I feel I don't belong here . . . not without Tom and my mother. I really feel I belong at Manorleigh and in London . . . with you, Lucie. I wonder if I shall see you soon. I know it is what I want more than anything . . . if I lose my mother.

With my love and memories,
Belinda.

Memories indeed. I could see her in my mother's clothes which she had taken from the locked room, sitting on the haunted seat in the garden where ghosts had been said to gather long ago. I saw her, too, swearing that Pedrek Cartwright had attempted to molest her when she did not want him to marry Rebecca. I could see her when we were very young, dancing round me with a lighted candle in her hand, which suddenly sent the flames running up my dress. I could see Jenny Stubbs, who had loved me better than her own life, dashing to me, smothering the flames with her own body . . . giving her life that mine might be preserved.

Yes, Belinda, I thought, you have brought back memories to me.

I talked of Belinda to Celeste and to my father.

'Poor, poor Leah,' said Celeste. 'I wonder if there is any hope of her recovering. She does not say what is wrong.'

'No. But she is too ill to travel. I am sure that if she were well enough she would bring Belinda to us.'

'All we can do,' said my father, 'is to wait and see what happens. In any case we have offered her a home here. It is all we can do.'

So it was left at that.

Soon after that there was talk of an election and that, as usual, dominated everything else.

The mission to Buganda would naturally have to be postponed until after we knew what government would be in power.

'I have to make sure that I hold my seat before it is decided whether I shall be a member of the mission,' said Joel.

'Of course you'll hold your seat,' I replied. 'It's a tradition that a Greenham shall represent Marchlands.'

'One can never be entirely sure.'

The excitement was growing. It was nearly six years since the last election. I was an adult now with a keen interest and some understanding of what was going on.

We studied the papers every day. Gladstone's age was often referred to. The man was undoubtedly grand but was he too old? He seemed vigorous enough in mind even if he was rather bent and walked with a stick.

'And it's the mind that counts,' said my father.

The Queen's comment to her secretary was reported. 'The idea of a deluded, excited man of eighty-two trying to

govern England and my vast Empire, with miserable demo-
crats under him, is quite ridiculous. It is like a bad joke.'

'Unfortunate,' said my father. 'First that she said it, and
secondly that it was allowed to leak out.'

'But it is the people who choose the government, not the
Queen,' I added.

'For which we have to be thankful,' he added wryly.

Soon the action started. The Greenhams went down to
Marchlands and we to Manorleigh. The campaign had
begun in earnest.

Celeste and I sat on platforms with my father. It created a
pleasant family atmosphere which the people liked their
member to have. We played our small parts, riding round
the country in our dogcart – for Manorleigh was a straggling
constituency and contained many outlying villages – and
telling people why they should vote for Benedict Lansdon.

My father was a dynamic speaker. He could hold an
audience, in vast assembly rooms or village halls, absolutely
spellbound. Listening to him, one realized the power of
words and the gift of using them which was surely essential to
a man who wanted to rise in politics. My father had all the
assets except one: prudence. Instead he had a rashness
which had tripped him up once or twice and which was the
reason why people were not looking to him to follow
Gladstone.

He did spare time from his busy campaign to go down to
Marchlands to speak for Joel.

I was surprised really, because although he was certain
that he would retain his own seat, he had always said that no
prospective candidate should relax even for a short time.

But he had a special feeling for Joel; and I believed I knew
why. It was because of me. He had made up his mind that I
was going to marry Joel and I had a fancy that he wanted to
mould Joel into his *alter ego*. Joel was going to catch all the

plums which had failed to fall into his own hands, and he was going to enjoy the act of putting them there. He wanted to see Joel as his creation. It was a passing thought, but men such as my father must have power. Perhaps he saw that certain events in his life had prevented him from snatching the top prize and that irked him.

I was nearer to him than any living person and I believed he was planning to marry me to a man made in his image. I had heard stories of his grandfather – Uncle Peter, as everyone in the family called him. He had made his daughter's husband into a politician because he himself had failed to achieve his ambition – through scandal again. I had heard it said that Benedict was very like his grandfather.

When I heard my father speaking and holding an audience, I felt contented and happy. He would always be there to look after us, Joel and me. Joel already admired him almost to idolatry, and he was my beloved father.

So we went to Marchlands and stayed one night only before we went back to Manorleigh. I always enjoyed being at Marchlands and since my conversation with Joel it had become even more exciting to me, for when I married Joel this would be my home.

It was a wonderful old house with a battlemented tower which gave it the appearance of a castle. Its grey stone and the fact that it was built on a slight incline gave it a proud and dominating look. The countryside around it was beautiful – wooded hills and meadows and a delightful little village close by with a Norman church and a pond on a green.

It had been the Greenham home for centuries.

We sat in the village hall and listened to my father using all his persuasive and dynamic powers. They seemed overwhelming in such a setting and the applause was vociferous. Joel spoke well – less flamboyantly than my father but he had a quiet confidence which was convincing.

It was a successful evening and walking back to the house I thought how romantic it looked by starlight.

I felt very happy and contented.

When the election was over it was almost certain that Joel would go to Buganda . . . perhaps for a few months; and when he came back we should announce our engagement.

Afterwards I often remembered that night and I never ceased to marvel how speedily – in the space of a few seconds – change could come.

I remember sitting in the cosy little room which led off from the great hall and how delicious the hot soup and sandwiches which had been prepared for us tasted.

'This reminds me of Lucie's little suppers,' said my father. 'Do you know, this daughter of mine waits up for me when I'm late at the House with a delicious supper.'

'Shades of that excellent lady, Mrs Disraeli,' said Sir John. 'You're a lucky fellow, Benedict.'

'I know.' He was smiling at Joel. 'Lucie knows how to treat a jaded politician. One never wants to go straight to bed after an exciting debate. One wants to talk. So . . . I talk to Lucie.'

'Lucie is wonderful,' said Joel.

Our elders exchanged conspiratorial smiles which betrayed the fact that they were making plans together for us.

'Buganda is almost certain,' said Sir John.

'If I get in,' added Joel.

'My dear boy,' said my father, 'you don't think you are going to break the tradition, do you? There's been a Greenham in Parliament for the last two hundred years.'

'Well, it doesn't do to count one's chickens before they're hatched.'

'No need to worry about those chickens, son,' said Sir John.

'I think we're safe enough,' put in my father. 'Of course there's a feeling for change in the air. A lot of foolish people talk of change. They like it for its own sake . . . never mind if that change is for the better. It's just a matter of change for the sake of change.'

'Well, we shall have to wait and see,' said Lady Greenham. 'Some people might want a change but I cannot believe our tenants and the people here would be so foolish.'

Nor could any of us visualize Joel's not holding his seat.

There came the thrill of Election Day. We were gathered in the town hall at Manorleigh to hear the result. It was as we had expected – a decisive victory for my father.

That night a messenger came over from Manorleigh with the news that Joel had sailed safely through, his majority intact.

Alas, the party did not fare so well. Gladstone had his majority but it was a small one and that meant that the future did not look so promising.

He went down to Osborne in the Isle of Wight to kiss the Queen's hand, at which she showed no great pleasure. So there was the Grand Old Man ready to take office once more, and if his health was feeble, his convictions were as strong as ever. So the Liberals were in power, in spite of an election victory with such a slender majority, which meant that the reforms they wanted to get through would stand a good chance of being thrown out by the Opposition. It boded ill for the length of the Parliament. It was a Pyrrhic victory.

The government staggered along and, perhaps because of its difficulties, almost a year elapsed before the question of the mission to Buganda was raised.

It was late August, which was a year since Mr Gladstone had gone to Osborne to kiss the Queen's hand when the mission was ready to depart, and Joel was one of the chosen six.

Two days before his departure, my father gave a dinner party so that all friends and well-wishers could say goodbye to Joel.

It was a wonderful evening, although there was some depression among members of the government, for they were wondering how long they could totter on; but it was a triumph for Joel, as one of the younger members of the House to have been selected for this important mission.

After the men had left their port and joined the ladies in the drawing-room, Joel and I sat together.

'Everything is going well,' he said. 'I don't know how long I shall be away. Not more than two months, I imagine, and then . . .'

'I don't think they will be very surprised,' I said.

'Isn't it comforting that we shall be doing what they all want?'

'Oh yes. It is nice to please people.'

'Though,' added Joel, 'I want you to know, Lucie, that if we had had to face opposition – even from your father – it would have made no difference.'

'I'm glad of that,' I replied. 'Yes, I am so glad.'

My father came over to us. 'You sound very vehement,' he said. 'May I ask what you are so glad about?'

I hesitated.

'Secrets?' he asked.

I looked at Joel and I knew he understood what I was asking. Tacit agreement passed between us.

I said: 'When Joel comes back from Buganda we thought about becoming engaged.'

My father's pleasure was apparent.

'That,' he said, 'seems to me an excellent idea.'

'We had already fixed it and were saying how pleased we were because we knew it was what you all wanted.'

'So that is what you were so firmly glad about. How right you are. It is what we have always had in mind for you both.'

'It's a secret at the moment,' I said. 'Between just the three of us. We want to wait until Joel comes back from Buganda.'

'Wonderful timing!' He was beaming at us. I had rarely seen him so pleased.

I was glad afterwards that we had told him that night.

My father, Celeste and I went to Southampton to see Joel off. There was quite a celebration. The press was present to report the departure of the Members of Parliament, and to give their views on the Buganda project with some enthusiasm.

My father said a few words to them and we went on board and drank champagne before the vessel sailed.

'This will be the making of Joel,' he said as we travelled back to London. 'He is very young and to be chosen for such a mission is an honour. I do wish our hold on the government was a bit more firm. Salisbury is determined to get us out and with our tiny majority how can we stop him? We're powerless to do so.'

It was very shortly afterwards when Mr Gladstone introduced his Home Rule Bill for Ireland. My father was very preoccupied. He told me during one of our sessions that he was convinced the Irish question would destroy Gladstone and put the party out of office.

He was becoming increasingly aware that he was in something of a dilemma, which was unusual for him. Generally he was so certain that he was right. He at length admitted to me that he was not at all sure that Gladstone's solution was the right one.

He was torn with doubts. He felt the government was going in the wrong direction and could not last much longer. His own hopes of Cabinet rank were slipping farther and farther away from him. He was a man who, once he had determined to achieve something, could not lightly give up.

I began to realize that during that time he was trying to come to a decision.

He admitted to me on one occasion that he shared the view of the Opposition on the Bill. What if he went against his leader? What would his hopes be for further advancement in the party then? Did he owe his loyalty to his leader or to his conscience?

Could he give his support to something he did not believe in? On the other hand, could he be disloyal to the party?

We talked about it endlessly. His opinion swayed. He was, after all, a very ambitious man; and he was no longer young. He could not change sides now. There was something suspect about a man who changed sides. People usually said it was done to gain advantages.

But he did feel strongly about the Irish question.

'You see,' he said to me, 'the PM is growing old . . . many say too old. He had great flair in his heyday. I'd say he was one of the greatest politicians this country has ever known; but he gets obsessions. After all, there were those years when he embarked on his crusade to save the women of the streets.'

I knew of this. I had heard it discussed how Mr Gladstone would go out late at night and stroll about round Piccadilly and Soho, those areas which were the stamping grounds of the prostitute population. When he was accosted – as any man who showed an inclination to loiter would be – he would question the young woman, making sure not to adopt a moral tone, offer sympathy and invite her to his house. The women who went with him must have been amazed to find a genteel Mrs Gladstone waiting to offer supper and good advice, joining with her husband in the attempt to set them on the road to a more virtuous way of life.

This he had done over forty years – whenever possible dedicating one night a week to his self-appointed task.

'Of course, he has always been different from other men,' said my father. 'He is way above most. He has an idea and he clings to it. It never occurs to him that he may be doing harm to himself. He must follow what he believes to be right. And just as he had his crusade to rescue women of the streets, now he is determined to give Ireland Home Rule. Trafficking with fallen women might easily have ruined his career. In fact certain rumours regarding his intentions were inevitable, but he shrugged all that aside. He had a mission and he was determined to carry it out. You see, in some ways, he is far from being a normal man.'

'He believes firmly in Home Rule for Ireland,' I said, 'just as you are beginning to feel it is not the answer. His obsession with it could bring him down. Yet he will not hesitate.'

'I fear there may be civil war. He forgets that there are many in Northern Ireland particularly who do not want Home Rule. He will destroy himself if he continues.'

I said: 'He is something of a saint. He must do what he feels right whatever the consequences to himself.'

My father was increasingly becoming aware that he could not go along with Gladstone this time; and at length he came to his decision – and it was to prove fatal to him.

His conscience won.

His first step was to speak at a meeting declaring his opposition to the Bill. It was reported in all the papers, as his speeches usually were. He had always been a powerful and witty speaker; he had great charisma; he was the kind of man who drew attention to himself. There was his somewhat shady past and the fact that he had missed a brilliant opportunity because of it that made him a focus of attention; and, moreover, he was always eminently quotable.

The morning after he had made his speech, his name was well to the fore.

LANSDON OPPOSES BILL. GLADSTONE'S HENCHMAN MAKES A RIGHT TURN. CONSERVATIVES JUBILANT.

I went to his study where he was reading the papers.

'So you have done it,' I said.

'I believe it was right to do it,' he said. He seemed relieved.

It was a tense and exciting time. We followed the progress of the Bill through the House. It passed in all its stages – though, my father pointed out to me, with minute majorities.

Then . . . it was rejected by the Lords.

The thick black headlines stared at us from all the papers.

They were all about the Bill and Gladstone's defeat. In several columns the view was stressed that it was my father's outspoken opposition to it which had done a great deal to bring it to defeat.

The tension increased. My father admitted to me that he had lost all chances of Cabinet rank.

Gladstone was bitter. He wanted to call an election

and go to the polls on a slogan: 'The Country versus the Lords.'

'The Old Man doesn't realize that the country is heartily tired of the subject. He thinks everyone is as engrossed in the Irish question as he is.'

'And how is he feeling about you?' I asked.

'Oh . . . he's bitterly disappointed in me. Hurt, too. I wish I could make him understand. He really is looking very old and tired these days.'

'What are you going to do?'

He looked at me and shrugged his shoulders. It was one of the few times I had seen him uncertain.

Then he said: 'For now . . . carry on. Disagreeing with the PM doesn't mean I'm not still member for Manorleigh.'

'Shall you give up politics in time?'

'Indeed not! Accept defeat? Certainly not, and I shall not hesitate to voice my opinions.'

'Well, isn't that what all members should do?'

'They should, but sometimes one's views do not always coincide with those of the party. Then one has to make a choice.'

'As you have done.'

I felt I wanted to be with him at this time . . . always ready if he wanted to talk to me; and he did talk to me, more freely than ever. It was not only politics that we were discussing.

So we came to that particular evening when I was waiting for him to return from the House.

As usual, I had prepared the supper in his study. I had the soup waiting to be heated up on the little stove, some cold chicken and home made crusty bread.

The time was getting on. It was almost ten o'clock. I wondered what was happening in the House. I fancied some of his fellow members were not very pleased with

41

him. But he had done right, I assured myself. People must act according to what they believed even if by doing so they went against the policy of the party. Parliament was the place for discussion. That must be understood.

I tried to settle down to read. I started to think about Joel and wondered what he would be doing at this moment. How long would the mission take? At least six weeks after he arrived. It would be some time before he came home.

The time passed slowly. It was nearly eleven o'clock. Sometimes the House would go on sitting into the early hours of the morning. If he did not come by eleven-thirty I would go to bed. It was the rule. If he were as late as that he would stay at the Greenhams', according to the custom. But there was still a little time to go.

I went to the window and looked out. There was a high wind which had taken most of the leaves off the trees; some lay on the pavement on the opposite side of the road. They came from the trees in the garden which was for the use of residents in the square.

I noticed a man standing by the railings of the gardens. He was dressed in a cape and an opera hat. He took a few paces to the right, then he turned and walked a few more in the opposite direction. Afterwards he stopped and stood still looking along the road.

I could see him quite clearly for there was a street lamp close by. And as I stood there I heard a cab coming along the road.

This must be my father, I thought. I looked down, expecting it to slow down and my father alight; but it went straight past the house.

Disappointed, I stood there; then I noticed that the man had come to the edge of the pavement, his hand in his pocket; he was staring after the cab, and oddly enough I seemed to sense an exasperated frustration –which

42

suggested that he, too, might have been disappointed that the cab had gone by.

While I was thinking how strange it was and wondering what he could be waiting for, there was a gust of wind which lifted his hat and sent it rolling along the pavement under the street lamp.

For a few seconds I looked straight into his face. I noticed at once that his dark hair grew rather low on his forehead into what I had heard called a widow's peak; and there was a white mark on his left cheek which looked like a scar.

Then he was running along the pavement to retrieve his hat. This he did and slammed it back on his head.

I had become quite interested in him by this time and was wondering whether he intended to wait there the whole night. He must be waiting for someone. I wondered who.

I went back to my book and attemped to read for just a little longer. I was soon yawning. My father would not come now. Obviously he had gone to the Greenhams'. It must have been a very late sitting.

I went back to my bedroom, but before retiring for the night I went to the window to look out on the square.

The man had gone.

At above eleven o'clock next morning my father came home.

'It was a very late night sitting,' I said.

'Yes, it went on until one.'

'How are the Greenhams?'

'Delighted about Joel. They can't talk of anything else.'

'Can you guess how long it will be before he comes home?'

'I imagine it will be quite six weeks out there and then of course there is the journey to and from. I must say it is very convenient to have their hospitality. Their place is only five minutes' walk from the House, and there's always someone to let me in and the room is kept ready. I think Sir John likes to hear all that went on the previous night. He's always wanting a good chat in the morning.'

'I suppose Bates could bring you home.'

Bates was the coachman who drove him to the House, but he always came home by cab because of the uncertainty of the time.

'It would be impossible,' he said now. 'He might be there all night. No. This is an excellent arrangement. I'm lucky to have friends so near. It's become a custom. I think they'd be hurt if I didn't make use of it.'

'Will you be going to the House this afternoon?'

'Oh yes.'

'Another late sitting?'

'Who knows? But I expect everyone will be a little weary after last night. There's a great deal going on, though. I don't think the government can last. Salisbury is eagerly waiting in the wings, and this defeat from the Lords over the Bill . . .'

I said nothing. I did not want to stress his part in the defeat.

He was ready to leave in mid-afternoon.

'I can't believe it will be another late night,' he said, 'but have my supper waiting just in case.'

'I will,' I promised.

In the hall I helped him into his coat and put the white silk scarf about his neck.

'You need that,' I said. 'This horrible wind cuts right through you.'

He smiled indulgently at me, pretending to laugh at my coddling; but I knew he liked it.

Bates, the coachman, had brought the carriage round

from the mews and was waiting for him; the horse was pawing the ground impatiently.

I went down the four steps with him to the carriage door; he turned to me to smile as he prepared to get in. Then it happened. I heard the loud explosion. I saw the look of surprise on my father's face. The blood was spurting over his coat, staining the white silk scarf which I had just a few moments before put round his neck.

Then I saw the man standing there . . . the gun in his hand.

My father swayed towards me. I put out my hands and held him as slowly he slipped to the ground.

I knelt beside him and looked about me helplessly. I was stunned.

Briefly I saw the man, then I knew that although he was dressed differently, he was the one I had seen last night, waiting. He had changed his opera cloak and hat for a cloth cap which was pulled down over his eyes. For a second we looked fully at each other. I could not see the widow's peak, but I did recognize the scar on his left cheek; and instinctively I knew that he was the man who had stood on the other side of the road and that last night he had been waiting for my father so that he might do then what he had done today.

He had turned away and made off.

People were shouting. They were all round us. Bates was kneeling by my father and servants were dashing out of the house.

It was like a nightmare . . . fearfully real. A terrible fear had come over me. I might never wait for him to come home to a late supper . . . never again talk to him of his ambitions.

I had never known such desolation.

*

45

My memories of that time come back to me like a series of bad dreams – overshadowed by a terrible sense of loss. I found myself trying to cling to the past, telling myself that it had not really happened. But it had.

Celeste was beside me. She clung to me. She was as dazed as I was.

They had taken him to the hospital. Celeste and I went with him. We sat side by side, holding hands, waiting.

I think I knew from the start that there was no hope. He had been shot through the heart and was dead by the time they got him to the hospital.

Celeste, I am sure, found a grain of comfort in looking after me. I had been there at the vital moment, I had seen it happen. Small wonder that I was in a state of shock.

I was taken back to the house. There was a hushed atmosphere there. It did not seem like the same house. The servants were silent. There was tension everywhere.

I was given something to drink and made to lie on my bed; and after a while I slipped into blessed oblivion.

But soon I was awake again. My respite was brief; and the nightmare continued.

I soon realized that I was to play an important part in the drama, for I was the one who had been with my father when it happened. I was the one the police wanted to talk to.

I soon found myself in their company. They asked questions which I tried to answer. The conversation kept going round and round in my head.

'Did you see the man with the gun?'

'Yes. I saw him.'

'Would you recognize him again?'

'Yes.'

'You seem certain.'

'I saw him the night before.'

They were alert. I had said something of the utmost importance and I had to explain.

'I was waiting for my father's return from the House of Commons. When he was late home I kept a little supper for him in his study. It was a custom between us. While I was waiting for him I looked out of the window and saw a man. He was waiting on the other side of the road by the railings of the garden. He looked as if he were waiting for someone.'

'What was he like? Was he tall?'

'Of medium height. His hat blew off. There was a strong wind. I saw him clearly under the lamplight. He had dark hair which grew to a peak in the middle of his forehead. And there was a white scar on his left cheek.'

They were very excited now. They looked at me in wonder and then exchanged glances. One of them, the Inspector, I think, nodded his head slowly.

'This is excellent,' he said. 'And you saw the same man when the shooting took place?'

'Yes, but he was wearing a cloth cap pulled down over his face. I did not see his hair, but I saw the scar. And I knew he was the one who had waited last night.'

'Very good. Thank you, Miss Lansdon.'

There were headlines in the papers.

BENEDICT LANSDON ASSASSINATED.

Benedict Lansdon was shot dead outside his home today. His daughter, Miss Lucie Lansdon, was at his side.

The newsboys were shouting in the streets. All London was talking of the death of Benedict Lansdon who had so recently been making the headlines with his opposition to Gladstone's Home Rule Bill.

Late in the afternoon of the second day, my half-sister Rebecca arrived from Cornwall. The very sight of her lifted

47

my spirits a little, and I remembered how in my childhood I had always gone to her for comfort.

She came to my room and we clung together.

'My poor, poor Lucie,' she said. 'This is terrible. And you were with him at the time. What does it mean? Who could have done this?'

I shook my head. 'The police have been here. There have been a lot of questions. Celeste didn't want me to see them but they insisted.'

'They are hinting that this is something to do with his opposition to the Irish Bill.'

I nodded. 'They are saying that the Bill failed to get through the Lords because of my father's speaking out against it. And, of course, he was one of those who voted against it.'

'Surely that could not be a reason for murder!'

'I don't know. It's probably some wild conjecture. The press have brought it up to make it more sensational. There is a mention of the Phoenix Park murders.'

'That was years ago.'

'About ten. And then Lord Frederick Cavendish and his Undersecretary were shot . . . just as my father was.'

She nodded.

'So it seems possible,' I said. 'Who else would do it?'

'Perhaps someone he knew long ago. Perhaps it was some personal feud. Did you know of anything? I suppose a man such as he was might have enemies.'

'I don't know, but I expect the police will find out.'

'Lucie, you must come back with me to Cornwall.'

'I couldn't go yet, Rebecca. I have to wait here for a while. The fact that I was with him when it happened . . . they co me here and ask me questions. There will be an inquest and after that . . . what do you think will happen? Will they catch this man?'

She lifted her shoulders.

'I saw him, you see,' I went on. 'I saw him clearly.'

I told her about the man who had waited by the railings the night before the shooting, and how I had seen him next day kill my father.

She was astonished. 'He would obviously have done it the night before, if your father had come home. Can you be sure it was the same man?'

'Absolutely. He had such distinguishing features. Moreover, there was something about him . . . something I can't describe . . . something purposeful.'

'You have told the police this?'

'Yes, and they are very excited about it.'

'Do you think it could be that this man is known to them?'

'I hadn't thought of that. But I see that it could be. Oh, Rebecca, it was so good of you to come. I feel better now that you are here.'

'I know,' she said gently.

'Will you stay?'

'I shall until after the funeral. Then I shall take you back with me.'

'I suppose there has to be an inquest.'

'Certainly there will be. I'll stay till it's all over and then you can come back with me to Cornwall.'

'What of Celeste? I feel I should be with her.'

'She could come, too. You will both want to get away from this house for a while.'

'There will be changes everywhere,' I said. 'I suppose we shall have to think of what we are going to do. At the moment I can think of nothing but his standing there. He looked surprised. I suppose it was less than a second but it seemed longer and there was my father . . . staggering, covered in blood. Oh, Rebecca, it was terrible.'

She put her arms about me and held me tightly.

'You must try to put that out of your mind. It's over and there is nothing we can do about it. We've got to think of the future.'

'Yes. But later . . .'

'The children would love to have you with us,' said Rebecca. 'And so would Pedrek.'

I nodded. I always enjoyed my visits to Rebecca. They were such a happy family. She had two lovely children, Alvina who was about six and Jake aged four. I found them interesting and amusing; I loved the sea and the moors and the air of remoteness; but all the time I was there I used to think of my father who, I knew, would be growing more and more restive, as he always was when I was away. So I had not been with Rebecca as much as I should have liked to be because of my father's reluctance to let me go.

I could hear his voice coming to me now. 'Going to Cornwall?'

'It's some time since I've been.'

'Well, how long will you be away?'

'At least a month. It wouldn't be worth while going for less.'

'A whole month!'

I knew that all my life I would be remembering such conversations and with them would come the heartbreak, the reminder that he had gone forever . . . killed by a man who did not even know him.

Rebecca knew well the state of affairs and she had never persuaded me to stay on, though she always hinted that she would be delighted if I did. There had always been something motherly about Rebecca as far as I was concerned. I had even seen it in her attitude towards my father. She had understood him as few people did, and that understanding had made her tender towards him.

London was obsessed by the news of my father's assassination. It was not only the papers which were full of it. People strolled past the house, looking up at it and whispering. We could not help seeing them from the windows. I often found myself looking out at the pavement where my father had lain covered in blood, and across the road by the railings where that man had waited for him. If only I had known and been able to warn him.

There was the inquest – a painful ordeal which I had to attend. All interest was focused on me, for it was my evidence which was of the greatest importance. I had been there. I had had a good view of the assassin whom I recognized as the man who had waited for my father on the previous night.

The verdict of the inquest was 'murder by some person or persons unknown'.

My name was blazoned across the papers. *Miss Lucie Lansdon, eighteen-year-old daughter of Benedict Lansdon.*

'He doted on her,' said Emily Sorrel, parlourmaid.

'She was the apple of his eye,' said the housekeeper. 'I never knew a father more devoted to his daughter,' the butler told our reporter. It came out about the little suppers I had waiting for him. *Miss Lucie Lansdon was with her father in his dying moments.*

Celeste said the papers should be kept from me, but I wanted to know.

The day after the inquest Inspector Gregory came to see me. He was a big man with piercing blue eyes, a stern profile but a kindly manner; and he was very gentle towards me.

He said: 'I shall be frank with you, Miss Lansdon. Your evidence has been of the greatest help to us. You gave us an accurate description of a man we want to interview and we believe we know who he is. He is Irish, a fanatical 'campaigner for Home Rule who has been under suspicion more than once. There seems an indication that your father's death might have been brought about because of his opposition to the Home Rule Bill. The man we suspect has been involved in other outrages of this nature. We have wanted to interview him for some time. This has given us the chance to get him. We would have something concrete to bring against him. As a matter of fact, we are detaining a man at the moment. I want you to come along and identify him. He will be with others. I want you to pick him out and if he is the man who shot your father we shall then have our man.'

'So . . . you have caught him, then?'

'We are not sure. Of course, we are hoping he is our man. What we need is an assurance that he is. You were a witness of the murder and you saw this man quite clearly the night before. So we want you to tell us if the man we show you is the same one you saw with the gun in his hand the night before from your window. You will just have to pick him out of a group. It is very simple. I know it will be something of an ordeal for you, but it will be quickly over. I can tell you it will be a great relief to us and all law-abiding people if we can have this man in custody. We want to prevent him from committing more crimes like this one.'

'When do you wish me to come?'

'Tomorrow morning. We will send a carriage for you at ten-thirty.'

'I will be ready.'

He touched my hand lightly. 'Thank you, Miss Lansdon,' he said.

When he had gone, I kept thinking about the man and I wondered how he could have shot cold-bloodedly a fellow human being whom he did not know. He could not have paused to think of the misery he might be causing to a number of people. The opinion seemed to be that he did it to serve a cause. What causes were worth human lives and all the misery such crimes like this one could bring about?

I slept little that night. Once I got out of bed and went to the window. I looked out on the deserted street where the light from the lamp shone on the damp pavement. I was shivering, half expecting to see that man there.

The next morning the carriage arrived.

I was taken into a room where Inspector Gregory was waiting for me.

'Thank you for coming, Miss Lansdon,' he said. 'It's just along here.'

He took me into a room where eight men were standing in a line.

'Just walk along and see if our man is among the others,' murmured the Inspector.

I approached the line. Some were tall, some short, some of medium height, dark and fair. I walked slowly along.

He was there – the fifth. I knew him at once. He had attempted to disguise the peak of hair by shaving it but by looking intently I could see its outline; and there was a faint white scar on his left cheek, which I could see he had attempted to conceal by some colouring matter. There was not a doubt in my mind as I went back to the Inspector.

'He is there,' I said. 'The fifth in the line. I could see the outline of the peak of hair and he has tried to conceal the scar. The second time I did not see his hair, yet I knew he was the same man. And I know it now.'

'That is good. You have been of the greatest help to us, Miss Lansdon. We are extremely grateful to you.'

They took me back. I was exhausted. I kept thinking of that moment when his eyes had looked into mine. I could not explain the expression I saw there. He knew that I was aware of who he was. He must have seen me at the window that night; we had looked full at each other when he held the gun in his hand. His eyes were defiant, mocking, faintly contemptuous. Oh yes, he knew that I had recognized him.

I went to my room when I arrived home. Celeste came in with a glass of hot milk on a tray.

'Was it such an ordeal?' she asked.

'It was just walking along a line of men and picking him out. He knew that I recognized him. Oh, Celeste, it was frightening. It was the way he looked at me . . . defying me, mocking me.'

'I expect he was very frightened.'

'I am not sure. Perhaps people like that who take life lightly don't overvalue their own. What do you think will happen to him?'

'He'll be hanged if he's proved guilty.'

'He is guilty. It's rather a sobering thought. But for me, it might not have been proved against him.'

'He would probably have betrayed himself in some way. He must have been caught up in that sort of thing before. The police are very clever. After all, they suspected him and got their hands on him very quickly. They must have known what he was and probably had been watching him, for it seems he was not unknown to them. The fact that you recognized him has made it easier for them to bring this charge against him.'

'But if they do hang him, it will be because of me.'

'No. It will be because he is a murderer who must die so that he cannot murder others as he did Benedict. You've got to see it that way. If he were allowed to escape there could shortly be another death, and other bereaved relations suffering because of his wanton act.'

'That,' I said firmly, 'is how I must see it.'

Celeste said: 'When it is all over you will go to Rebecca's, I suppose.'

'Perhaps for a short stay.'

'We shall have to decide what we are going to do. I hope you won't go away altogether.'

'You should come to Cornwall with me, Celeste . . . for a while at least. Rebecca suggested it.'

'I don't know. I feel lost . . . unable to make decisions. I am so lonely . . . without Benedict . . . although I know he never really cared for me. But he was always so much a part of my life.'

'He did care for you, Celeste. It was just that he did not show it.'

'He could not show it because it was not there. He showered his affection on you . . . and your mother.'

'But, Celeste, he did love you. He was grateful to you, I know.'

'Well,' she said ruefully, 'that is all over now.'

'And there are the two of us left. Let us stay together.'

She put her arms about me.

I said: 'You are a great comfort to me, Celeste.'

'And you to me,' she replied.

My father was buried with a certain amount of ceremony. We should have liked it to have been done quietly, but in view of the circumstances we had realized that that would be impossible.

His coffin was hidden by flowers and there had to be an extra carriage to accommodate them all. Many, I thought ironically, had been sent by those who had been his enemies in life; but those who had been envious need be so no longer. Who could be envious of a dead man? He could now be remembered for his brilliance, his wit, his shrewdness, his hopes of a high post in government now cut short. They were talking about the certainty of his becoming

Prime Minister one day . . . if he had lived. It was a great career cut short by a senseless murder, they said. My father, by dying, had become a hero.

The eulogies in the press were almost embarrassing. There was no mention of that early scandal which had blighted his hopes, the resurrection of which he had always dreaded. It would appear now that he had been loved and admired by all.

Such is the glory attained through death; and the more sudden and violent the death, the greater the glory.

I read these accounts. Celeste and Rebecca read them. We knew them for the clichés they were, but did we allow ourselves to be swept along on the tide of insincerity? I suppose we did a little. But there was no comfort for me. I had lost him for ever and there was a terrible emptiness left.

When the will was read we realized how very rich he had been. He had rewarded all his faithful servants with substantial legacies. Celeste was well provided for; Rebecca was left a considerable sum. As for the rest of his fortune, there was to be some sort of trust. It was for me during my lifetime, and after me it would go to my children; and if I failed to have any it was to be for Rebecca or her children.

The house in London was left to Celeste; the one at Manorleigh to me.

I had never thought a great deal about money and at such a time, with so much else to occupy my thoughts, I did not fully realize what this would mean.

The solicitors said that when I had recovered a little they would talk with me and explain what had to be explained. There was really no hurry. I could hardly give my attention to such matters now.

Rebecca said: 'When this is all over, you will have to start thinking what you want to do. There will be changes, no doubt. The best thing for you – and for Celeste, too – is to come back to Cornwall with me . . . away from all this. Then you will be able to see everything more clearly.'

I had no doubt that she was right, yet I hesitated. Joel would be coming home soon. I clung to the thought that I should be able to talk with him.

I had been so stunned by my father's death that I had been unable to think of anything else. Now memories of Joel were coming back. I would not be alone. Joel would return and when he did he would help me to recover from this terrible shock.

In a way I longed to leave London. I should feel better in Cornwall. I loved Cador, the old family home, and I was always happy to be with Rebecca.

But I must be in London for the trial, and until that was over there could be no peace for me. I was sure my presence would be required; I was a key witness. There would be no point in going to Cornwall with this ordeal hanging over me.

I am sure, for the rest of my life, I shall never be able to escape from the memories of that courtroom. I would never forget the sight of the man in the dock. I tried hard not to look at him, but I could not help myself; and every time it seemed that his eyes were on me, half-hating, half-amused, half-mocking.

His name was Fergus O'Neill. He had been involved in similar trouble before. It was, no doubt, how he had received the scar on his face. He had served a term in an Irish jail where he had been involved in a riot; he was a member of an organization which took the law into its own hands. He was a killer who served a cause; and he had no compunction in taking life to do so. The police had had him under surveillance; it was the reason why through my description they had been able to arrest him so quickly.

Mr Thomas Carstairs, QC, Counsel for the Crown, opened for the Prosecution. He spoke for what seemed like a long time setting out what had happened. Benedict Lansdon, a well-known member of the Liberal Party, highly respected in the political world – and indeed destined for Cabinet rank – had been wantonly done to death outside his own house in the presence of his daughter.

He went on talking about my father's openly stated opposition to Mr Gladstone's Home Rule Bill, and how Fergus O'Neill, already known to the police as an agitator, had waited on the night previous to the murder, with intent to kill. He had been foiled by the late sitting of the House of Commons on that night, for on these occasions Mr Lansdon stayed at the house of friends in Westminster and did not come home. He referred to the fact that I had seen Fergus O'Neill loitering outside the house. It had been a windy night. O'Neill's opera hat had blown off and, as there was a street lamp nearby, I had had a clear view of his face. The next time I had seen him was at the time of the murder and with a gun in his hand.

And so on.

Then began the evidence for the Prosecution. Several people were called. There was the landlady in the house where Fergus O'Neill was lodging. He had come over from Ireland a week before the murder and had apparently spent the intervening time preparing for it.

There were two people who had rented rooms in the house; there were the pathologists and the doctor who had attended my father; and a few others. I was to be the most important witness because I had actually been present at the time of the murder and had seen and identified the assassin. It was clear, even to myself – and I knew little of court procedure – that it was my evidence which would prove the case against Fergus O'Neill.

After the first day I arrived home exhausted. Rebecca and Celeste sat by my bedside and talked to me until I fell asleep.

But even in sleep I was haunted by that man. I knew that I had had to do what I did. I could not have withheld anything. I was as certain as I could be of anything that the man was my father's murderer; but I kept imagining the rope about his neck, and I could not stop telling myself that I was the one who would put it there.

When I told Rebecca this, she said: 'That's nonsense. He has put it there himself. The man's a murderer and if he is guilty he must be punished. You cannot allow people to go free so that they can go round killing people just because they disagree with them.'

She was right, I knew, but how could one drive morbid fancies out of one's mind?

'As soon as this is all over,' announced Rebecca, 'I am definitely going to take you to Cornwall. And you are coming with us, Celeste. You need a break. You need to get away from all this. And it is no use saying you cannot come, because I am going to insist.'

'I think I should be here,' said Celeste.

'And I think you should not,' replied Rebecca firmly. 'You need not stay long, but it is necessary for both of you to get away from here for a while. It has been a great shock to you both. You need a break . . . right away.'

We both knew that she was right and I must say that, for me, the prospect of getting away was enticing.

But the trial was not yet over. I should have to return to the courtroom. Mr Thomas Carstairs thought that the Defence might want to put me in the witness-box and endeavour to discredit my evidence.

And so it had to be. The solemn atmosphere of the courtroom was awe-inspiring with the judge sternly presiding over the barristers and the jury; but the one I was constantly aware of was Fergus O'Neill, the memory of whose face would, I began to fear, haunt me for the rest of my life.

The Defence, after all, did not call me. I suppose they thought that anything I could say would only be damning against the prisoner.

The Prosecution, however, put me briefly in the box. I was asked to look at the prisoner and tell the court whether I had seen him before.

I answered that I had seen him the night before my father died and at the time of the shooting. I told how I recognized him.

It was over very quickly, but it was the deciding factor.

The judge gave his summing up. The verdict was inevitable, he said. The case had been proved (not only, I kept telling myself, by me). The man was a fanatical terrorist and anarchist. He had very likely killed before. He was a man already wanted by the police.

I wished I was anywhere but in the courtroom when the jury came back and gave the verdict of guilty and the judge put on the black cap.

I shall never forget his voice: 'Prisoner at the Bar, you have been convicted by a jury, and the law leaves me no discretion and I must pass on to you the sentence of the law and this sentence of the law is: This Court doth ordain you to be taken from hence to the place of execution; and that your body there be hanged by the neck until you are dead; and that your body be afterwards buried within the precincts of the prison in which you have been confined after your conviction and may the Lord have mercy on your soul.'

I took one last fearful look at him. His eyes were fixed on me – venomous, revengeful and mocking.

*

Rebecca wanted us to leave at once, but I could not go. I had to stay.

'Sometimes there is a reprieve,' I said. 'I want to be here . . . so that I know.'

'There would not be a reprieve in a case like this,' said Rebecca. 'For Heaven's sake, Lucie, the man deserves to die. He murdered your father.'

'It was for a cause. It wasn't for personal gain. It's different somehow.'

'Murder is murder,' said Rebecca firmly. 'And the punishment for murder is death. Let's leave soon. The children and Pedrek think I have been away too long.'

'You go back, Rebecca. Celeste and I will come when this is all over.'

Rebecca shook her head. 'I have to stay with you, Lucie. Pedrek understands.'

Three weeks had passed since the judge uttered that sentence and the day for the execution came. There had, of course, been no reprieve; in my heart I had known there could not be.

I sat in my room. Rebecca and Celeste wanted to be with me. But they understood my feelings. I wanted to be alone, and they respected that.

So I sat there while it was happening. This man, this Fergus O'Neill, a man to whom I had never spoken, was dying and I was the one who, figuratively, had put the rope round his neck.

Rebecca was right. I was being foolish to think that. Her calm common sense should be like a douche of cold water to my fevered fantasies. And so it was . . . at times. Yet at others these thoughts would come back to me.

Who would have believed this time last year that I, a simple girl, happy in the life she shared with her brilliant father, had lost him and gained a terrible burden of guilt?

How could it be possible for life to change so drastically in such a short time!

'There is nothing to detain us,' said Rebecca. 'What we must do now is plan for the future. And you will do this better away from here. You will be able to think more clearly in Cornwall.'

I knew that she was right.

'So pack what you need,' she went on. 'We'll catch tomorrow morning's train.'

'There is something I have to tell you, Rebecca,' I said. 'It's about Joel Greenham.'

She smiled and I saw the understanding in her eyes.

'Before he went away,' I added, 'we became engaged . . . secretly.'

She turned to me, smiling. I had not seen her look so happy since the tragedy.

'Oh, Lucie,' she said, 'I am so pleased. This is wonderful. Of course, I knew there was something between you and Joel. He will take care of you. When is he coming home?'

'I don't know. I haven't heard anything yet.'

'These missions don't usually last very long and he has been away some time. I wonder whether he will have heard . . . he can't have done so. If he had I am sure he would have come home right away.'

'It seems so long since he went away,' I said.

'As soon as he comes home you can go back to London . . . or he could come down to us. Oh, Lucie, I can't tell you how happy this has made me.'

'I should have told you before only we didn't intend to announce it until he came back.'

'It will help so much. You'll be able to start afresh. I can see that you don't want to make too many plans until he is with you.'

Her mood had changed. She was clearly thinking what a help Joel would be to me.

She was right, of course.

'So,' she went on, 'we'll leave tomorrow morning.'

Celeste was coming with us. We had insisted that she did; and I think she was relieved to do so; although she was a little diffident, as was her way; she confided in me that she was not sure whether Rebecca really wanted her or was asking her out of kindness.

Poor Celeste! Her life with Benedict had nurtured this feeling of being unwanted; although in the last years he had tried hard to make things different between them.

So we prepared to leave. I was telling myself that in the peace of Cornwall I should see everything more clearly. I would be able to convince myself that I was foolish to harbour these uneasy feelings about a man who had deliberately set out to kill my father, shattering his life in a matter of seconds and bringing misery to his family.

I had packed and we were ready to leave.

'We should get a good night's sleep,' advised Rebecca.

She herself brought a glass of milk to my bedroom. She stayed by my bed and talked to me.

'Everything will be different in Cornwall,' she said soothingly. 'The children will love to see you. They are rather adorable. And the grandparents, ours and Pedrek's – you know how they love it when you come. Ours will be trying to snatch you away from us and get you to Cador. But I shan't allow it.'

'It all sounds so cosy.'

'It will be best, Lucie. And soon we shall be hearing from Joel. I am sure he will come straight to Cornwall when he knows you are there.'

'I'm getting rather worried about him. It seems so long since he went.'

'Well, it is a long way off, and I don't suppose getting letters through is very easy. Soon he'll be home. Oh, I am so glad you and Celeste are such friends. Poor Celeste!'

'I always feel that I want to look after her,' I said.

Rebecca nodded. 'Now drink that milk and get off to sleep. We'll have a long day tomorrow.'

She took the glass, set it down and tucked me in as she used to do when I was a child.

I put my arms round her neck.

'I am so glad to have you, Rebecca,' I told her.

'And I to have you, little sister,' she replied.

Then she kissed me and went out.

I think I dozed a little. Then . . . something wakened me. It sounded like a scratching on the window. I lay staring into the darkness. The light from the street lamp showed me the outline of familiar furniture. It was something I had found comforting when I was very young. I was thankful for that street lamp. It had played a part in my life. And then it had shown me clearly the face of my father's murderer. I could not have been so sure of him if I had not seen him standing hatless under it on that fateful night.

Again that scratching on the window. I looked and was in time to see that it was a handful of small pebbles which had been thrown at it.

I got out of bed and went to the window. My heart seemed to stop for a second as I caught my breath, for standing there, under the street lamp, was a figure in an opera cloak and hat. It was a man. He looked straight up at me as I stood at the window. For a few seconds we remained motionless, then suddenly he took off his hat and bowed. As he was standing under the street lamp I could see him clearly. I saw the widow's peak, even the faint outline of the scar.

He was smiling at me, mockingly.

I could not move. I just stood there, limp with horror.

The man put his hat on his head and slowly sauntered out of sight.

I was shivering; my limbs were shaking. What had I seen? Was it a ghost? That was my first thought. He had come back to haunt me.

For a few moments, I stood there staring down at the deserted street. Then I went back to bed.

I was still trembling. Then another and more terrible thought occurred to me. Was the man I had condemned *not* my father's murderer? That man was still here. I had seen him this night, *after* the other had been hanged.

Oh, God help me, I thought. I have condemned an innocent man.

But the man I had seen in court *was* the man I had seen in the street on those two occasions. But if that were so, how could he have been down there on this night?

He had meant me to see him. He had thrown pebbles at my window.

Had he been real or was he a phantom come back to haunt me?

Belinda

Pedrek was waiting at the station with the carriage when we arrived. The journey had seemed long and all through it I had been trying to forget what I had seen on the previous night. There were moments when I almost convinced myself that I had imagined the whole thing.

I was certainly in an unusual state. I had been terribly shocked. It was just possible that I had suffered from some hallucination. That was the happiest conclusion to which I could come, although I hated to think of myself being so mentally disturbed.

I wanted to tell Rebecca. I felt sure she would have some explanation. Indeed, I had had to restrain myself during that night from going along to her bedroom to tell her all about it.

As we sped across the country past green fields and wooded hills, through villages and the outskirts of towns, I began to get a sense of normality, and the more I thought of what I had seen last night, the more reasonable it seemed to believe that I had imagined the whole thing.

Pedrek embraced us all.

He said to Rebecca: 'It's been a long time.'

Rebecca replied: 'Yes, I know, but . . .' and he nodded, understanding, I felt, as he always would.

We got into the carriage and our luggage was put in beside us.

'The children are all agog,' said Pedrek. 'Nanny Billings has made a great concession. They are going to be allowed to sit up a little later tonight because you have come home.'

'The darlings!' said Rebecca. 'I've been away so long. I hope they haven't forgotten me.'

'They certainly have not!' Pedrek assured her. 'Every morning Nanny Billings tells me she is asked "When is Mummy coming home?"'

'That's a relief,' said Rebecca. 'I should have hated to have my children look on me as a stranger.'

'Well, High Tor waits to welcome you. I can tell you, the entire household has been in the throes of feverish preparation ever since it was known you were coming.'

'What a lovely homecoming,' I said.

'It's true, Lucie,' said Rebecca. 'I know how pleased everyone will be to see you and Celeste.'

We drove through narrow lanes where the hedges brushed against the carriage; we wound round and round and caught glimpses of sea and moorland, until we came into open country and there was the house in all its glory – the happy home of my dearest Rebecca and her family.

Even the horses seemed pleased because they were near home; and in spite of everything I was beginning to feel more at peace and more remote from the scene of sudden death.

Rebecca and Pedrek had chosen this house because it was more or less half way between Cador and Pencarron, the house of Pedrek's grandparents. Pedrek now, of course, ran the Pencarron Mine which he had inherited from his grandfather – although I think the old man still had an interest in it. It was about a mile or so from High Tor, so within easy distance for Pedrek.

High Tor was a misnomer really as it stood on a slight incline which could hardly be called a tor. It was an interesting house. Celeste had once lived in it, for it had belonged to her family, the Bourdons, before they went to Chislehurst and later to Farnborough with the exiled Empress Eugénie.

I remember that at one time Pedrek and Rebecca had decided against it and then afterwards had fallen in love with it again.

It was an old house, having been erected in the late sixteenth or early seventeenth century. I had always been told that it was in the Inigo Jones style. It was the first time I had heard his name and I was very impressed because I could see that everyone else was. But I had always been enchanted by the leaded windows, the gables and the pediments; and I loved old houses; they set me thinking of what had happened to all the people who had lived in them over the years.

High Tor was especially interesting to me because it was in one of these rooms that Belinda had been conceived. It was here that Leah Polhenny had come to repair the tapestries which the Bourdons had brought from France, and while she was here had been seduced by Jean Pascal, Celeste's brother, and the son of the house. So it was really in this house that our story had begun – mine and Belinda's.

No wonder it had a fascination for me.

We went through the gateway into the courtyard. A groom came running out.

'Welcome home, Mrs Cartwright.'

'Hello, Jim,' cried Rebecca. 'It's good to be back.'

Rebecca could scarcely wait for the carriage to stop before she leaped out. She was longing fervently to see the children.

And there they were, one on either side of Nanny Billings, and when they saw Rebecca they rushed forward and threw themselves at her.

They were all talking at once. The children were squealing with joy. Alvina wanted to show her mother her new painting book, Jake his toy engine.

Lucky Rebecca, I thought, to have such a family. And, indeed, as she held them to her the sorrow and drama of the last months seemed to pass away from her.

'And what have you to say to your Aunt Lucie and your Aunt Celeste?' she asked the children.

They came and stood before us. I knelt and put my arms about them.

'Now,' said Nanny Billings briskly, 'we mustn't get too excited. We are going to stay up a little longer because this is a special day.'

The children laughed together and we went into the house.

The hall was large, as they usually are in such houses, with a high vaulted ceiling supported by thick oak beams. The butler and housekeeper had appeared to welcome us and tell us that our rooms were ready and we could go to them right away.

'We'll have a quick wash and then something to eat,' said Rebecca. 'It's been a long journey and we're a little tired.'

'In the small dining-room in half an hour,' said Mrs Willows, the housekeeper. 'Unless that will be too soon.'

'Oh no, that will be just right,' said Rebecca.

The children came with us up the stairs. My room was next to that of Celeste. It was the one I always occupied on my visits to High Tor.

Rebecca was looking at me anxiously. She had been aware of my preoccupation on the train. I was thinking of the number of times I had stayed in this room. Everything will be different now, I reminded myself. We can never go back.

'Come along, children,' said Nanny Billings.

Alvina looked as though she were about to protest. Rebecca knelt down to kiss her and whispered that that night she would come along to tuck her in and perhaps tell her a story, and that seemed to satisfy her.

When Rebecca and I were alone in my room, she said: 'Something's happened, hasn't it?'

I looked at her in surprise and she hurried on: 'I mean yesterday . . . last night. I felt there was something . . .'

I nodded.

She said quickly: 'Tell me later. I'll come along tonight for a chat.'

I felt suddenly relieved. I had been wondering whether to share my misgivings with Rebecca, and now I knew that I would.

'I'll have to leave you now,' she went on. 'See you downstairs in half an hour.'

When I had dressed I tapped on Celeste's door. She was ready and waiting.

'How does it feel to be in your old home?' I asked.

'A little strange,' she replied.

'It must be very different now.'

'Very different.'

'I suppose it was rather grand when your parents had it – all that Gobelin tapestry which Leah came to repair.'

'There were some fine pieces, but here . . . there is . . . love.'

I was silent as I went downstairs with her. Lucky Rebecca! I was wondering whether Joel and I would be able to build ourselves a life like this.

Joel was my hope now. It was a sad quirk of fate that he should happen to be out of the country at the time when I needed him so much. But he would soon be home, and it would be different then. We would start at once to build a new life together.

I fancied the conversation at dinner was a little laboured. I guessed that Pedrek had made up his mind not to talk of my father's murder, and as all that had followed as a result of it must be uppermost in our minds, a restraint was put upon us.

I think we were all relieved when the meal was over.

'It has been a long day,' said Rebecca. 'We shall all feel better after a good night's sleep.'

I had not been in my room more than five minutes when there was a tap on the door. I knew it was Rebecca who had come for our talk.

I was at the dressing-table brushing my hair and she came and sat in the armchair facing me.

'What's happened, Lucie?' she asked.

I told her and she was clearly shocked.

'But . . . who could it have been?'

'I don't know, but I have a terrible feeling that they have hanged the wrong man.'

'But you recognized him. You picked him out. He had the sort of appearance which could be easily recognized. The way his hair grew was enough and then there was the scar. All that is not very usual. And he was known to the police as a terrorist. He had been involved in that sort of thing before.'

'I know. It seemed certain. But if he were dead and buried, how could he have been down there in the street?'

'Let's try and look at this clearly. I think you may have imagined you saw this man.'

'But, Rebecca, he threw pebbles at my window. He was down there. He took off his hat and bowed to me . . . as though he were mocking me.'

She was silent for a few moments, then she said: 'You were – still are – in a highly emotional state, Lucie. Most people would be. That sort of shock has its effect. You were actually there. You saw the whole thing . . . and you and your father were very close. You were closer to him than anyone else. It's bound to have a deep effect.'

'Rebecca, if you think I imagined I saw that, you must also think that I am unbalanced mentally.'

'Of course I don't. It could happen to anyone.'

'Do you mean to tell me I *imagined* I heard pebbles at the window?'

'I think you might have been dreaming. You went to the window and there was a man. He may have seen you . . . and bowed.'

'He took off his hat. He was standing under the lamp. I saw his widow's peak quite clearly. It was what he wanted me to see.'

'You must have imagined it.'

'I tell you I saw it clearly. Rebecca, there are only two explanations. One is that what I saw was his ghost and he has come back to haunt me, or they have hanged the wrong man . . . and I am responsible.'

'I don't believe either.'

'You believe that your mother came back after death and made you look after me.'

She was silent.

I went on: 'So you *do* believe that the dead can return . . . if there is something which is very important to them. Our mother did when I was left with Jenny Stubbs. She wanted me in the house where I belonged and she came to you and put all that into your mind. That's what you've always believed, Rebecca. Well, if she could come back, why shouldn't he? Our mother came back to do good, but she was a good woman. Fergus O'Neill was a man who killed people because they did not believe what he believed, because they did what he did not want them to. He killed for what he would call a cause. He would come back for revenge.'

'Lucie, you must put the whole thing out of your head. You're overwrought. You have been through a greater ordeal than you realize. You've got to get back to normality. I'm so glad you're here. You'll be better quickly here . . . I shall look after you.'

'As you always have, Rebecca. I can't think what my life would have been like without you.'

'We're sisters, aren't we? I suffered terribly when our mother died. I hated your father for marrying her and taking her away from me. That was bad for me. Then it began to be better between us and that made me a lot happier. Lucie, we have to remember that we go through a great drama when we suffer a terrible loss. We are not quite ourselves. Yes, we can become a little unbalanced. We see things out of proportion. We don't always see clearly . . .'

'You think I saw nothing last night, don't you?'

'I don't know. I think you may have had a nightmare . . . that you awoke startled and were half dreaming when you went to the window and you saw the man in the street. He was dressed for the opera. That's not surprising. He was probably returning from the opera. He looked up at the window. He saw you and took off his hat and bowed. Well, he'd probably had a little too much to drink. He was in a merry mood . . . he saw a young woman at the window . . . and, well, he bowed.'

'But his face . . .'

'My dear Lucie, you saw the hat and the cloak. There was just the light from the street lamp. You imagined the rest.'

'Do you really think that could be so?'

'I think it is the most likely answer.'

I closed my eyes. It was what I hoped. Rebecca's calm common sense was beginning to have its effect.

Of course she must be right. It had been no ghost I saw. It was not Fergus O'Neill who had been down there. Fergus O'Neill was dead. He had paid the penalty demanded by the law. He was a murderer.

Rebecca saw that she was convincing me and she was pleased.

73

'Now,' she said, 'I am going to bring you something to drink.'

'The inevitable hot milk?' I asked.

'It's the best thing. Trust Rebecca.'

I flung myself into her arms. 'Oh, I do,' I assured her. 'I always have. You have always been there when I needed you.'

'And always will be. You know that.'

I did. I was feeling a great deal better; and when she appeared with the hot milk, I drank it and was soon fast asleep.

Rebecca had been right. Cornwall had a healing effect. We had crossed the bridge between tragedy and the new life which we had to make for ourselves.

I was thinking more and more of Joel. Soon he must be home and then our engagement would be announced. We would plan our future. We would have a house in London and, I supposed, live at Marchlands. He would have to be in both places . . . convenient for Parliament and for his constituency. I should wait up for him when the House was sitting late; I should have a supper waiting for him. It would be the familiar pattern, with Joel instead of my father.

I must stop thinking of the past. I had to plan for the future. It would be wonderful. It was just the present that was so hard to live through.

But the bridge was here and we were crossing it.

I had always been fascinated by Cornwall. It was, I supposed, natural that I should be, since it was in the Duchy that I had been born. Rebecca saw that my days were full. I was glad I had told her about my experience. She understood now my preoccupation, my nervous tension; and she had done her best to wipe it away with her sound common sense. Which she had done . . . almost.

It was not difficult to fill our days. There was so much to do. The gardens at High Tor were a delight. There were no orderly flowerbeds; shrubs and trees grew naturally; and in a way it resembled the gardens of Manor Grange at Manorleigh. The children loved to play in the gardens and I was with them a great deal. There was the paddock round which they rode their ponies on lead reins. Both Celeste and I were expected to watch their performance and applaud. We also rode. Of course, we had to visit Pencarron, the home of Pedrek's grandparents who made a great fuss of us.

Then there were trips to Cador to my own grandparents. Cador I loved especially, for it was in that grand house that I had spent the greater part of my childhood. I did not remember very much of those early days in Jenny Stubbs's cottage; but to be in Cador again with its battlemented tower and its view of the sea always affected me deeply.

There seemed to be an understanding between my grandparents and Pedrek's that the subject of my father's death should not be referred to. But there were often times when it seemed to be there, and it put such a restraint on us that sometimes I felt that it would have been better to say what was in our minds. He was always in my thoughts, though . . . and in theirs too, I imagined.

I had to make a pilgrimage to Branok Pool. Rebecca and I went there together.

She understood. It meant a great deal to us both. For her it held terrible memories, for it was there that Belinda had said that Pedrek had attempted to molest her and that had almost ruined Rebecca's life. So the Pool had a special significance for her. As for me, it had been close to my first home – that cottage in which I had lived with Jenny Stubbs.

We rode the horses close to the Pool. It was grim as ever with the willows trailing into the muddy water which had been churned up by the recent rains. An eerie spot, full of secrets and memories, the place where legends would be born.

'The cottage is still there,' I said.

'Yes. It is occupied sometimes. It's useful when it is needed. There are emergencies. The Blakeys are in it now. They have been there for a year or more.'

I nodded.

She must be thinking of the people who had been there at the time when Belinda had set the Pool for the scene of her cruel melodrama, which fortunately had been revealed in time for what it was. And I was thinking of poor, mad Jenny Stubbs – a vague and shadowy figure to me . . . a soft singing voice, tender hands . . . Jenny, who had taken me so happily as her own when I was a sickly baby and had nursed me back to health.

With such events to remind us, both Rebecca and I had plenty to think about when we came to the Pool. Perhaps it was not very wise of us to come here.

Mrs Blakey came out of the cottage while we were standing by the pool.

She called: 'Good day to 'ee, Mrs Cartwright. I see you've got Miss Lucie with 'ee. Good day to you, Miss Lucie.'

'We must go and speak to her,' whispered Rebecca and we walked over.

'Miss Lucie is here for a little holiday,' Rebecca explained.

'Oh, my dear, I did hear . . '

Rebecca said quickly: 'Yes, it was all very sad. You seem to have settled into your cottage very well now.'

'It will be a year or more since we came here, Mrs

Cartwright. Now you must come and take a glass of my cider. My Tom do say that it be better than anything they do serve up at the Fisherman's Rest.' She assumed a touch of modesty. 'Well, maybe that's for other folks to say.'

Rebecca was always tactful with the local people. She had learned that from my grandmother.

'Well, that would be nice, wouldn't it, Lucie?' she said.

Mrs Blakey was all smiles. She was clearly proud of her home, and it certainly was a picture of shining neatness. The warming pan hanging by the fireplace gleamed and shone like gold; the fire irons were the same; the linoleum gleamed and the furniture was highly polished.

'You have certainly made it comfortable,' said Rebecca.

Flashes of memory came back to me. In the first years of my life this had been my home. It was familiar and yet strange. It must have been very different when Jenny Stubbs lived here.

The cider was brought and placed on the table.

'Now, if you'd care for a little pasty . . . I be right down proud of my pasties. My Tom do take one with him every day . . . when he be working. He says it do keep him going until he do come home.'

'I'm afraid we can't manage the pasty,' said Rebecca, 'much as we should like to. They'll have a meal waiting for us when we get back and we shall be expected to eat that. This cider is delicious.'

'Delicious,' I echoed.

Mrs Blakey was a garrulous woman and I sensed at once that she was grateful to Pedrek, and wanted Rebecca to know that she had not forgotten what he had done for them.

'It was a terrible blow to Tom,' she confided to me more than to Rebecca, who must have heard the story many times before, 'when this here rheumatics struck. Sudden-

77

like it came . . . just a little pain here and ache there. And then came the time when he could hardly get up again if he knelt down. The doctor, he said, "It's this 'ere rheumatics, Tom. It seems your mining days are over." We were in a rare old trouble, I can tell 'ee. Tom had been in the mines all his life and his father before him . . . and his grandfather before that. Doctor said a little light work was all he'd be able to do. It broke Tom's heart. He's always been a good workman, always brought his pay packet home regular . . . a proud man, my Tom. "What be I going to do, Janet?" he said. "Where'll we be to?" "Well, I be a good hand with the needle," I said. "We'll pull through." Well, there was our home. The cottage near the mine . . . that goes with the job. That would be wanted for him as took Tom's place. Then Mr Cartwright says, "I'm sure I can arrange that you have that place at Branok. It belongs to Mrs Cartwright's family. It's empty now and I'll have a word with them." And so he did and we come here . . . thanks to Mr Cartwright and them up at Cador.'

'Our grandparents,' said Rebecca with a little smile at me.

'Well, they did say, "You just have the cottage, Tom, and never mind about rent and such. It's there for them as needs a roof over their head. You take it while you do want it." And there's little jobs Tom can do . . . on the farms and at Cador. They've kept him busy ever since, and my bit of sewing brings in a tidy bit. So there, you see . . . we're better off than we was when Tom was in the mines.'

'And how is the rheumatism?' I asked.

'On and off, Miss Lucie. You can tell the weather by it. "Going to have a bit of rain tomorrow," Tom will say. "My leg's giving me gippo." It's a sure sign. And do you know, he'll be right. He's a real weathercock, our Tom, since he got his rheumatics. And now let me top you up, Mrs Cartwright.'

'Oh no, thanks, Mrs Blakey,' cried Rebecca in alarm. 'It's strong, your cider.'

Mrs Blakey laughed happily. Then she looked at me solemnly and said: 'Oh, we be happy here. There's some as say it be a gloomy old place and there's ghosts and such like on the prowl. Tom and me, we don't mind the ghosts.'

'Do you ever hear the bells?' I asked. 'You know, the ones which are supposed to ring from the monastery at the bottom of the pool.'

'That old tale! How could monks live down there for hundreds of years? It's just a lot of nonsense, I say. So does Tom. No, we don't hear no bells. We're settled here and I don't mind telling 'ee that, if it wasn't for them old rheumatics giving Tom gip now and then, I'd be glad. Mines are dangerous things. Terrible things can happen to miners. I used to worry about Tom down the mine. But we were lucky. Tom happened to work for a good owner. I'll never forget Mr Cartwright and your grandfather, Mrs Cartwright. Mr Cartwright, he be a good master.'

'I am so glad you feel like that,' said Rebecca. 'I shall tell Mr Cartwright. He will be very pleased. He always wants to do what is right for the miners.'

'The Lord will bless him,' said Mrs Blakey, 'for what he has done for us.'

On that happy note we left.

As we made our way back Rebecca said: 'She has transformed that place. I always used to think it was rather eerie. It looks so warm and cosy. I wonder how many hours she spends polishing the furniture and the brass.'

'It makes her happy,' I said.

'Oh yes. And talking of mines reminds me. We shall have to go to Pencarron. It's a week since we were there. We must take the children. The Pencarrons get a little hurt if they don't see them frequently.'

79

'Could we go tomorrow?'

'I'm sure we could,' said Rebecca.

The next day Rebecca and I with the children went over to Pencarron Manor. Celeste had said she wanted to go into the Poldoreys to shop. She was anxious not to intrude. The children were excited. They always enjoyed visiting their grandparents, for at Pencarron they were apt to be spoilt.

Pencarron Manor lacked the antiquity of Cador and High Tor. It was a solid Victorian edifice, as Josiah said: 'Built for use.' And what it lacked in fancy battlemented towers it made up for in modern improvements. 'A bit of comfort's worth a houseful of ghosts,' was his favourite comment.

He was bluff, kindly and somewhat contemptuous of the fanciful Cornish folk, with their piskies and what he called fancy tales about this and that happening to folk who didn't look out. Mining had been his life; and he had come to Pencarron after his marriage, built the house and turned a failing old mine into a prosperous one.

He and his wife had longed for a child and had had to wait some time for Morwenna. When she came she had been the centre of their lives and now Pedrek and the children made up for the fact that she lived chiefly in London, where her husband managed the transport of tin and matters which could not be so easily dealt with in Cornwall.

We were all welcomed warmly, but I noticed the Pencarrons could not take their eyes from the children.

They wanted to know how Pedrek was, although they must have seen him a few days before. We all had a lavish meal which was typical of Pencarron hospitality. The children had to be at the table with us, for their grandparents could not bear to be deprived of their company even for a short while; and there was a great deal of laughter.

When this was over the children wanted to play in the garden and were allowed to do so; and we sat before the french windows so that we could watch them while we talked.

Coffee was served and Mrs Pencarron was saying that we should come more often, and weren't the little ones growing, and Jake was going to be the image of Pedrek. You could see it already, and Alvina was a little madam, wasn't she?

'The country air is so good for them,' said Josiah.

'I can't tell you how relieved we were when Pedrek decided he wanted to take over the mine,' added his wife.

'We thought he might have wanted to join his father in London, but he had the good sense to choose this.'

'It wouldn't have been any good for the children up there.'

'We do have our parks, you know,' I said.

'Parks,' snorted Josiah. 'You can't compare them with the moors and the sea.'

'They are very pleasant,' said Rebecca.

'I reckon the country air is better,' insisted Josiah. 'Life's safer here, I reckon.'

'Well, there is the occasional accident in the mines and then the fishermen have a bad time when the storms arise.'

'You get disasters everywhere. What about those Members of Parliament?'

'On the whole they're safe enough.'

'I was talking about those two. It was in the papers this morning. Have you seen the morning paper?'

'No, not yet. We thought we'd better get here early. We didn't stop for very much.'

'You wouldn't have seen it, then. Apparently they were in Africa or somewhere. Two of them . . . they're missing.'

I said quickly: 'Where were they?'

'They were visiting there with some others –'

'Was it Buganda?'

'Now you come to mention it, I think it was. Gone out for the government or something, some fact-finding mission, they called it. Well, two of them have disappeared. The rest of them are coming home – quick. It seems they were not well received by the natives.'

'I . . . I know the mission you are talking about,' I said. 'In fact, I know very well one of the members who went out. He was a friend of . . . my father . . . of the family . . . Who are the two who are missing?'

'It did say their names, but I don't remember.'

He could see that I was uneasy.

Rebecca was looking at me anxiously.

'Perhaps we could see the paper?' she suggested.

'I'm sure you can find it, can't you, Mother?' said Josiah.

'Of course. Have some more coffee, Rebecca . . . Lucie?'

I could not concentrate on what they were saying. I kept thinking of Joel and the conversation we had had before he left, when we had declared our feelings for each other and our intentions. Two of them missing, I thought. Oh, not Joel!

It seemed a long time before the paper was found; and when I saw it I almost wished I had not.

I read: *The government mission to Buganda has not been an unqualified success. Some of the natives objected to what they call interference, and there was not always a warm welcome for the delegation. In fact they were often met with some hostility and will be returning home within the next day or so . . . unfortunately without two members of the party. They are Mr James Hunter and Mr Joel Greenham . . .*

My heart beat faster as I read and the paper trembled in my hands.

It appears that the whole party were at a meeting and,

when it was over, prepared to return to their hotel. There was not room in the carriage for them all, and Mr Hunter and Mr Greenham, being the youngest members of the party, decided to walk to the hotel. They have not been seen since. Enquiries are being made.

I kept staring at his name. I kept seeing him as he had been when we had planned our future together. 'When I come back we will announce our engagement . . .'

But he would not come back with the others. What could be happening to him?

Rebecca was saying quietly: 'Are you all right, Lucie?'

'It . . . it's a shock. This . . . er . . .'

'Well, it's what I was saying,' said Josiah. 'Life's better in the country. You know where you are.'

I don't know how I got through the time before we left. Rebecca came to my aid and did what she could.

As we drove home she said: 'Of course, we know very little yet. It's probably very exaggerated. We must hear more news later on.'

But I felt bewildered and lost. I was beginning to ask myself what dire tragedy could happen next.

It was indeed hard to imagine that this had happened, following so soon after that other tragedy.

Celeste, who had guessed what the relationship between Joel and me was blossoming into, was most upset. She had had so many troubles of her own that she was always ready to sympathize with others.

'I can't believe it,' I said. 'It's so soon after. Didn't Shakespeare say that when troubles come they come not as single spies but in battalions?'

'This is different,' Celeste assured me. 'He'll come back.'

'What could have happened to him?'

We read more in the papers. But of course it was only speculation. The mission had been unpopular, and there was some anxiety expressed concerning the whereabouts of the two missing Members of Parliament.

'There must be an explanation,' said Rebecca. 'There will be news soon, I'm sure.'

'But what explanation?' I asked. 'What news?'

Rebecca could not reply.

'I must go home soon,' I said.

'Oh no, not yet. You are not ready.'

'I want to be there. I want to know what's happening. I want to see his family. They might know something.'

'I doubt they will know any more than the authorities.'

'They will be desolate. They dote on him. He's such a wonderful person, Rebecca.'

'You'll be better here,' she advised. 'Don't rush away. I can't bear to think of your going back to that house.'

'I must go, Rebecca.'

'Think about it for a few days.'

I promised I would, and each day I scoured the papers for news. There was none. All I read was: *There is still no news of the missing James Hunter and Joel Greenham.*

I knew that I must go. There was no peace for me here any more. What I could achieve by going to London I was not sure, but I felt I wanted to be there.

While I was in this state of uncertainty, letters were forwarded on from London. There was one for me and one for Celeste. They were both from Belinda.

Eagerly I slit the envelope.

Dear Lucie, [I read],
    My mother died last week. It has been terrible. I

miss her so much. You know she had been ill for a long time and it had to come. I feel lost and lonely. She has always been there for me, and I don't know what I shall do without her. It's a great shock, though I have seen it coming for months now. She made me promise that I would come back to England. I said I would and she was so happy and relieved when she had letters from you and Celeste saying that I could come.

Well, the time is here. There are some people from England who were out here visiting their relations in Melbourne. We knew the Melbourne family and, before she died, my mother asked them that if it were possible – by which she meant that if she died before the visitors left – she would be grateful to them if they would let me go back to England with them. She had all the instructions written out and I believe she wanted to die in good time, so that I should be able to go with them. Well, it did work out that way, and I am leaving next month, so – unless I hear news from you and Celeste to say you won't have me – I shall be coming with them.

I heard what happened to your father. It was in the papers here, not much about it, just that he had been shot by a terrorist because he had obstructed some Bill. It must have been a shock for you as you saw it happen.

Lucie, I do so much want to see you. I have often thought of you and wondered about you. In all this terrible time there is one thing I look forward to and that is seeing you.

I'll let you know dates and arrangements when I am more certain.

In the meantime, I send my love and the hope
that I shall be with you before long.

Belinda

I showed the letter to Celeste, who gave me hers to read.
It was more brief.

Dear Aunt Celeste,

My mother is dead now and her last wish was
that I should come to England. She said you had
very kindly promised that I could come to you. I
will try not to be a burden, but if I can stay until I
know what I have to do, I shall be very grateful.

I have written to Lucie and told her about Mr
and Mrs Wilberforce who have been visiting
relations in Melbourne and are going back to
England next month. They have promised to let
me travel with them, which will be easier for me.

I will let you know details of our sailing soon.

Your affectionate and grateful niece,

Belinda

My spirits lifted a little at the prospect of seeing Belinda.
The thought kept me from wondering all the time what was
happening to Joel.

Celeste was uneasy. I could understand that. She could
not help thinking that Belinda had been a source of trouble
in the past; but I think she too felt that the prospect of her
arrival did stop us brooding all the time as to Joel's fate.

We showed the letters to Rebecca.

I said: 'We shall have to go now. I don't know how long
these letters have taken to get here, but Belinda may well
be on her way by now.'

'She says that she will let us know when she is coming.'

'She will. But in view of the distance and the time letters take to get here, she may have started by now.'

It seemed that events were making up my mind for me.

'Don't go to the London house,' advised Rebecca. 'Go to Manorleigh.'

'I feel I have to be in London. I want to see Joel's parents. And I want to be there . . . to get ready for Belinda.'

She sighed.

'There will be too much to remind you . . .'

'I have to go back, Rebecca.'

'How I wish I could come with you. But I can't leave Pedrek and the children again so soon.'

'Of course you can't. Dearest Rebecca, I am very much able to stand on my own feet. I can't rely all my life on my big sister.'

'You know I'm always there. You know this place is waiting for you if ever you found it intolerable . . . elsewhere.'

'It won't be intolerable. I've got to grow away from it. I can't hide in a shelter for ever. Besides, I do want to find out all I can about Joel. And there will be Belinda.'

Rebecca frowned. 'I wonder if she will still be the same.'

'We shall both come down to see you, of course.'

She kissed me tenderly. 'Take care of yourself, Lucie,' she said. 'Remember, I shall be thinking of you.'

My return to London meant that my uneasiness was increasing.

As soon as I was alone in my room, I went to the window, half expecting to see a figure there under the street lamp, although it was broad daylight. The thought occurred to me that I ought to change rooms. That would be cowardly, I decided. No. I must fight against my fears.

I was becoming more and more convinced that Rebecca's theory was correct. I must have imagined those pebbles at the window; a man had been down there, true, and he was in a merry mood. He had bowed to me and I had thought I saw the widow's peak, and the scar.

I must take a firm hold on my imagination. I must make it work for me, not against me.

I was glad that Celeste was with me. She had her own sorrow to contend with. But at least there was no sense of guilt attached to hers. That was what was for ever in the back of my mind. Was it possible that I had helped to send an innocent man to the gallows?

The day after my arrival in Town I went to see Sir John and Lady Greenham.

Theirs was a house of sadness and terrible apprehension. They greeted me with affection.

'My dear, dear Lucie,' said Lady Greenham. 'This is a great blow to us. I was all against his going from the first. How I wish I had managed to persuade him.'

'Is there any news? All I know is what I saw in the Cornish paper.'

'There is very little known,' said Sir John. 'He just vanished into thin air. He left this meeting with the others . . . when he and James Hunter decided to walk.'

'They should never have done that,' said Lady Greenham, 'in those foreign places.'

'But what is being *done* about it?'

'All sorts of things are in motion,' said Sir John. 'You see, it is a political matter. The government wants to get at the truth . . . diplomatically. It is, after all, a government matter. At the same time they don't want to put a strain on our relations with Buganda.'

'So they think it is entirely because of the business on which he is engaged?'

'That seems to be the official view. I shouldn't think it is just an ordinary case of robbery . . . and . . . er . . . disposing of the victims.'

'Oh John!' cried Lady Greenham. 'For Heaven's sake, don't talk like that.'

'We have to face facts, my dear. In some of these places it's not safe to walk out at night.'

'Joel should have known better,' said Lady Greenham.

'You can see how it happened,' went on Sir John. 'The carriage took as many as it could, and the two youngest members of the party naturally agreed to walk.'

'And during that walk they disappeared,' I said.

'That's about it.'

'But you say the authorities are doing something about it. They are not just letting it pass.'

Sir John nodded. 'You can be sure that all that can be done is being done.'

'It is good of you to come and see us,' said Lady Greenham. 'There has been too much horror lately. I think you did right to go to Cornwall.'

'My sister wanted me to stay, but in view of this . . '

Sir John leaned over and patted my hand.

'We always knew you were fond of him,' he said.

'As a matter of fact . . . we talked together before he went. We were going to announce our engagement on his return.'

They were both smiling at me.

'He'll come back,' said Sir John, 'and then we shall have wedding bells. Alas . . .'

I knew what he was thinking. It would be so different from what we had all had in mind. My father, one of the architects of the plan for us, would not be there. He had been done to death by an assassin's hand; and the bridegroom was missing in a foreign country.

I asked myself how much more disaster could strike.

While I was talking to Sir John and Lady Greenham, Gerald Greenham arrived. There was only about a year's difference in his and Joel's ages and I knew there was a strong friendship between the two brothers. Gerald was in the Army. He was likeable and full of vitality, though he lacked that inner gentleness which I found so appealing in Joel.

He talked about his brother's disappearance. Naturally it was the chief topic of conversation in that house. He was of the opinion that not enough was being done to find out what had happened.

Sir John said that naturally plans of action would not be blazoned from the rooftops and in such cases there was bound to be a certain amount of secrecy.

Gerald stuck to his view. He asked me how I was getting on, remembering suddenly, it seemed, that I had endured an even greater tragedy, for while they could retain hope, I could have none.

When I rose to go, Sir John suggested that Gerald should take me home, to which Gerald responded with enthusiasm.

When we came out of the house he hailed a cab and, as we jogged along together, he said: 'This is a great blow to the parents. They hide it . . . but I know what it is doing to them.'

'I understand.'

'I get impatient. *I* want to do something.'

'What could you do?'

'That's the important question. What I can't endure is sitting at home here waiting for something to happen. I get impatient.'

'Understandably.'

'You must feel the same. I know how you felt about Joel.'

'I do wish he would come back.'

'I'd like to go out there, make a few investigations, in secret . . . you understand. Not letting on that I was his brother.'

'I suppose the government could achieve more than a private detective.'

'That depends. I'd like to have a good go anyway.'

I glanced sideways at him. He had a very firm jaw; and there was speculation in his eyes.

I liked him very much. He really cared about his brother. When I said goodbye I felt a little better . . . because of him.

The weeks began to pass. There were letters from Belinda, one for me, one for Celeste. By the time they reached us she was on her way.

I visited Manorleigh briefly, but I felt I wanted to be in London. I no longer looked fearfully out of the window at night. I had done so during the first weeks and been confronted always by the empty street.

I had one or two sessions with the solicitors who talked at great length about the Trust and what should be done about that money that was now virtually mine. I could not give my thoughts entirely to such matters; they seemed of little importance when compared with my fears for Joel.

It had been more than a month since his disappearance and a melancholy possibility had occurred to me that I might never see him again.

I visited the Greenhams from time to time. They continued to be hopeful, but I sometimes wondered whether that was a pretence. I saw Gerald once and he was still obsessed by his brother's disappearance.

Time was going on.

Celeste said that we should bestir ourselves. She looked upon me as her responsibility. She said on one occasion that girls in my position had a Season and she was sure it was what my father had been planning for me.

'Though I believe,' she added, 'that he wanted to shelve the matter for a while. He was afraid someone would marry you and take you away from him.'

I put my hand over hers and we were both too emotional to speak.

She recovered herself and said: 'Well, with all this hanging over us, we couldn't possibly do it. We'll have to wait.'

'I don't need a Season, Celeste,' I said. 'I should hate it. If – when – Joel comes back, we shall marry, he and I, and Seasons are not for married women.'

'He must come back,' said Celeste.

And we looked at each other sadly.

'And,' went on Celeste, 'soon there will be Belinda.'

'A Season for Belinda,' I murmured. 'The two of us together.'

It was surprising how often Belinda cropped up in our conversation.

And then one spring day, the *African Star* sailed into Tilbury with Belinda on it.

Celeste and I went to Tilbury to meet her. I knew her at once. Dark-haired, dark-eyed, with something of Leah's beauty, and an indefinable touch of the exotic which perhaps came from her French ancestors. Her main characteristic was that immense vitality which had always been apparent when she was a child. She sparkled with a love of life. She had not changed and she was very attractive.

We were introduced to Mr and Mrs Wilberforce, who seemed rather relieved to hand over their charge. Not that Belinda would regard herself as such. For her they had not been guardians but travelling companions.

She rushed at me in the old exuberant way.

'Lucie . . . Lucie . . . the same old Lucie! I should have picked you out anywhere. Oh, it *is* wonderful to see you!'

Celeste regarded her rather shyly.

'Welcome home, Belinda,' she said.

'Well, thank you,' replied Belinda, and kissed her. 'I'm so glad to be here.'

Celeste turned to the Wilberforces and thanked them for looking after Belinda.

'Actually,' Belinda informed us, 'it was I who looked after them, wasn't it?' She smiled archly at Mr Wilberforce, who returned the smile indulgently. Already I had had a glimpse of her power to charm. 'We had some rough water,' she went on to explain. 'Poor Mrs Wilberforce. She wasn't the only one. Half the ship was prostrate. Mr Wilberforce and I were almost the only ones who were not.'

'The Bay,' murmured Mrs Wilberforce. 'Well, we must be getting along, I suppose.'

'You must come and visit us,' said Celeste. 'We want to thank you properly.'

'Belinda has our address.'

Goodbyes were said and arrangements made for Belinda's luggage to be collected and brought to the house; then, with Belinda seated between Celeste and me, we rode along to the house.

Belinda kept pointing out landmarks that she remembered. She was clearly delighted to be back.

We came into the square. I glanced about quickly, as I always did, at the railings of the gardens and the lamp post, even at this time half expecting to see the man standing there.

'The old house!' cried Belinda. 'I remember it so well. And there's the house at Manorleigh . . . Manor Grange. Do you go there often?'

'Yes, now and then.'

'I loved it. All that antiquity and the ghost . . . the ghosts. You remember the ghosts, Lucie.'

Indeed I remembered. So did Celeste, I saw from her expression. She was remembering Belinda's playing the ghost of my mother, which had given her such a fright.

I wondered that Belinda, who could not have forgotten the incident, should have had the insensitivity to mention it. I thought then: She hasn't changed at all.

We alighted from the carriage.

Belinda looked at me and suddenly said: 'This must be where it happened.'

I nodded.

'It must have been terrible for you.'

'Please,' I whispered, 'not now . . .'

'No, of course not. This is a homecoming, the return of the prodigal. But I am not that, am I? My departure was all quite natural and seemed so right at the time.'

'Come along in,' I said. 'The servants are all agog to see you.'

She smiled, well pleased, and, with Celeste, we went into the house.

Celeste had decided that Belinda should have a room close to mine. Hers also had a balcony which looked down on the street.

'Oh, it's lovely,' she cried. 'I shall be able to look down and see what is going on. And I shall love knowing that you are close, Lucie.'

There were just the three of us for dinner that night.

Belinda talked more than Celeste and I did. She told us about the goldfields and what a strange life it was. She spoke sadly of Leah. I do believe she had really loved her mother; and she was affectionate about Tom Marner.

'He was wonderful to us both,' she told us. 'And at first it was very exciting. Then I began to get homesick. We weren't so far from Melbourne. Tom used to take us there and we would stay for a few days. That was the highlight. We entertained now and then in the house we had there. It was quiet by goldfield standards. What about Rebecca? She'd remember it, of course.'

'She will be coming up to London some time.'

'How is she? She has children, hasn't she?'

'Two. Alvina and Jake. They are darlings.'

I fancied she felt a little uneasy about Rebecca, as well she might. I supposed Rebecca had forgiven her. I wondered if Pedrek would ever be able to forget. There would almost certainly be a little embarrassment between them when they met.

'Does . . . my father ever come here?' she asked suddenly.

Celeste looked a little flustered.

Belinda noticed this and went on: 'Well, he is my father, isn't he? He doesn't deny it, does he? My mother told me all about it – how young and innocent she was, and how it never occurred to her that he would not marry her. Do you think he will want to see me?'

'I . . . I don't know,' said Celeste.

'*I* want to see him.'

'Perhaps . . . one day . . .' murmured Celeste.

'It was all so dramatic, and it all happened so quickly. One day I was the daughter of the house and the next Leah was my mother and Monsieur Bourdon my father. Then I was whisked away. I often thought how strange it all was and wondered how he and I would get on if ever we met.'

'We shall have to see how things turn out,' said Celeste vaguely.

It was an uncomfortable meal. Belinda had always been outspoken and had never shown any respect for conventional modes of behaviour.

I was glad when it was over and I was sure Celeste was, too. She suggested we retire as we must all be tired after the excitement of the day.

I had not been in my room long before there was a tap on the door. I knew at once that it was Belinda.

'A bit stilted, wasn't it?' she said. 'Dear old Celeste! I don't think she wants me here.'

'She does. You are her niece. You're related to her as you are not to me.'

'Oh, but you and I were always special, weren't we? We didn't need family ties. We were brought up together. Then we swopped families. That never ceases to make me marvel. Tell me about everything. What a lot of deaths! First . . . I always think of him as our father, for I believed he was mine for so long. Well, he's dead now. I always hated him and he hated me too. He thought I killed your mother by getting born. And I was not the one after all. It was you.'

'He never held it against me.'

'No. I was the one he hated. He couldn't believe that his sainted Annora had given birth to such a monster.'

'You were indeed a little monster at times, you know.'

She laughed. 'I know. I was a monster by nature. No wonder he was relieved when he found out I wasn't his.'

I was silent. I knew that was true.

'Then he got his dear little Lucie; and he seemed to be rather pleased about that.'

'He was,' I said defiantly. 'We were very good friends.'

96

'The Wilberforces knew all about the way he died. They brought newspapers with them when they came and I was able to read about those little suppers and everything and how you were with him when it happened. What an awful thing!'

'It *was* awful.'

'Somebody didn't like him . . . besides me.'

'Please don't be flippant about it, Belinda. I just can't endure that.'

'Sorry. I'm really sorry, Lucie. But as I was saying, all those deaths. Dear Leah . . . I couldn't bear that. Not to have her there any more. She had always been there. I loved Leah. I loved her for all she went through for me. It was bad enough when Tom died, but Leah . . .'

'I understand, Belinda. Only it's hard to talk about it now. It seems too soon.'

'Everything is different now, is it not? Little Lucie . . . you were always so meek, just asking people to put on you . . . always the little waif.'

'I thought I was. And you took pains to remind me of it if I were inclined to forget.'

'That was the little monster again. I'm sorry, Lucie. I'm going to be different now.'

'I hope you will be. We have suffered a great shock, Celeste and I. He meant a great deal to us both. We are having to readjust ourselves. Please don't make trouble.'

'Trouble! My dear Lucie. I am going to help you, to take your minds off it.'

'Our minds are so much on it that it will be very difficult to take them off.'

'Leah used to say that I'd be better in London. I'd meet people. She wanted a good future for me.'

'Of course. She was your mother.'

'I suppose he wanted the same for you.'

97

'I don't think he thought about it much. We were very important to each other.'

. 'He wanted to keep you with him, I expect. The devoted daughter and all that. He wouldn't want to share you with a husband.'

'I don't know. But he has gone now . . .'

'And in a most horrible fashion. Everything that happened to him had to be dramatic. He was, as they say, larger than life, so spectacular things had to happen to him. And his going was the most spectacular of them all.'

'Belinda . . .'

'All right. I won't talk of it. You and I, Lucie, are growing up. If all this hadn't happened, people would be saying it was time we thought about getting married. Has anyone asked you?'

I was silent for a while, then she cried out: 'Someone has! Oh, Lucie! Just fancy . . . you! Tell me about it.'

I hesitated, but I guessed that she would hear sooner or later, so I told her about Joel.

She was intrigued. 'Disappeared! My dear Lucie, you do attract disaster. Disappeared in Buganda! On a mission! It's so thrilling. Oh, he'll come back, then you can be married. It will be a wonderful wedding. All the press will be there. He . . . a Member of Parliament . . . and all this happening to him. He must come back. It's hard to think of you – *you*, Lucie – in the midst of all this.'

'And what of you?' I asked.

'Well, I haven't lived in such exciting surroundings, have I? There are no Members of Parliament, terrorists and expeditions to Africa. Just imagine the goldfields . . .'

'My mother used to tell Rebecca about them and Rebecca told me. The campfires and the celebrations when someone found gold. I heard about the songs they used to sing and the shacks the miners and their families used to live in . . .'

I paused and she went on: 'Yes, it was like that. I expect it has improved a bit. I was in the big house, of course, and it wasn't so bad, but I used to long to come home, except when we went to Melbourne. That's a fine city. I used to look forward to our trips there. But then Tom became ill.'

'He always seemed so hale and hearty when he was here.'

'It was his heart. He had to have a manager. That was when Henry Farrell came.'

I waited eagerly, for clearly she wanted to talk about Henry Farrell.

'He was good-looking. One of those men made to command. Very sunburned, as most of them are over there. He took over from Tom. He knew how to deal with men.'

'You sound as though you were attracted by him.'

'I was.'

'And he?'

'He was besotted about me.'

'I guessed that was coming.'

'He wanted to marry me. You see, you are not the only one who has had a proposal.'

'And you declined?'

'I knew in time that I did not want to spend all my life in the goldfields. I had already made up my mind that I wanted to come home. I would have persuaded them to pay a visit to England. I thought Tom ought to have treatment in London. But then he died and we found out that the mine wasn't doing as much as it should, but Henry Farrell stayed on . . . and then he asked me.'

'He probably had his eye on the mine.'

'Well, you might expect that. But I wasn't Tom's daughter, only his stepdaughter. But there was no one else and he'd always looked on Leah's daughter as his. I liked Henry. He was a fine man. If things had been different . . .'

'What did he think about your leaving?'

'He was devastated, poor man. Tell me, what do you think about my father?'

'I don't know very much about him. He's in the wine business, I think. He goes to France now and then. I believe he has a house in London. We don't see much of him. I believe he goes to the family in Farnborough quite a lot. They moved from Chislehurst when the Empress Eugénie did. I believe there is a sort of court there.'

'How exciting! I'd love to go there.'

'It's only a court in exile. Don't expect Versailles in the time of the Sun King.'

'I wonder if he ever thinks of me. Where does the family live in Farnborough?'

'In a house called The Red House, I believe. I've heard Celeste mention it. That would be their parents' home. I don't know if he has his own house there. I dare say he moves around too much to want a place of his own.'

'A man ought to be aware of his daughter's existence. I must get his address and write to him. I wonder if Celeste will give it to me. I fancy she does not want to bring us together.'

'Well, he knows of your existence. If he wants to see you I dare say he will.'

'Some people need a bit of prodding. Give me his address.'

'I don't have it.'

'I expect The Red House, Farnborough would be enough.'

'Why don't you ask Celeste?'

'I think she might warn him and put him on his guard.'

'Well, if you think it would have that effect, wouldn't it be better to leave it alone?'

'But I don't want to leave it alone. I want him to be aware of me. I want to visit the court at Farnborough.'

'Why?'

'I rather fancy moving in royal circles. I am sure everyone must know The Red House, Farnborough. After all, in a way it would be connected with the resident royalty.'

Her eyes were dancing with excitement and she brought back many memories of the past. I knew then that her life in the Australian goldfields had not changed her one bit.

She said: 'You are looking sleepy, Lucie. I am going now, so I will leave you to your slumbers.'

I knew she wanted to get away. In the past, I remembered, when she had made up her mind to do something she would have no delay. It had to be done immediately.

I knew she was going off to write a letter to her father.

A few days had passed. There was still no news of Joel. I had to admit that having Belinda in the house did ease the tension to some degree, and that certain melancholy was less apparent. Belinda refused to be sad; and somehow she carried us along with her.

She was delighted with London and I could not help being caught up, to some extent, in her enthusiasm. There were only occasional moments when she slipped into solemnity, thinking of Leah; but it was only a passing sadness and she seemed determined to throw it off quickly.

There was no doubt that she was overjoyed to be back. Even Celeste cheered up a little. She could not help smiling at Belinda's exuberance. I think she felt mildly intrigued because Belinda was her niece. She had always craved affection, which she had never received from her rather formal parents, and as for her brother, I imagined he was far too immersed in his own affairs to think much about his sister. Celeste would have liked to bestow her affections on Belinda; I was a little dubious whether that would bring her satisfaction. I knew too much of the old Belinda not to know that she could not give Celeste the affection she craved.

Belinda wanted to see London, she said. She had missed it and so often thought of it. She loved the parks and the shops – particularly the latter, I discovered. I went with her one day. We looked at fashionable clothes but we bought nothing.

We went into a tea-shop and over tea and cakes Belinda grew a little mournful, and began to confide in me.

'I suppose I shouldn't have come home,' she said.

'What do you mean?' I asked. 'I thought you were so happy to be back.'

'Oh, I am. It's where I have longed to be. But . . .' She bit her lip and, shaking her head, went on: 'No, I can't tell you. You wouldn't understand. You're so rich.'

I looked at her in surprise. 'What are you talking about?' I asked.

'Well, I know how rich your father was, and most of it is left to you. Just think of that. Anything you want, you can buy. Whereas I . . . Lucie, I am poor, terribly poor.'

She stirred her tea thoughtfully. Her expression was one of abject misery. I remembered I had always been amazed at how quickly her moods could change.

'You see,' she went on, 'I only have the tiniest income. One of the reasons for Tom's heart attacks I always felt was the tension. He was dreadfully worried about the mine. Mines are gambles. They can make men's fortunes and break them. It did very well just after Tom bought it and then it began to decline. Trust your father to have got out in time. Poor Tom was so worried he got ill and died. He left everything to my mother, of course . . . and she got rid of the mine. It was the only thing she could do. Henry Farrell took it over. That was one of the reasons why she was so anxious for me to come to England. She thought Celeste – who, after all, is my aunt – would look after me, I'd make a grand marriage and live in luxury for the rest of my life.'

'Well, perhaps that will come to pass.'

'Look at me!' she said. 'How do I strike you?'

'Well, I suppose you would be reckoned quite good-looking.'

'Don't mock! I look like a provincial. How can I get into London society?'

'Who said you were going to get into London society?'

'I shall be living in the house. After all, we'll get back to normal in time . . . and there'll be entertaining, won't there?'

'I don't know. There was a great deal of entertaining when my father was alive.'

'Well, there will be again.'

'Celeste is not a very social person.'

'I suppose you'll be having a Season.'

'Really, Belinda! With everything that has happened I haven't thought about that.'

'No. I suppose not. But in the meantime . . . Oh, I feel so wretched! I don't want to be here, not as some shabby poor relation. I shouldn't be living in that house with you and Celeste.'

'What nonsense! As you are short of money, I can let you have some. I have enough.'

'I know you're rich. Lucky old Lucie. Isn't life ironical? We thought you were the waif and I was the daughter of the house. Not that he would have left all that money to me . . . even if he had gone on believing I was his daughter.'

'Stop talking about money. Look, I'm going to give you some.'

'How could I take it?'

'Well, make it a loan and then you can pay me back if you must.'

'How?'

'You'll find a way, I am sure. Didn't you always? And now I don't want to talk about it any more.'

She looked at me with the utmost tenderness. 'Oh, Lucie,' she said, 'I do love you. I always did, you know. In spite of the fact that I was such a beast to you.'

'Well, that's settled, then.'

'Lucie, do you really mean you'll give me money?'

I looked at her in exasperation, but her face expressed such joy that I smiled.

'Do you remember that dress with the little pleats . . . in that lavender shade . . . ?'

I nodded, smiling at her enthusiasm.

'If we could go back to that shop . . . if I could have that, and that cape and that costume with the severe-looking blouse and the frilly one as well . . . if I had those, I could get by for a little while.'

'You shall have them.'

'Oh, Lucie – you angel! It's only a loan, though. I insist.'

'Only a loan,' I agreed.

So we went back to the shop and bought the clothes which were charged to me; and I felt happier than I had for a long time. It was good to see Belinda so delighted.

When we returned to the house we were met by one of the maids.

'Oh, Miss Lansdon,' she said. 'A Mr Gerald Greenham has called. He wanted to see you specifically.'

My heart began to beat faster. My one thought was: Can there be news of Joel?

Belinda, still gloating over her new acquisitions, took them upstairs; and I went into the drawing-room.

'Gerald,' I cried. 'How nice to see you.'

He came forward and took both my hands. I saw at once that he was excited.

'Is there news?' I asked eagerly.

'Yes, but nothing of Joel yet. The fact is I am going away. I've got special leave. I'm going out there, Lucie.'

'You really are! How have you managed it? I should have thought the regiment . . .'

He smiled at me and grinned. 'I've got leave. It's a special case. After all, he is my brother. Anyway, I'm leaving tomorrow. I had to come and tell you.'

'What are you going to do when you get there?'

'I'm going to find him, Lucie.'

'Oh, Gerald, do you really think . . . ?'

'I'm full of hope and I had to come and let you know.'

'Thank you. It was kind of you to think of me. And your parents?'

'They think I'm going to find him . . . and I shall, Lucie.'

'Oh, I do hope so.'

He told me of his plans. It was a pity the journey would take so long. But he would have plenty to think about on the way. 'I am determined to find him . . . or at least to find what has happened.'

'Wouldn't it be wonderful if he came back!'

He nodded. 'Well, wish me luck, Lucie.'

'With all my heart.'

He was so certain that he was going to succeed that he made me feel more hopeful than I had since I had heard of Joel's disappearance.

Just as he was leaving Belinda came into the room. She was wearing the lavender dress with the pleats. It fitted her somewhat voluptuous figure perfectly and she looked very attractive.

'Oh, hello,' she said, 'I didn't realize your visitor was still here. I had to try it on, Lucie. I was so thrilled.'

'This is Mr Gerald Greenham,' I said, 'and this is Celeste's niece, Miss Belinda . . . Marner.' I hesitated over her name. She had been called Lansdon while she was with us, but of course that had not been her real name. She was, I supposed, Belinda Polhenny for that was her mother's name; it did not fit her at all and she had taken Tom Marner's name when Leah had married him, which seemed a sensible thing to do.

She was smiling at him in a way with which I was to become familiar – provocative, inviting admiration.

Gerald certainly gave it.

'I'm delighted to meet you, Miss Marner,' he said.

'I'm delighted, too,' she replied, and they stood smiling at each other with mutual approval.

'Mr Greenham and his family were great friends of my father,' I said.

'So are you in politics?' said Belinda. 'How exciting!'

'Sorry,' said Gerald. 'Army. But politics runs in the family. My father, my elder brother . . .'

'And you escaped that fate,' said Belinda. 'Are you leaving now?' She gave a little pout as though she objected to that.

'I have to,' he told her regretfully.

'Mr Greenham is leaving the country tomorrow,' I told her.

'How exciting! Is it permitted to ask where you are going?'

'To Africa.'

'How thrilling! Of course, people in the Army do travel about . . .'

She had certainly impressed him. I could see that he was very reluctant to go; he seemed temporarily even to have forgotten the project about which he had been so excited on his arrival.

When he had gone Belinda stood before me smoothing down the pleats of the dress. 'Well, what do you think?' she asked.

'That you made a great effort to attract his interest,' I said. 'And you managed to do it very effectively.'

She looked at me mischievously. 'Oh . . . I was talking about the dress.'

'It suits you,' I told her.

And I thought: She hasn't changed one little bit. She has come home not so much to see us as to find a husband who will keep her in luxury for the rest of her life.

A few days later there was another visitor to the house. This was Jean Pascal Bourdon. He had written to Celeste to say that he would be in London for a brief spell and would like to come and see his sister.

When she told me this I immediately thought that this sudden interest might have something to do with the letter I was sure Belinda had written to him.

When she heard that he was coming, Belinda was very excited. She became pensive. She asked me a great many questions about him, and brought the subject up with Celeste, who was somewhat non-committal, so she turned back to me.

I told her that he was interested in wine and that the family owned a château in the Médoc. 'That,' I said, 'I believe, is the greatest wine-growing country in France . . . or one of them. I believe the place is called Château Bourdon and has been in the family for years. I think he has a small pied-à-terre in London, for he does not stay here in this house which might be expected, Celeste being his sister. It would be quite convenient for him. I believe he spends some time in Farnborough where his parents have their home.'

'In the court of the Empress Eugénie,' said Belinda, her eyes sparkling. 'Celeste does not go there.'

'No, she never did . . . and they did not come here. In any case his father died a little while ago and his mother is too feeble to travel.'

'My grandparents,' murmured Belinda.

'I believe they are very formal. In any case you will see Monsieur Jean Pascal Bourdon when he comes here. He'll be dining with us on Tuesday.'

I could see that she was already making plans. She was deciding what she would wear. She bought a book on wines and spent some time studying it. She was determined to impress him.

She wore the lavender dress with the pleats and piled her dark hair high on her head. She looked very arresting.

'I wish I had some piece of jewellery,' she sighed. 'Pearls would look just right with this.'

'You don't need any further adornment,' I told her.

'Lucie, *you* haven't any idea.'

'Thanks,' I said. 'Then I won't interfere. I was going to say I have a pearl brooch which my father gave me.'

'Oh Lucie . . . really! Show me!'

I brought it out and she pinned it on her dress. 'It's lovely,' she cried. 'It's perfect. Elegant simplicity, is it not? You're going to lend it to me, I know.'

I nodded and she threw her arms about my neck, perfunctorily kissing me. Her thoughts were far away, thinking of the effect she would have on her father.

We went down to the drawing-room together.

He was there with Celeste and rose as we entered. He was of medium height, with dark hair and lively dark eyes; he was handsome in a way, with well-defined features in a somewhat classic mould; he spoke English well with only the faintest trace of accent. He was elegant and suave, and

108

there was something about him which slightly repelled me. I was not sure what, but I did know that whenever he was mentioned Rebecca's attitude showed me clearly that she did not like him, and I think that this attitude of hers had sown seeds of mistrust within me.

'Here are Lucie and Belinda,' said Celeste.

He turned to us. 'Lucie!' He took my hand and kissed it. 'Enchanted,' he murmured. And then: 'Belinda.' He took both her hands. 'Why . . . you are beautiful. I think we should get to know each other, don't you?'

Belinda sparkled. Her eyes danced. I, who understood her well, knew she was thinking that it was going to be easy to make a conquest of this man. I was not so sure. I felt I knew a little of him – not much, but enough to tell me that one could not take him entirely for what he appeared to be. He could not be easily understood. He was Belinda's father and I imagined they might have similar characteristics in some respects. That might draw them together.

'Dinner will be served very soon,' said Celeste.

He looked at his sister. 'Will there be guests?'

'No, I thought we might just be . . . the family.'

'Excellent idea. It is what I hoped.'

'Well, in a few minutes, I think, we should go in. It will be the small room tonight.'

'Delightfully intimate,' he said.

His eyes were on Belinda – admiring, I thought, though one could not be sure with such a man.

'I am so pleased you have come home,' he said to Belinda.

'So am I,' she answered.

'You don't look as though you have come from – what is it they call it? – the Outback?'

'Yes,' said Belinda, 'they do call it that.'

'Rather you look like a young lady of fashion.'

109

'What one is depends upon oneself,' responded Belinda.

'How right you are.'

'Belinda has told us a great deal about her life on the goldfields,' said Celeste. 'It was very interesting.'

'You must tell me . . . some time,' he said to Belinda.

It was an indication that they would meet again and that he was not particularly interested in goldfields. Belinda got the message. She was beaming. I fancied she was deciding that it was all going according to her plans.

At dinner there was an animated conversation, generally between Belinda and Jean Pascal. It was clear to both Celeste and me that he was delighted with her and amused and rather pleased to be presented with a grown-up daughter.

Belinda had always been without reticence. She talked animatedly, showing a lively interest in the château in France and the wine industry.

'It's not far from Bordeaux,' he said. 'Wine-growing country. Everything there is suitable for it.'

'It produces the best wine in the world,' said Belinda.

'We think so, naturally.'

'So does the whole world. I think it must be fascinating watching over the grapes . . . making sure that everything is all right. How wonderful!'

'It can be far from pleasant sometimes,' he told her. 'There are forces to contend with . . . weather and disease.'

'But that makes it all the more exciting.'

'I am not sure that my workpeople would agree with that.'

'Well, if everything runs smoothly, it must be less rewarding when it all comes right in the end.'

'A philosopher, I see.'

'It's just plain common sense.'

'There are things you do not know of, Belinda. Why, some ten years ago the vine louse destroyed most of the grapes in France. That was a far from exhilarating experience, I can tell you. Just imagine the wretched creatures getting to the vines underground and sucking the sap at the roots. There is only one way of getting rid of them, and that is to flood the grounds.'

'How terrible!' said Belinda. 'But how fascinating! Do tell us about Château Bourdon. Is it really a castle?'

'Not on the scale of Blois or Chambord – much, much smaller. There were many castles in France and they were not all destroyed during the Revolution. Bourdon is a medium-sized château. It is rather pleasant. It is set in attractive country and our own vineyards are quite extensive.'

She clasped her hands and gazed at him ecstatically.

I thought he was rather attracted by his daughter, but I was not sure, for he was the sort of man who would hide his true feelings under a cloak of sophistication. No doubt he was seeing all sorts of traits in her similar to his own.

He did bestow some attention on me.

He asked me what I intended to do, and I told him that as yet I was unsure.

'Lucie has suffered a great shock,' said Celeste. 'She needs time to recover.'

He nodded sympathetically.

'My dear Lucie,' he said, 'I feel for you. Celeste has told me how brave you have been. I must apologise for bringing up this subject on a happy occasion, but when it is so much in our thoughts it seems unnatural to make a studied effort not to mention it. I feel deeply for you . . . and my sister. I do indeed. But you have to grow away from it.'

I nodded in agreement.

'Belinda will help you, I'm sure.' He turned to her. 'I am so glad you came home, my dear.'

'We are glad too,' said Celeste.

'Now we are going to make you put the past behind you,' he went on to me. 'Are we not, Belinda?'

'Of course we are,' said Belinda. 'Lucie and I are very special friends.'

'I'm glad to hear it, and I am sorry to have introduced such a sombre note to our happy evening. However, I just did not want you and Celeste to think me hard-hearted.'

'I understand,' I said.

'Tell us more about the château,' pleaded Belinda.

He did so cheerfully. It had been in the possession of the Bourdons since the days of Charles the Wise and that was in the fourteenth century. It was a typical French château. 'There are hundreds of them throughout France,' he went on. 'Most have the rounded towers at each end which come to a point at the top.'

'They have been described as pepperpot towers,' I said.

'A good description. Grey stone . . . with that medieval look. It has been restored in places, of course, so you will find touches of later centuries here and there, but nothing has been done to it for the last hundred years. Such places are built to stand for ever. We even survived the Revolution. I hope you will see it one day.'

Belinda exuded satisfied excitement. It was better than she had expected, I was sure. There *was* a similarity between them and I felt they would understand each other – a fact which made communication between them easy.

She was delighted with her father, and I had the impression that he was not displeased to discover he had such an exhilarating daughter.

It was late when he left the house. Belinda came to my room and sat on my bed.

'What an evening! I have never known one like it.'

'Well, it is very rare for a young woman of your age to come face to face with a father whom she has never seen before.'

'Do you think he liked me?'

'Like might be too strong a word. I think he found you . . . interesting.'

'*I* thought he liked me. He kept talking to me and watching me.'

'You kept talking to him and watching him.'

'Do you think he'll take me to Château Bourdon?'

'I don't know.'

'And to the court at Farnborough?'

'It might be rather difficult to explain an illegitimate daughter in formal society.'

'You beast, Lucie.'

'I'm only stating a fact. The French are very formal and I should imagine particularly so in royal circles . . . even though in exile.'

She looked momentarily downcast and I went on: 'Yes, Belinda, I think he was impressed. I feel absolutely sure that he will want to see you again . . . soon.'

She put her arms round my neck and kissed me.

'You're an angel,' she said.

'I'm glad of the remarkable transformation. All this for just stating the obvious.'

'Yes,' she said musingly, 'I think he liked me, too. He also likes you, Lucie.'

'He likes all young women, providing they are not outstandingly unattractive. But daughters would come into

113

a different category. Yes, I am absolutely certain that he was not displeased with his daughter and I have a feeling that he will want to see her again . . . very soon.'

On that note she said goodnight and went to her own room.

He did come again. In fact he allowed only one day to pass, during which Belinda's mood changed from despair to hope, and then he arrived.

It was obvious to me that he was rather amused to discover a grown-up daughter, and Belinda was just the type of whom he could be proud. She was vivacious and, if not exactly conventionally beautiful, very attractive. She had something more than beauty. Leah's charm had been her gentleness, which had given her the look of a madonna – particularly in the days when we were young and I had often seen the tenderness in her eyes when they rested on her daughter. But there was nothing of the madonna about Belinda. Hers was a flamboyant charm; she was a little mysterious, promising all sorts of excitement to those who went along with her. As soon as she entered a room one was aware of her; the atmosphere changed; she had some special quality. Even here, to this house of mourning, she had brought some relief from gloom.

I was glad for her sake that Jean Pascal Bourdon was ready to recognize her as his daughter. He was the sort of man who, if she had been unappealing, would have gone away and forgotten all about her. But he was intrigued by this dazzling girl who had suddenly presented herself to him. I guessed he was thinking the situation rather piquant.

He had never married. I wondered why. I had heard that he had intended to marry someone connected with the royal house of France, some relation of the Emperor

Napoleon III and the Empress Eugénie, but of course the 1870 débâcle had put a stop to that. Jean Pascal was not the man to attach himself to a falling star. At least that was the impression I had and which I realized had been given to me by my sister Rebecca. She had clearly not wanted to talk much of him. She disliked him intensely.

During the next weeks we saw a great deal of him, for he came frequently to the house. Belinda was radiant. Her plans were working out – even better than she had hoped.

I think he rather liked to be seen with her. He bought clothes for her. He was delighted with her choice. She had French elegance, he said, which she had inherited from the paternal side of the family. She was learning French, and when Belinda applied herself to anything she did it with such enthusiasm that she was certain to succeed.

Now her great aim in life was to please her father, to bind him to her; she was determined to be part of the château life in France and finally to be received at Farnborough.

She lived in a whirl of excitement during those weeks and, I must say, to a certain extent carried me along with her; and Celeste was not far behind. She was delighted by her brother's interest in Belinda.

Belinda's joy was overwhelming when he suggested that she should have an allowance.

'Do you know what he said to me, Lucie?' she asked.

'I have no idea,' I replied.

'He said, "I can't have my daughter living with rich little Miss Lucie as a penniless dependant." Isn't that wonderful? Isn't it the most exciting thing to find you have a marvellous father! I have had three fathers – the first I didn't like much; the second was all right but he was not exactly a gentleman; and now I have the perfect father.'

I said: 'You are not being fair to the first two.'

'Oh, shut up, Lucie. You always argue about everything. I have now found my real father and he is the best of the lot. Isn't that something to be pleased about? I shall be able to buy some marvellous clothes. I think I shall be going to France soon.'

'Has he said so?'

'Not in so many words, but he talks about it . . . just as though I'm going to be there.'

'Well, I suppose you will soon be leaving us and going to your grand château. And then, of course, you'll be joining the royal circle. I wonder what it's like at Farnborough. How does royalty live in exile? Farnborough must be a change from Versailles.'

'I shall probably invite you.'

'That's gracious of you. Oh, Belinda, I am so pleased, I really am, that it is working out well for you.'

I believed, as Belinda did, that her father was making some plans for her future. He was spending so much time at the house, which in the past he had rarely visited. My father had never liked him, and had not been a man to assume an affability he did not feel. That may have been one of the reasons why in the past we had seen so little of Celeste's brother. However, that was changed now.

He took us to the opera and to the theatre, following with supper. They were very enjoyable and interesting evenings.

He liked to hear Belinda air her views, and he always listened intently with an amused smile on his lips. *La Traviata* was the opera we saw, and I remember sitting in the restaurant with the red plush, comfortable divan-like seats, while we discussed it.

Belinda's eyes shone. She had enjoyed the evening thoroughly.

'But I think she was rather silly to have given up her lover just because of that old father,' she said. 'I didn't like *him* at all. What business was it of his? To come and spoil it all!'

'You think she should have sent him on his way?'

'*I* would have.'

'Of course *you* would.'

'Well, if they had not parted they would not have had long together,' I pointed out. 'She was going to die soon in any case.'

'You see, Lucie has a logical mind,' said Jean Pascal. 'Now that is rare in a woman. I admire it very much, Miss Lucie.'

Belinda hated his attention to be turned away from herself for a moment.

'Oh, I thought that, too,' she said.

'Then we have two logical women. Don't you think that is something to celebrate, Celeste? Let us have some champagne.'

I watched Belinda. She never seemed tired, while poor Celeste wilted. As for myself, I was still in the theatre, thinking about poor Violetta, her exquisite voice still ringing in my ears. It was wonderful; even when she was on her deathbed, she sang with power and clarity.

When we arrived back at the house Belinda came as usual to my room. It was becoming a habit for her to do so, for she liked to comment on the day.

'What a wonderful evening!' she said. 'I expect you were thrilled to be part of it.'

'I certainly enjoyed the opera.'

'He's going to take us to the play. We're going to see Ellen Terry and Henry Irving. Isn't that exciting? I'm so glad I wrote to him. Don't you think, Lucie, that most people don't *make* things happen. They just go on accepting what is. I like to say *I want* that to happen and then I'm going to make it happen.'

117

'I think you are the sort of person who has always done that.'

'Isn't it clever?'

'Not always, Belinda.'

I was wondering whether she remembered what she had done to Rebecca and Pedrek. That was one of the occasions when she had attempted to arrange life as she wanted it to go; and she had succeeded temporarily. She was fortunate in having to deal with forgiving people like Rebecca and Pedrek.

Now she was thinking that if she had not written to her father and implied she wanted to see him all this would not be happening now, so I supposed she had a point.

True to his promise, Jean Pascal took us to the theatre. It was a wonderful experience because we saw the unique Ellen Terry as Katharine in *Henry VIII*. We were all entranced and even Jean Pascal dropped his mood of cynical sophistication, and became engrossed in the performance. There was the usual supper afterwards.

'I liked her,' said Belinda. 'She wasn't going to give in.'

'But in the end she had to,' I pointed out. 'He was too powerful for her.'

'That is because he was a king and a man,' replied Belinda. 'They have all the power.'

'So you think that men have too much power?' asked her father.

'I think they do not have as much as they think they have . . . and they can be made to do things which women want as long as they don't know they're doing it.'

Jean Pascal laughed. 'She's a devious creature, this daughter of mine,' he said. 'I am beginning to wonder whether I shall have to be on my guard against her.'

'Oh, I wouldn't do anything you didn't approve of,' said Belinda quickly.

'How should I know that? Would it all be part of the guile to deceive?'

'You'd know. You're clever.'

'Still leading me on?'

Belinda was a little nonplussed. She was wondering, I guessed, whether she had betrayed too much of herself.

We went on discussing the play but she was a little restrained and uneasy.

It was during supper that Jean Pascal said: 'I shall have to be going back to France very soon.'

Belinda's expression betrayed her bitter disappointment.

He put on a doleful look and went on: 'Well, you see, I have to find out what's going on there. I have been away rather a long time.'

'When will you be coming back?' asked Belinda.

'That is something I cannot be sure of.'

Melancholy settled at the table. It was amazing how Belinda carried us along with her moods.

Then he said: 'I've been wondering . . .' He paused for some seconds. 'I rather think you would enjoy the château.'

Belinda's eyes opened wide. Joy flooded back. He was smiling at her and I knew he found her enchanting.

'Well,' he went on, 'it is the country . . . of course, we are not so very far from Bordeaux . . .'

'Do you mean . . . I could come with you?'

'I was wondering . . .'

'Oh, how marvellous! When do we go?'

'The end of the week. Is that enough notice?'

'It's wonderful. I'd be ready to go tomorrow.'

'Then it is settled.' He paused. 'There was something . . .'

Belinda looked worried. Then he said, looking at me: 'Perhaps Lucie would like to come, too?'

'I?' I said, surprised.

'Well, you are Lucie, are you not?'

'Oh, Lucie,' cried Belinda, 'you must come. Oh, you must. I'd hate for you not to. It would do her good, wouldn't it, Aunt Celeste?'

'I think it would be a change of scene and that would be good for her,' said Celeste.

'Go to France,' I began. 'But . . .'

'Oh, don't be so stodgy, Lucie,' cried Belinda. 'She is a bit stodgy, you know,' she said to her father. 'She dithers. She always did.'

'You must be nicer to Lucie,' admonished Jean Pascal. 'She has been a very good friend to you.'

'I am nice to her. Aren't I, Lucie? I want her to come with us. You will, won't you, Lucie? Say yes.'

'I . . . I'd like to think about it.'

'What do you want to think about? It's marvellous. *I* want you to come.'

'You'd be very welcome,' said Jean Pascal. 'And it wouldn't be the same for Belinda without you.'

'What about Celeste?'

'Let Celeste come, too.'

'No . . . no,' protested Celeste. 'I couldn't think of it. But, Lucie, I think it might be good for you to get away for a while.'

'I did get away to Cornwall.'

'Yes, but it wasn't long enough.'

Jean Pascal leaned across the table and took my hand. 'Think about it,' he said warmly.

'Thank you,' I replied. 'I will.'

Later Belinda stormed into my room.

'Of course you'll come,' she announced. 'Why not? You are an old spoilsport. I don't understand why you hesitate. Do you want my father to go down on his knees and *beg* you to come?'

120

'No, of course not. But he really doesn't want me. He wants you. He is only asking me to be company for you.'

'But he does. He's always talking about you. Asking questions about you. He likes you . . . because you've been so good to me.'

'I'll think about it. It was all so sudden. I am just not sure.'

'Oh, you are an old stick-in-the-mud. You must come, Lucie. I want you to. It will be more fun if you are there.'

'What? Such an old stick-in-the-mud?'

'Of course. The contrast draws attention to my superior charms. Moreover, I shouldn't like it half as much without you.'

'I've said I'll think about it.'

'Well, go on thinking and tomorrow we'll talk about what we'll take with us.'

I did think about it. I kept waking up and asking myself: Why not? Poor Celeste would be lonely; but she did seem to want to be alone. I should miss Belinda. I had felt more alive since she came. I could ask the Greenhams to let me know at once if there was any news, and if Joel came home I could come back straightaway.

By the morning I had convinced myself that it would be a good idea to go to France with Belinda and her father.

Encounter with a Swan

Belinda greeted my decision with delight. Then she said scornfully: 'I knew you'd come to your senses. It will be such fun. Oh, how glad I am I came to England.'

Then she started to talk about the clothes she would take. She planned to go shopping that afternoon and she wanted me to go with her.

Celeste thought it would be a good thing for me to go to France.

She said: 'It has been different, hasn't it, since Belinda came? She's good for us, Lucie. She does stop our brooding a little. I am sure you will feel better in France. You see, you'll get right away from this place and that must be good for you. You know I told you you should get down to Manorleigh for a time, but I suppose there are too many memories there. This will be a complete change. I'll send Amy up to help you pack.'

'I'm not ready yet.'

'Well . . . when you need her.'

In spite of myself, during the next few days I was caught up in the excitement. Belinda talked constantly about our trip to France. She was so happy, it was a joy to watch her. I thought how much better she managed her life than I did mine. She had lost her mother not long ago and the man whom she had regarded as a father and of whom she had been fond, yet she was able to cast off the unhappy past and

122

look forward to the future. Perhaps it was a wonderful experience to find a long-lost father – after all, in a way I had known what that meant myself, for I, too, had discovered *my* father and we had become important to each other. So perhaps it was not so surprising after all.

Preparation for the visit took my mind off constantly wondering what was happening to Joel. I had told myself that there was nothing I could do by staying in London.

Belinda's arrival had caused a great deal of excitement among the servants and I knew she was the main topic of conversation in their quarters. Amy, the girl who was to help me with my packing, was taking the place of one of the parlourmaids who was leaving in a month's time to get married.

She was about sixteen years of age, fresh-faced and pretty; she came from the country, she told me. She was rather loquacious and, I suppose, excited about coming to London.

She was getting on very well, she told me. She found the people very friendly. She had been told it would not be like that in London, but she had nothing to complain of.

She had brought in some cases from one of the attics and had set one on the bed. I noticed that she kept glancing towards the window, and I asked if she was expecting to see someone down there.

She blushed faintly. 'It . . . it's a friend,' she told me.

'Oh. You've quickly made friends.'

'This is a special friend, Miss. I've known him for about three weeks.'

'A young man?'

She blushed deeper and giggled.

'Jack is his name,' she said.

'How did you meet him?'

'It was my afternoon off and I was just going for a walk in

123

the park. He said he was walking that way. So . . . we got talking.'

'And you found you had a lot in common, did you?'

'You might say that, Miss. He was ever so interesting. I told him where I came from . . . and he was very pleasant, like.'

'I suppose you've been told to be careful of strange men?'

'Oh yes, Miss, but he wasn't like that. He was ever so nice. He said we'd meet again and we did. He's round this way quite a lot. He delivers things, you see . . . papers in envelopes . . . documents, I think he said . . . from some solicitor. He said people don't like to trust them to the post.'

'That's interesting.'

'Do you want to take this skirt, Miss? If you're going to, you'll want the jacket that goes with it. Oh, here it is. I'll fold it in tissue, then it won't get creased.'

I went to the window and looked down. A young man was standing on the opposite side of the road in almost exactly the same spot as that other had stood.

'There is a young man down there, Amy,' I said.

'I wonder if . . .' She was beside me. 'Oh, that's him. That's Jack.'

'Do you want to go down and have a word with him?'

'Oh, could I, Miss?'

'Go on,' I said; and she went.

I thought I could easily do the packing myself. It had been Celeste's idea that I needed help.

I smiled to myself, contemplating Amy and her young man. I expected there would be more; she was an attractive girl.

The day arrived for our departure. Jean Pascal came to the house with the carriage which was to take us to the station.

'I feel honoured to escort two beautiful young ladies,' he said gallantly.

As we settled into the carriage Belinda said: 'This is an adventure. Not for you, *mon père*. You have had too many adventures to get excited about one – if it is an adventure for you, which this is not, of course.'

She had decided to call him '*mon père*'. 'Father' seemed wrong somehow. She said, you could not suddenly start calling someone father. She thought '*mon père*' more suitable and he seemed to like it. So that was what he had become.

He said now: 'I can still get excited about adventures and I do admit that this one is filling me with elation.'

We all leaned forward to wave to Celeste who was standing at the door. As we did so, I caught a glimpse of Amy's Jack, the deliverer of documents. He was standing on the other side of the road.

'Did you see the young man?' I asked Belinda. 'He's waiting for a glimpse of Amy.' As the carriage moved off I told them about my conversation with Amy. 'He delivers documents,' I added.

'An odd occupation,' said Jean Pascal. 'I've never heard of that.'

'It may be that Amy didn't get it right or he is trying to impress her.'

'I dare say that was it. What of your sister Rebecca? What does she think about your coming to France?'

'It was all arranged so quickly. I have written to her, but I am wondering whether she will have received my letter by now.'

'I always had such a great respect for Rebecca. A wonderful lady. And now she is living in my old home. I find that rather amusing.'

'Oh, they love High Tor. It's a fine old house.'

'I agree.'

'It's a very special place for me, I believe,' said Belinda somewhat roguishly.

Her father chose to ignore that remark and, always alert for his reaction, Belinda did not pursue it.

'Everything looks different this morning,' she said. 'That's because we are leaving London.'

In a very short time we had reached the station. We were in good time but the boat train was already waiting. A porter took our luggage and we were conducted along the platform to a first class carriage.

'I expect you two young ladies would like corner seats,' said Jean Pascal.

'Oh yes, please,' cried Belinda.

She got into the train and I was about to follow her when some instinct made me turn my head. I looked along the platform and, to my astonishment, I was sure a young man I saw not far from us was Amy's friend, Jack.

No, I thought. We left him near the house. It couldn't possibly be. What would he be doing here at the boat train?

'Come on,' said Belinda. 'What are you waiting for?'

I got into the train.

'Here is your window seat,' said Jean Pascal. He took my arm and as I sat down his hand lingered on mine.

'Comfortable?' he asked.

'Yes, thank you.'

I could not stop thinking of Amy's Jack. It must have been someone who bore a resemblance to him. He was really quite an ordinary young man and the mistake was understandable.

Belinda sat back in her seat and closed her eyes.

'Isn't this wonderful?' she said.

*

It was during the Channel crossing that I met the Fitzgeralds.

The sea was smooth and Belinda and I were sitting on the deck with Jean Pascal. Belinda was talking animatedly with her father. I sometimes felt I was a little *de trop*. It was easy for me to understand that. Belinda wanted to be alone with the father whom she had recently discovered. She had wanted me to come along with them, true, and she had been very insistent that I should, but there were moments when they wished to be alone together and this was one of them.

I stood up and said: 'I am going to take a little walk.'

'Don't go too far away,' cautioned Jean Pascal.

'No, I won't. I'll keep you in sight.'

I walked a little way and paused to lean on the rail and look at the sea. There was no sight of land and only the faintest breeze to ruffle the waves a little. I stood, filling my lungs with the fresh air. Where was Joel now? I wondered, as I did constantly. How was Gerald faring with his what could be called a wild goose chase? How could he discover what others had failed to do?

'Lovely day, isn't it?' said a voice beside me.

I turned. A young woman was standing beside me. She was taller than I, fair-haired, and had a pleasant smile.

'Very,' I replied.

'We're lucky to have it so smooth. It can be quite rough really.'

'I'm sure it can. You cross often, do you?'

'Not often, but I have done it before . . . when it wasn't so pleasant. Is this your first crossing?'

'Yes.'

'Oh, then I'm glad it is a good one.'

There was silence while we both looked out to sea. Then she said: 'Are you staying in France?'

'Yes . . . for a time.'

'Beautiful country.'

'You know it well?'

'Not really. But I have visited it several times. This time we are going farther south than usual. Near Bordeaux.'

'Oh, so are we!'

'On holiday?'

'Yes, I suppose so. Visiting.'

'I'm convalescing.'

'Have you been ill?'

'My brother says I need a rest away from the damp of home. He thinks this is the place. He says the climate is good for the vines, so it will be for me. That's why he's taking me.'

'How nice of him.'

'He's a very good brother, but he fusses a little. I'm not complaining. It's comforting. Well, there are just the two of us now, you see. Oh . . . here he is.'

A man was coming towards us. He was tall and had the same pleasant smile which I had thought attractive in his sister. He was a few years older than she was, I imagined.

'Oh, there you are, Phillida,' he said, not noticing me for a few seconds. 'There's a chill in the air. Button up your coat.'

She looked at me and smiled as though to say: There, I told you so.

I was about to move away when she said: 'This is my brother Roland . . . Roland Fitzgerald.'

'How do you do?' I said.

He took my hand and shook it. He was looking at me questioningly: 'I'm Lucie Lansdon,' I said.

'We were just chatting as we looked at the sea and congratulated ourselves on its calmness,' said Phillida.

He looked at her with mock exasperation which told me

128

that it was a habit of hers to chat to strangers and one of which he did not entirely approve.

'She's going to stay near Bordeaux,' announced Phillida.

'Oh, not exactly Bordeaux,' I said. 'It's a place near, I think. A little place called Bourdon. I imagine it's a sort of hamlet.'

'I believe I've heard of it,' he said. 'We shall be a few miles further south. Isn't there a château there? Château Bourdon, I believe.'

'Yes, that's right. I suppose I ought to be going. It won't be long before we are disembarking.'

'It was very nice to have a chat,' said Phillida.

Her brother put his arm through hers and, smiling, I turned away and went back to Belinda and Jean Pascal.

I wondered during the long journey down to Bourdon whether I should see the Fitzgeralds again as they were travelling in the same direction; but I did not.

There were so many hours in the train. First to Paris, where we had to change, then to Bordeaux where a carriage was waiting for us, to take us the several miles to Bourdon.

It was late at night when we arrived, so I could not see the full glory of the château at that time. We turned into a long avenue with big trees on either side and we seemed to drive for at least a mile before we came to the château.

As we pulled up several people came running towards us and there appeared to be a great deal of bustle from within. I was aware of a dark imposing building. We mounted several stone steps to reach the door. Belinda was awestruck and for once silent.

Two men appeared with lanterns to guide us into an enormous hall. A sudden feeling of dread came over me, and a ridiculous impulse to turn and run back home, down to

Cornwall and Rebecca. It was an absurd feeling which I dismissed at once. I was overwrought. Too much that was tragic had happened to me in too short a time. My father . . . Joel . . . I felt an almost unbearable longing for them both. My father's shrewd common sense. Joel's gentleness. If only I could enjoy them again.

I glanced at Belinda. She clearly felt no such misgivings: her mood was one of sheer enchantment.

People were scurrying about in all directions; and Jean Pascal was giving orders in rapid French. Thérèse . . . Marie . . . Jeanne . . . Jacques . . . Georges . . . there seemed to be so many of them. I gathered that first we were to be shown our rooms where we could wash and change before eating.

I was given into the care of Thérèse who was middle-aged and brisk. She took me up a wide staircase to a corridor which was long and dark. She set down a candelabrum which she was carrying and lighted its three candles, then she held it high and I followed her to the room which had been chosen for me.

I shivered a little. I thought: It will be different in daylight. I was trying to shake off that sense of foreboding.

Thérèse indicated the hot water and towels which had been set up in a little alcove, and which I later learned was called a *ruelle*. I managed to understand what she was saying, which was that she would return for me in fifteen minutes and take me to the dining-room.

There was a basin and ewer, so I washed and combed my hair. My face in candlelight looked back at me from an antique mirror; it seemed mottled and unlike me . . . almost a stranger.

Why had I come here? I was asking myself. I might now be at High Tor with Rebecca. I had hesitated, it was true, but Belinda had been persuasive and I was as easily influenced by her as I had ever been.

I told myself that I was being foolish. It had been a long and exhausting journey; I was in a strange land; I had suffered a great shock from which I had not yet recovered. I would feel differently in the morning.

Thérèse came and took me down to the dining-room where Jean Pascal was waiting. He took my hands and held them firmly.

'It is my earnest desire that you should be happy here, Lucie,' he said.

'Thank you.'

'I shall do my best to make you like this place.'

'It is kind of you.'

Belinda had arrived.

'What an exciting place!' she cried. 'I long to explore.'

'Which you shall do in the morning,' her father assured her. 'I myself will take you on a tour of inspection . . . and Lucie as well, of course.'

'I long to see it all,' enthused Belinda.

'For tonight you must content yourself with what my servants have prepared for you. I will not have you see too much of my château for the first time in the dark.'

Belinda laughed with pleasure.

The meal seemed to go on for a long time. I felt a little better. I had simply had an attack of nerves – something which I had thought could not happen to me. I was just tired and could not feel the exuberance that Belinda did.

Jean Pascal was eager for us to taste the wine. It was one of the finest vintages, he told us, and he had ordered it to be served tonight because this was a special occasion.

'And this is your own wine?' cried Belinda.

'My dear child, did you think I would allow anything else to be served in my château?'

Belinda laughed. I liked to see her happy. She had an effect on me, for she helped to lift my spirits.

When the meal was over Jean Pascal suggested we retire.

'We are all feeling the effects of the long journey,' he said. 'All those hours on the train . . . they are a trial of endurance.'

So we said goodnight and Jean Pascal summoned the servants to conduct us to our rooms. Thérèse took me to mine. I could see why this was necessary. I should not have been able to find it by myself.

Candles throw shadows over a room and somehow they disturb the imagination. The drapes had been drawn across the windows. I undressed but before getting into bed I went to the window and drew back the curtains. I could just see a green expanse, in the middle of which was a fountain. There was no moon, but the stars were bright; and I felt happier with the light from them in my room.

I wondered if Belinda's room was close to mine. She seemed to have gone in another direction when we had been escorted up after dinner.

The place seemed very quiet.

I looked at my door, which was heavy, with intricate carving. It seemed to me that some of the flowers had human faces. It was beautiful, I supposed, but in a way menacing – as I saw it that night.

That was the mood I was in.

Then I noticed the key in the lock. I turned it. Now I had locked myself in.

It was amazing how much better that made me feel.

I got into bed, but it was a long time before I slept.

When I awoke the sun was shining.

The room looked quite different. I unlocked my door

and went back to bed. I saw that it was seven o'clock. I lay there wondering what life would be like here. I started thinking of how much everything had changed since my father's death. I was longing for the old days . . . the familiar house, the conversations we had had. I wanted to wait up for him on his late nights at the House, to enjoy once more those evenings when I sat opposite him watching him eat while he told me about the day's proceedings; I wanted to think of a settled future with Joel, marrying with the approval of both families . . . settling into a way of life which was already familiar to me.

I had believed it was there, waiting for me, but with two blows, fate had decided otherwise; and here I was in an ancient château which echoed with memories of the past. It seemed to me that there were ghosts here, ready to emerge. Many stirring events must have happened here . . . death . . . unhappiness . . . dark secrets. Pleasures too . . . joys . . . happiness. Why, in such places, did one always thing of the unpleasant things? Perhaps because they were more obtrusive.

What was I expected to do? I presumed a maid would come in with hot water. In the last few days I had tried to improve the French I had learned with Miss Jarrett; speaking it – particularly with the natives – was quite different from reading and speaking it with Miss Jarrett.

At about eight o'clock there was a tap at my door. I called for whoever was there to come in.

It was Thérèse with a tray on which was a brioche and pieces of hot crusty bread, a little pot of butter, a cup and saucer and two jugs, one containing coffee, the other hot milk, both covered with woollen cosies to keep them warm.

'*Petit déjeuner, Mademoiselle,*' she told me.

With her was another maid who carried a big metal jug full of hot water which she placed in the *ruelle*.

I thanked them and, smiling, they departed.

The coffee was delicious, so were the hot bread and brioche.

While we were at dinner on the previous night our luggage had been brought to our rooms. I had been too tired to unpack last night and had just taken out things I needed for my immediate use.

I put on a dark blue dress and hung up the rest of my clothes in the wardrobe. While I was doing this, there was a knock on my door and before I could answer Belinda walked in.

'Aren't you ready yet?' she demanded. 'Isn't it fun? Do you like your room? It's very like mine.'

'I suppose most of the rooms are rather alike.'

'I'm longing to explore. Aren't you?'

'Yes, of course.'

'It's all so fascinating. You are very lucky, Lucie.'

'Am I?'

'Oh, poor Lucie.' She rushed at me and put her arms round me in a protective gesture. 'I do put my foot in it, don't I? But you've got to stop thinking of all that. Life goes on. *Mon père* says we've got to make you see that. We're going to make you happy here. He says so.'

'That's very good of him.'

'He is good . . . really. Oh, I know he sounds a little cynical sometimes, but he has *lived*, Lucie, really *lived*. That doesn't mean he isn't kind. He talks a lot about you. He says you ought to be enjoying life because you've got so much to make you.'

'It is certainly good of him to give so much attention to my affairs.'

'He likes you. He wouldn't have asked you to come here if he didn't.'

'Oh, that was to please you.'

'Oh no it wasn't . . . although it does please me. He was the first one to suggest it.'

'Well, here I am.'

'And we're going to have a lovely time. I'm going to make you enjoy it.'

'Thank you, Belinda.'

'Hurry up and finish and we'll go down. I wonder if *mon père* is already up?'

'Where is your room, Belinda?'

'On the other side of the château.' She went to the window. 'I've got a different view. I look out on the lake. Well, it's like a lake. There's a stream, too – part of the river, I think – and it flows into the lake. There are swans on the lake. Two black ones. I haven't seen black ones before. It's lovely.'

'So, we are quite a way from each other.'

'Well, it is a big château.'

'Your father said it was of medium size.'

'He was comparing it with the royal ones – châteaux of the Loire, Blois and places like that. This is a nobleman's château, not a king's.'

'I see.'

'Hurry up. I'll be down in the hall. You'll find your way down?'

'I hope so.'

'And don't be long.'

The morning was spent exploring the castle.

'It is essential that you do so, otherwise you will be hopelessly lost,' explained Jean Pascal. 'I am going to take you outside and bring you in as though you are just arriving.'

'It was too dark for us to see properly last night,' said Belinda.

'I want you both to like the château. It's very important to our family.'

135

'And yet,' I said, 'you left it.'

'Ah, Lucie, it was a wrench. But our country was in turmoil. We did not know which way we were going. Memories are still with us of the great Revolution, which took place only about a hundred years ago. When the Emperor and Empress went into exile you cannot imagine what that did to our country. We thought it was coming again. Fortunately, tragic though this was . . . it was not of the same magnitude as that which our country had suffered before.'

'But you were able to keep the château,' I said, 'and it is still yours.'

'Yes, and I am a frequent visitor here. In fact, I believe I am here more than anywhere else. The wine well, shall we say it is a kind of hobby. I wish I could persuade my mother to return, but she is there with the Empress. Perhaps one day it will change.'

'Celeste never comes here,' I said.

'Celeste . . . oh, poor Celeste! Her marriage took her away and she became a politician's wife.'

'Perhaps now she would like to come back?'

'She does not say she would.' He lifted his shoulders. 'She knows it is her home – the family home. If she wants to come, she can return.'

'It may be that she will. She is not very happy in London.'

'No. But we are not here to talk of sad things. This has to be a happy time. I insist. So does Belinda, do you not?'

'Yes, I insist. So stop being morbid, Lucie. You've got to enjoy all this.'

'You see,' said Jean Pascal, 'it is an order. Now we are outside we will approach the château as though we are entering it for the first time.'

We ascended the imposing marble steps, at the bottom of which stood two huge marble containers full of green shrubs which trailed their leaves over the pedestals on which they stood.

Looking back, we could see that the tree-lined drive opened on to the lawn which was immediately in front of the house.

Jean Pascal made us turn our faces to the château.

'You see, the building is dominated by the tower,' he said. 'In the old days it was called the watch tower; and in times of trouble a man would be posted up there, his sole duty being to watch and give warning of any suspicious person or persons approaching. He used to while away the time by singing songs or playing the flute. A musician always had to be chosen for the job because he could practise his art while watching. I remember its being done when I was here in the 'seventies, at the time when we were expecting trouble. People would hear the singing or the flute-playing and know that all was well. We had our watcher. The songs were called Watchman's Songs and they were often his own compositions. In French we called them *chansons de guettes*. You see, the tower is right in the centre . . . just below is what is called the palace. That is the part where the family live.'

He waved his arms towards the lawn and went on: 'Tournaments used to be held here . . . tilting and jousting. The château was the centre of life in the neighbourhood in the Middle Ages. You see how the staircase is supported by the vaults. Beggars and hangers-on used to congregate there. They were given the remains of food after meals. Everything is different now.'

We mounted the steps and went into the hall.

'This was the main living-room in medieval days,' he continued. 'Look up and you will see the hole in the roof where there was once a vent to let out the smoke. But that was changed a hundred years ago and we have our big fireplace over there, you see, and our chimney to take away the smoke. If you look closely you can see, in the centre of the hall, where the fire used to be. You see those hearth tiles? The château has indeed changed since medieval times, but we are still proud of the past and my family have always kept as much intact as possible. But when it was excessively uncomfortable, then we felt it advisable to move with the times.'

So he talked and I could visualize what it had been like in the old days. I could see the beggars under the steps, the guests in their brilliant costumes sitting on those same steps on a warm summer's evening. I wondered about the long-dead Bourdons and what their lives had been like. They seemed to linger on . . . even in daylight.

He showed us the *salon* and the *salle à manger* which had been introduced into the château within the last two hundred years; we saw the extra wing which had been added to make more bedrooms. It was a mingling of the ancient and . . . well, not exactly modern, but later periods than those when the Château Bourdon had been erected.

I could see why he was proud of it, and how great a tragedy it must have been to his family when they had felt obliged to leave it.

I wondered why they had not been lured back.

Jean Pascal said: 'My parents were devoted to Napoleon and Eugénie. They spent a great deal of time at Court – far more than they did here and when the Emperor and Empress were forced into exile, they had to join them.'

There was so much to see that the tour of the castle lasted a long time.

'Years ago,' he told us, 'noble families would send their sons and daughters to be brought up away from their own homes. I don't know why this was the custom; perhaps it was thought that parents would be too lenient. Young girls and young men were brought up here. The men would learn courtly manners, how to joust and so on, to make them worthy to go to Court when the time came.'

'And what of the girls?' asked Belinda.

'Oh, they were taught how to be good wives and mothers and please their husbands.'

'Were the men taught to please their wives?' I asked.

'Ah, Miss Lucie, that was something they knew how to do without tuition. I see you are sceptical. You do not believe that is something which comes naturally to a man?'

'I am sure it does not. I just wondered whether it might not have been a good idea to give them a little tuition, as it was thought necessary for the women.'

He smiled benignly at me. 'I think you may be right, Lucie,' he said. 'Now let me show you where the girls used to come to learn how to embroider, how to sing, how to play some musical instrument and how to charm the men. It is called The Maidens' Room or *La Chambre des Pucelles*. We always keep it just as it was. I like to think of the girls here . . . so young . . . so pretty . . . so docile . . . all so eager to learn.'

He was regarding me with an expression I did not understand, but it made me a little uneasy.

I wished that I could cast off that sense of foreboding which the place seemed to inspire in me. It was not as intense as it had been on the previous night, but it lingered. I told myself it was the strangeness of the place – and, of course, my fanciful nature.

We had explored the château and were back in the hall when the door was suddenly opened and a woman came in. She was in a riding habit of silver-grey, and her hair, which was luxuriant and golden, showed beneath her grey riding hat.

'Jean Pascal!' she cried, coming towards him, smiling. 'I heard you were home.'

Jean Pascal looked distinctly annoyed. I had never seen him look like that before. He seemed really angry.

'Oh, Clotilde,' he said. 'I am busy now . . . showing my guests round the château.'

'How amusing!' She waited expectantly.

'I'll see you later on.'

She looked amazed. I wondered why he did not introduce us. So did she evidently, because she came forward and stood looking at us expectantly.

There was no alternative then but for Jean Pascal to act as we all expected.

'My daughter Belinda . . . Mademoiselle Lansdon,' he murmured. 'And . . . er . . . Madame Carléon.'

In our somewhat laboured French Belinda and I said we were enchanted to meet her.

'Well, we must go,' said Jean Pascal. 'I'll see you at some other time, Clotilde.'

She stared at him for a second or two and then, turning, walked out of the hall. I listened to her footsteps on the marble steps.

Jean Pascal quickly recovered from what seemed to have been for him an unpleasant experience.

'You haven't seen it all yet,' he was saying. 'We have some magnificent stables and plenty of horses. So you will be able to ride round and explore.'

I heard the sound of horse's hoofs and I guessed that Madame Carléon was departing in anger.

I wondered what that was all about.

A few days passed. Jean Pascal seemed determined that we should enjoy our stay. I wondered whether he had it in his mind that Belinda should live here permanently. I had an idea that he was interested in her . . . and perhaps asking himself whether he wanted a grown-up daughter in his household. He might find it amusing for a while, certainly, but would he grow tired? I was sure that Belinda wanted to be with him. His mode of living would suit her. It would be more exciting residing in the château, visiting royalty at Farnborough and travelling with her father. Quite different from the comparatively dull lives we lived in London.

But he did include me in everything. He would ask my opinion and always considered it carefully. He really did seem as though he were trying to please me. In fact there were times when I think Belinda grew a little impatient because he bestowed so much attention on me.

He told me that he had a few friends and acquaintances in the neighbourhood and that we should have a dinner party; and he had no doubt that there would be invitations for us to visit.

Belinda was much looking forward to that. She had already been to Bordeaux and bought some clothes. She regretted that we were so far from Paris. How she would have loved to see the shops in that city!

I still kept to my plan to escape from them from time to time. I found a need to be alone. Every day I hoped there would be news of Joel. Celeste had assured me that she would let me know at once if she heard anything; and the Greenhams would of course keep her informed, knowing I was as anxious as they were.

The grounds about the château provided me with great pleasure. They were extensive; there was a small pine wood to which one could retreat and feel as though one were a long way from any habitation; it was always a pleasure to emerge from the trees and see the central tower of the château and the two round ones at either end of the building. Standing some distance from it, the symmetrical beauty of the place struck one forcefully.

I liked to wander along the banks of the lake and to watch the swans; both remained aloof and rarely came to the water's edge. The big one, the cob, was always followed by his smaller mate. He looked very dignified, with her always following in his wake. The little ducks were more friendly. They would come close, always hoping for some little titbit to eat, I imagined.

On this particular day I was unusually deep in thought, telling myself that there must be news of Joel soon. Time was passing. Surely if anything was to be discovered it must be in the near future. It had been so long that I was beginning to despair and feel I might never see him again.

I had wandered to the edge of the lake as I watched the swans. The large one was coming purposefully towards me, the little one docilely swimming behind him. I thought how beautiful they were, so exquisitely graceful and serene. They were coming nearer and nearer. I was surprised. Previously they had seemed somewhat disdainfully aloof.

Then I heard the sound of horse's hoofs. I turned. Jean Pascal was galloping towards me. He was alone.

I did not know why I had that sudden feeling of uneasiness. I was subject to strange moods in the château. Often I felt this sense of foreboding which I found impossible to shake off. It seemed to me that the servants watched us, Belinda and myself, closely – as though they were speculating. Once or twice I caught the whispered words 'les anglaises' so I knew we were the subject of their conversation.

'Lucie!' Jean Pascal was calling my name and there was an urgent note in his voice. 'Come here. Come to me . . . quickly!'

I did not move . . . and then I heard the sound of flapping wings. I turned sharply. The big black swan was flying straight at me. Jean Pascal had leaped from his horse. He pushed me roughly to one side. The swan turned its attention to him. Fortunately there was a fairly stout branch of a tree lying on the ground and with great presence of mind Jean Pascal picked it up. He was just in time to be able to protect his head by striking out at the swan. He took a few paces backwards and hit out.

For a few seconds the black swan continued to attack him; and then suddenly it turned and flew back to the lake. I stood still, shocked, while it swam back to the middle of the lake, its meek mate following in her usual fashion, just as though nothing untoward had happened.

Jean Pascal put his hand on my shoulder. He whistled. 'That was rather uncomfortable,' he said.

He took both my hands. 'You're trembling,' he said.

'It happened so quickly . . . I didn't realize what it was all about.'

He dropped my hands and put an arm round me.

'Dear little Lucie, it is all over now.' He held me tightly against him and I wanted to cry out in panic, for he alarmed me as much as the swan had.

I tried to break free but he held me firmly. 'You see,' he said, 'I was there. I hope always to be at hand when you need me.'

I managed to free myself. 'It was good of you,' I said. 'Why did the swan try to attack first me . . . and then you?'

'You should have been warned. He's a wicked old fellow, that swan, for all his good looks. We call him Diable. His little mate is so charming. She would never indulge in tantrums. She wouldn't dare to with old Diable around. As a matter of fact her name is Ange. So you see, we have a devil and an angel. You went too near the lake,

143

which Diable regards as his property. He doesn't like people intruding. We have to be careful not to offend him. You should have been warned.'

'He's quite dangerous, and he was ready to attack *you*.'

'Oh, he is no respecter of pesons. He is quite ungrateful to those who provide for him. There's a certain arrogance about him. Heaven knows what would have happened to you if I hadn't come along just in time. He would have attacked your face . . . pecked at your nose or your eyes. His wings are strong. He's a magnificent creature. *Mon Dieu*, the thought of your being hurt . . . I am so annoyed with myself. We're so used to Diable here that we forget to tell people how vicious he can be. He's a menace to the unwary. Never go near the edge of the lake again, and when you are out walking, find a stout stick just in case you encounter Diable.'

'Why do you have such a dangerous creature on your lake?'

'He keeps it clean . . . and you must admit he is rather majestic.'

'I admit that . . . but so dangerous!'

'Well, we accept him. The servants all know Diable, and now . . . so do you. You are becoming one of us, Lucie.'

'You have been most hospitable.'

Belinda was coming towards us. She frowned to see us together. I wanted to tell her how pleased I was to see her as I did not feel happy when I was alone with her father.

We told her about the adventure.

'Trust you, Lucie, to provoke him,' said Belinda.

'It could have happened to anyone. Even to you.'

'I knew swans could be like that – male ones, anyway.'

Jean Pascal laughed. 'You see, Belinda knows the ways of the world. She recognizes the dangerous male who is so different from the gentle, charming female.'

'It's not always like that,' said Belinda.

'That's one thing you have to learn in life, isn't it – not to generalize,' he said. 'There will always be exceptions.'

And so we came to the château. I went to my room. I was still shaken, not only by the swan's attack but by the manner in which Jean Pascal had held me to him and the look in his eyes when he spoke to me.

The Fitzgeralds

When we were at Manorleigh both Belinda and I had ridden frequently, in London less so. It was necessary, as my father said, to 'nurse' the constituency and I, with Celeste later, used to ride round to the various villages which were part of it; so I had become a quite skilful horsewoman.

I went riding now and then with Belinda and Jean Pascal, but I looked forward to those times when I could be alone. I was becoming increasingly uneasy because of Jean Pascal's attitude towards me. I might be innocent but I was not ignorant. I had already discerned that he was the sort of man who would be interested in any woman who crossed his path. I did not think that I was particularly attractive, but I was there . . . actually living under his roof. I began to think that it was time I went away.

The truth was he alarmed me. I admonished myself. I had only to convey to him that I was not one of those people who indulged in the light love-affairs of which I was sure he had had great experience. He was Belinda's father and that meant that he was old enough to be mine. Not that age would be so important, I supposed, if one truly loved. Love Jean Pascal? The thought appalled me. Of course, he was good-looking, suave, a man of the world. Some people might have fallen in love with him. As for myself, I felt only revulsion when he came near me.

146

And here I was, a guest under his roof! No wonder I felt uneasy.

I did suggest to Belinda that we could not stay here indefinitely. Perhaps we should think about making a date for our return.

She looked at me in amazement. 'We haven't been here two weeks yet.'

'That's quite a long time to stay in people's houses.'

'*People's* houses. This is my father's.'

'Yes. Your father, but not mine. I was just wondering, I was thinking it was about time I . . .'

'What do you want to go back for? You're supposed to be enjoying yourself. You are putting the past behind you and where could you do that better than here?'

'I was just thinking . . .'

'You're an idiot, Lucie. Stop thinking! Just enjoy all this. I think it's wonderful. Don't grudge me my father.'

'As if I would.'

'He's been very nice to you. He always brings you in to everything.'

'Yes, I know. But I think I ought to go and leave you two together.'

'Don't talk nonsense,' she said; and as usual, when she had decided something, she assumed that settled the matter. So I knew it was useless to talk to her about going home.

I cherished those days when I could get away on my own. On this particular one I had gone into the grounds and into the little wood. I knew that Jean Pascal and Belinda were going to the vineyards that morning. The implication had been that I should go with them, but it had not been absolutely arranged. So I went off and was not to be found when they were ready to go.

After they left I experienced a wonderful sense of

freedom. I went to the stables where a groom saddled a horse for me at my request; and I had the pleasure of riding out alone.

It was a lovely morning. It would probably be too hot later in the day but at that time it was perfect.

I told myself I must remember which way I came for the country was unfamiliar to me. I must not get lost or there would be a ban on my riding alone, which was my chief pleasure.

I left the château grounds and after about ten minutes, I came to a little wood of pine trees. A rider was coming towards me. There was something familiar about her. She drew level and we looked at each other, both a little puzzled, trying to remember, I supposed, where we had met before.

The woman smiled suddenly. 'I know,' she cried. 'Of course, it was on the Channel steamer. I'm Phillida Fitzgerald. Do you remember? We talked for a few minutes.'

It was coming back. The pleasant-faced woman who was going with her brother to recuperate near Bordeaux.

'I remember well.'

'And you were . . . ?'

'Lucie Lansdon.'

'That's right. What a coincidence! Well, perhaps not so . . . as we are in the neighbourhood. Isn't it lovely country?'

'It is. Are you better?'

'Yes. Did I tell you I was convalescing? I really am much better. Even my brother is pleased.'

'Is he here?'

'He's at our place.'

'Are you staying near here?' I asked.

'Yes, quite near. We've rented a house. We didn't

148

greatly care for the hotel. So we looked round and found this place. There's a good deal of letting goes on nowadays in these parts. Some people prefer it to staying in a hotel.'

'I suppose they do.'

'My brother likes it much better. It's a nice little house . . . lovely setting. Not far from here. There are a couple who live in a sort of cabin in the grounds. They look after us. They go with the house. They're quite good. We like it.'

'How long are you staying?'

'For a few more weeks, I suppose. Nothing definite. We've taken the house for a month and if we want to renew at any time I don't think there would be much difficulty.'

She nodded. 'What of you?'

'I'm staying at the Château Bourdon.'

'With friends, I think you said. That must be wonderful, really. Look, why don't you come back with me and have a cup of coffee? Angélique – the female of the couple – makes excellent coffee.'

'It sounds like a good idea.'

'Come on, then. Roland will be amused. He says I pick up people. Well, I like meeting people. I like talking to people. And after all, we're not strangers, are we? We met on the boat.'

'I certainly don't feel we are.'

She laughed and turned her horse back the way she had obviously come. I followed. We rode for about a mile until we came to the village of Lengore.

'It's charming,' she told me, 'particularly on market days. I love shopping. They all laugh at my atrocious accent. But I can laugh with them. I know how awful it is. The house is just on the outskirts of the village.'

We came to it. It was small and of grey stone, surrounded by a pleasant garden. She pointed out to me what she called

149

'the cabin' where Angélique and her spouse lived. There was a stretch of grass on which a few chickens scratched while a rooster perched proudly on a low stone wall watching over his hens.

'It's a little primitive in some ways,' said Phillida. 'But my brother says that this is what we have come here for. There are two or three barns . . . good for storage . . . and a field, too, so we have plenty of space. We hire the horses for the time we are here, and Pierre –that's Angélique's husband – looks after them as he does the chickens and a couple of geese. So you see, it really is the country life.'

She pushed open a door and we were in a room with stone walls and tiled floor. There was an enormous fireplace and a kettle hanging on a chain. Leading from this was another room into which she led me. It was fitted with two armchairs and a sofa. Her brother stood up and laid aside the book he had been reading. He looked puzzled at first until Phillida explained.

'Look whom I have found,' she cried. 'It's Miss Lucie Lansdon. Come on, Roland, you remember. On the boat coming over.' She turned to me. 'Roland doesn't remember people like I do. But then, of course, we had a long chat. He only saw you briefly.'

'But I do remember,' he said. He held out his hand. 'How do you do, Miss Lansdon. How nice to see you.'

'Wasn't it a coincidence?' said Phillida. 'We just happened to come face to face near that pine copse. Then it all came back to me . . . how we'd met and talked.'

'Well, it's a pleasure,' said her brother.

'What about some coffee?' said Phillida. 'I've lured her here with a promise of Angélique's special brew.'

'Come and sit down,' he said.

'Yes, that's right, and I'll go and see about the coffee.' She went and I was left alone with Roland.

I said: 'You seem to be comfortable here.'

'Oh yes. It's pleasanter than a hotel.'

'I can see that.'

'And the couple take on everything, so there is nothing for my sister to worry about.'

'Is she better? I gathered she had come here for some sort of convalescence.'

'The place suits her. But I don't know how long we shall be able to stay. I shall have to go back eventually, but I do want to make sure she is quite well before we return. It's a weakness in the chest. Our climate is too damp for her. This dry heat suits her better.'

'She seems absolutely well.'

'That's Phillida. She refuses to accept ill health. She has a wonderful spirit.'

'You and she are obviously very good friends.'

'Brother and sister. But I admit there is a special closeness. Our parents died. They were killed together in a railway accident. To lose them both at one time . . . well, you can imagine what that meant. She said she would look after me. I said I would look after her.'

'Well, you both seem to be making a good job of it.'

Phillida came back. 'Coffee will be served very shortly,' she said. 'I want to show Miss Lansdon the house.'

'After coffee,' said Roland.

'Oh, come. It won't take more than a few minutes.' She grimaced at me. 'There's not much of it, and there is just time before coffee arrives. I'll whip you round in five minutes. It's not Château Bourdon, you know. It was Bourdon, wasn't it? I remembered because I'd heard it before.'

'Yes, that's right.'

'Vast and imposing, I believe.'

'I suppose it is . . . rather.'

'Well, come and see our humble abode. You stay here, Roly, in case Angélique brings the coffee in.'

She took me up a spiral staircase which led from the sitting-room. There were two rooms on the next floor. 'This is the best bedroom, my domain. Roland insisted on my having this room. The other room is a sort of dressing-room – sitting-room. Then there's another floor . . . to the attics, really.' We climbed the stairs to a room in which on one side the ceiling sloped and one had to stoop to approach the small window which looked down on the patch of green and the hens. The geese were down there too.

She laughed. 'It's fun in a way. Different from your château, I dare say. Roland sleeps up here. It's difficult for him to stand upright all the time . . . and it's amusing, for a holiday, of course. And that's all. Château Fitzgerald. Now let's get down to that coffee.'

She was right about the coffee. It was delicious.

I found them both interesting and I liked their obvious affection for each other. They made me feel that it was a special pleasure to have a visitor from home.

'Isn't it wonderful to be able to talk naturally, Roland? Rather than to have to stumble over your words, and when you do get a comprehensible sentence they come back at you with such a rush – thinking mistakenly that you have mastered their language. And then you are completely lost.' Phillida laughed.

They wanted to know about me. I could see that they remembered the tragedy by the pains they took to avoid mentioning it.

At last I said: 'My father was shot outside our house. You probably read about it.'

'Yes,' said Roland quietly. 'It must have been a terrible shock for you.'

152

I nodded. 'But I have so many kind friends. There is my sister particularly. She lives in Cornwall, though, and that is quite a long way from London.'

'I suppose you visit her often,' said Roland.

'Yes, and I expect I shall more and more. I think she would like me to go and live with her and her family.'

'But you are as yet undecided?' asked Phillida.

'Well, I feel a little . . .'

They exchanged glances and I knew a message passed between them. It was to drop the subject.

'The rural life is very amusing and interesting for a time,' said Roland, 'but I wonder how long one could find that sort of thing amusing.'

'Where is your home?' I asked.

'Well, we really come from Yorkshire. We are in wool, actually. But I am in London a good deal. We have a small *pied-à-terre* there. Everyone has to be in London sooner or later. It was my father who decided that we must have an office there to deal with the business – most of which is conducted in Yorkshire, of course. He died just as he had set up the office . . . and I was to be in charge of it.'

'Have some more coffee,' said Phillida. 'Angélique gets quite cross if people don't show they appreciate what she produces.'

'It's a failing with good cooks,' added Roland.

'How long do you intend to stay in France?' asked Phillida, filling my cup.

'I am unsure. So much depends on Belinda.'

'She is travelling with you, I suppose.'

'Yes.' I felt the need of a little explanation. 'She is my stepmother's niece. It is her father who owns the château.'

'I see,' said Roland.

'I hope you don't go too soon,' added Phillida. 'It's great fun to meet one's compatriots in a foreign land.'

153

Roland smiled indulgently at his sister.

'Well, you agree with me, don't you Roland?' she insisted.

'I do on this occasion,' he replied.

'You must come and see us again,' said Phillida.

'I'd like to,' I told them. 'But this reminds me . . . I ought to be going.' I looked at the clock on the wall. '*Déjeuner* will be served in an hour. They will be wondering what has become of me if I am late.'

'We'll take you back,' said Roland. 'It's about half an hour, I reckon, wouldn't you, Phillida?'

'I should think so. We are really quite close neighbours.'

'Well, there is not much time.'

'I can see Miss Lansdon is getting anxious,' said Roland, 'so we'll leave now.'

I thought how kind and gentle he was. He reminded me of Joel. He was a complete contrast to Jean Pascal.

Within five minutes we were leaving the house. We chatted about the countryside as we rode along. It had been a very interesting morning.

They left me within sight of the château. It was Roland's suggestion that they should do so. Phillida would have liked to come closer, I was sure, with a hope of meeting Belinda or Jean Pascal. But, firmly and quietly, Roland insisted. He was so tactful. He thought it was better for me to arrive alone, and not have to give an immediate explanation of our meeting.

So I was back in good time. I felt better than I had for a long time. It gave me a comfortable feeling to remind myself that I had friends in the neighbourhood.

When I went down to *déjeuner* Belinda and Jean Pascal were already there.

'What happened to you this morning, Lucie?' asked Jean Pascal.

'Oh . . . I went for a ride.'

'We couldn't find you,' scolded Belinda. '*Mon père* was most put out.'

'I knew you were going to the vineyard. I didn't think you would want me with you.'

'Of course we expected you to be with us,' said Jean Pascal.

'It was very interesting,' added Belinda. 'You missed something very good.'

'I had an interesting morning, too.'

'Doing what?' asked Belinda.

'I met some people.'

There was silence for a few seconds. Then Jean Pascal said: 'People? What people?'

'There was a young woman whom I met on the Channel boat. We had chatted for a while. Didn't I tell you?'

'I didn't know you'd met anyone,' said Belinda.

'It was when we were on deck and I wandered off on my own. I was leaning over the rail and so was she. We talked. She said they were staying near Bordeaux.'

'And you just met by chance?' said Jean Pascal.

'Yes. They are actually staying quite nearby.'

'They?'

'She and her brother. They've rented a house for a month or so. She took me back with her and they gave me coffee.'

'Wasn't that rather rash of you?' He was looking at me with concern.

'Rash? I don't see anything rash about it.'

'But . . . people you don't know!'

'I told you, I met them on the boat.'

'That is not knowing them.'

'Oh, you are so formal. I could see they were perfectly nice ordinary people. They invited me to see the place they had rented and to have some coffee. That's all. It was a very pleasant morning.'

'What is their name?'

'Fitzgerald.'

'I've not heard of them.'

'It's hardly likely that you would. They are visitors from England just on holiday here.'

Jean Pascal looked displeased. I thought he was a little annoyed because I had not accompanied them to the vineyard.

'By the way,' he said, 'I've asked some people to dine with us tomorrow night. The Comte and Comtesse de Grellon and Monsieur and Mademoiselle du Pont. Just a small dinner party to begin with.'

Belinda looked excited. 'A real Comte and Comtesse!' she cried.

Jean Pascal smiled at her indulgently. 'There are some still around, you know.'

'Tell us about them,' pleaded Belinda.

'The Comte is about sixty, the Comtesse a year or so younger. They have a château about five miles from here. They will stay the night. Then there are the du Ponts. Monsieur is about forty, a widower, with a charming daughter Geneviève. I am sure you will like them all. The rest, my dear Belinda, you must discover for yourself.'

He was smiling blandly now. I believed his vague annoyance that I had eluded them and spent a pleasant morning elsewhere had passed.

Belinda was very excited at the prospect of a dinner party although, as she said to me, the guests did not appear to be very exciting.

'How can we tell until we meet them?' I asked.

156

'An old Comte of sixty and his Comtesse! Another old man with his daughter! I should have thought *mon père* would have invited some young people . . . young men.'

'I dare say some will be provided at a later date.'

'Why waste time?'

Early in the morning a man arrived at the château with a special message for Jean Pascal. We learned what it was at *déjeuner*.

'There will be an extra guest tonight,' he told us. 'I have had a note from the Comte. He tells me that a friend from England has arrived unexpectedly and he is asking if he might bring this guest along tonight. I have said that of course I shall be delighted. I am sure you young ladies will be pleased that you will be able to speak to someone in English.'

We admitted that we would. 'French people speak too fast,' said Belinda.

'No faster than you do, my dear,' her father retorted. 'It is just that you can't follow quickly enough.'

Belinda dressed with care. Her father had a Frenchman's eye for what was chic and he was inclined to be critical. I often watched the manner in which he took notice of our appearance; and I must admit that at times I felt an inclination to wear something of which he would not approve. Belinda, on the other hand, set out to please him, which was not difficult for her. She had a natural flair for choosing what suited her, and dressed with a certain panache and a touch of flamboyance which was in keeping with her looks and personality.

We went down to the hall to receive our guests. The du Ponts arrived first. He was a small man with sleek dark hair and pince-nez which gave him a somewhat severe look. His daughter Geneviève I imagined to be in her early twenties; there was a certain primness about her and she appeared to be devoted to her father.

I saw Belinda study them and dismiss them as dull. I had a notion she might be right.

Then the Comte and Comtesse arrived and with them their mystery guest.

I was aware of Belinda's excitement. He was tall and very fair with a fresh complexion, light blue eyes, and features set in a somewhat classical mould. I guessed him to be in his twenties – good-looking in a bland way. The Comte and his Comtesse could not be anything but French. Aristocratic, both of them, unconsciously implying that they were accustomed to deference and formality. They were both silver-haired, elegantly dressed, immaculate.

The Comte kissed our hands and we murmured that we were enchanted to meet him. Jean Pascal looked on with approval.

Then the Comte presented his guest. He was Sir Robert Denver, whose father had been a great friend of the Comte. Sir Robert always visited the Comte when he was in France and so here he was.

Jean Pascal said how pleased he was that Sir Robert's visit had coincided with that of the Comte and Comtesse to Bourdon. These platitudes continued for some little time and then we all went in to dinner.

Sir Robert was seated between Belinda and me.

Dinner was served with special formality. I had not realized how many servants there were at the château. They tiptoed about the dining-room, unobtrusive and efficient.

Sir Robert was as glad as Belinda and I were to have someone to whom he could chat in English.

There was something charming about him. This was particularly noticeable in the somewhat formal company. He was without pomposity and completely unpretentious.

'How jolly,' he said, 'that I happened to be staying with

the Comte when this invitation came. To tell the truth, I was dreading it. My French is appalling. I don't get half what is said. I can't tell you what a relief it is to be able to talk in English!'

'We find that too,' Belinda assured him.

'So you see,' I added, 'the relief is mutual.'

'My father, of course,' went on Belinda, 'speaks perfect English. Well, he has been so much in England.'

'Yes. So the Comte told me.'

'Do you often come to France?' I asked.

Belinda frowned at me. *She* wanted to talk to him and there were too many interruptions coming from me.

He said: 'No, not often. Before he died, my father came frequently. Sometimes I came with him. He had a feeling for France . . . and he had one or two good friends here. The Comte, for instance, was one of them. He was a special one. On the rare occasions when he came to England he stayed with us. So when I come to France I always visit them and stay a few days.'

'So you are only here for a few days,' said Belinda, a little crestfallen.

He nodded. 'That is why it is so lucky that I came here.'

Belinda sparkled. 'Isn't that a nice thing to say, Lucie?'

I agreed that it was.

'And where is your home?' asked Belinda.

'It's in Hampshire.'

'Oh, not so very far from London.'

'That's true.'

'Do you ever come to London?' Belinda asked.

'Not often. Occasionally.'

There was a brief silence while the fish was served.

'There is quite a lot to do on the estate,' he went on. 'Since my father died . . .'

'Was that recently?' I asked.

'About a year ago.'

'Are you a sort of . . . squire?' said Belinda.

'Sort of,' he answered.

'How exciting!'

He shrugged his shoulders. 'I haven't had a lot of experience.'

'Well, I suppose you have people to help. Have you a family?'

'No. I was the only one. My father died suddenly. It was a terrible shock. Everyone thought he had years ahead of him.'

'So you are all alone. No wife to help you, no children?'

'All alone,' he said.

I could see that Belinda's interest was increasing. Sir Robert Denver – owner of a title and estate in Hampshire, good-looking enough. Quite an eligible bachelor.

She gave me a venomous look, realizing that I was reading her thoughts.

I watched her setting out to charm him, and I guessed she was making a success of it.

I wished her luck. There was something very pleasant about him. He was not exactly worldly and this was particularly apparent in the company of such men as the Comte and Jean Pascal . . . and, I dare say, Monsieur du Pont. Of course, he was a good deal younger than they were, but I could not believe that Jean Pascal had ever been innocent as this young man appeared to be.

From then to the end of the meal Belinda took charge of the conversation, chattering away, telling him, in the most interesting manner, of her life in the goldfields and how different it was in London; he listened avidly and before it was time for us to leave the table, I could see that she had woven her special spell about him. He looked a little bewildered . . . but enchanted.

160

When I was in bed that night I kept thinking about the evening and the guests, particularly Sir Robert.

I heard the door rattling and my heart began to beat with alarming rapidity. I sprang out of bed.

'Who is that?' I cried.

'Belinda, of course.'

'Just a moment.' I unlocked the door and she came in, clad in dressing-gown and slippers.

'Why do you lock your door?' she demanded.

'I don't know. A habit, I suppose.'

She was too concerned with herself to give more than a passing thought to my little fancies.

I got back into bed and she sat on the edge of it, watching me.

'What did you think of him?'

'Of whom?'

'Don't be silly! You know very well.'

'I presume you are referring to that eligible bachelor with a nice title, an estate in Hampshire and no encumbrances.'

'Of course.'

'Well, I think he is a very pleasant young man . . . rather too innocent to be let loose into a world of predatory females.'

'Oh, stop being pompous! He's nice, isn't he? What do think he thought of me?'

'One of the females I just mentioned whose attitude towards him brightened considerably when he disclosed his position in the world.'

'Stop it. I liked him.'

'Well, so did I.'

'Lucie, don't you dare! Well, you wouldn't have a chance if you tried.'

'Certainly not against you with your wiles.'

'So don't attempt it.'

'I had no intention of doing so.'

'I think he is just right.'

'I am sure he is.'

'And *I* am going to make sure that we see more of him.'

'Yes. Don't let him slip through your fingers. That would indeed be a tragedy.'

'I don't intend to listen.'

'And it was to tell me this that I owe the pleasure of this visit from the future Lady Denver.'

'It sounds rather good, doesn't it?' she said with a giggle.

'Belinda! One word of caution.'

'What?'

'Don't be too blatant. I don't suppose you are the first who has tried to snare him. All that eligibility, you know. So don't be too obvious.'

She laughed. 'I don't know why I tell you all this.'

'I do. You've got to talk to someone on this all-absorbing subject.'

'What subject?'

'You, of course. My dear Belinda, you are obsessed by Belinda, and naturally expect everyone to be the same.'

'Oh, shut up. I am going to ask *mon père* to invite him over again. Or perhaps we can go riding over to the Comte and see him then.'

'Do that. I am sure *ton père* will agree.'

'I'm going now.'

'Good night. And good luck in the campaign.'

She went and I got out of bed and locked the door.

We did not have to go looking for Sir Robert. He rode over the next day. Belinda sparkled. It was even better than she had thought.

Jean Pascal was amused and Sir Robert was pressed to stay to *déjeuner*, an invitation he was delighted to accept.

Belinda chatted animatedly all through lunch while Jean Pascal looked on benignly. I presumed from his demeanour that he approved of Sir Robert as a prospective son-in-law.

Later we all walked in the gardens together and Jean Pascal talked quite knowledgeably about the flora and fauna of the neighbourhood, to which Sir Robert muttered and murmured his appreciation, but I was sure his thoughts were elsewhere.

Belinda was radiant, and when at length our guest left – most reluctantly – it was with an invitation from Jean Pascal to call whenever he felt inclined to do so.

I guessed the next visit would not be long delayed. Nor was it.

The next day he came again.

I was walking in the grounds which I loved to do. They were so beautiful and because of the many shrubs and trees and the copse one could be shut away from the château and enjoy a pleasant feeling of solitude.

My thoughts were wandering. I was thinking of Joel, for he was never long out of my thoughts; then I fell to wondering whether this obvious attraction between Belinda and Sir Robert would result in an engagement. I heard footsteps. They were coming towards the copse. I was certain they belonged to Jean Pascal and decided to emerge into the open, as I felt reluctant to be alone with him in the copse.

I quickly made my way in the direction of the lake.

He called to me and I paused, looking back.

'Lucie, I was hoping to catch you,' he said. 'I saw you walking this way. You love the grounds, don't you?'

'They are very beautiful.'

There was a seat under one of the trees. He indicated it and we sat down. 'I wanted to talk to you,' he said.

We sat side by side. I had moved away from him as unobtrusively as I could because he had sat too near.

'What do you think of this Sir Robert?' he asked.

'I think he is a very pleasant young man.'

'Belinda seems to think so, too.'

'Belinda is . . . impressionable.'

He laughed. 'You are not, I am sure.'

'Not so much as Belinda, perhaps.'

'Do you think anything will come of it?'

'I don't know.'

'I think it would be rather a good idea. He seems eligible.'

'That's the word I used to Belinda.'

'So you have been discussing it. She seems to like him, wouldn't you say?'

'Whether she likes his eligibility or his personality I am not sure.'

'Don't the two go hand in hand?'

'Not for some, I imagine. But I am inexperienced in these matters.'

'Lucie, you amuse me. And I think you are wiser than you make out to be.'

'I do not make out anything. I am just as I am.'

'And may I say I find that delightful.'

'It is good of you to say so.' I looked at the watch pinned on my blouse.

'There is no great hurry,' he said. 'We can talk awhile and still be in time for *déjeuner*.'

'You are concerned about Belinda?' I asked.

'No, not really. I think she can take care of herself. I just wanted to know what you think of this – shall we say whirlwind courtship.'

'You think it is a courtship?'

'Well, we have our English gentleman . . . and the English are said to be an honourable race.'

'Do you believe in generalizations?'

'No. But Sir Robert seems to fit the mould.'

'Yes. I am sure he is honourable.'

'Then I think we may have a match on our hands.'

'And that pleases you?'

'It does not displease me.'

'Then I suppose you will give your consent?'

'I have a notion that Belinda is one to act as she wishes, and would not be concerned with the consent of others.'

'You are her father. I am sure she would want your approval.'

'She would like it, but if she made up her mind and my wishes did not accord with her desires, she would dispense with such a formality. Don't think I would blame her. I like her spirit. She has plenty of that. She is, after all, my daughter.'

'Then you must feel very happy about what is happening.'

'I am not unhappy.'

'It will save you a great deal of planning for her future, I dare say.'

'I suppose you are right. I have already discovered all I can about Sir Robert. There is my good friend the Comte. I could learn more if this becomes a serious matter. But what I know already is in his favour.'

'Well, this seems a wonderful piece of good fortune for Sir Robert . . . and for you.'

'It is stimulating talking to you, Lucie. You have such an air of reserve, almost a meekness. Yet you are in fact a spirited young lady and it excites me to talk to you. By the way, have you seen any more of those people?'

'People?'

'Those two you met on the boat and had coffee with a few days ago.'

'No.'

'Well, they were hospitable to you. Would you like me to ask them here?'

'That is kind of you. I am sure they would enjoy that very much.'

'We'll ask them to lunch. After all, you must return their hospitality, you know.'

I was pleased at the prospect of seeing the brother and sister again. It had been a very pleasant encounter. They had become so friendly in such a short time; and I liked to feel that I had friends close by.

'No more trouble with Diable?' he said.

'No. I have been very cautious and haven't ventured too close.'

He gazed across the lake and just at that moment the two swans came into sight.

'They look so graceful,' I said, 'so utterly beautiful.'

'You would not believe, would you, that there could be so much venom in such a magnificent creature,' he said. 'Never forget that you must be watchful of him, for he can suddenly attack. He vented his spite on one of the maids a few years ago. She lost the sight of one eye.'

'How dreadful! Thank you for coming to my rescue.'

'You were unprepared. But remember it for the future. Swans – like some people – are not all they seem.'

'Well, I hope there are not many around like Diable.'

He leaned towards me and took my hand. 'Be on the watch, Lucie, for the Diables of this world,' he said.

I was puzzled and he continued to smile at me.

'I shall always be at hand,' he went on, 'whenever you need me.'

He had said that once before. I supposed I should be

grateful to him. He had certainly saved me from the swan; he had made me welcome at his château; and now he was prepared to entertain two strangers, merely because they had shown me some hospitality. Yes, I should be grateful but I could not throw off this feeling of revulsion.

It was with great pleasure that I rode over to the Fitzgeralds.

Sir Robert was now a frequent visitor at the château. He had postponed his return to England, and the reason was, of course, Belinda.

He told us he was known as Bobby, which seemed to suit him. The more I saw of him, the more I liked him. There was a certain innocence about him – rare in a young man – and I subconsciously felt he would have no defence against Belinda's wiles.

She would marry him, I was sure, for that was what she had made up her mind to do.

When I arrived at the Fitzgeralds' house, Phillida was out, but Roland was in and clearly delighted to see me.

'How very nice of you to call,' he said. 'We were talking of you only this morning. Phillida was wondering whether we dared send a note to the château asking you to come over for lunch.'

'What a coincidence!' I cried. 'For I have an invitation for you. Monsieur Bourdon wondered whether you would care to come over to the château for lunch.'

'That would be delightful. I feel sure Phillida would love it. As for myself, I should enjoy it very much.'

'Then that's settled. Would tomorrow be all right?'

'We have no engagements here, so I can assure you that it will be very convenient for us. Do sit down. I'll ask Angélique to make some coffee.'

I sat down and we talked. He thought that his sister should stay a little longer, he said. 'Phillida is getting restive, though. She won't admit that she is ill.'

'Well, she is not now, is she?'

'Oh no. She has recovered. But I think she needs to be in this climate a little longer. She has this weakness, you know.'

'She seems so full of life.'

'I know. But I have to watch over her.'

'She is fortunate to have such a devoted brother.'

'I am the fortunate one.'

'Well, let us say you both are.'

The coffee arrived and while we were drinking it he said: 'You haven't told me much about yourself. Are you feeling better?'

I hesitated. Then I said: 'What happened to me is not easily forgotten.'

'I understand, and you must forgive my speaking of it. Please do not talk of it if you would rather not. I think a great deal about all you went through. That – and the aftermath – must have been terrible for you.'

'Yes, it was.'

'The trial and everything. The part you were called upon to play in it . . . to come face to face with . . .'

I nodded.

'I am upsetting you,' he went on. 'I just wanted you to know I understand . . . and sympathize. But we should not be talking of it now. It does no good.'

'No, it does no good. Oh, listen, that must be Phillida.'

It was. She came in, flushed and laughing, and when she saw me her eyes lighted up with real pleasure.

'Oh, how wonderful to see you! We were talking of you.'

'Yes, I told her,' said Roland. 'It was only this morning.

What do you think? We are invited to luncheon – invited to the château!'

'Really?'

'And I, your brother, have accepted on your behalf. Was that right?'

She laughed joyously. 'Need you ask? I accept with alacrity.'

I stayed with them for some time. We laughed a great deal, and my previous conversation with Roland was forgotten.

I could see that Roland was blaming himself for bringing up the subject, and I tried to convey to him that it was not important. It was never far from my mind, in any case.

I was thinking what pleasant people they were, and I was glad our friendship was growing.

It was a comfortable feeling, when I was at the château, to remember that I had friends close by.

Roland and Phillida Fitzgerald visited the château as arranged.

I met them in the gardens where I had gone to wait for them. A groom was ready to take their horses to the stables, and I took them into the hall and introduced them to Jean Pascal, Belinda and Sir Robert Denver, who was at the château every day. It was accepted now that he was Belinda's suitor.

Jean Pascal was charming to the visitors, and was clearly determined to make them feel welcome.

'Miss Lansdon was so delighted to meet you again after your brief encounter on the Channel boat. It is fortunate for us all that you met there and then again ran into each other.'

'It was certainly very pleasant for us,' said Phillida. 'And 'so kind of you to ask us to visit your wonderful château.'

'I have to confess,' Jean Pascal told her, 'that I am rather proud of it, and you have given me the opportunity to show it off. *Déjeuner* will be served almost immediately.'

It was a very pleasant meal. Both Fitzgeralds obviously enjoyed the conversation, as did Jean Pascal, so it ran smoothly.

Jean Pascal discreetly set about discovering as much as he could about them, never for one moment appearing to be curious. They told him what they had already told me . . . about the death of their parents and how Roland was carrying on with the London branch of their business, although he paid periodic visits to Yorkshire.

'So it is wool with you and wine with me,' said Jean Pascal. 'Two very useful commodities. Neither of which I believe the world could be happy without.'

'We have been most impressed by the wine we have been having here,' Phillida told him.

'We of the Médoc believe it is the best in the world. You must forgive our pride.'

'It is natural to be proud when pride is merited,' said Roland gravely.

He asked a great many questions about the wine-growing industry and Jean Pascal said that, if they cared, he would take them for a tour of the vineyard. Phillida expressed her delight at this and Roland accepted the invitation with more subdued but no less enthusiasm.

Then the talk was general, in the midst of which Sir Robert said that he had had news from home and would have to be returning before the end of the week.

Belinda looked shocked, so I knew she had not been prewarned; and I noticed that Robert avoided looking at her.

'I hate to go,' he said. 'I'm having such a splendid time

here. But, of course, I didn't intend to stay so long in the first place.

'Well,' said Jean Pascal. 'It's not so very far away, and the Channel is not always in one of its ugly moods.'

I began to wonder whether the courtship was not going as well as I had thought, and whether he was seeking an excuse to end it. Knowing Belinda, I realized that she was far from pleased.

There was a brief but awkward silence which Roland broke by commenting once more on the excellence of the wine; and Jean Pascal immediately told them its vintage and said that it had been brought up from the cellars because it was a special occasion when Lucie's friends came to the château.

Roland was looking at me intently. He seemed to be faintly puzzled. I had a notion that he was wondering about the relationship between Jean Pascal and myself.

When lunch was over, Jean Pascal suggested that we accompany our guests on the tour and we went among the vines and watched the men and women at work, pruning and examining the plants for signs of disease, tying the vines to stakes and repairing trellises.

I had rarely seen Jean Pascal so enthusiastic about anything as he was on this subject. He was clearly very knowledgeable and took great pleasure in explaining to people who knew little about the matter. He talked at great length about the dreaded pests, fungicides, and all the evils which could befall the grape.

I could see the Fitzgeralds were enjoying the tour. Phillida could not restrain her excitement and kept asking questions.

'I know you must think me very stupid, Monsieur Bourdon,' she said. 'I am such an ignoramus. Yet it is *so* interesting and I *do* want to know.'

Jean Pascal was only too happy to instruct. In fact, he seemed a different person. It was the first time I had seen him really enthusiastic. That cynical languor dropped from him. I liked him better that afternoon than I ever had before; perhaps I was grateful to him for being so charming to the Fitzgeralds whom I looked upon as my friends.

Jean Pascal showed us the winepresses which they had used before the wooden cylinders were put in.

'These are quite effective,' he explained. 'They press the grape in the best possible way and so ensure that all the juice can be made use of.'

We saw men clearing the great vats and preparing them for the harvest.

'They are made of stone, you see,' said Jean Pascal. 'When they have been well scrubbed, they will be put in quicklime to saturate the acid still existing in the cask.'

'It's quite fascinating,' said Roland.

'How can we thank you, Monsieur Bourdon,' added Phillida, 'for giving us such an instructive and entertaining afternoon?'

'By coming again, Miss Fitzgerald,' said Jean Pascal gallantly.

We walked back to the château past the lake. Diable, with Ange in attendance, looked at us suspiciously as we passed.

'What beautiful swans!' cried Phillida. 'And black, too. I don't think I have ever seen a black swan before. I have seen plenty of white ones. They look so serene.'

Jean Pascal looked at me and smiled. 'Lucie will tell you that you cannot always judge by appearances. The cob, the male, may be beautiful to all outward appearances, but he has an evil nature. He objects to anyone encroaching on his territory. He gave Lucie a fright not long ago.'

'Yes,' I explained. 'I was standing admiring him when suddenly he decided to attack me.'

'Fortunately I was at hand,' went on Jean Pascal, 'and I rushed to the rescue. I beat the old devil off with a stick. I had to.'

'So he would have attacked you!' cried Phillida. 'I should have thought he would have known you.'

'Diable – that's our name for him: apt, don't you think? – Diable is no respecter of persons. I told Lucie it is a lesson for her. Don't be beguiled by beauty, for you never know what lurks beneath it.'

'I think you are a cynic, Monsieur Bourdon.'

'Shall we say a realist? But Lucie will be very careful in future. Is that not so, Lucie?'

'Certainly where the swan is concerned.'

When the guests left we all went to the stables to see them off. It had certainly been a most enjoyable afternoon.

'Pleasant people,' was Jean Pascal's comment.

Sir Robert was invited to stay to dinner that evening, which he did.

Conversation was a little less fluent than usual. The prospect of his departure hung over us. Jean Pascal said how sorry we should be. We should miss him.

He replied that he would miss us all . . . very, very much. His eyes were on Belinda who was unusually quiet.

'Well,' said Jean Pascal lightly, 'you'll be coming over again sometime, I expect.'

'Oh yes . . . yes indeed.'

I was glad when the meal was over and I retired early. Poor Belinda, I thought, although I suspected that her feelings had not been very deeply involved. She had just liked the idea of marrying a presentable young man with an even more presentable background.

I lay in my bed reading and was not surprised to hear a tap on my door.

I said: 'Who's there?'

'Belinda, of course.'

I unlocked the door and she came in. 'I expected you to come,' I said.

She sat on my bed and she looked radiant.

'I'm engaged,' she announced. 'Bobby has asked me to marry him.'

'Well! Congratulations! You managed it after all.'

'What do you mean – managed it? You are jealous, Lucie Lansdon.'

'Not in the least. Only full of admiration.'

'I'm so happy. Bobby is such a darling. He wanted to ask me before . . . only he was afraid it was too soon. Then he got this message. He has to go home and he didn't like to tell me . . . because he was wondering whether to ask me to marry him and was afraid I'd say no.'

'What? With a title and a handsome face and some fortune, I imagine! The man must be mad.'

'Don't tease. It's too important.'

'All right. So he has asked you to marry him and you have said yes please. And now all we have to do is wait for wedding bells.'

'You've got a sharp tongue sometimes, Lucie. No one would guess it. You look so meek.'

'I understand you too well, Belinda.'

'Well, Bobby likes me.'

'Evidently. Now tell me in detail.'

'He was very quiet after letting out at lunch-time that he was going home. He was making up his mind whether he could ask me or whether he ought to go home and then come back to France and ask me then. You see, we have known each other such a short time, really.'

'True love transcends time and space,' I said.

'Shut up. It was after dinner. You'd gone off and *mon père* – he's very tactful – he guessed that Bobby and I would

174

want to have a talk together, so he left us, said he had some work to do or something and would join us later. It was then that Bobby blurted out that the moment he had seen me he had known. It was sudden like that.'

'And as you had already marked him as your victim, there was nothing to prevent the course of true love running smoothly.'

'We're so happy, Lucie. And *mon père* joined us and we told him. He said, "It seems I have only just found Belinda to lose her to another." Wasn't that sweet? But he was pleased. He wants my happiness – and I suppose it will save him an expensive Season and all the fuss of finding a husband for me.'

'Satisfaction all round,' I commented.

'You like Bobby, don't you, Lucie?'

'Yes, I do. I have one fear, though.'

'What's that?'

'That he is too good for you.'

She laughed at me and then went on to talk of her plans.

'We shall be married with the minimum of delay. I expect it will be in London. Celeste can arrange it. It could hardly be here. So many people don't know *mon père* has a daughter, whereas Celeste *is* my aunt. Bobby is coming back as soon as he can and then we'll make the arrangements. One thing we are both determined on. It is going to be soon.'

After she had gone I lay in bed, feeling, I must admit, a little bitter. Here was Belinda with life flowing so smoothly for her; and I had lost not only my beloved father, but the man I had believed I was going to marry.

Poor sad Lucie . . . and lucky Belinda.

It was ironical that the next morning the blow should fall. It came with a letter from Celeste.

My dear Lucie [she wrote],

Gerald Greenham has returned home. I am afraid the news is bad. There seems to be no doubt that Joel is dead. Gerald has found proof. Apparently Joel and James Hunter were set upon when they left for the hotel. They were robbed and must have put up a fight, for they were killed by the robbers. They were traced by a ring James Hunter was wearing at the time. It is rather an unusual one and the authorities have a description of it. Apparently it is a family heirloom – plain gold with an inscription inside. In the family it was considered a sort of talisman. James was pressed to take it by his mother before he went on the mission. I am afraid, dear Lucie, there cannot be any doubt.

Gerald is home. The family is very sad. Don't write to them. It will only distress them more. They have asked me to tell you what happened. The robbers have been caught and were sentenced to death. They confessed . . . so you see it is true.

I don't know how you feel. Perhaps it would be better for you to stay in France for a while. It might be easier for you there. There would be so much to remind you here.

It is for you to decide. Rest assured I want you to do everything that is easiest for you. You are young and will grow away from the tragedy . . . in time.

God bless you.

With my love and thoughts,

Celeste.

I did not want to speak to anyone. I took an opportunity of escaping. I went out and sat some little distance from the lake, watching the swans as they sailed majestically across the lake. I fancied Diable was keeping a watchful eye on me.

They looked beautiful, so graceful, so much a part of the idyllic scene. Who would believe that the beautiful creature could suddenly be a symbol of hatred?

Yet it was so.

But then, who would have believed that a comparatively short time ago my life had been happy and contented and I saw before me only a continuation of that contentment, and that it had changed drastically?

I sat for a long time looking over the lake.

I did not mention Celeste's letter. I could not bring myself to talk of Joel. Belinda continued in her euphoric state and naturally did not notice my sadness.

I would sit listening to her talking incessantly about plans for the wedding, of the ancestral home which she had yet to see, of the honeymoon which would be of her choosing. Venice, she thought. A romantic city. Or perhaps Florence. Italy certainly.

'*Mon père* is very helpful,' she told me. 'He has made discreet enquiries about Bobby's standing and background . . . financial status and all that, and apparently everything is impeccable and suitable, even to his French mind.'

'How conveniently wonderful,' I murmured, but I was thinking all the time of Joel . . . deciding to walk back to that hotel . . . and going off with James Hunter . . . to death.

I must admit to a certain bitterness. I felt life was so cruel to me while it was benign to Belinda, and I could not help that twinge of resentment towards a fate which could be so unkind to me and benevolent to her.

I took to sitting by the lake. I found a certain satisfaction in watching the swans. On one or two occasions I ventured near to the edge of the lake into Diable's territory. It was only when he came swimming towards me that I retreated.

I was fascinated by the swans. Oddly enough, in those sad days they helped to cheer me in some way. They seemed to tell me that I must be prepared for life, which was not always what it appeared to be, that it was no rare thing in the midst of happiness to find the canker which would erupt into fearful disaster.

I thought often of that maid who came out, in all innocence, to admire the beautiful swans and had ventured too close to the water's edge. Consequently she had been viciously attacked and had lost an eye.

I had come near to disaster, too . . . saved by Jean Pascal.

I was sitting there, watching the swans, when Jean Pascal himself came along.

'Oh, there you are, Lucie,' he said. 'This lake fascinates you, doesn't it? I really believe you have quite a fondness for old Diable.'

'He interests me. He's so beautiful. He looks so calm and harmless . . . right out there in the middle of the lake.'

'Yes, I know, Lucie. You seem a little preoccupied lately.'

'I? I'm sorry.'

'It's nothing to apologize for. I was just wondering whether there was any trouble. If there was something I could do to help?'

'You have been most kind.'

'It has been a great pleasure for me to have you here.'

'It must have been a great joy to you to have your daughter with you.'

'I was thinking of you, too.'

'You have been very kind to me, but it has occurred to me that I must not abuse your hospitality. I think it is time I returned home.'

'You can't go, Lucie! What of Belinda?'

'It would not be necessary for Belinda to come with me.'

'She would be terribly upset if you went. So would I. Robert is coming back as soon as he has settled his business. Then they will announce their engagement. I wanted to talk to you about the arrangements and so on.'

'Belinda will talk to you about them. I really think —'

'Lucie, there is something I have wanted to say to you for some time. I have grown very fond of you. I know I am a few years older than you, but I am young in heart. Lucie, I want to marry you.'

'Marry me!'

'You sound surprised. We have always got along well together, haven't we?'

'Of course, but . . .'

'Well, why not? You have been happy here in the château, have you not?'

I did not answer. I could not truthfully say I had. I had always felt that sense of foreboding. Was it because I had subconsciously felt he was too interested in me for my comfort? Was it because I had come here mourning my father's death and uncertain of the part I had played in convicting the man suspected of murdering him; and that the man I was going to marry was missing? I had come here with all those burdens on me. No, certainly I had not been happy here.

'Oh Lucie,' he said, 'I have failed, then.'

'You have been a kind host and it was good of you to invite me with Belinda. But I could not be happy. My father . . .'

179

'Of course. Of course, I understand. I have been tactless and foolish.' He took my hand. 'Lucie, I love you. I know I could make you happy. I can give you a full and happy life. We will have a happy family. I promise you your welfare shall be the main concern of my life.'

I felt a desire to run away – up those marble steps into the château, to my room, to pack my bag and get right away.

The idea of marrying him filled me with dismay.

'I am sorry,' I said. 'But I could not think of marrying.'

'Perhaps I have spoken too soon.'

'No. It is not that. I do not want to marry. I appreciate your kindness, but I could not marry you.'

'Give it a little thought.'

'That is not necessary. No amount of thought would make me change my mind.'

His face darkened. I felt a twinge of that foreboding which came to me now and then. I was sure that his anger would be something to fear.

He sat back in the seat, glaring out at the lake.

Diable began to swim towards the shore. It occurred to me that the swan sensed Jean Pascal's anger and believed it was directed at him.

I said: 'Look! The swan is coming.'

I stood up and was preparing to move away, for I knew that as soon as we showed that we were not approaching, the swan would turn back to the middle of the lake.

Jean Pascal had risen also; but he showed no sign of retreating. He was looking about him for a weapon. With a quick movement he broke a branch from one of the trees and strode towards the water's edge. The swan flew towards us suddenly and attempted to attack Jean Pascal, who beat at it viciously.

For a few seconds, it was not clear who would win, but Jean Pascal was in command. The swan realized this

180

perhaps, for suddenly he flew back and settled on the lake where his mate was patiently waiting for him.

I felt frightened. The attack had been deliberately provoked and I fancied there was some meaning in it. Jean Pascal was angry, furiously angry, and with me, of course, for refusing his proposal. He had had to vent his anger on someone and he had done it on the swan.

I was shaking with fear. There was something maniacal about the manner in which he had attacked the beautiful creature. Was he imagining that he was beating me?

I started to walk back to the château. He was beside me very soon, smiling, suave as ever.

'It is time someone taught Diable a lesson,' he said.

I did not answer and he went on: 'Lucie, I don't take no for an answer. Think about it, will you? Just give me that promise. Give it thought. Just consider what it would mean to you. We could be happy, Lucie, I know it. Promise me you will think about it.'

I was a coward, I knew. But I was in his house. I was his guest and I was terribly shaken by what I had seen. I could not tell him of the revulsion I felt, so I nodded my assent.

I wanted to get away and I was unsure how to act. I had travelled with Belinda. Could I undertake the journey back alone? Could I try to explain to Belinda? She would never understand.

I rehearsed what I might say. Something like: 'Your father has asked me to marry him. I can't, so I cannot stay in his château.' No. That would not do. Belinda would think I was a fool to refuse her father. I could imagine her comment. 'It would be wonderful for you. My father is rich and important. As for you, Lucie, you're hardly Helen of Troy or Cleopatra. You ought to marry an older man.

You're a bit of an old sobersides yourself. Young men don't like that. I reckon it's the best thing that could happen to you.'

How could I explain to her: he frightens me. My flesh creeps when he comes near me. I had no idea that he had marriage in mind. I must go quickly.

The best thing to do was to get away by myself to think. If I walked in the grounds there was a good chance that I would come face to face with Jean Pascal. I went down to the stables and managed to ride off . . . unseen.

I found myself riding towards the Fitzgeralds' house. I could not confide in them, of course, but I did feel the need for company. I experienced a great sense of relief when I met them. They were on horseback and obviously on their way somewhere.

They hailed me with pleasure.

'Were you coming to visit us?' asked Phillida.

'Well, not exactly. I thought it would be nice if I saw you . . .'

'It certainly is. Unfortunately we are just going visiting. What a pity!'

'Come tomorrow afternoon,' said Roland. 'We shall be at home then.'

'I should love that. What time?'

'Two . . . no, two-thirty?'

'Thanks. I'll see you then.'

They waved and rode off. I was rather relieved in a way. I wanted to think of the position. I did not want to do anything rash. I could perhaps ask their advice about returning home. Jean Pascal had looked after us on the journey out. I must remember that I should have to get myself across the country and my knowledge of the language was far from perfect. I was not sure of trains and so on. I would need help. I was not sure that I could ask Jean Pascal. I had a feeling that he might try to hinder me.

I wondered whether I could put the matter of my departure to the Fitzgeralds. I needed time to think . . . to ponder, so it was just as well that our meeting had been postponed until the next day.

I got through that day somehow. I was on tenterhooks wondering whether I should be able to escape without Belinda and Jean Pascal knowing what was going on.

The next day, immediately after luncheon, I was on my way to the Fitzgeralds. I was surprised on my arrival to find that they had a visitor. It was a young woman who was vaguely familiar to me: and as soon as I heard her name, I remembered.

'This is Madame Carléon,' said Roland. 'She is a neighbour of ours.'

'I picked her up,' explained Phillida, 'which was really very clever of me.'

'Phillida is very good at that, as you know yourself,' added Roland.

. I knew now where I had seen her before. She was the young woman who had come into the hall of the château and displeased Jean Pascal by her presence.

'This is Miss Lucie Lansdon,' went on Roland.

'I am very pleased that we meet,' said Madame Carléon in very accented English.

'I, too,' I replied.

'We met before at the Château Bourdon,' she went on.

'Very briefly,' I said.

'This will not be so brief,' said Roland. 'Do sit down. Madame Carléon has told us so much about the country-side. We have been so fortunate in the friends we have made here.'

Madame Carléon was very attractive. She had abundant

183

blonde hair which was beautifully dressed and she wore a riding habit of light navy which accentuated her fairness; her eyes were deep blue and she had a short nose and a rather long upper lip; this gave her a kittenish look, which was appealing. She was animated in conversation, now and then breaking into French, but making a great effort to speak our language.

She asked me how I liked the château.

'It's a wonderful place,' she said. 'I know it well. And you are a friend of Mademoiselle Bourdon . . . the new daughter, I believe.'

'Yes. We were brought up together until we were about ten years old. Then Belinda went to Australia and she has been back only a short time.'

'Very *intéressante*. And she is a very attractive girl, this Miss Belinda.'

'Oh yes. She has just become engaged.'

'Here?'

'Well, he was not exactly a friend of Monsieur Bourdon. He is English and was visiting friends here. They brought him along to dine . . . and it was love at first sight.'

'But that is charming,' said Madame Carléon.

'And there is family approval on both sides?' asked Roland.

'Certainly on this side. I think Sir Robert does not have much family.'

'How very exciting,' put in Phillida.

And we went on to talk about the various places of interest in the neighbourhood. Madame Carléon lived in Bordeaux and had already taught the Fitzgeralds a great deal about the town.

'I was always interested in Bordeaux,' said Roland, 'because it belonged to England once. It came to us with

184

the marriage of Eleanor of Aquitaine to Henry II, and Richard II was born there.'

'So we became enormously interested in the history of the place,' went on Phillida. 'We really have had a wonderful time in France. Roland and I were wondering whether we would go along the old pilgrims' way to St Jacques de Compostela.'

'A very daunting journey, I'm afraid,' said Roland. 'It takes you right through the Médoc to the Dordogne valley.'

Madame Carléon lifted her shoulders and spread out her hands.

'Oh, but you are the adventurous ones.'

'Perhaps we'll do it one day,' said Roland.

And so we talked until tea was served.

'Angélique does not approve,' said Phillida. 'But she humours our English custom of afternoon tea.'

'I think it is a very charming custom,' said Madame Carléon.

I found it interesting but I had wanted to talk to the Fitzgeralds about the journey home, and I felt I could not speak of this in the presence of Madame Carléon. I thought: I will come here tomorrow perhaps, for I must get away soon.

When we were leaving, Madame Carléon said: 'I will go part of the way with you. There is someone I have to see before going home and it is on my way.'

We left together and before we had gone very far it occurred to me that our meeting had been contrived, for almost immediately she began to talk of Jean Pascal. She said: 'I hope you are comfortable at the château.'

'But . . . yes.'

'I hope you will not be angry with me . . . for what I say.'

'Angry? Why should I be?'

'It could seem perhaps – how do you say in English? – a little impertinent. Is that the right word?'

'I can't tell you that until I hear what it is you are going to say.'

'I must tell you that I know Jean Pascal very well indeed.'

'Oh?'

'Yes . . . as well as two people can know each other. You understand?'

'Yes, I think so.'

'He is a man not to trust . . . *particulairement* a young girl.'

'I understand what you mean.'

'He can be . . . dangerous.'

'Yes.'

'I feel I must tell you . . . must warn . . . Is that what I mean?'

'I believe it is.'

'There have been so many. This girl, your Belinda, she is not the only child. There are many of them in the country here. He thinks because he owns the château he has the right . . .'

'*Le droit de seigneur*, you mean?'

'*Exactement*.'

'I understand fully what you are trying to tell me. I have guessed something of this.'

'He and I, were lovers for a long time. My husband . . . oh, I am a wicked woman . . . I deceive him. I did not mean to. I love him . . . in a way . . . but I was fascinated, you understand?'

'Yes.'

'My husband . . . he find us. It break his heart. He die soon. He was very sick. I think we kill him. And Jean Pascal . . . he does not care. He snap his fingers. He has promised marriage . . . but no. Not now. He is tired of me. He look round for new people.'

'Why do you tell me this?'

'To warn.'

'I don't need warning.'

'You are so young, and believe me, Mademoiselle Lansdon, youth is very attractive to one so . . . jaded? . . . is it?'

'Yes,' I assured her. 'Jaded. I know all this and I am not in the least tempted.'

'Then I am happy for you. I need not have spoke.'

'I appreciate it very much. It was kind of you . . . but, because of my feelings, quite unnecessary.'

'Then I am glad. He would be no good. He makes no woman happy. Oh, he is very charming . . . in the beginning . . . but after . . .'

'It was good of you to want to warn me.'

'I see you so young . . . so fresh . . . so innocent.'

'I am all these, but I do know something of the world and I am not in the least likely to become one of his victims.'

'And you forgive me?'

'There is nothing to forgive. I thank you for your kindness. You were not to know it was not necessary.'

'I am hurt, you see.'

I did understand the feeling of a discarded mistress. An unpleasant thought occurred to me. Had he dispensed with her because of his designs on me? I must get away. I could not stay longer in the château.

Madame Carléon said: 'I will turn off here. I am content. I have spoken. My conscience is happy now. I say goodbye. Perhaps we meet again, eh?'

I said I hoped we would, and rode back to the château.

Belinda wanted to know where I had been.

'I looked everywhere. I wanted to talk to you. I've

187

written to Celeste. *Mon père* thinks it would be best for us to have the wedding there.'

'Good Heavens! You're just engaged and that was all fixed in a hurry because poor Bobby had to go back. He's the one you'll have to consult about the wedding.'

'Oh, he'll want to have it just as I want it.'

'I think his opinion might be asked.'

'Well, it will be . . . But after we've made the plans.'

'Just the same old Belinda,' I said. 'Everything must fit in with you.'

'Of course,' she replied.

Jean Pascal expressed displeasure, too.

'What happened to you this afternoon, Lucie?' he asked.

'I rode out and met the Fitzgeralds.'

'That seems to be becoming a habit.'

'It is pleasant to meet one's compatriots abroad.'

'I suppose so. But I missed you.'

I could not bear that look in his eyes. I thought about Madame Carléon. What would he say if he knew I had spent the afternoon with her? Moreover, what would he say if he knew that she had told me of him? It was nothing I did not already guess, of course, but it was a confirmation.

I must get away.

I wondered whether to consult Belinda. No, that would be useless. In any case she was too immersed in her own affairs. She did not want to leave yet. She must wait for Bobby's return and the plans they would make. How long, I wondered, could I endure to stay in the château?

Then I thought of Rebecca. I had turned to her all my life when I was in difficulties. I should have done so before.

I would write to her. I would explain that I had to get away quickly. I knew what Rebecca would do. She would come to France – Pedrek with her – and they would take me

188

back to safety and Cornwall. On the other hand, could I travel alone?

I decided to try Rebecca first. That night I wrote to her.

Dear Rebecca,

I have to get away from here. Belinda has become engaged and will not leave just yet. I could, I suppose, travel on my own, but I feel very uncertain. I should have to get the train to Paris and then from Paris to Calais and so on. Once I was on the Channel ferry I should be all right. It is the uncertainty of the language which daunts me.

Dear Rebecca, I need to come home at once. Do help me. If you could come out – or Pedrek – perhaps both of you. I know I am asking a lot, but I have always known that you were there to help me, and I feel very shaken in view of everything that has happened. I have just heard the terrible news that Joel was killed. It seems too much. I feel weak and foolish, but I know you will understand. I so much want to come home . . . to be with you.

Love from your sister,

Lucie.

I felt better when I had written that letter. I thought of all Rebecca had been to me through my life and I knew she would not fail me now.

It was a great comfort to have taken some action. I would post the letter tomorrow. How long would it take to reach her, I wondered? But at least I had taken some action.

I got into bed. I could not sleep; and suddenly I was alert, for I heard a faint noise outside my room. I sat up, startled. Someone was on the other side of the door.

Silently I leaped out of bed. I went to the door. Slowly the handle turned.

189

I stood leaning against the door. I could hear the sound of breathing on the other side. I knew who was there and I was trembling with fear.

Belinda would have spoken sharply, demanding to be let in. Moreover, it was late. She would have come earlier.

I knew who was there. It was Jean Pascal, and he was trying to surprise me in my sleep.

I waited. I heard the frustrated sigh . . . and then the sound of retreating footsteps.

He had gone.

I leaned against the door, still shaking. I thought of him, angry and frustrated, beating the swan.

Had I not locked the door he would have been in the room. The thought of that filled me with horror.

I must get away. I could not stay here another night.

Tomorrow I must take action.

I had a sleepless night, but I grew calmer in the morning. If necessary, I must make my own way home. I could find out about trains. Anything was better than spending another night in this château. I had been lucky. He had not knocked and asked to come in. He had known what my response would have been. He had planned to come into my bedroom, catch me asleep, surprise me . . . and then what?

I was limp with horror at the images which my tortured mind conjured up.

I rose and unlocked the door and in due course Thérèse came in with my *petit déjeuner*.

I forced myself to eat it. I washed and dressed and put on my riding habit, for an idea had come to me.

I was going to leave, and I could find out about the journey from the Fitzgeralds. They travelled a great deal and would be the ones to advise me.

I made my way down to the stables. The household was not yet awake. I saddled a horse and rode over to them.

They were just finishing breakfast when I arrived.

'Lucie!' cried Phillida. 'This is a surprise!'

Roland stood up to greet me.

'I hope I'm not disturbing you . . .' I began.

'Nonsense. We're delighted to see you at any time.'

'Perhaps I am making too much of this . . .' I stammered. 'But . . . er . . . I want to get away from the château. I have to go at once.'

'What's happened?' asked Phillida.

Roland held up a hand to silence her. 'You will take the train to Paris,' he said. 'It's a long journey. Then you will have to change trains . . . from Paris to Calais. There you get to the docks for the Channel ferry. Did you say you wanted to go today? I don't think that would be possible. The train leaves for Paris at ten o'clock. No . . . you couldn't possibly do that.'

'I'll go tomorrow then. I'll have to have one night more . . .'

'Something has happened, hasn't it?' said Phillida.

'Let us get you some coffee,' said Roland, 'and then you can tell us what you want to.'

'I don't want any coffee, thanks.'

I looked at them steadily. They were good friends, I was sure. I decided to trust them.

I said: 'Jean Pascal Bourdon has asked me to marry him.'

Phillida could not hide her dismay and I guessed that Madame Carléon had been talking to them about Jean Pascal.

'You have not accepted him!' she cried in dismay.

'No. I could never do that.'

I noticed they exchanged a glance and I fancied it was

191

one of relief. I warmed towards them. They were my good friends – even though I had known them such a short time I could confide in them.

'In fact,' I went on, 'he alarms me. I know the sort of man he is. I have known for a long time. He ruined Leah's life so that she was persuaded to take part in something which was really wicked. She was Belinda's mother. She was a good woman and would never have acted as she did if she had not been desperate . . . made so by him. But this doesn't concern us now. Leah is dead and things have worked out well for Belinda.'

I realized I was talking thus because I found it difficult to speak of Jean Pascal. They seemed to understand.

'Well, you have refused him,' said Roland, 'and I think you were very wise to do that. And now you feel that you do not want to stay under the same roof with him. That is clear enough.'

'Yes, but last night – I locked my door, you see. I always have, right from the first. It seemed like some premonition. I had to do it. But – he tried to get into my room last night and then I made up my mind that I had to get away. I have written to my sister, my best friend in the world now, and I have asked her to come here so that I could go back with her. But after last night I felt I couldn't stay – and I haven't even posted the letter yet.'

'So you are leaving tomorrow?'

'Yes. I'll manage somehow. I want you to tell me exactly how to do it. My French is not very adequate and being on my own . . .'

They exchanged glances.

'It's just a suggestion,' said Roland.

'Go on, Roly!' cried Phillida. 'I know what you're going to say. And I don't see why not. We were going anyway, next week.'

192

Roland said: 'If we left tomorrow, you could travel with us.'

I could not restrain my joy and relief. I wanted to hug them both.

'You – you really would do that?' I murmured. 'But you were not going tomorrow.'

'Why should we not?'

'Oh, it's so wonderfully good of you.'

'No, it's not,' said Phillida. 'We'd enjoy the company. It will be great fun, won't it, Roland? I'm ready to go home anyway.'

'There'll have to be one more night in the château, I'm afraid,' said Roland.

'I'll manage that. I'll keep my door locked, and I shall tell them I am leaving tomorrow. I'm sure there won't be any trouble.'

'You could stay here perhaps,' suggested Phillida. 'Or perhaps in Bordeaux?'

'I couldn't very well do that. After all, I did not actually see him last night. It might have been just a fancy of mine. No, I shall feel quite safe – if I can leave tomorrow.'

'Well then, that's settled,' said Roland. 'Now let us plan how we will set about it.'

I could not believe it. I was sitting in the train which was carrying me to Paris. Phillida sat beside me, Roland opposite. Phillida was clearly excited by what she called 'our adventure', while Roland smiled benignly at her, including me in the smile. I felt so fond of them. They had come to my aid when I most needed friends; and now I was on my way home; and I had no anxiety about the journey. Everything was taken care of.

Yesterday had been difficult, and I had left the château

193

under a cloud. I could not help feeling that I had behaved rather ungraciously in making such a hasty departure.

When I had ridden back after having made all the arrangements with the Fitzgeralds I found consternation in the château.

I had been missed. One of the servants had seen me on my way to the stables. I had left early in the morning without telling anyone where I was going. At the least it was most inconsiderate.

I could not explain to Jean Pascal that it was because he had attempted to get into my room the previous night.

Belinda cried: 'What on earth made you go off like that?'

I replied: 'I have to tell you that I shall be leaving tomorrow.'

Both she and Jean Pascal stared at me in amazement.

'Tomorrow?' echoed Jean Pascal.

'Why?' demanded Belinda.

'I think it is time I left, and as I did not care to travel back alone, I have arranged to go tomorrow with the Fitzgeralds, who will be leaving then.'

'I don't understand,' said Jean Pascal coldly.

'I have been thinking for some time that I should not continue to encroach on your hospitality indefinitely, and when the opportunity came, I took it. So we have made arrangements to leave tomorrow on the ten o'clock train from Bordeaux.'

'But it is so sudden,' said Jean Pascal; though I could see by the expression in his eyes that he knew it was because he had attempted to come to my room the previous night. I could also see the smouldering anger in his eyes, and I thought again of how he had attacked the swan. I believed then that he would have liked to take a stick to me.

194

How glad I was . . . how grateful to my good friends, the Fitzgeralds.

'I think it is very ill-mannered of you to make all these arrangements without telling us,' said Belinda.

'I have only just discovered that the Fitzgeralds were going and I thought it would be a good idea to go with them.'

'We oughtn't to allow it,' said Belinda, looking at her father.

'I'm afraid you can't stop me,' I said sharply. I turned to Jean Pascal. 'I hope you don't think it ungracious of me. In view of the circumstances . . .'

He knew full well what I meant and was fast getting the better of his anger.

He said coolly: 'You must do what you want, of course. If you had told me, I would have made arrangements for you. I would have escorted you back myself.'

'Oh, I could not have allowed that. You and Belinda want to be here. You will have so much to do when Robert returns. But thank you all the same. Now I will go to my room and pack.'

'How will you get to Bordeaux tomorrow?'

'We have arranged for a carriage to pick me up and then the Fitzgeralds. It will then take us to Bordeaux.'

'You seem to have become very friendly with them. Do you think it wise to put so much trust in them? You don't really know them very well, do you?'

'I feel they are good friends and in any case what harm could befall me? I am only travelling back with them. And now I really must begin to pack. There is so much to do.'

Belinda kept away from me during the day; she was very upset with me. Jean Pascal also left me to my own devices, which pleased me very much. I returned early, locked my door and was ready to leave next morning.

I felt I was coming very well out of a delicate situation.

I had had a rather restless night which was to be expected. When I did doze I had a nightmare in which Jean Pascal suddenly broke into my room and I awoke in the dream to find him at my bedside. Suddenly he turned into the black swan. It was a great relief to wake up and know that it was only a dream. And after that I scarcely slept at all.

How relieved I was when morning came!

Thérèse knocked at my door an hour earlier than usual. She had coffee and a brioche for me.

'You'll need something inside you, Mademoiselle,' she said. 'You've got a long day ahead.'

She was smiling sympathetically. I wondered if she knew the real reason for my departure. It would not surprise me if she did. She probably knew a good deal about the habits of the master of the château. I thanked her warmly.

When I went down to the hall, Jean Pascal was there.

He said: 'I'll send someone to bring down your bags.'

He took my hands and looked earnestly into my face. 'I'm sorry you are leaving us like this, Lucie,' he said.

'I'm afraid . . . I felt I had to.'

'My dear child, I understand. I hope you will try to understand me. I love you very dearly. I have been overhasty. I do realize that now. Please remember that I shall always be there to help you if you need me. You understand that, don't you, Lucie?'

'It is good of you . . .' I began.

He shook his head. 'I would care for you . . . always. One day I am going to make you change your mind.'

'Thank you for your hospitality. I am sorry if I seemed churlish.'

'No, my dear, the fault was mine. I understand. I am considerably chastened. Give yourself time. My poor

196

Lucie, you have so much to contend with and I was impatient. It was because I cared so much. But we will leave it . . . for a time. And then I shall come back and try to win what is so important to me.'

I had a great desire to get away. The carriage was at the door. He kissed my hand as they put the luggage into the carriage.

Belinda did not come to say goodbye. That was typical of her. She was very annoyed with me and was not going to hide it.

The carriage moved slowly away. Jean Pascal stood there, looking so sad that I could not help feeling a little contrite.

When the Fitzgeralds joined me and we rattled along to Bordeaux, I began to feel better.

And there we were in the train speeding along to Paris.

A Quiet Wedding

The journey went smoothly. Roland got us across Paris and we caught the train to Calais in good time. I realized often during that journey how lost I should have been without the Fitzgeralds.

Then there was the task of getting on the ferry. I felt so relieved when we came in sight of Dover.

The Fitzgeralds said they had a *pied-à-terre* in London which Roland used when he was there on business; but he did pay frequent visits to the headquarters in Bradford.

When we arrived in London, he said they would drop me and then go on to their little place. They would not come in with me as I should be unexpected and it would be better for me to arrive alone and make the explanations. They would call next morning to make sure everything was all right.

They accompanied me to the door of the house where my bags were deposited. The cab waited at the door until it was opened by the butler.

I turned and waved to them and the cab drove off.

The butler was clearly astonished. 'Miss Lansdon, we weren't expecting . . . We didn't get a message . . .'

'No,' I replied. 'There wasn't time to send a message. Is Mrs Lansdon at home?'

'Yes, Miss Lansdon. I'll inform her. And I'll send someone to take your bags up to your room.'

'Where is Mrs Lansdon?' I asked.

'I think she would be in the drawing-room, Miss.'

'I shall find her. If you will see about the bags . . .'

'I will, Miss.'

I went past him up the stairs.

Celeste had heard the sounds of arrival and was at the top of the stairs to see what it was all about.

'Lucie!' she cried.

'Oh, Celeste, I'm so glad to see you.'

She put her arms round me and held me tightly.

'But why?' she said. 'Where are Belinda and my brother?'

'They are still in France. I came back with friends.'

'You must be very tired.'

'I suppose so, but at the moment I'm so glad to be back that I don't feel the least bit tired.'

'Something has happened . . .'

She hesitated and then went on: 'I'm so sorry. It's Joel, of course. I hope I did the right thing in letting you know. I wasn't sure. I ought to have broken it gently. But I thought you would have to know.'

'Oh yes. Dear Celeste, I had to know. How . . . how are the Greenhams taking it?'

'Badly. I've only seen them once. I called . . . but I think they do not want callers. One understands. Sir John, well, you can't tell with him, but Lady Greenham cannot hide how sad she is. I felt I shouldn't have called. It seemed like bringing it all back, but I suppose it's in their minds the whole time. I left very soon.'

'Did you see Gerald?'

She shook her head. 'It is so very tragic. There was such excitement when Joel went. It was going to be so important for his career. It all seemed so happy then. And it has all changed. But we must not speak of it. I am so pleased to see you. It has been so quiet without you and Belinda.'

'Belinda is going to be married.'

'Yes, I know.'

'It is all so suitable. It happened very quickly. Her father approves. Sir Robert seems acceptable in every way. It was love at first sight and I suppose there will be a grand wedding.'

'Yes,' said Celeste with a faint note of alarm in her voice. 'It will be here.'

'You'll do it beautifully,' I assured her.

'And you, Lucie?'

I hesitated and then decided to tell her.

'It became a little awkward. Your brother asked me to marry him.'

'No!'

'He did. And, Celeste, I could not accept his proposal. He seems to think I shall change my mind, but I shan't. I never shall.'

'No. I understand.'

'Well, I couldn't really stay in the house with that sort of situation and I had met some people who were coming back, so I travelled with them.'

'French people?'

'No. English. It was rather a coincidence. I met them first on the ferry going over – just briefly, you know, and it turned out that they were staying near us. We became friendly. You know how it is, meeting your fellow countrymen in a foreign land. I saw them several times and when I heard they were coming back, I thought I'd take the opportunity to travel with them. They will be calling tomorrow, so you will meet them.'

'It's lovely to have you back,' she said.

'It is wonderful to be back,' I replied.

'It's been rather lonely without you.'

'Dear Celeste, you should have come with us. The château is so beautiful. You must know every inch of it.'

'Well, it was where I was born, where I lived my early days. But I made a new life here. This is my home now.'

I thought then that her life was as tragic as mine.

We went up to my room together. My bags were already there.

'I'll send one of the maids up to help you unpack,' said Celeste.

'I'd rather do it myself.'

'Would you like something sent up on a tray . . . and then you can get to bed?'

'Hot water to wash off the stains of the journey. Then the tray.'

'It shall be done. Then, later, we'll talk.'

'Thank you, Celeste. It was a nice welcome home.'

I washed and the tray came up. I was surprised to find I was really hungry.

I did not feel sleepy so I wrote a letter to Rebecca telling her I was home. I had a great desire to go and see her, and toyed with the idea of going down to Cornwall the very next day.

I could not do that, though. The Fitzgeralds were coming tomorrow, and I could not leave Celeste who was so delighted that I was back.

I would stay in London for a week at least, so in the meantime I would console myself by sending a letter to Rebecca.

I wrote to her at some length, telling her that I was home. But I did not mention Jean Pascal. That was something I could only convey to her when we were alone.

The letter would be posted next day.

One of the maids came in, took the tray away and asked

if there was anything I needed. I told her there was not.

How peaceful it was! How different from that room in the château which had aroused in me such feelings of foreboding. It was as though it were warning me. Of marriage with Jean Pascal? Even to contemplate that sent a shiver down my spine. Why should I be so scared? People could not be made to marry where they did not want to.

Here I felt safe from Jean Pascal. There would be no need to lock my door.

That night, before getting into my bed, I went to the window and looked out across to the enclosed gardens and the street lamp. Just for a moment I fancied I saw a figure lurking in the shadows. It was merely the effect produced by the light, but for a second or so it startled me.

I thought: Am I going to be haunted all my life?

The next day the Fitzgeralds called, and Phillida's gaiety and Roland's quiet charm made a good impression on Celeste.

Phillida talked amusingly about her adventures in France and the trouble she had had with the language; and Celeste laughed a good deal, which was rare for her.

Before they left they received an invitation to dinner the following night which they accepted with alacrity.

Celeste said: 'I want to thank you for looking after Lucie.'

'It was our pleasure,' replied Roland.

'The journey was such fun,' added Phillida, 'particularly when we thought we were going to miss the train in Paris. Then we realized we had misunderstood the time. It is so difficult, you know, when they let out that stream of words . . . and numbers are particularly tricky.'

Celeste was quietly animated.

'They are so charming,' she said, when they had gone. 'The sort of people you become very friendly with quickly. I look forward to seeing them tomorrow night.'

I was delighted to see how much they all seemed to like each other.

That afternoon I called on the Greenhams. I knew it was going to be painful but I wanted to find out all I could about Joel, and I guessed, in view of my relationship with him, they would regard me as one of the family.

I was shown into the drawing-room. Lady Greenham was not there and Sir John was alone.

He took both my hands in his and said: 'How are you, Lucie?'

'I am well,' I replied.

'My wife is very poorly,' he told me. 'She is really not well enough to see anyone.'

'I understand. It must have been a terrible shock for her.'

'For us all. I'm afraid she is taking it rather badly.'

'I was wondering if you have any details. Gerald . . .'

'Gerald is back at his duties. We only know what you have been told. There is nothing more to be said.'

'It is all rather mysterious.'

'It happens, Lucie.'

'I thought perhaps . . .'

'We are trying to grow away from it. You understand what I mean. It is over. There is nothing we can do.'

We were silent.

'Would you care for a glass of sherry?' he asked.

'No, thank you.'

I had an idea that this interview was as painful for him as it was for me, and I wanted to end it as soon as possible.

'I think I should be going,' I said. 'Do give my best wishes to Lady Greenham.'

'I will,' he said, and looked relieved.

I felt a little hurt, and that my call had been unwelcome.

It was very strange. In the past they had always been so friendly. They had behaved as though I were a member of the family. Of course, that friendship had been with my father; but whenever we had visited I always felt very welcome; and in view of my relationship with Joel I really did feel very close. I was a little subdued and surprised that now I felt like a stranger intruding on their grief, which surely they knew was mine also.

I was pensive as I drove home. Then I began to realize that seeing me must have brought back the tragedy more vividly.

I mentioned this to Celeste.

She replied: 'You noticed it too. I did not see Lady Greenham either. I was told that she was not well and was resting in her room. But Sir John . . . well, he hardly seemed overjoyed to see me.'

'I can understand it in a way. They were so friendly with my father and first he went . . . and now Joel. We must try to realize how they must be feeling. They don't want to see anyone who reminds them. I had the feeling that I did not know the whole truth.'

'What was there to know? He went out there full of promise and he came to this dreadful end. It's a bitter tragedy for his parents.'

'Yes, I understand their feelings. But I hoped to hear something. Now it is left at Joel's just going over there and then . . . disappearing.'

'Well, that is what happened. I think, Lucie, you will have to try to forget Joel. We both have to shut off the past. We've got to look ahead. Now those very nice people you met . . . I think we could be really good friends. The girl is amusing and he is rather serious . . . but I like him for that.'

'I am glad you like them. I do, too.'

'Well, we'll see how this dinner goes.'

It went extremely well; and after that the Fitzgeralds became frequent visitors to the house. They took us out to dine. Their *pied-à-terre* was not suitable for entertaining, they said.

Our pleasant friendship was developing fast.

To my great joy, Rebecca paid us a visit.

As soon as she had received my letter she had prepared to come to London.

I could talk to her as I could to no one else, and I was soon confiding to her what had happened with Jean Pascal.

Her face darkened as she listened.

'Oh, you did well to leave, Lucie. It was absolutely the right thing and how lucky that those nice people were leaving at the same time.'

'I don't think they planned to do so, actually. They just put their return about a week forward so that they would travel with me.'

'Then I like them the more.'

'You'll be meeting them soon. They have become great friends. Celeste, I am glad to say, likes them very much and so will you. I wrote to you at the château but I did not post the letter. I was asking you to come there and then of course I saw the Fitzgeralds the next day and realized I could leave with them.'

When I told her how Jean Pascal had tried to come into my bedroom, her face darkened.

'How glad I am your door was locked! He is a man to avoid. I was quite worried when I heard you were going to France with him. I did think, though, that his main interest was in Belinda.'

'So did I. I think he is proud of his daughter. She is like him in lots of ways and she is, of course, very attractive.'

'And he really asked you to marry him!'

'I was astonished. Of course, he had been very considerate towards me all the time . . . and then that happened
and I just wanted to run away.'

She nodded. Then she said slowly: 'A thought has
occurred to me, Lucie. You could now be called a rich
young woman, I suppose.'

'You think it was that . . .'

'He is what he would call a realist. He was once going to
marry a girl with royal connections . . . but that sort of
thing has gone out of fashion in France. I always thought
that was why the marriage was delayed and later abandoned. It may be that now he is ready to settle for a fortune.
On the other hand, you are young and he would find youth
very appealing at his time of life.'

'He said that he was in love with me.'

'He falls in love as naturally as he breathes. It doesn't
mean much more to him than the fancy of the moment. But
to propose marriage . . . well, I don't like it, Lucie. I can't
tell you how relieved I am that you had the good sense not
to be fascinated by him.'

'I was repulsed.'

'I know. So was I. He made suggestions to me once. Oh
no . . . not marriage. He had the temerity and insolence to
suggest that he could initiate me into the art of being more
seductive to my husband. I was furious with him. And then
– it was in High Tor – he tried to rape me. It was to give me a
taste of the irresistible pleasures which he could provide
and which I was too stupid and unsophisticated, in his
opinion, to know anything about.'

'How arrogant! He can be courteous and behave sometimes with such a sense of chivalry outwardly while he plans
those things. He reminds me of the swan.'

'Swan?'

'Yes, there was one on the lake in the château grounds. It is beautiful . . . so majestic. It gives an air of peace gliding there across the water. Then suddenly, it becomes vicious. One of the maids lost an eye when it attacked her – so he told me.'

'How absolutely terrible! I think it is a very good thing that you have come home. Now, Lucie, you have to look ahead. There must be no more brooding. It's a mistake to live in the past. You have lost two people you love . . . cruelly and violently. But there are good things in the world. You've got to look for them.'

'I know, Rebecca, and I am going to try.'

She leaned forward and kissed me and, as I had all my life, I felt comforted by Rebecca.

We knew that Rebecca's stay would be brief as she could not leave her family for long. Two weeks was the most we could expect.

She said that when she left she was hoping to take me with her. I felt it would be restful to be at High Tor for a while.

When she met the Fitzgeralds she liked them very much. We saw them every day and a firm friendship was fast growing between the two families.

They would come to luncheon or dinner and repay our hospitality with visits to the theatre or the opera.

Rebecca said it had been a wonderful gesture of theirs to return home with me so that I did not have to travel alone. That was a test of friendship; and, of course, at that time I did not know them as well as I did now. And the more we knew them, the more our respect for them grew.

It was so pleasant, said Rebecca, to see a sister and brother so fond of each other; and it was rather touching to be aware of how they attempted all the time to look after each other. It had come about, of course, through the tragic loss of their parents. They were really very nice people. That was the general verdict.

I had almost made up my mind that I would go back with Rebecca when the letters came. One was from Jean Pascal to Celeste, the other was for me from Belinda.

Dear Lucie [she wrote],

I am going to be married in six weeks' time. Isn't that exciting? Bobby insists. He is so impatient.

He came down to the château as he had said he would and then we were officially engaged. There was a grand party to celebrate it. It was wonderful. Musicians playing in the great hall and in the gardens. Lots of grand people and *mon père* displaying me with pride as his dear daughter. Nobody asked awkward questions as to where I had been all this time. They understand these matters in France. However, there I was, his dear daughter and her lovely fiancé.

Bobby is a darling. He does everything I want. He said he was sorry you weren't here, and I told him how awful you had been, an absolute *pig*. After all we'd done for you – making a fuss of you, looking after you – and then you went off suddenly just because those people were going home. Bobby said he thought pigs were rather nice. He's got a lot of them on his estate. But Bobby is like that. He likes everything. That's because he's so happy about us.

The fact is, we are coming home. *Mon père* is giving Celeste instructions because I'm to be married in London. I wish it were here in the château . . . but *mon père* says no. We have to

208

remember Bobby and he couldn't very well be married in France. So, London it is. I shall need you to help me with my trousseau. I've decided on the wedding dress. It's going to be – No, I won't tell you. You don't deserve it after the way you've behaved. *Mon père* will tell Celeste what has to be done. It will be the wedding of the year. That is what we intend to make it.

You are a silly old thing, just going off like that. *Mon père* says you thought you were intruding. What a lot of nonsense! He said you were mistaken, but he understood your feelings and he has forgiven you for going off like that. I haven't, though. Never mind. You shall help me to get ready.

Isn't it fun? We are coming home next week, and by the time you get this it will be very near.

Till then,

Belinda.

Celeste was a little dismayed when she read her letter.

'This wedding is going to be rather a grand affair,' she said. 'My brother wants me to arrange it.'

'I gathered that from Belinda. She seemed very happy.'

Celeste nodded and continued to look worried. 'You'll help, won't you, Lucie?'

I thought of the peace of Cornwall in Rebecca's company which I had been contemplating but there was pleading in Celeste's eyes.

'I shall if I am of any use . . . of course.'

I was rewarded by the immense relief in her eyes.

The Fitzgeralds were very interested when I told them the news.

'Do you think we shall be invited to the wedding?' asked Phillida.

Roland looked shocked but Celeste said quickly: 'You are invited now.'

Phillida clapped her hands. 'What a wonderful day that was,' she said, 'when we met on the Channel ferry.'

Rebecca understood now that I should not be accompanying her to Cornwall.

'But you will come later on,' she said. 'It will be something for us to look forward to.'

Belinda arrived at the house with Jean Pascal. I was not looking forward to seeing the latter but when he appeared he was gracefully charming, and no reference was made to my unconventional departure from the château. I was glad, however, that he did not stay at the house, although I expected him to be there frequently during the coming weeks.

Belinda was in a state of bliss. She chattered endlessly and the subject was always that of the imminent wedding. She had changed the venue of the honeymoon five or six times.

First it was going to be Rome. 'The catacombs and all that. The Colosseum. We shall see where the Romans sent the Christians to the lions.'

Then a few days later: 'I don't know. I don't think I want to see all those old ruins. But I believe there is rather a nice fountain. You throw a coin in and it means you will come back. I think I'd rather like that. But perhaps Florence . . .'

Then we heard of the glories of Florence for a few days until she thought of Venice.

'All those canals. Fascinating. Drifting along in a gondola with a handsome gondolier.'

'You shouldn't be interested in handsome gondoliers, only in your new husband.'

'I shall have to make him jealous now and then, don't you think?'

'No, I do not.'

'Of course *you* wouldn't . . . and what do you know about it?'

'Enough to know that it is not a very propitious start to a honeymoon for the bride to be planning conquests of other men.'

She put out her tongue at me as she used to do when we were children.

Finally Venice was the favourite.

'Doesn't poor Bobby get a choice?' I asked.

'He just wants to do what I want.'

'I can see that he is determined to keep you contented.'

She loved that sort of banter and she could get it only from me. I believe she was fond of me in a way, just as I was of her. In spite of everything that had happened, there was a bond between us and it was impossible to break it.

The days began to slip by. There was so much to do and it all seemed so important that I have to admit that there were periods – quite long ones – when I stopped thinking of my father and Joel.

Celeste noticed and said it was the same for her. She said to me: 'This wedding is good for us, Lucie.' And I knew what she meant.

'It's an indication,' she went on. 'It shows that, in time, we can grow away from the past.'

Jean Pascal had decided that it should be a grand occasion. I think he had become quite fond of Belinda. She amused him and he liked to be amused. She was really very attractive and that made him proud of her, I imagined. I wondered what Leah would have said to see her daughter now.

The wedding gown had arrived. It was beautiful and

made of Valenciennes lace and satin; there was a wreath of orange blossom for her hair and her bouquet was to be made of gardenias.

'Everything will be white,' she said.

'A sign of purity,' I reminded her.

I was surprised at the effect my words had on her. She looked at me sharply. 'Why did you say that?'

'Because it is true, isn't it?'

'I thought you were . . .'

'What? What did you think?'

'Oh, nothing.'

'You looked quite fierce.'

'I thought you were making fun.'

'We're always making fun, aren't we?'

'Yes, but that was different.'

'Whatever has got into you?'

'Oh nothing, pre-wedding nerves.'

'You! With pre-wedding nerves? You're joking.'

'Of course, you idiot.'

But there was something on her mind. I wondered what for a while and then I forgot it.

The wedding day dawned. There were a good many guests and of course the press was in evidence. Belinda was referred to as the niece of Benedict Lansdon. The press was interested on this account. It was recalled that Belinda was married from the very house outside which the assassination had taken place.

'*Happier Days*', commented one newspaper. '*The ghost of the past exorcised. Today, from the door from which Benedict Lansdon had emerged on that fatal day to meet his assassin came a charming bride. Miss Belinda Bourdon, niece of Mrs Celeste Lansdon, was married today from the very house outside which Benedict Lansdon was shot not quite two years ago.*'

It was a pity they had to bring memories back to us.

So Belinda became Lady Denver. She was a very beautiful bride. I shall never forget the sight of her standing beside Robert while they cut the cake. She looked radiantly happy and I was sure she was.

Celeste and I helped her change into what she called her going-away costume. It was peacock blue trimmed with miniver. She looked enchanting in the close-fitting hat made of matching blue feathers.

She kissed us fervently and told us how much she loved us, which was rather touching coming from Belinda. Then we were all waving them off on their way to Venice.

I was with Roland and Phillida afterwards.

'It was a wonderful wedding,' said Phillida. She looked a little wistful. 'It is marvellous to be as happy as that.'

Roland agreed with her.

'It's always something of an anti-climax at this moment,' I said. 'The bride and bridegroom have departed. And here we are left.'

'With friends,' said Roland looking at me steadily.

'Yes, of course,' I replied. 'With friends.'

There was indeed a feeling of anti-climax after the wedding. I missed my verbal battles with Belinda. They had somehow brightened the days. Jean Pascal was in London, which made me feel I wanted to get away.

Rebecca was preparing to go back to Cornwall and urged me to go with her. I hesitated. Much as liked to be with her and her family, I did not think it was what I needed just then. I told myself that Celeste needed me here. There was another thought which occurred to me. I should not see the Fitzgeralds and it brought home to me how much their friendship meant to me.

Then I thought of Manorleigh. I had loved that house in my childhood. It had seemed full of mystery, and life had been exciting there. Belinda and I used to ride round the paddock on our ponies. There was the haunted garden with the oak tree and the seat on which Belinda had once played the ghost. It was *my* house now; and that gave it an added attraction.

I told Rebecca that I should like to stay there for a week or so.

'A good idea,' she agreed. 'It will get you out of London and you are not so far away.'

'I shall ask Celeste to come and stay for a few days when she wants to. I think she would be rather lonely if I went far away.'

Rebecca understood.

Celeste said she would love to come to Manorleigh.

'Any time you feel like it, Celeste. It is your home . . . just as I think of this house as mine.'

I saw Rebecca off to Cornwall and I should have felt very melancholy at her departure if I had not been making plans to go to Manorleigh.

When the Fitzgeralds called I told them that I was going away for a while and could not help being pleased by the blank dismay on their faces.

'Actually it is only a little way out of London,' I told them. 'Manorleigh was my father's constituency. He bought Manor Grange because of that. And now it is mine. It's a lovely old place and it is quite a long time since I've seen it. I am going down there for a while.'

'We might be able to visit you perhaps,' suggested Roland.

'But of course. I shall expect that. I am going on Monday. Why don't you come down at the week-end? That will give me time to settle in and prepare the

214

servants. You could come on Friday if that is convenient.'

Roland looked at Phillida whose eyes were shining with delight.

'We shall be there, shan't we, Roland?' she cried.

He looked at me steadily. 'That is one thing of which you can be sure.'

So I left for Manorleigh. Celeste came with me. She said she would go back on the Wednesday. She just wanted to see me settle in.

We had a good welcome when we arrived. Mr and Mrs Emery, who had been with us for years, were waiting in the hall with the parlourmaid, two housemaids and Mrs Grant, the cook.

It was rather formal at first. They had known me as a child and as the outsider at that, the child their beloved Miss Rebecca had unconventionally brought into the household; they had not known then, of course, that I was Benedict Lansdon's daughter; and I don't think they ever really got used to this fact.

Mrs Emery had adored Rebecca. I was sure she would have been delighted if my half-sister had inherited the house. However, here I was.

As head of the staff, Mr and Mrs Emery were very much aware of their position in the house and constantly afraid that it would be assailed in some way. I imagined they were wondering why I had suddenly decided to come.

We were installed in our rooms. Mine was the one which used to be next to Rebecca's. It looked down on the oak with the wooden seat under it. It was the spot where the ghosts were said to gather.

I stood looking out of the window for some time, remembering so much of the past. I had known memories would come flooding back in this house.

I slept well and was awake early. I was reminding myself that it would not be long before the Fitzgeralds came. What fun it would be showing them the house!

After breakfast Mrs Emery asked me if I would come to her room for a little chat.

'It was Miss Rebecca's way to do that,' she said. 'She and I got on like a house afire. What a lovely young lady! I trust she and Mr Cartwright are well.'

'They are very well, Mrs Emery. My sister would have liked to come and stay here for a few days before going back to Cornwall after the wedding, but she felt she had left her family too long.'

'Yes, of course.'

'Neither Mr Cartwright nor the children like her to stay away too long.'

'No. I am sure he doesn't and as for the little ones – God bless them. As long as she is well and happy . . .'

'She is, Mrs Emery.'

She was looking at me anxiously. 'You have had a terrible time, Miss Lucie.'

I nodded. 'I have to put that behind me, Mrs Emery.'

'I was wondering, Miss Lucie, if you have any plans . . .'

'Plans?'

'About the house. I mean, Emery and me, well, we've been wondering . . .'

'Oh, I see what you mean. I'd always want you here, Mrs Emery – you and Mr Emery. No, I haven't any plans. I've been so shocked by everything. Then I went to France, and almost immediately there was Belinda's wedding.'

'Well,' said Mrs Emery, 'that was something, that was. And Lady Denver she is now. I remember her well, though it's years since I've seen her. She must have changed a bit.'

'She's grown up. But she is still . . . Belinda.'

'I see what you mean,' said Mrs Emery, nodding sagely. 'Will you be living here now, Miss Lucie?'

'I'm very unsure at the moment. It is my home now, I suppose. I think Mrs Lansdon would like me to be with her. I expect I shall be between here and London and go now and then to Cornwall. It will be like the old days.'

'I see. I reckon it will all work out. You were always so fond of Manorleigh . . . and now it's yours! It's a wonderful house. Emery and me, well, we've come to feel rather settled here, if you know what I mean.'

'I do, Mrs Emery. Don't think for a moment that I want to change anything. I have a feeling that this will be my home really. By the way, I have some guests coming for the weekend.'

She brightened considerably. 'Oh, that's good. How many, if I may ask?'

'There are two, a brother and a sister. I met them in France.'

'Are they French, Miss Lucie?'

'No. They're English. They were staying in France near where I was. I had met them on the Channel crossing. It was quite exciting when they turned out to be staying near. Well, the fact is they visited us in London and I want them to see this place.'

'Brother and sister. The Blue room, I think for the lady and I'll talk to Emery about where we'll put the gentleman. So Friday . . . and that will be for luncheon, will it?'

'Yes, it will.'

'It's nice to have things going on in the house,' she said. 'I can't tell you how glad I am you've come. So is Emery.'

Celeste went back to London and I waited for the arrival of the Fitzgeralds with an impatience which amazed me.

217

They came in the morning. It was wonderful to see them and my spirits immediately rose. I took them up to their rooms where everything had been made ready for them; and then I showed them the house, which delighted them.

Phillida wanted to hear the story of the haunted garden and listened intently when I told her of the young wife who had died when her daughter was born and came back to comfort her; and how the daughter grew into a strange woman who used to sit on the haunted seat under the oak tree and talk to her dead mother.

Phillida said it was a delightful story. 'You believe it?' she asked.

I replied: 'I don't know. Would you?'

'Yes. I think I would,' she replied. 'I think people might come back . . . in special circumstances. If they suddenly left the Earth . . . like the woman who left her child. That would be love, wouldn't it? Some might come back for hate.'

'Phillida,' chided Roland.

'Well, suppose someone had been murdered, mightn't that person feel that he – or she – had to come back and haunt the one who had sent him to the grave?'

'Or her,' said Roland lightly.

'Well, of course. You're laughing at me. He does laugh at me now and then, as you know, Lucie. I suppose I'm full of fancies. That is what my dear brother thinks. But I am not sure about such things. *You* see what I mean, Lucie, don't you? I believe you have an open mind, too.'

'Yes, I believe I have.'

'What a morbid conversation,' said Roland. 'And in this beautiful house!'

'Well, it was this beautiful house which started it,' pointed out his sister. 'Those people under the tree and all that.'

Roland looked at her in affectionate exasperation. Then he said: 'Oh, I see you have some good stables here, Lucie. Do you ride much?'

'Yes. I've always loved it. It was one of the main attractions of Manorleigh for me.'

'Then perhaps we can ride while we're here?'

'That would be wonderful.'

'We'll find one of those inns we're always hearing about,' said Phillida. 'You know the sort. They've been there for the last three hundred years; there are underground vaults where they used to hide the goods which had been smuggled into the country; they lured ships on to the rocks and led seamen to their deaths; they hung the excise men on gibbets and buried their corpses in the cellar.'

'Except,' I said, 'that we are miles from the sea and I don't know where your wreckers could have done their evil work.'

'You have started something,' said Roland, laughing. 'You've brought out Phillida's unhealthy taste for the supernatural.'

'That's right,' went on Phillida. 'You hear the moaning in the night of those who died violent deaths.'

How we laughed that weekend! We explored the house. There were lengthy discussions during meals. There was always something to talk about. We rode through the countryside visiting those little villages where Celeste and I used to go canvassing during election time. We found an inn which appealed to Phillida, but the landlord was very prosaic and not given to conversation – which disappointed her. It was a wonderful weekend and I was very sad when it came to an end.

'Couldn't you stay another day?' I asked when Monday came.

'Oh yes, please. Do let us, Roland,' cried Phillida.

He looked rather sad. 'I shall have to be going up to Yorkshire very soon,' he said.

My look must have betrayed my disappointment, for Phillida came to me and put an arm round my shoulders. 'It has been so wonderful knowing you,' she said rather huskily. 'I marvel at my luck that day on the boat when I spoke to you. Roland says I shouldn't do that sort of thing, but I always have and you see how well it has worked out this time. I was right, Roland – you have to admit it – because if I hadn't been like that we should never have met Lucie.'

'Let us say that you were very right on this occasion,' admitted Roland.

'Please show you mean that by staying another day,' said Phillida.

He hesitated. 'Well . . .'

I cut in: 'Oh, please do. It would give me so much pleasure.'

'Perhaps, then . . .'

So they did.

Phillida had become a favourite with Mrs Grant the cook. From the first she had complimented her on her various dishes and admitted that she herself – as she put it – liked to try her hand at special dishes, something unusual.

On Sunday for lunch Mrs Grant had served a soufflé. Phillida had praised it and wanted to know exactly how it was done.

Mrs Grant was enchanted. She was a garrulous woman who came of a family of cooks; her mother had actually cooked in this house and so had her grandmother before that. She it was who had first told Rebecca the story of the haunted seat.

The outcome of this was that Mrs Grant said that she would make a soufflé for lunch on the Monday and if

Phillida would come to the kitchen she would show her exactly how it was done.

Phillida delightedly accepted the invitation.

'So you are going to desert us,' said Roland. 'I had thought we would go for a long ride on Monday morning. I'd like to see that village again, the one with the Norman church.'

'Well, there is no reason why you and Lucie should not go,' said Phillida.

Roland looked at me.

'No reason at all,' I said.

'If Phillida prefers the kitchen to the open countryside, so be it,' added Roland.

That was how it was that Roland and I were alone that morning.

We visited the Norman church and came out to the ancient graveyard. The yew trees had been there for many years and so had some of the gravestones. Many of the inscriptions were almost entirely obliterated; some of the dates were just visible and it was sobering to realize that many of them had been put up two hundred years before.

'How peaceful it is here,' said Roland.

'You really feel you are here with the dead,' I said.

'Does that sadden you?'

'No. I just feel the peace of it.'

We made our way along the path, past the well where visitors to the graves found the water for the flowers they wished to put there. There was a wooden seat close to it.

'Could we sit here for a while?' suggested Roland. 'There is something I want to say to you.'

'Yes, let's do that,' I replied.

So we sat there.

'How quiet it is,' I said.

'People are all working. Remember it's Monday. I

expect on a Sunday there are many people here. Lucie . . . I want to talk to you.'

'Yes?'

'It's difficult,' he began. 'I know what you have gone through . . .'

'You and Phillida have helped me a lot.'

'Phillida is very bright. It is difficult to feel unhappy in her company. That does not mean she does not feel . . .'

'Oh, I know. It has been wonderful for me to have been with you both.'

'We feel the same. And it is because of this that I want to talk to you. You have made a lot of difference to us. I know Phillida loves you. And, Lucie . . . so do I.'

I was silent, for I was not sure to what he was leading.

The fact that he mentioned Phillida's love for me with his own suggested that they shared an affection for me like that of brothers and sisters. I was already aware of that. On the other hand . . . could he mean that he was in love with me?

He went on: 'We have come to know each other very well over the last months. I know you have suffered a terrible tragedy, and you feel that your old way of life has been completely shattered. But you cannot go on living in the past, Lucie. You've got to break away. I know you are feeling a little uncertain. I understand you well. But I'm in love with you, Lucie. I have been thinking of you almost from the first day we met . . .'

'You are asking me to marry you?'

'Yes. It is what I want more than anything on Earth. And I think it would be a way for you to start a new life . . . to put the past behind you.'

I was silent thinking about it. I could not say I was in love with him. I liked him very much and I had been melancholy at the thought of his and Phillida's going back to Yorkshire.

He was of course aware of my hesitation. 'Lucie,' he said anxiously, 'what are you thinking?'

'I don't know what to say.'

'You do like us, Phillida and me . . .'

'Of course. It has been wonderful knowing you.'

'I promise to make it more wonderful yet.'

He took my hand and held it firmly while he leaned towards me and kissed my cheek gently.

'Have you told Phillida you were going to ask me?' I said.

He nodded. 'Phillida is very perceptive. She said to me, "I know you are in love with Lucie. Ask her to marry you. It is only right that you should." Phillida is hoping you will say yes. You know what she is. She said she would go away and leave us together. Married people should be alone together, she says. She is a wonderful person, Lucie. We've always been together, as I told you, and since our parents' death . . . Well, you know how that is. I don't know what she would do, but . . .'

'I would not dream of separating you.'

'Then we should all be together, the three of us. Oh, Lucie, it would be a good life.'

'You two,' I said, 'you are so happy together. As for myself . . .'

'I should have waited,' he said. 'But as I shall have to go to Yorkshire I felt I could not go without asking you.'

'How long will you be in Yorkshire?'

He lifted his shoulders. 'I can never be sure. I am in London nowadays most of the time, but I do have to pay these occasional visits to the North and then I am not sure how long I shall be away. That's why I felt I had to speak to you this morning.'

I thought of what it would be like when they had gone. Celeste was in London. I could go there but there were so many memories. Every morning I would have to pass the

223

spot where my father had fallen. I would look out of my window and wonder if the man in the cape and the opera hat were there.

Or I could stay at Manorleigh. But that was different now. If Belinda had been here . . . But she had now become Lady Denver. And I was alone. But I need not be.

And yet . . . I was not in love with Roland. I liked him. In fact I was very fond of him. I enjoyed his company so much – and that of his sister. When I looked back over the last months I realized that they had been the ones who had made life tolerable for me. I did not forget how they had cut short their stay in France so that I need not travel back alone.

If I said I could not marry him, what would happen?

He would go to Yorkshire and I should not see him for a while. I would probably not see much of them again. The thought depressed me.

He was waiting for me to say something.

'I'm sorry, Roland.' I turned to him and it hurt me to see the expression of misery in his face. I knew then that I did care for him. I was very fond of both him and his sister. Her lively conversation, his calm strength, had meant a good deal to me during those days in France. I did not want to lose them. I went on: 'You see, Roland, what happened was so devastating. It was so sudden.'

'I know. I understand perfectly.'

'I feel that I am still reeling from the blow.'

He nodded.

'It was not only my father. There was something else.'

'Please tell me, Lucie.'

'My engagement was going to be announced.'

'Your engagement!'

'Yes. It was to someone I had known for a long time. His people were great friends of my father's. He was in politics. He went to Buganda . . . and was murdered.'

224

'Oh, my poor Lucie. I had no idea. I remember something . . . was it a group of MPs on some mission?'

'Yes. Joel and I were going to announce our engagement when he returned.'

'And you were in love with him?'

'Yes.'

He put his arm round me and held me against him. I felt comforted.

'And you feel you could not love anyone else,' he said bleakly.

'I . . . don't know.'

'You must have been very young.'

'Well, it was not so long ago, but I seem to have grown up a good deal since then.'

'I understand. You have not recovered from this blow. But you do like us – you like me and you like Phillida, don't you?'

'Of course I do. I'm very fond of you both.'

'You have been so badly hurt. First your father and then this young man . . . and in such a short time.'

'Life is like that, I believe. When misfortunes come it is not always singly.'

'I'm glad you told me. You were very much in love with him, weren't you?'

'I thought so.'

'But you were very young.'

'I know that I was very happy when he asked me to marry him; and now he is gone. He is dead, just as my father is.'

'I want to care for you. I want to bring you back to happiness. I want to show you that life can be good again.'

I just sat there with his arm about me while I stared at the graves and found myself wondering about the life and loves of those who were lying under the gravestones. They also would have had their tragedies to face; they would have

225

been brought face to face with decisions which could shape their lives.

I knew that I wanted to stay there with him beside me. I did not want him to go away. I wanted a chance to forget the tragedies of the past and when I was with him and Phillida I could laugh and forget for a while.

He was right. I did need to start afresh, and even Rebecca could not help me with that because she was too close to the tragedy.

Yet I hesitated. Thinking of Rebecca, I knew I must talk to her.

I said: 'Roland, I have grown so fond of you and Phillida. But I am unsure. Marriage is not something which can be undertaken lightly.'

'By no means. You are going to say you need time to think about it. That is right, of course. You should think about it. That was what you were going to say, wasn't it, Lucie?'

'Yes,' I answered.

He held me tightly to him. 'Then I can continue to hope,' he said.

'I think that when you leave for Yorkshire I shall go down to my sister Rebecca in Cornwall.'

'That seems a good idea.'

'She has been like a mother to me.'

'She is a wonderful woman. Both Phillida and I said that of her. We loved her because we could see how much she cared for you.'

'Yes,' I said. 'I shall go to Rebecca.'

'And when you come back I shall have my answer?'

I nodded.

He kissed my cheek again lightly. 'Oh, Lucie,' he said, 'you can't know how important it is to me that you say yes.'

As we walked slowly back to our horses, he slipped his arm through mine. I felt a great urge to say yes; but something restrained me. I did want to talk to Rebecca first.

When we arrived back we were just in time for luncheon.

Phillida was waiting for us. She searched our faces eagerly. She had known Roland was going to ask me to marry him. I was not surprised at that. They were so close and she was the sort of person who would know exactly what was going on, so she would be aware of his feelings for me. I could see by the expectant look on her face that she very much wanted us to marry. I felt then how good it would be if the three of us were together. I could visualize a happy life with them.

'How was your morning?' she asked.

'Interesting,' Roland told her.

'The church is so ancient,' I said. 'It is amazing how those Norman buildings stand up to time. How did the soufflé go?'

'You'll be able to judge that for yourselves.'

I sensed that she was disappointed.

It was wonderful to be with Rebecca again. There was a warm welcome for me at High Tor. Alvina and Jake wanted to take me off to the nursery so that they might show me their toys and Pedrek said how nice it was to see me and that I did not come to Cornwall often enough.

Rebecca, who knew me so well, realized at once that there was something on my mind, and on the very first night after I had retired she came to my bedroom for the customary chat.

'Something's happened,' she announced. 'Is that why you are here?'

'I very much wanted to talk to you.'

'Well?'

'Roland Fitzgerald has asked me to marry him.'

227

I could see that she was pleased. 'Such a nice man. I liked him . . . and his sister. The way they brought you back from France is an indication of the sort of people they are.'

'Yes, I know.'

'Well, are we going to have a wedding?'

'I don't know, Rebecca. I'm so uncertain.'

'You are thinking of Joel still?'

'Of course.'

She took me by the shoulders and looked into my face. 'You can't go on grieving for ever, Lucie,' she said.

'I know. That is what Roland says.'

'He knows . . . about Joel?'

'I told him.'

'Lucie, the sooner you break away from the past it is going to be easier for you.'

'That's what Roland implies.'

'He's right. He's a good man and he loves you.'

'Yes, I think he does. But there is more to it than that.'

'You mean you don't care for him?'

'I do . . . in a way. They have been so good to me . . . both he and his sister . . .'

'Oh, there is his sister. I suppose she feels a little put out.'

'Oh no, no. I am sure she knew he was going to ask me. You see, we went out riding, just the two of us . . . but I felt he had talked it over with her beforehand. Which was natural. She had made an excuse not to come. She was waiting for our return and when there was no announcement I think she was a little disappointed.'

'Oh! So you really think she wants you to marry him?'

'Yes, I do. You see, the three of us get on so well together. She was so much a part of the trio. Roland is rather quiet. She does most of the talking. She is very jolly.'

'And you are fond of her.'

228

'It would be difficult not to be. She is so charming and so kind. She is really a delightful person.'

'It seems to me that you want to be part of that trio,' said Rebecca.

'I rather think I do. But . . . I am not sure. It is not so very long since I was thinking of marrying Joel.'

'You must stop thinking about Joel. Couldn't you have a tentative engagement, something like that?'

'I think Roland wants a definite answer.'

'Of course he does. But he'll understand that you are not ready yet.'

'I think he does understand that. It is just that I am so unsure.'

'I think it would be a wonderful idea if you made a fresh start, if you put the past behind you. You'll never get over it while you go on brooding. There is so much all round you to remind you of it. I don't think it's good for you to be in that house in London. I think Celeste should sell it and get right away. It is, after all, where it happened. And then Manor Grange . . . you were there so much with your father.'

'I could never sell Manor Grange, Rebecca. What about the Emerys?'

'Yes, I know. It would break their hearts. How they used to love all the entertaining which was done there! They've been through so much with us.'

'Mrs Emery adores you.'

'We always got on well together. We'd talk in her sitting-room . . . over her Darjeeling tea.'

'I think she likes me, too, but for her there is only one – and that is you, Rebecca. You see that I could not bear to disturb them.'

'Well, why don't you go and stay down there while you make up your mind?'

'And your opinion is that I should marry Roland?'

'Well, we don't know much about him, but he is certainly very charming and really everything I want for you. I like his relationship with his sister, and she obviously adores him. Well, that shows something of his character, doesn't it? When you see devotion like that . . . it has to be earned and in their case it is mutual. Yes, I do think it would probably be the best thing for you to marry him.'

'It's so soon. That is what I think.'

'But you've got to grow away from it and the sooner the better. I am so glad you came here.'

'I had to talk to you, Rebecca.'

'Well, let us get some sleep. We've plenty of time to talk later on.'

She kissed me goodnight, and to my surprise, I slept through the night without waking.

There was certainly something comforting about being with Rebecca.

The days began to speed past. I spent a good deal of time with the children.

Rebecca and I went riding together and visited some of the people on the neighbouring farms. There was always a welcome and we were usually given something to drink – usually homemade cider and home-baked cakes, which it would have been churlish to refuse.

Rebecca loved the country life; but then, of course, she had Pedrek and the children.

She had admitted that she had discussed my affairs with Pedrek and he thought that Roland – and his sister – would be just right for me. In fact, the more I saw of the family life Pedrek and Rebecca enjoyed, the more I came to believe that the best thing I could do was marry Roland.

I liked Roland. I loved Roland, I supposed. I realized how desolate I should be if I never saw him again. It was brought home to me how much I enjoyed his and his sister's company. Phillida could always make me laugh and it was indeed a fact that when I was with them I could more easily forget the past than at any other time.

I had been romantically in love with Joel, but I had been young and inexperienced then, and although I might not now be so very much older, I had known such tragedy as few are made to face and that must inevitably force me into maturity.

Rebecca and I discussed the future constantly. We went over the same ground again and again; but Rebecca did not mind. What she wanted most was to find the right solution and I realized she had made up her mind that it was marriage to Roland.

I knew she was looking into the future and she saw me in a cosy home with Roland and Phillida . . . and children. Rebecca was a great believer in the solace that children could bring.

And so the days passed and I began to believe that she was right; and by the time I left Cornwall I had made up my mind.

I would marry Roland.

I went back to Manor Grange and I had only been there a few days when Roland and Phillida came down. They had had a trying time in Yorkshire, they told me; and they were delighted to be back in the South.

When I told Roland I would marry him, he looked so happy that my spirits were lifted. He held me tightly in his arms and kissed me tenderly.

'I want to tell Phillida first, Lucie,' he said.

231

We went to her room. He knocked and we stood on the threshold hand in hand. I saw her eyes light up with joy.

'It's true!' she cried. 'It's really true!'

She flew at me and hugged me.

'I'm so excited!' she cried. 'I've been so terribly afraid. Oh, Roland, isn't it wonderful? Now there'll be three of us.' She stopped and released me, her face grave. 'There will be, won't there? But . . . perhaps you won't want me. Two's company, three's a crowd . . .'

'What nonsense!' I said indignantly. 'We're no ordinary three.'

'No, we're us!' She kissed me again and her jubilation delighted me.

'Phillida has been a little anxious,' explained Roland.

'Anxious!' she said. 'I was terrified. I was afraid you were going to pass over the chance of a lifetime and refuse the most wonderful man in the world.'

'Phillida,' protested Roland with a little laugh.

'Well, it's true. And who should know better than I? Oh, Lucie, I'm so happy. You must forgive my being a little silly. I am like that when I am happy. But I know this is going to be the most wonderful thing that could happen. We missed you so much in Yorkshire. I said to Roland, "It isn't the same without Lucie. Something's missing." And of course I was right. Lucie was missing. Are you sure you'll want me with you? I shan't spoil it, shall I? Oh, I do hope –'

I laughed at her with Roland. 'Of course we shall want you,' I said. 'It wouldn't be the same without Phillida.'

The news was out. Mrs Emery thought it would be 'very suitable'.

'I hope you'll be living at Manor Grange, Miss Lucie,' she said.

'I don't know. We haven't made arrangements yet . . . but rest assured I shall keep Manor Grange just as it is.'

Celeste was delighted. I had written to her and my letter brought her hurrying down.

'I'm so pleased for you, Lucie,' she said. 'It really is the best thing possible. You have to put everything that has happened behind you.'

'It's what Rebecca tells me.'

'You'll start a new life. You'll be happy, I know. Roland is such a good, kind man.'

She spoke wistfully. I wondered whether when she thought of my father, she remembered the years of frustration and loneliness she had endured. Poor Celeste, I wished she too could find happiness.

It was to be a quiet wedding. We did not want a renewal of that publicity which Belinda's wedding had provoked.

'It is too soon after everything,' said Celeste. 'It was different with Belinda. She wasn't so close to your father. But I realized that was a mistake and should have been done more quietly.'

Roland said he did not mind what sort of wedding it was so long as it took place.

When Belinda heard that I was to be married she and Bobby paid a flying visit to Manor Grange.

Her marriage appeared to have been very successful. She had grown even more attractive. She had acquired some very fashionable and beautiful clothes, was as vivacious as ever and had thoroughly enslaved Bobby.

'Marriage suits you,' I told her.

'I made up my mind that it should.'

'Bobby is charming.'

'He's rather a pet and it is all such fun. He has the most fantastic house in the country . . . You're coming to stay, you and Roland. Mind you, between ourselves, I found the country a trifle dull. I'm persuading Bobby to

233

buy a house in London and we shall be there most of the time.'

'Bobby has agreed, has he?'

'Bobby always agrees.'

'I can see why the marriage is so successful.'

'Now don't be acerbic. Is that the right word? You would know, you old sobersides. I never thought you'd get married. But now there is this nice Roland. Celeste says he is very charming and suitable. He comes from Yorkshire, doesn't he? Does that mean you'll live in Yorkshire? I hope not. It's much too far away.'

'Roland is mostly in London and he and his sister have a little *pied-à-terre*. He doesn't have to go to Yorkshire so very often. So I expect we shall be round about here most of the time.'

'A house in London, I suppose, and Manor Grange as the country residence. Well, it's yours anyway. Lucky old Roland, to marry an heiress.'

That remark upset me a little. I was sure Roland hadn't thought of me as an heiress. He knew little of my affairs and had never asked. All the same, Belinda had planted an uneasy thought in my mind. Trust Belinda to introduce an unpleasant note!

'Are you going to have a grand wedding?' she asked.

'No. A quiet one.'

Belinda grimaced.

'I should have thought that with all your money you would have wanted something really grand.'

'We are not all as ostentatious as you like to be,' I reminded her.

She laughed. 'I recommend Venice for the honeymoon. Ours was wonderful. But I expect you would prefer Florence. Dante and Beatrice and all that. It was all there, wasn't it?'

'We have not decided yet.'

'Well, you should. It's such fun planning. I am wondering what to wear for this wedding.'

'That should keep you occupied for a while.'

She laughed and gave me an affectionate push. 'Honestly, Lucie. I never really thought you'd make it. You never set out to attract men and they do like to be chased, you know.'

'I thought they were supposed to do the chasing.'

'That shows how little you know of the world.'

It was amusing talking to her as always, and I was glad she would be there. It was unfortunate that Jean Pascal had come back with her.

Celeste told me that he had asked all sorts of questions about Roland.

'It is not his affair,' I protested.

'He says he feels a certain responsibility for you, as he does for Belinda.'

'Well, there is no need.'

I hoped he would not approach me, but he did. He caught me when I was alone.

'So,' he said, 'you are going to be married!'

'Yes.'

'I feel considerably jealous of my successful rival.'

'It was never a matter of rivalry.'

'You made that clear to me. I should be very hurt with you. But I do really care for you, Lucie, and I want to assure myself that all is well.'

'Then I can assure you that all is well.'

'This man, your fiancé, he seems to have come out of the blue, as it were. He was on the Channel ferry; he was in France. Is that all you know of his background?'

'I know what I wish to know,' I replied. 'Really you must not concern yourself.'

'But I do. You see, you are Celeste's stepdaughter and that makes some sort of relationship between us, doesn't it? Who is going to look after you if I don't? Rebecca's husband? Well, he is far away in Cornwall.'

'Why do you think I need a masculine protector?'

'Most women have one. If your father were alive . . .'

'But he is not, and I assure you that I do not need your protection.'

He bowed his head and then lifted his shoulders.

'In fact,' I went on, 'I would prefer it if you did not attempt to, as you say, protect me.'

'I must accept your decision, of course,' he said. 'But you must remember that you are not exactly penniless. There might – with some people – be a certain temptation.'

I looked at him coldly, and said pointedly: 'I feel sure there may well be some . . .'

He smiled at me, cynically, taking my meaning. He did not look in the least offended and I felt that my suspicions that my newly inherited wealth was the main reason for his offer of marriage were not without foundation.

I felt disgusted with him. I compared him with Roland who was so different and who, I was sure, had no ideas of the size of my fortune. I felt very happy and secure then.

Every day I was thinking more and more of how good life would be when I was Roland's wife.

It was, to Belinda's disgust, a very quiet wedding. We had decided that it should be at Manorleigh which would ensure that the press was not so likely to get wind of it. I could not fancy walking out of the London house over that spot where my father had been struck down. Not on my wedding day! It was Celeste who had suggested Manor

236

Grange. She had been staying there for a week before the wedding, planning everything.

Rebecca had come, too, with Pedrek and the children. This was a very special occasion, she said; and we had decided that Alvina should be a bridesmaid and Jake a page. Pedrek would 'give me away' and Jean Pascal had offered to be Roland's best man.

'Roland doesn't have anyone else here,' explained Celeste, 'and Jean Pascal offered himself, half in fun, and was accepted.'

It seemed ironical that a man who, a short time ago, had asked me to marry him, should take that role; but I believed it was a situation which would appeal to Jean Pascal's type of humour.

Belinda and Robert were staying at Manorleigh, too. We had invited very few other guests.

'It is really just our immediate circle,' said Celeste.

Mrs Emery had prepared for us what she insisted on calling the Bridal Suite. It was on the floor above my old room – one of the largest in the house with a dressing-room attached. It had big windows which looked down on the oak tree and the haunted seat. In fact, the view was exactly the same as mine below.

Fresh curtains had been hung and the carpet cleaned. In the room was a large four-poster bed, the one which had been used by Sir Ronald Flamstead and his young wife – that Lady Flamstead who, it was said, had come back from the dead to be with the child whose birth had killed her.

After the ceremony we were to spend one night before leaving the following day for our honeymoon, which, after a certain amount of debate, we had decided should be spent at Amalfi.

We were to leave early on the morning following the wedding; and Phillida would stay on at Manor Grange with

Celeste. They had become very good friends, although they were so different – Celeste so quiet and restrained, and Phillida so ebullient. I was surprised at the friendship which had sprung up between them, but of course delighted.

I mentioned it to Roland. 'Oh, Phillida is determined to be friends with everyone,' he said. 'She is so happy about us . . . and she has made up her mind to love everyone connected with you.'

'What a wonderful nature she has! Life must be easy for her.'

He looked at me tenderly and said: 'Since the death of our parents she has not had to face tragedy. It is my earnest wish that she will never again have to. And that is how I want it to be for you, my dearest Lucie, and I am going to do all in my power to make it so.'

I thought then: Yes, I was right. This was the way for me.

The wedding was over. I was Mrs Roland Fitzgerald; there was a gold ring on the third finger of my left hand to prove it.

It was the first step away from all that unhappiness. Of course I would be reminded of it from time to time. Such momentous happenings cannot be dismissed so easily . . . but I *was* moving away from them. I *was* going to start a new life.

I was a little afraid of the inevitably intimate nature of my relationship with Roland. I felt so ignorant. I thought of Jean Pascal. Suppose I had married him! I should have been terrified of a man like that. But of course I would never have married Jean Pascal, and my husband was Roland . . . dear, kindly Roland, whose only concern was to comfort me and make me happy.

I need not have feared. Roland was tender and understanding, as I had known he would be. He realized my uneasiness and respected my innocence.

238

When I looked at the big four-poster bed I wished that we had had another room. I kept thinking of the beautiful young Lady Flamstead and I did not want ghosts on my wedding night.

I went to the window and looked out on the oak tree and the seat below. Roland came and stood beside me.

'There is nothing to be afraid of,' he said. 'All I want in the world is to make you happy. What is it about that spot which seems to have a morbid fascination?'

I told him of the ghost who had sat there; and while I was talking I was thinking about my own mother who, Rebecca had said, had come to her, although she did not see her, but had insisted to her that she must take me into the household.

Did people return after death? If so, what of the man whom I had helped to condemn?

I dismissed the thought, or tried to. It was an unsuitable subject for a wedding night.

I turned to Roland who took me into his arms.

'Dearest Lucie,' he said, 'don't be afraid of anything. It shall be as you wish. I am going to take care of you from now on.'

He led me back to the bed. I lay quietly in his arms for a time and later, gently and tenderly, he made love to me. And I was not afraid any more.

I often look back on the two weeks spent in Amalfi. In spite of everything it was a wonderful honeymoon.

It was an excellent choice. There can be few more beautiful spots in the world. It was warm without being too hot; we stayed in a charming hotel near the Cathedral and from the balcony of our room we looked out on the bluest of seas.

Everyone seemed friendly and glad to see us. We went for long walks and revelled in those magnificent views of high precipices and little white houses on the hillside. We would sit for hours talking idly . . . just being happy. I had not felt such peace since my father's death.

I felt I could not be grateful enough to Roland for what he had done for me. He was very moved when I told him how I felt. He took my hand and kissed it.

'I have never known such happiness,' he said. 'Thank you, Lucie.'

'I have a feeling now,' I replied, 'that everything is going to change for me. I am going to be happy. I really believed that I never could be again. It was terrible, Roland. My father was so important to me . . . and to have him taken away like that. If he had been ill, if I had been prepared, perhaps . . . I don't know. But to go like that. And then the trial . . .'

He put his hand over mine. 'Don't think of it. It's over, Lucie.'

'It must be. But I can't stop thinking of it. You see, it was my evidence. That man . . .'

'He died,' said Roland in a quiet voice.

'He had killed my father. What could he expect?'

Roland did not answer. He was staring out at the blue sea with a strange expression on his face. Then he turned to me, smiling. He kissed me, lightly at first, then with passion.

'Roland,' I said in surprise.

'Dear Lucie,' he replied. 'Please don't worry.' Then he added slowly, and there was a note of something I did not understand in his voice: 'What has to be has to be.'

We sat for a long time looking over the sea.

I loved exploring the town. There was so much of interest to see; both Roland and I were enthralled by the past and loved to make discoveries. Amalfi had been just a name to us before. Now we learned that the little town had become

240

quite important in the sixth century under the Byzantines, and later it was one of the first maritime republics in Italy.

I loved to visit the Cathedral of St Andrea with its beautiful bronze doors which, we learned, had been standing there since the eleventh century; then there was the campanile and the cloister near the Cathedral. There was so much to see and how I loved to linger in those little streets and to sit under a blue and white sunshade drinking wine or coffee.

We talked about most of the places we had seen and made plans to see more.

Roland said as we were nearing the end of our stay that we should visit Naples. We spent a few days there and each morning would look out over the bay at the menacing peak of Vesuvius. We spent an exciting day at Pompeii. It was exhilarating and at the same time sobering to pick one's way over those excavated ruins of what had once been a great city until the molten ash from the giant volcano had destroyed it. It brought home to me how precarious life was and how in one day death and disaster could change the whole course of a life.

Roland said: 'I think Pompeii, while it interested you, saddened you a little.'

'How could anyone look at such destruction and not be saddened?' I asked. 'How could one walk over those cobbles which had once been streets, and not think of that terrible day when disaster struck?'

He knew, of course, that I was thinking of another disaster which had struck, perhaps even more suddenly.

We were a little sombre that evening when we returned to Naples; and I could not forget while we stayed in that town, for everywhere I looked I felt the scene to be overshadowed by the looming, menacing volcano.

We went back to Amalfi – beautiful, peaceful Amalfi; and there we spent the last few days of our honeymoon.

Fire!

I had become a different person. I was no longer an ignorant girl. I was a woman. I was seeing things differently. Roland and I were lovers; and love, people say, and I suppose they are right, is the most wonderful thing in the world. I felt that I was no longer alone. My husband was closer to me than anyone had ever been before – even my father, Joel and Rebecca. This was a relationship of greater intimacy; and I felt more at peace than I had felt would be possible since my father's death. Roland had given me all this and there was nothing I needed more.

I tried to explain this to him and he was very moved.

Everything seemed different now. I was looking forward to being home. We had to make plans and decide how we were going to live. I wanted to keep Manor Grange and why should we not? It would be difficult to find a more attractive house.

I had seen what he called his *pied-à-terre* in London. It was a narrow house with two rooms on each floor – there were eight in all, and that included two in the basement.

'It seemed quite enough for Phillida and me while we were up here,' he explained, 'and we saw no reason to change.'

He had recently sold the country house in Yorkshire, he told me. 'That was about a year ago. It seemed the wise thing to do. We could not get there very often. We were never very happy there after our parents died. We should have sold it long ago. When I am in Yorkshire now I stay at an hotel in Bradford.'

So the *pied-à-terre* was his only home.

'Phillida and I never cared much about possessions,' he explained.

'In that case, we'll make Manor Grange our home, and when you have to be in London there will be the *pied-à-terre*.'

'Yes. Perhaps it is best to leave it like that for a while. Let's see how it goes. We're together. That's all that matters.'

There was a great welcome for us at Manor Grange.

Phillida was in the hall, her eyes wide with excitement. She hugged us both.

'I'm so glad to see you,' she cried. 'I've missed you so much. I've just been counting the days. My goodness, you look well . . . both of you. You've had too much sun. You have to be careful of foreign sun.'

'It's the same old sun, you know,' said Roland.

'Yes, but at a different angle or something. However, I must say you look well.' She looked a little anxious for a moment. 'And you *have* had a wonderful time.'

It was almost as though she were urging us to tell her so that she could be reassured that everything had gone well. I thought what a delightful person she was to care so much for us.

'We *have* had a wonderful time. We've seen Naples,' I told her.

'Don't they say "See Naples and die"?'

'That means it's so wonderful you must see it before you die.'

'It's an odd way of expressing it, don't you think, Lucie? "See Naples and die."' She laughed as though it were a great joke.

Roland said rather sharply: 'It was all wonderful. We've had a most thrilling time.'

'And now you're back, and it is lovely to see you. I've a hot bottle put in your bed.'

'Was that necessary?' I asked.

'I thought it might be a little damp. And I told them to light a fire. It's chilly in the evening.'

'How have *you* been getting along?' I asked.

'Splendidly. I love it here. It's a wonderful old house.'

We went to our room. It looked comfortable and inviting. I resisted the temptation to go to the window. Roland would know why I did it, so I desisted.

Roland left me alone to unpack and while I was doing this there was a knock on the door and Mrs Emery came in.

'I trust everything is satisfactory, Miss Lucie. Oh . . . I suppose I mustn't call you that any more. It's Mrs Fitzgerald, I suppose, now.'

'You may call me what you like, Mrs Emery. I think it is going to take a little time to get used to Mrs Fitzgerald. Everything is fine.'

'Oh.' She nodded, but I could see that something was wrong because of the pursed lips and the tilt of the head. I was on the point of asking but I decided to postpone it, for there was little time now as dinner would be served in half an hour.

I said: 'We'll have a little chat tomorrow, Mrs Emery.'

'Yes,' she replied. 'Thank you, Miss Lucie. I'd appreciate that.'

'It's good to be home.'

'I hope it was a happy honeymoon.'

'It was wonderful.'

'Emery will be glad to hear of that . . . and so am I.'

'Tomorrow then, Mrs Emery, we'll have our little chat.'

She was satisfied temporarily, but I was faintly disturbed. What could be wrong? However I did not give a great deal of thought to the matter, for I knew that, good housekeeper that she was, she easily took offence if she thought her authority had been flouted.

Phillida chattered throughout dinner – in fact, she scarcely stopped.

'My tongue is running away with me,' she said. 'I can hear Roland saying, "Nothing extraordinary about that," but I *am* so glad to have you back. I've spent the time thinking about what I could do to make things comfortable for you. Oh, I don't mean that this isn't a comfortable house – and the servants are just wonderful – but, you know what I mean, that extra something. I put flowers in the room. I hope you liked them, Lucie.'

I said indeed I did and I thanked her. It was true that I had noticed them in passing but I had been so eager to unpack and, when Mrs Emery had come in nursing some grievance, I had forgotten about the flowers.

'I thought they would be a little extra welcome home.'

'They were,' I replied. 'It was thoughtful of you.'

'I do want to be useful here. You see, Lucie, this is your house . . .'

Both she and Roland were looking at me anxiously.

'But that makes it so convenient, doesn't it?' I said. 'Roland and I have been talking about where we would live, and this seems ideal. There is plenty of room. And then there is your little place in London when Roland is there on business. He can get there so easily from here.'

'We decided we would try it like that and see how it worked,' put in Roland.

'And you won't mind my being here?'

'My dear Phillida, of course I *want* you to be here. How could it be otherwise? Do understand that.'

'Yes . . . I think I do. I just wanted to hear you say it.'

'This reminds me,' said Roland. 'I shall have to go to London in the morning, just for the day to see how things are.'

'There's something I have to tell you,' said Phillida, a little shamefacedly. 'I've brought Kitty here.'

'Really!' said Roland.

'Who's Kitty?' I asked.

'She's a woman who works for us in London. We have a Mr and Mrs Gordon who live in the basement there and Kitty who comes in every day to help. She's been like a personal maid to me and I did miss her. So I've brought her here. I hope you don't mind.'

'What do you mean – to work?'

'Well, only for me. She does all sorts of things with my clothes, sewing and all that. She's very handy. I missed her . . . and, of course, with my being down here and Roland on his honeymoon, there really wasn't anything for her to do in London. She got restive, so I brought her down here. I hope you don't mind.'

'Of course not,' I said. 'What is she like?'

'Middle-aged, very clever with her hands – needlework and all that. She's really a treasure. I am sure you will find something you'd want her to do for you.'

'Well, I can't think of anything at the moment,' I said.

Phillida went on, 'She was getting a bit worried, with all this change. I knew she relies on what she earns. I couldn't let her go, and as we shall be here such a lot . . .'

'I understand, of course.'

Phillida looked immensely relieved. 'I didn't want you to think I was interfering – or behaving like the mistress of the house.'

'Of course I wouldn't do that!'

'Phillida is rather impulsive, I'm afraid,' said Roland.

246

'Perhaps it would have been better, Phillida, if you had waited to ask Lucie.'

'I knew it would . . . as soon as I'd done it. But the poor woman was so worried. I just had to tell her it would be all right. Forgive, Lucie?'

'Of course it's all right. Have you met many people round here yet, in the village for instance, while we've been away?'

'I haven't. I have been too busy, exploring the house for one thing. Isn't it fascinating? I'm so excited because I'm going to live here – at least until other plans are made.'

We retired early.

'Travelling is more exhausting than one realizes at the time,' said Roland.

We had not been in our room for more than a few minutes when there was a knock on the door. It was Phillida. She was carrying a tray with two glasses on it.

'I want you to try this,' she said. 'It's really very nice. It's what they call a nightcap. There is a shop in St James's where they sell it, a health shop, they call themselves. They have all sorts of herbs and things. I bought this and tried it. It's a sort of gruel, only much nicer. You take it in hot milk every night and it gives you peaceful sleep.'

'And you believe it?' asked Roland.

'My dear brother, I know it. I would not suggest you take it if I had not first tried it out myself.'

She set the tray on a table while Roland and I sat side by side on the bed.

'You stir it,' she said, 'and there it is. Lucie . . .' I took the glass she offered. 'And Roland.'

'I always have it last thing before I get into bed,' she told us. 'Now drink it.'

She watched us while we obeyed.

'It's rather pleasant, isn't it?'

We agreed that it was.

247

'Now I'll go.' She kissed both of us. 'Good night, my precious ones. I can't tell you how happy I am to have you home. I was rather worried about you . . . wandering about in foreign parts.'

She smiled at us rather tremulously and, taking the tray, went out.

The next morning Roland went off early to catch the train, promising he would be back in the evening.

I remembered that I had an appointment with Mrs Emery, so I went to her sitting-room where she asked me if I would like a cup of her Darjeeling, and, knowing that she might be even more put out if I declined, I said that I should.

There followed the ceremonial of making the tea and when we had our cups before us, she came to the point.

'I've been in this house a good many years, Miss Lucie,' she began. 'And I trust I know my place and do my work well.'

'But of course you do, Mrs Emery.'

'There have never been any complaints that I have known of.'

'Certainly there have not. Everyone, including my father, had nothing but praise for all you did.'

'I've run this house for more years than I care to recall.'

I was getting uneasy. This long preamble suggested something more serious than I had imagined.

'Do tell me what has upset you, Mrs Emery.'

'Well, Miss Lucie, it is the task of the housekeeper and the butler to engage staff. The housekeeper for the females and the butler for the men . . .'

'Yes.'

'It seems there are some who think they can come in and change all this.'

I knew now what was wrong. 'You object to this new maid whom Miss Fitzgerald has brought with her?'

'I do that, Miss Lucie. I've always engaged the staff in this house, and I see no reason why there should be changes.'

'I don't think Miss Fitzgerald meant to interfere with your rule, Mrs Emery.'

'*I* didn't employ this Kitty, or whatever her name is, to come here.'

'Has she done anything to which you object?'

'Well, I wouldn't say that. But she does come into the kitchen. Mrs Grant won't like that.'

I could not imagine Mrs Grant, our fat and comfortable cook, would have any objections. She did not have Mrs Emery's rigid code of protocol.

'I've spoken to Mr Emery about it and he agrees with me,' she went on.

Didn't he always have the good sense to agree with Mrs Emery? I could see now that she felt her dignity had been affronted and I had to put that right.

'I think I can explain this to you,' I said. 'Mr and Miss Fitzgerald only have a small house in London. They have a man and his wife living in and there was Kitty who came in to help. There wasn't enough for Kitty to do and she does, of course, act as a sort of personal maid to Miss Fitzgerald . . . so she came here. She's not really concerned with the household. She will just be attached to Miss Fitzgerald, you understand?'

'Well, I wasn't asked, Miss Lucie.'

'I am sure Miss Fitzgerald thought that as Kitty was really her maid it would be all right. She would be most upset if she knew she had hurt your feelings.'

Mrs Emery was a little mollified.

'Well, I'm glad you're back, Miss Lucie. You're the

mistress of the house and that's something everyone should remember.'

'Oh, I'm sure they do. Miss Fitzgerald did mention Kitty to me and she was most apologetic for what she had done. She said she acted on the spur of the moment. There was no work for Kitty and she did not want to dismiss the poor girl.'

'She's no girl. She's a woman close on forty, if you ask me.'

'I see. I haven't met her yet. But Miss Fitzgerald really meant no harm. And Kitty must stay here. Don't hold it against her, Mrs Emery.'

'Well, as long as I know where I stand, Miss Lucie.'

'I think you know how much I appreciate you and it upsets me very much to know that you are unhappy.'

'Oh, I didn't say that. But I've always done my work here as well as I could and I've always felt people knew that. I was aware of just where I stood and I thought everyone else was. I just didn't like strangers coming in and setting up their own rules.'

'Well, you see, Miss Fitzgerald is hardly a stranger. She is now my sister-in-law; and I hope we are all going to get alone well together.'

'Now that you put it like that, Miss Lucie . . .'

'Well, that's how it is, Mrs Emery. And I must say, you make one of the best cups of tea I ever tasted.'

She was mollified.

It was a storm in a teacup, I thought, smiling to myself.

During the day I met Kitty. She was different from what I had been expecting. She was a big woman – quite forty, I should say. She had little to say for herself when Phillida introduced us.

250

'This is Kitty,' said Phillida. 'She is really making herself useful.'

'I hope you like it in the country, Kitty,' I said.

'Oh yes, M'am,' she replied.

And that was all.

Roland returned that evening. I had missed him even in that short time. I told him this and it delighted him.

At dinner he explained that there had been quite an accumulation at the office. The clerk had had to leave a good many matters for him to attend to; and he thought he would have to go up for a short spell, perhaps four or five days.

'I suppose you'll be hard at it all day and half the night,' said Phillida. 'I know you work in an erratic fashion and seem to take a lot of time off.' She turned to me. 'But when he works he works.'

'She's right,' said Roland. 'That is how it goes. It's spasmodic in a way. But I really must go soon. In a day or so – I think on Monday – and I shall probably be up for the whole week.'

'As long as it is no more we'll allow it,' said Phillida. 'Lucie and I will be counting the days till your return.'

'Can't we go with you?' I asked.

Roland hesitated and Phillida said: 'Well, from experience, I know it will be better for him to get the work done quickly. He'd be worrying about us all the time if we went. It would take two or three weeks instead of not quite one. You go on Monday, Roland, and then you can be back by Friday and we can all have a lovely carefree weekend.'

He was hesitating, looking at me apologetically.

'I think it's for Roland to decide,' I said.

'Well,' he replied, with reluctance in his voice, 'I suppose Phillida is right. Perhaps it's better to get on with it quickly, without distractions – very welcome ones, I hasten to say.

251

But this does need a great deal of concentration and I shall be working all hours.'

'Go and come back soon, then,' I said.

'It's settled, then.' Roland sounded gloomy.

'It will soon pass,' I assured him.

Phillida came to our room that night with glasses of her special beverage.

'Now did you feel the benefit last night?' she asked.

We looked at each other and smiled.

'Oh, come on,' she said. 'Of course you did. I know, I tell you. I've studied these things. This is good for you. It's got all the ingredients on the packet and they all have special virtues. And promise me, Roland, when you are in London, you will take it. I shall make you take some with you and I shall want your solemn promise.'

'All right, I promise.'

She was looking at him quizzically.

'Do you want him to swear on the Bible?' I asked.

'My dear Lucie, if he promises me, he will do it. My brother is a man of honour. Now, drink up like good children.'

'We are not good children,' said Roland. 'At least, we are not children.'

'I know I can be a fussy old hen. But you see, I love you both so much, and I have missed you, and now I have you back. And Roland is going away!'

'Never mind,' said Roland. 'You will still have Lucie to coddle.'

She flew at us and kissed us both, her eyes misty.

'My dears,' she said, 'I love you both so much.'

We drank our beverages which were really rather pleasant and, as she had on the previous night, she took the tray away and left us.

*

After the weekend Roland left for London. I knew that I was going to miss him, for there was no doubt in my mind now of the deep affection he had aroused in me. It was not what I had felt for Joel. I supposed I had been innocent and romantic when I had fallen in love with him. This was a more sober affection. I felt peaceful with Roland; and I realized that this was what I had needed for so long.

I had written to Rebecca telling her how I felt, for I could open my heart to her. She replied at once and said how happy she was for me. She was sure I had done the right thing and had known as soon as she had seen Roland that he was the one for me.

I spent a lot of time with Phillida. She was very interested in every subject raised and she wanted to hear all about the places we had visited in Italy. We went to the library – my father had built up quite an extensive one at Manor Grange – and there we were about to find some references to Naples, Pompeii and Amalfi. Phillida said how wonderful it would be if we could all go back there together.

'But you might not want there to be the three of us,' she said a little wistfully.

'Of course I should love it,' I assured her. 'And so would Roland. As a matter of fact, while we were in Italy, we were constantly talking of you and Roland was always saying, "Wouldn't Phillida have liked this?"'

'Sometimes I worry about it. I wonder whether I ought to get away . . . get a place of my own. It seems unfair to you two, always to have me tagging along with you.'

'Will you please put such nonsense out of your head?'

'Oh, Lucie, I'm so glad Roland married you.'

I asked how Kitty was getting on.

'Oh, quite well. She's got a skin like a rhinoceros. It's a good thing. She doesn't notice the occasional barb sent in her direction.'

'Barb?'

'From the dragon, Mrs Emery. I don't think the lady likes Kitty very much . . . and it's not Kitty's fault. It's mine really, for bringing her in like that. But she was a sort of maid to me and it didn't occur to me that I ought to have consulted the oracle.'

I sighed. 'Oh, that little upset!'

'Did she speak to you about it?'

'Yes, she did. Very ceremoniously, over a cup of her best Darjeeling which is only brought out for special occasions. Apparently it was an offence against protocol to bring a servant into the house without prior consultation with an Emery.'

'The fault was entirely mine. Should I apologize to Mrs Emery?'

I hesitated. 'It might not come amiss. It might even set the matter right. All Mrs Emery wants is recognition of her status.'

'I'll do that and be as tactful and respectful as I can.'

We laughed together.

That night she brought up what she called my nightcap and we sat talking while I drank it. It had become a ritual.

I missed Roland very much during the days which followed. I was looking forward to his return and I thought that, next time he went to London, I would go with him. I could find plenty to do there while he was working. I could go to see Celeste and shop. I would suggest it to him when he returned.

That night it was Kitty who brought my nightcap.

She was a big woman with strong, capable hands, I noticed; she was deferential, speaking only when spoken to, which was a trait in her favour.

I thought I ought to have a little chat with her, however,

254

and as she set the glass down on the table, I said: 'Oh, it's you, Kitty.'

'Yes, M'am. Miss Fitzgerald said to bring it up.'

'Thank you. Are you settling in all right?'

'Yes, M'am.'

'It must be a little different from London.'

'Yes, M'am.'

I could see that I was not going to learn very much from her, so I said goodnight.

I almost forgot to drink the nightcap since Phillida was not there to talk to me while I did so.

I quickly drained the glass and put it on the tray to be collected in the morning.

Roland had been three days in London. He will soon be home, I kept telling myself.

I had been out riding, as I so liked to do. Phillida had not come with me on this occasion, and when I returned to the house one of the maids dashed out to tell me that a visitor was waiting for me with Miss Fitzgerald in the drawing-room.

I went there and, to my surprise, Belinda rose and came towards me.

'Hello, Lucie,' she said. 'I've come to see you.'

'So I see. How lovely! What a surprise! Are you well?'

'Oh yes,' she replied, but I knew at once that something was wrong. There was a subdued air about her; and I asked myself: Why should she have come, if she did not want something?

'Miss Fitzgerald told me how wonderfully you are settling in here and what a marvellous honeymoon you had.'

'I've also been telling her that she should have brought her husband,' said Phillida.'

'Yes,' I said. 'Why didn't you?'

'Oh, he's got some business to attend to . . . on the estate, of course. And I thought I'd snatch a day or so to see how you were getting along.'

'You are going to stay a little while, I hope.'

'If I may . . . just for a few days.'

'Of course. We'll be delighted to have you, won't we, Phillida?'

'But of course. Roland will be disappointed if you don't stay. He's not due back until Friday or maybe Saturday. But you will stay as long as that, won't you?'

'I . . . I don't know. I'll have to see . . .'

I guessed she was desperately wanting to be alone with me.

I said: 'I think we'll put you in the Red Room. I'll go and see Mrs Emery.'

'I'll do that,' said Phillida, and hesitated.

'Perhaps I'd better,' I said quickly.

Phillida understood. Although she had spoken to Mrs Emery about bringing Kitty into the house, Mrs Emery's attitude towards her was still somewhat frosty.

'Shall I go and tell her you want to see her?' suggested Phillida.

'Yes, please, do that. And will you tell one of the maids to get the room ready?'

Phillida left us together.

'What's the matter, Belinda?' I asked.

'Something terrible.'

'Well, you'd better tell me.'

'But Mrs Emery will be here in a minute.'

'Let's get your room settled and then we can be alone and talk.'

It was not long before Mrs Emery appeared.

'Well,' she cried, 'if it's not Miss Belinda. I beg your pardon . . . Lady Denver, I should say.'

'It is,' said Belinda. She went to Mrs Emery and kissed her.

It was not quite protocol but entirely forgivable, and Mrs Emery looked pleased.

'Well, it's nice to see you, Miss Be- . . . your ladyship.'

'Miss Belinda to you always,' said Belinda. 'Belinda, the wicked one.'

'Well, you could be a bit naughty. I'm not denying that. But it's nice to see you here. Like old times, Miss Lucie and you together.'

'Belinda is going to stay for a few days, Mrs Emery.'

'Well, that's nice.'

'Yes, isn't it? I thought the Red Room.'

'I'll make sure it's all put to rights. Well, I must say, it's a pleasure.'

When she went out, Belinda looked at me and I thought she was going to burst into tears.

'Do tell me, Belinda.'

'I can't here . . . someone might come in.'

'They'll soon have your room ready. You know where it is. It's close to ours.'

'The bridal suite?'

'Call it that if you like.'

'It's the best bedroom in the house, with that balcony looking down on the garden.'

'You don't forget the old house then, Belinda?'

'How could I ever? I wish they'd hurry up with that room.'

'Mrs Emery will tell us when it is ready. Would you like a drink . . . some refreshment?'

'I couldn't eat a thing.'

'Is Bobby all right?'

'Yes, and it's true, he is rather busy on that old estate. There are always people coming and he rides round and attends to everything. He's very keen on the estate. It's been

257

in the family for generations and all that . . . a solemn duty to carry on . . .'

'And what about you, Belinda? Aren't you happy?'

'I was.'

'You mean you're not now?'

'I tell you, I can't talk to you here.'

'It's all right, isn't it . . . with you and Bobby?'

She nodded. 'It's just that I'm afraid . . . I want to keep it right. I do, really.'

'Well, why shouldn't you?'

'I keep telling you, I can't talk now.'

It seemed a long time before Mrs Emery came in.

She said: 'The Red Room has been prepared now, Miss Belinda, your ladyship. I think you'll be very comfortable up there.'

'Oh, thank you, Mrs Emery,' said Belinda.

'I must say, you're looking beautiful, Miss Belinda. Married life suits you. Miss Lucie, too. I was saying to Mr Emery how nice it is to see Miss Lucie a married woman . . . and now there's you, Miss Belinda.'

'We do you credit then, Mrs Emery,' said Belinda.

Mrs Emery laughed and shook her head. 'You were always a caution, Miss Belinda. We never knew what you'd be up to next.'

'No,' I said. 'That's true. Well, let's get you to the Red Room. Is Belinda's case up there?'

'Yes, it is,' replied Mrs Emery.

'Well, I'll take her up now.'

'She wouldn't like something? A cup of tea or coffee, or a glass of wine?'

'No, thank you,' said Belinda.

'Come along, then.'

We went up the stairs. Belinda knew the way, of course.

'How familiar it all is!' she said. 'How it takes me back.

No matter how long I was away, I'd find my way about this house blindfold.'

We were in the Red Room. She shut the door and sat on the bed. I took the chair opposite.

'Now,' I said. 'I want to hear what it's all about.'

'I'm in terrible trouble, Lucie. I don't know what I'm going to do. This can be the end of everything.'

'Then tell me, for Heaven's sake.'

'I don't know where to begin. It was in Australia. I told you about Henry Farrell, didn't I? Oh, you've forgotten. He was the one who took over the mine.'

'I remember. Well, what about this Henry Farrell?'

'He was very much in love with me and for a time . . . I thought I was with him. I was only sixteen. He was a good deal older . . . in his mid- twenties. He persuaded me.'

'To what? Don't be bashful, Belinda. That's not like you.'

'I hate to say it, Lucie. It's awful. We – we were married.'

'Married!'

She nodded wretchedly. 'In Melbourne. Secretly.'

'And he's still alive! So how . . . ?'

She nodded again wretchedly.'

'Then,' I added, 'if you are married to him, you can't be married to Bobby.'

'That's what I'm telling you. What am I going to *do*?'

I stared at her in blank dismay. Then I said: 'Does Bobby know?'

'Of course not.'

'Then you'll have to tell him.'

'Henry wants me to go back with him.'

'Back with him? Is he here?'

She nodded once more. 'What am I going to do, Lucie? I had to get away. I had to come and tell you about it. I want you to help me.'

'Help you? How can I? What can *I* do about it?'

259

'I don't know. I thought . . . together . . . we might think of something.'

'Oh, Belinda, how could you have done this? Didn't you think of Henry Farrell when you went through this form of marriage with Bobby?'

'He was so far away . . . and it was long ago. I thought no one need ever know about it. And I'll tell you something else, Lucie. I'm going to have a baby. Bobby is so thrilled. So what now?'

'I . . . I didn't imagine anything like this. How could you have got yourself into such a mess?'

'I feel as if I'm going mad.'

'You'll have to tell Bobby right away.'

'I just couldn't do that. It would break his heart. He's so pleased about everything. I just could not tell him, Lucie.'

'Have you seen this Henry Farrell recently?'

'Yes. He's in London. I saw him today. Then I came straight down here.'

'I thought he was still in Australia.'

'He was. It was all that stuff in the papers when I was married. One of the newspapers turned up over there, and it would be the one with that in it. He said he didn't believe it at first. Then he had someone make enquiries and found out it was true. He found Celeste's address and wrote to me, saying he was coming over. Celeste sent the letter on to me. I told Bobby I wanted to shop for the baby. I knew Bobby couldn't leave the estate at this time, so I came to London. And I met Henry Farrell in London. He said I was his wife anyway and he wanted me to go back to Australia with him. I had to get rid of him, Lucie. I told him I'd think about it. I won't go back, though. I'm married to Bobby now.'

'But you're not, Belinda. You've just committed bigamy and that's against the law.'

'I won't go back. I'm Bobby's wife.'

'Look, Belinda, it's no use hiding from the truth. What you've just told me is that you married this man in Australia long before you even met Bobby. Therefore Bobby is not your husband. That's the plain truth. If we are going to find some solution we won't do it by shutting out the facts and pretending they do not exist. Tell me exactly what happened.'

'I wanted to get away after Tom died. It wasn't bad when the mine was doing well, and we had trips to Melbourne. I liked it then. We'd stay there for a week or so sometimes when Tom was doing business, and we'd meet people and it was fun. But then the mine started to fail . . . and Tom got ill and there we were, stuck in that awful little mining town. There was nothing to do . . . and then Henry got friendly and at the time it seemed quite exciting. I was only sixteen and Henry said we could get married quietly and we did. I never told my mother. Her idea was for me to come to England and make a great marriage. I had been brought up as a Lansdon and she wanted me to have the sort of life I would have had if I had really been Benedict Lansdon's daughter as everyone thought I was in the beginning. So I didn't tell her. I didn't want to upset her . . . because she was ill. It was so dreary . . . I had to *do* something and it seemed exciting at the time.'

'I can see exactly how it happened,' I said, 'but the point is, what are we going to do about it?'

She looked at me helplessly.

'I think you ought to tell Bobby,' I said.

'I just *couldn't*.'

'It concerns him.'

'I know. But I couldn't tell him. He's such a darling. He's so happy . . . and what about the baby?'

'Oh, Belinda,' I said. 'What a mess!'

261

'I thought you might have some suggestion.'

'Why me?'

'Well, you're calm and reasonable and all that. You would never have got yourself into a mess like this. I thought you might see a way out.'

'There are only two ways out, as far as I can see.'

'What? What?'

'You go back to Australia with Henry Farrell as his wife, because he is after all your husband . . .'

'That's right out of the question. What's the other?'

'You explain everything to Bobby. Get the marriage with Henry Farrell dissolved and remarry Bobby.'

She breathed a deep sigh.

'That's it,' she said. 'That's what we have to do. We *must* do that.'

'You've forgotten, of course, that you would have to get Henry Farrell's agreement.'

Her face darkened. 'He . . . he won't let me go. He said he won't. He said he loves me. He wants me back.'

'But he did let you go. He was ready to part with you before.'

'I know. We quarrelled terribly, you see. I soon realized what a mistake I'd made.'

'And you let him know it!'

'He used to get really angry. Sometimes I thought he'd kill me. I got really frightened. And it was all so secret because I didn't want my mother to know. We never set up house together. It wasn't really like a true marriage.'

'Oh, Belinda, how could you be so feckless?'

'Because I'm a fool. You know how I always took some action before I'd thought very much about it.'

I nodded.

'Well, what am I going to do?'

'Do you really love Bobby?'

'More every day. I like being with him, and he thinks I'm wonderful.'

'And it is rather nice being Lady Denver?'

'Well, yes, it is,' she said defiantly.

'Better than being Mrs Farrell, which I suppose you really are?'

'It's not only that. If you saw Henry Farrell you would know why I want to be with Bobby.'

'Didn't you realize . . . Oh, but it's no use going over all that. The point is, what are you going to do? And how do you think I can help?'

'Henry is in London. If someone could talk to him . . .'

'You, for instance?' I suggested.

She shook her head. 'No. When I'm there he's just mad. I think he hates me at the same time as he loves me. He knows what I'm like. He wouldn't trust me . . . and in a way I think he hates himself for wanting me. You've always been so calm and logical. You wouldn't understand that . . .'

'Oh, but I do. I know how exasperating you can be and yet I quite like you myself. You've done some dreadful things in your life, Belinda. Think of Pedrek and Rebecca . . . and yet they forgive you. I don't know why. But yes, I think I do understand how Henry Farrell feels.'

She came to me and hugged me in her impulsive way.

'You will help me, won't you, Lucie? You can . . . I think.'

'How?'

'He might listen to you.'

'Why? Why should he? He doesn't know me. We've never met.'

'He knows *of* you. I used to talk about you. He said, "Your Lucie sounds a very nice person. From your descripton I think I'd like her."'

263

'I'm surprised that your description of me engendered such respect.'

'Stop talking like a governess. This is too serious for that. I thought if you could see him and talk calmly to him . . . explain to him that I will never go back to him . . . that I'm happy with Bobby now. I've found just what I want. If he'd only go back to Australia and forget about me . . .'

'You'd still be married to him.'

'No one need ever know.'

'What of the child? It would be illegitimate.'

'I said, nobody need know.'

'It would be better to get it settled clearly and cleanly. Suppose Henry Farrell agreed to go away and withdrew his claim to you, you'd have this hanging over you for the rest of your life. You would never know when it might be discovered. And you have the child to think of.'

'What else can I do?'

'Well, you could confess to Bobby what you have done. I think you owe that to him. He is good and kind and he loves you dearly. He isn't going to let you go.'

She nodded slowly. 'Yes,' she said, 'and then?'

'You might persuade Henry Farrell to agree to this annulment. It could be arranged discreetly, perhaps. Then you and Bobby could be married quietly. And you'd go on from there.'

She clasped her hands and looked at me with admiration.

'That's it, Lucie. You've got it.' Her eyes were shining and it amazed me how quickly she could change.

'You'll have to get Henry Farrell's agreement,' I went on. 'That might not be easy. You've always thought everyone ought to do what you want.'

'He could be persuaded, I'm sure.'

It was typical of Belinda. I wanted to tell her that others had their lives to lead and they were just as important to them as hers was to her. She seemed to think that, now we had found a possible solution, all we had to do was manipulate the actors in the drama, as a playwright might – writing their lines for them so that they could meekly act out the play according to direction.

She was excited now. She sparkled. Her beautiful face was alight with purpose. I found myself smiling with her. I could understand her power to attract. She could be irresistible.

'I know what we have to do now,' she said.

I looked at her questioningly, and she went on: 'You will go and see Henry Farrell. You will tell him exactly what he must do.'

'Belinda! He isn't going to listen to me.'

'You can tell him how happy I am . . . that I am going to have Bobby's baby . . . how necessary it is for him to agree to a divorce . . . quietly . . . so that I can marry Bobby . . . because there is to be a child . . . and children must always be considered.'

'I think *you* should see him and explain all this.'

She shook her head dolefully. 'He wouldn't listen to me, Lucie. He gets mad with rage at me. Lucie, please, do this for me. Please go to see him. Explain in your lovely calm way . . . make him see it . . . You can. You explain so well . . . and you're so logical. You would make him see reason, I'm sure.'

'It sounds ridiculous to me. I don't know the man.'

'You know what I've told you,' she pleaded. 'Will you do it . . . for me, Lucie? Please, please . . . so much depends on it.'

'I . . . I'd have to think about it.'

A slow smile crossed her face. 'All right then. Think about it. But please, oh, please, think quickly.'

She was almost complacent, having a firm belief in her powers to persuade.

During the rest of that day I thought about Belinda and her problem. I could picture it all so clearly: the mining town, the dullness of the days, the failing mine, the desire for excitement.

And there was Henry Farrell. I imagined him, tall, masterful, and completely fascinated by the wayward Belinda. Then the suggestion of marriage, a secret marriage. She had been only sixteen; but Belinda had matured early. She would have been physically a young woman, though sadly lacking in a woman's judgement. I could imagine her dashing into marriage without a thought beyond the excitement of the moment. The passionate Henry Farrell, the meetings which had to be held in secret, would appeal to her sense of adventure; and then the death of Tom Marner, the illness of Leah; the talk then of what Leah wanted for her cherished daughter; the rich life in the wealthy Old Country which she remembered from her childhood; the dinner parties in the London house, the charm of Manor Grange, the grandeur of Cador . . . and then, the sudden realization of what she had done – in fact, ruined her chances of a cosy life in rich surroundings. She had married a man who had acquired a mine which was no longer prosperous.

I could imagine her dismay and her plans to extricate herself from what had become distasteful and an impediment to those plans.

She and her husband had quarrelled violently. She might well have provoked those quarrels; they had no doubt declared their regrets and vowed they never wanted to see each other again.

So . . . she had come to England and, Belinda-fashion, had dismissed the past as though it had never happened. Bobby came along – admiring her and so suitable, with his wealth, adoration and title. So, without a qualm – or perhaps just a few – Belinda saw no reason why she could not write off the disagreeable past and start afresh.

It was all typical Belinda.

And here I was, half promising to help her out of her trouble which she had created by her own actions.

During the day Belinda endeavoured to be alone with me and was impatient when others were present.

Phillida whispered to me: 'I can see she wants to talk to you. I'll leave you to yourselves.'

Dinner seemed to go on endlessly and I was glad when it was over. I was deeply disturbed. I had half promised to see Henry Farrell and I wondered whether I had been wise. I could not believe that I could bring about the miracle, but Belinda was sure I could.

I was rather relieved when we said goodnight and I could escape and be alone.

But I had undressed and was about to get into bed when there was a knock on my door.

I thought it was Phillida with her nightcap, but it was not. It was Kitty.

'Oh, thank you, Kitty,' I said. 'Put it on the table.'

She did so in silence.

'Good night, Kitty.'

'Good night, M'am.' The door shut.

I got into bed, still thinking of Belinda. Could I do it? Was it possible that I could persuade the man? I guessed I would have to try. Hadn't I always allowed Belinda to lead me?

I was very sorry for her. For Bobby, too. Perhaps more so for him. He was such a nice young man and I should hate to see him hurt. I could picture his joy over the coming child.

And, oddly enough, I thought Belinda had a fair chance of happiness with him. He was the sort of man who would be faithful and only see the beautiful, fascinating Belinda. I did wonder, though, what his reaction would be when he knew she had deceived him about her marriage to Henry Farrell.

There was a knock on the door. I guessed rightly this time. It was Belinda.

'I had to come and talk,' she said, sitting on the bed. 'I couldn't sleep. You will see Henry, won't you?'

I hesitated.

'Oh yes . . . please say yes. I'll be so wretched if you don't.'

'I really don't think it would do any good.'

'Yes, it will. Everyone listens to you. You're clever and you're nice. Look at your father.'

'What has he got to do with it?'

'Look how he was with you. Wasn't he glad that you turned out to be his daughter and not me?'

'That's not the point.'

'It is. It means you're sensible and reasonable. People listen to you. Oh, I'm so worried. I didn't sleep at all last night . . . and I shan't tonight.'

'Oh yes you will.'

'If you'll promise you'll go and see Henry . . .'

'Well, I will. But I don't think it will do any good.'

'You will do it! Oh, you are an angel. Let's go up tomorrow. He's at a little hotel in Bayswater. Oh, thank you, Lucie. I feel so much better already. I have such faith in you.'

'It's misplaced.'

She shook her head slowly and then suddenly saw the glass by my bed.

'What's that?' she said.

'It's Phillida's nightcap. She makes us take it . . . Roland and me. She says it's good for us. It gives us a good peaceful night's sleep, she says.'

'Does it?'

'I haven't noticed. I usually sleep well. Roland and I take it to please her.'

She took the glass and drank the beverage.

'Sorry. I need that peaceful night's sleep more than you do. It's rather nice. Now I'll tell you what we'll do. We'll go up tomorrow. We can stay with Celeste. I did last night. She's always glad to see me. Perhaps you could stay with Roland. Tell him that you couldn't be without him any longer. Then you can go and see Henry and tell him what he has to do.'

'You're incredible, Belinda. You think you can push us around like pieces on a chessboard.'

'I do nothing of the sort. But I think that if sometimes you try to make things go the way you want to, you can. And why shouldn't you? I've got to make this right, Lucie . . . for Bobby and the child.'

'And for Belinda herself,' I murmured.

She kissed me.

'I love you, Lucie. I can't tell you how happy you've made me. I know you'll talk to him in just the right way. You'll make him see what has to be done.'

'Don't hope for too much.'

'I feel so much better since I've talked to you. I feel I can get a good night's sleep because it's all going to come right now.'

'I'll do what I can.'

'Bless you, Lucie. See you in the morning. We'll have an early start, eh?'

'Yes,' I agreed.

She turned at the door to blow a kiss.

'Sleep well,' she said.

And she was gone.

What had I promised, I asked myself? What good could I possibly do?

Well, it was no use worrying about it. Tomorrow or the next day I would see Henry Farrell. It would, I supposed, be interesting to meet him and find out what sort of man he was.

Belinda was exhausting and I felt tired.

I blew out the candle and settled down to sleep.

I must have done so almost immediately, but suddenly I was awake. Something was happening. I could hear a strange noise. I opened my eyes and stared about me. There was a strange glow in the room. I must be dreaming. I could see the shapes of the furniture. They looked different in the strange light.

Then suddenly I was aware of the heat. I was wide awake now. I sat up and saw at once that the curtains about my bed were on fire. The acrid smell filled my nostrils. This accounted for the glow in the room. I saw a flame run right to the top of the tester.

I leaped out of bed and looked back. The curtains on one side of the bed were a mass of flames.

I ran out into the corridor, shutting the door after me and shouted: 'Fire!'

What followed was like a nightmare.

Emery was magnificent. He was a quiet man whose sterling qualities came to the fore in a crisis; and it was his presence of mind which saved what was a small incident from turning into a major conflagration.

It was fortunate that I had wakened in time before the fire had taken a real hold of the bed.

Emery had been the first to hear my call and was on the spot in a matter of seconds. He seized rugs and quickly beat out the worst of the flames, and by that time Mrs Emery with Phillida and most of the servants had arrived.

Mr Emery took charge of the situation and soon we were all bringing water to the smouldering bed; and within half an hour of the discovery of the fire it was out. Mr Emery was the hero of the occasion. Phillida kept telling him how wonderfully he had done and at the same time embracing me fervently. 'Thank God,' she kept muttering to herself. 'Thank God.'

It was about one-thirty when Mrs Emery took charge.

'Now, Miss Lucie, you can't go back there tonight.' She was ordering two of the servants to make my old room ready.

She said: 'As for the rest of you, it's time you were in bed. There's nothing more to be done till morning. We could have had a bad fire but for Mr Emery, and we should all be thankful to him that we are alive and kicking.'

Mr Emery said: 'It was nothing much. I'm only thankful Miss Lucie woke up when she did . . . before it got under way.'

'It was a blessing,' said Mrs Emery. She looked at me. 'I think a little something would be good for Mr Emery,' she went on. 'And you, Miss Fitzgerald and Miss Lucie, could do with a pick-me-up too.'

'Come to the library,' I said. 'And we'll have some brandy.'

We sat there together, the Emerys, Phillida and I.

'I can't stop asking myself how it could have happened,' said Phillida. 'What do you think it could have been, Lucie?'

'I've no idea.'

'Emery's theory was that it had been the candle. It had been hot and could have tumbled over and set the velvet smouldering.'

'But I had been asleep,' I said. 'It was some little while after I had blown it out.'

'It could have toppled at that time when you doused it. Sometimes things smoulder for quite a while before bursting into flames.'

'Well, anyway,' I said, 'it happened and we have to thank you, Mr Emery, for getting it under control before much damage was done.'

'The curtains are ruined,' said Phillida, somewhat ruefully. 'And imagine what the bed will be like after all that water!' She laughed a little hysterically. 'What does that matter as long as you are safe? I keep thinking what might have happened. How could I have told Roland!'

'Oh, Phillida!' I cried. 'It didn't happen. It was just . . . an accident. Thank goodness it was nothing more.' A sudden thought struck me. 'I haven't seen Belinda . . .'

Phillida cried out: 'Oh yes. I'd forgotten she was here. All this happening . . .'

'Surely she couldn't have slept all through this?' I said. 'I'm going to see if she's all right.'

I ran out of the room, Phillida close behind me, up the stairs, past the ruined bedroom to that of Belinda.

I opened the door, calling softly: 'Belinda.'

There was no answer.

Belinda was lying on her back, fast asleep. There was a faint smile about her lips, as though her dreams were pleasant.

Phillida was beside me. I glanced at her and put my finger to my lips. We tiptoed out.

'She must have slept through it all,' said Phillida.

'It seems incredible.'

The Emerys were just behind us.

'Is she all right?' asked Mrs Emery.

'She's fast asleep. Let's go back to the library and finish our drink.'

'She must be a deep sleeper,' said Mrs Emery. 'Some are.'

'I think she was rather exhausted,' I said. 'She mentioned having had a bad night previously.'

'If I'd known, I would have given her one of my nightcaps,' said Phillida.

'Obviously she didn't need it,' I said. 'Although, I remember now . . . she drank the one Kitty brought up for me. Perhaps that is why she slept through it all and I didn't.'

Phillida laughed. 'Thank God,' she murmured. Then: 'It's not meant to send you off like that. It's just to bring about a peaceful, natural sleep.'

'She's a heavy sleeper, that's what,' said Mrs Emery. 'Some people are like that.'

I yawned and said: 'I do think we ought to try and get some sleep now.'

'Your room will be ready,' said Mrs Emery.

'Thank you, Mrs Emery. Then I think I'll go up.'

So there I was, in my old room. I could not help going to the window and looking out at the oak tree and the haunted seat.

It had been a wild night and, as I expected, I slept little.

Belinda and I did not leave next morning. After what had happened it was not possible. The household was obsessed by the topic of the fire. Everyone had to inspect the damage. Phillida was really upset. She kept looking at me with a mingling of horror and affection.

'Oh, Phillida,' I said, 'it didn't happen.'

'No . . . but it might have. If you hadn't wakened . . . I keep thinking of it. I just could not have borne it, Lucie. I keep thinking of Roland. What could I have said to him?'

'But it did not happen.'

'Thank God.'

Belinda expressed amazement when she heard what had happened.

'A fire! In your room! Good Heavens! And there was I, fast asleep.'

She inspected the damage.

'Those curtains! And you lying there! You might have been burned to death, or badly scarred. Oh Lucie, and there was I, fast asleep all through it!'

I wondered whether she was thinking, as I was, of that occasion when she had taken a candle from the Christmas tree and touched my dress – a dress which Rebecca had given to the poor little cottage child so that she might come to the party. Did Belinda remember? She must, for her actions had cost Jenny Stubbs her life and it was the reason why I had been taken into Cador to be brought up with her.

But now I was sure that what was uppermost in her mind was the fact that our journey to London had been delayed.

Phillida said: 'How strange that you did not hear the commotion.'

'I was so tired,' replied Belinda. 'I was asleep almost as soon as I got into bed.'

Phillida looked at her intently. I had a notion that Phillida did not greatly care for Belinda.

Phillida then said that, if I would give her permission, she would have the bed taken away and a new one supplied.

'It just upsets me to look at it,' she said. 'I can't stop thinking of what might have been.'

'You've got to stop thinking about that, Phillida.'

'I wish I could. So – shall I get it taken away? Actually, I wouldn't want Roland to see it in that state. I know how upset he'd be.'

'Then do it, if you can, while I'm in London.'

'Oh, I will, Lucie. Of course, you'll be going with Belinda.'

'Yes, that's so.'

'I hope you'll be all right.'

'All right? Of course. What do you mean?'

'I don't know . . . exactly. I'm just fanciful after what happened.'

'Fanciful . . . about Belinda?'

'Well, there is something about her. She's a strange person. She's rather wild. I have a feeling that one would never really know what she was about.'

'Yes, Belinda is a little . . . unexpected. But I know her well. We are the best of friends really.'

Phillida nodded but she continued to look a little anxious.

The Return

The next day Belinda and I went up to London.

We went first to Celeste who was delighted to see us.

'Lucie as well,' she said. 'This is nice. I do hope you are going to stay a little while.'

'Well, Celeste,' I replied, 'I thought I'd go to Roland. He is in London now.'

'She couldn't do without him,' added Belinda. 'She has to come up to be with him.'

How could she diverge from the truth unnecessarily? I had come up at her request to see Henry Farrell, and she knew it. Why had she deliberately twisted the truth?

'So Roland will be expecting you?' said Celeste.

'No. He doesn't know I'm coming. It was arranged on the spur of the moment. I thought I'd just come to see you and then go along to him. He'll be busy during the day and Belinda and I have one or two things to do in London.'

It sounded reasonable enough.

We had luncheon with Celeste and by that time it was three in the afternoon.

Belinda was all impatience but I said I would go and see Henry Farrell on the following day, because I wanted to prepare what I would say to him. And first I must see Roland.

Belinda accepted my decision rather ungraciously, but

she did not want to offend me for fear I abandoned the entire exercise.

I left her with Celeste and took a cab to Welling Gardens where Roland and Phillida had their *pied-à-terre*.

It was a street of tall, narrow houses. I had been there only once before and then only briefly. Neither Roland nor Phillida had suggested that I should go again and it had not seemed necessary that I should. It was a rented house – a temporary residence – and when they had entertained us it had been in hotels and restaurants. We had always heard the place referred to vaguely as the *pied-à-terre*.

At No. 70 I alighted and paid the cab-driver. I mounted the steps to the front door and, looking down, I saw the shadowy figure of a woman in the basement. She would be the wife of the couple who took charge of the domestic arrangements and lived down there. Roland had told me that the man and wife team went with the house to those who rented it.

I knocked on the front door and after a while the woman opened it. She was middle-aged, rather plump, with reddish hair.

'I'm Mrs Fitzgerald,' I said.

The woman stared at me for a few seconds and then smiled rather expansively.

'Oh, come in,' she said. 'I'll tell Mr Fitzgerald . . .'

'Oh, he's home, is he? I wondered whether he would be at this time. My plan had been to be here and surprise him when he came in.'

Then I saw him. He was coming down the stairs and he paused to stare blankly at me for a moment. Then he said: 'Lucie!'

'I've surprised you, I know,' I explained. 'But I came to London and here I am.'

His surprise turned to warmth.

277

'Oh, Lucie . . .'

He had taken me into his arms. I was aware of the woman watching us, smiling.

'Thank you, Mrs Green,' he said, noticing her. 'This is my wife. We'd like some tea.'

He put his arm round me. 'Come upstairs. It's wonderful to see you. I can't tell you how pleased I am.'

'I thought you would be at your office.'

'Well, the fact is I've been hard at it . . . until today. Then I brought some work home. It was a change of scene and I thought I might get on quicker without interruptions. I was so anxious to get back to Manorleigh.' He opened a door. 'Come into the sitting-room. Not much compared with Manor Grange, I'm afraid.'

'Well, it is just the . . . *pied-à-terre*.'

'It suffices. It's not a home, really . . . but the Greens are good. They really take care of everything.'

'I think it's rather nice. Homely. You could make something out of it.'

'That's what Phillida used to say. But it isn't ours . . . just rented. We did talk about getting a house of our own, but we never got round to it. However, the great thing is, you are here. Tell me, what made you come? Did you want to see me?'

'Of course I did. But I don't think I should have disturbed your work if it had not been for Belinda. She came down to Manorleigh and more or less prised a promise from me to come to Town for a few days.'

'Belinda, the wild one,' he said.

'Yes, that's Belinda. We should have come yesterday but for the fire.'

'Fire?'

'Oh yes. I must tell you about it. It was in our room. The bed is ruined . . . all those lovely curtains are a mess. We

278

don't know how it started. Emery thinks it was a candle which fell over and caught the curtains, which smouldered for some time before bursting into flames. Anyway, we think that is what happened.'

'But when – when was this?'

'The night before last.'

'In the night . . . while you were . . . in bed!'

'It's all right, Roland. I woke up in time.'

'Oh, my God,' he murmured.

'The fire had only just started. I rushed out and woke the household. Emery was marvellous.'

He held me tightly against him. 'Lucie . . .'

'It's over, Roland. Phillida was in a terrible state about it.'

'Oh yes . . . Phillida.'

'She keeps talking about what might have happened to me. But it hasn't . . . and it's a lesson to me to be more careful in the future.'

'I – I can't understand how it could have happened.'

'Emery is sure it was the candle, and I suppose he's right. However, it was all over very quickly.'

He released me, sat down and covered his face with his hands.

I went to him and drew them away. His face was tortured with anguish. I felt a tremendous tenderness towards him. How he loved me, I thought. I must try to love him always. I must care for him. I felt suddenly very protective.

I said: 'Forget it, Roland. It's over. Phillida is getting rid of the bed. There'll be a new one when we get back.'

He did not seem to be listening. He was staring straight ahead and I knew he was seeing that room with the flames creeping up the curtains, and me . . . lying there, unaware.

He could not stop talking of it.

There was a tap on the door and Mrs Green came in with some tea.

As we drank it I told him that Belinda had come down to see me.

He did not pay much attention. I guessed that his thoughts were far away in that bedroom in Manor Grange.

'I am going out with her tomorrow,' I said. I wondered whether to tell him of her troubles and decided that they had been given to me in confidence and that I was not expected to divulge them even to my husband.

'I see,' he said.

'You'll be busy, of course. Do you think you will be finished by Friday?'

'Oh yes. We'll go back together.'

Then we talked of ourselves and he told me how much he had missed me.

'I should have come with you,' I said.

He smiled in agreement. Then he said: 'Phillida would have hated to be alone at Manor Grange. She has some notion that the servants resent her and think she is trying to usurp your place as mistress.'

I did not answer. I knew there was some truth in this.

Then I said: 'You know what servants are. The Emerys were there when my mother was alive. I never saw my mother. She died when I was born, but my half-sister Rebecca has talked to me of her so much that she is a real person to me. Before the Emerys came here they were my mother's servants in her small London house and she took them to Manor Grange with her. So you realize how long they have been in charge of things?'

'Oh yes. Phillida understands that. I think she would like to have a place of our own . . . start afresh . . .'

'She has said nothing to me.'

'No. She wouldn't. Sometimes she has a feeling that she is in the way . . . the third party . . . if you know

280

what I mean. It's on her mind quite a lot. She is always wondering whether, now we're married, she ought to leave us.'

'Oh no. Where would she go? I'm so fond of her, and I know you'd hate it if she went away.'

'We've always been together. It would be a terrible wrench for us both.'

'For me too. I love her dearly. I always think of her as my sister.'

'I know she feels the same about you.'

'She was so terribly upset about the fire.'

'I can imagine that. Well, what do you think of the idea? Say somewhere in Yorkshire? It would be near Bradford and convenient. It's beautiful countryside.'

I was silent. I should hate to be away from London and Manorleigh.

'We would, of course, keep on this place.'

I looked round it. I could not imagine it as a home. A tall, narrow house in a street of such houses, it seemed dark after the big airy rooms of the London house which was now Celeste's, and Manor Grange. The latter, with its spacious rooms and inescapable air of mystery, meant a great deal to me.

'You couldn't sell Manor Grange?' said Roland tentatively.

'No, I don't think I could. Even if I wanted to. I was so shocked when my father died that I am afraid I didn't take in everything about the will and the practical details. I've realized since that, although everything was left to me, it was left in trust. I can't touch the capital and I suppose the house would come into that category. In any case, the solicitors would have to be consulted before I made any move. I think my father thought I might be prey to fortune-hunters.'

Roland looked alarmed and I laughed.

'Oh, that couldn't apply to you, Roland. But there are people . . .' I thought of Jean Pascal. I had no doubt of his motives. 'My father was a very shrewd man,' I went on, 'and his great wish was to protect me. Of course, he hadn't thought of dying for a long time. In any case, he left everything in what is called a trust. It means that I can't do anything with the capital. It's for my children and if I don't have any it's for Rebecca's. So I don't suppose I could sell Manor Grange without a lot of fuss.'

'I see,' said Roland. 'Well, this was just an idea of Phillida's. And she loves Manor Grange. It is just because she feels there is some resentment . . .'

'That will pass. The Emerys are really a wonderful pair. But they have their set of rules and everyone is expected to keep to them.'

'And Phillida has stepped out of line.'

'It was because she brought Kitty into the house without consulting Mrs Emery. She is the one who expects to engage the staff and she feels it was an affront to her.'

'I wish we'd known.'

'It's a small matter. She'll get over it. Oh, it is good to be here. I'm glad I've seen you in your Welling Gardens home.'

'Hardly a home. Just a place to sleep in. That's how Phillida and I regard it. It seems different now you're here, though.'

I smiled happily.

The next day I kept my promise to Belinda. I took a cab and went to the address she had given me. It was, as she had said, a small hotel in Bayswater.

There was a reception desk and I asked there if Mr Henry Farrell was in. He was not but was expected shortly. I said I would wait.

I was reproaching myself for not having made an appointment with him; but, of course, if I had attempted to do that, there was a possibility that he might have refused to see me.

For ten minutes I sat rehearsing what I would say to him, and I grew more and more convinced that I had been misguided to give way. What sort of man was he? Forceful, I imagined. He had come over here to assert his rights. He was not going to listen to me. The best thing I could do was get up and leave now.

I should have discussed this with Roland, asked his advice. I knew what it would be: don't interfere. Leave Belinda to sort out her own troubles. Of course, that was what I should have done. But I did care for her . . . in an odd sort of way. I had really been delighted to see her, as I had thought, settled at last.

While I was ruminating, I heard a voice say: 'Mr Farrell, there's a lady to see you.'

He came towards me. He was of medium height, his fair hair bleached by the sun, his face clearly showing that he lived in a different climate from ours. He was deeply bronzed, which made his eyes look intensely blue. His features were clear-cut; and there was an undoubted air of strength about him. He was a pleasant-looking young man and I could understand Belinda's temptation to act recklessly before she realized that there could be a more splendid life ahead of her than one spent in the goldfields.

'Mr Farrell?' I said, rising.

'Yes,' he said, in a marked Australian accent. 'You wanted to see me?'

'Yes. I'm Lucie Fitzgerald. I was Lucie Lansdon. I don't know whether Belinda spoke of me to you.'

'Aw,' he cried, 'you're Lucie.' He took my hand and shook it heartily. 'Glad to meet you.'

I found I was liking him.

'So you've come to see me?' He looked surprised, but pleased.

'Is there somewhere we could talk?'

'Well, there's a lounge. Pretty quiet this time of day. That might do.'

'Thank you. I should be so glad if you would allow me to talk to you.'

He looked puzzled and led me to the lounge. He was right. It was deserted and I was glad of that.

'Come and sit down,' he said, 'and tell me what this is all about.'

We sat in armchairs in a corner of the room and I said: 'Belinda came to see me. She is very distressed.'

'So she ought to be.'

'Yes, I know. She told me all about it. It's a terrible thing she has done.'

He nodded and I was silent, wondering how to go on. He prompted: 'What is it you wanted to tell me?'

I hesitated. 'You . . . you see, she was very young.'

'That makes no difference. She was willing enough. She knew what she was doing. She was dead keen. If she's changed her mind now, well, that's too bad.'

'I know exactly how you feel.'

'I don't know why she sent you. What does she want you to do?'

'She didn't exactly send me. I agreed to come. She told me all about it. She's very unhappy. She deeply regrets –'

'She's said all this to me. But she's my wife and I'm going to take her back with me.'

'Do you think it would work?' I asked. 'Could it possibly be a happy marriage in those circumstances?'

'What do you mean?'

'Well, with your insisting while she is reluctant.'

'It's what is right.'

284

'Oh yes, I've no doubt of that. But what is right does not always make for happiness.'

'Look here, I don't really see –'

'I know how you feel. I'm interfering. It's no business of mine.'

'You're dead right, it's not.'

'But I do appreciate the fact that you listen to me . . . even to tell me it's no business of mine. It's just that I'm very fond of Belinda. We spent a great deal of our childhood together. There's a closeness . . . and she is very unhappy.'

'I tell you, she's married to me.'

'I know, but if people don't want to be with you, can you force them to be?'

'Yes,' he said sharply. 'You can. She'd change if she came back.'

I shook my head.

'I know her well,' he persisted.

'So do I. Would you let me say something? I do appreciate your seeing me. I do really. It must seem like a dreadful impertinence . . . and it is in a way.'

'Why don't you get on with it?'

I said: 'Belinda went to the goldfields when she was little more than a child. She was fascinated by the strangeness of it, the novelty. She was happy there for a time, but she had been brought up here and she knew there was a different way of life. I don't know what happened to your marriage. But it wasn't exactly idyllic, was it? I mean, before all this. Hadn't you agreed to part?'

'That was in a temper. I admit I've got one.'

'You agreed that you'd be better apart.'

He was silent and I continued: 'She came over here,' I went on, 'right to the other side of the world. All that had happened in Australia seemed remote to her. She put it out

285

of her mind. She met this man. They fell in love and she married him.'

'How could she, when she was married to me?'

'She went through a form of marriage with him. He believes he is married to her. She suits him . . . and he suits her. There is to be a child.'

'What? She didn't say.'

'Think of it, Mr Farrell. I believe you to be a kindly, good man.'

He stared at me in amazement. 'You don't know me.'

'I'm a good judge of character and I've summed you up.'

A faint smile touched his lips and my spirits rose a little. I believed that the mention of the child had had some effect on him.

I decided to press the point. 'Think of the innocent child,' I said. 'Are you going to let it be born with the stigma of illegitimacy?'

He continued to stare at me. 'What's that to do with me?' he demanded. 'It's her little bastard, ain't it? Not mine. She's married to me. That's how it is.'

'I know. I know.'

'What is it you're after?'

'I want to make it right for Belinda . . . for all of you.'

'Why should you?'

'Because I care about her. You understand that. You care about her, too.'

He was silent.

I went on: 'I know she's treated you badly. She hasn't always treated me well. But I am fond of her and I believe she has a chance of finding a way of life which will suit her.'

'Yes, Lady da-de-da.'

'Maybe. But that is what she wants. If you forced her to go back it would be a life of misery for you both. And what about the child?'

286

'She could have that and leave it here.'

'Mr Farrell, a mother does not leave her child.'

'Some of them do – and I've a notion Belinda might be one of them – if it suited her.'

'I don't believe that would be so. Well, all right. Break up this happy home. Don't consider the child at all. Be selfish. There's a recipe for a happy life for you!'

He smiled at me slowly. 'You talk like a lawyer! But, do you know, if I were in a spot of trouble, I'd like you to get me out of it.'

'Thank you,' I said. 'I wish you'd take me seriously.'

'I like to hear you talk. Tell me some more. Tell me, why she got you to come to me.'

'There is a way out of this,' I said.

'For her?' he asked, with a little quirk of his eyebrows denoting amusement.

'For her, for you and for everyone.'

'Yah?'

'Look. Your marriage is over, isn't it?'

'No, it's not. It's binding, ain't it? You're married . . . and it's forever.'

'Unless you decided to break the bond.'

'Divorce, you mean?'

'I see it this way. There could be a quiet divorce and Belinda could be quickly married to Robert Denver afterwards. It could all be done without too much fuss.'

'Divorce,' he repeated incredulously.

'You've reason to do this, surely?' I pointed out.

'Reason enough. But . . . divorce . . .' He shook his head.

'You'd never have any happiness together,' I pointed out. 'What was between you is over.'

'Why should I do this for her, while she treats me as she has?'

'Are you vindictive?'

'What do you mean? I only want my rights.'

'Your rights? What is the good of those without affection, without love?'

'She was supposed to love me once.'

'She was a child.'

'She's a selfish little she-devil.'

'Maybe, but she will not love you again. She would always hanker for a life she missed. You'd be better off without her. You'll probably find someone out there, someone you'll love. You could have a wonderful family. In fact, I think that is what you will do.'

'Why should you think that?'

'Because you are a sensible, reasonable man. A good man at heart.'

He burst out laughing. 'You certainly know how to get round a chap. Do you know, I'm getting to like you, Lucie.'

'I'm glad, because I'm getting to like you, too.'

'I reckon you're a good friend to her.'

'I know her well.'

'Then I'm surprised you're doing all this for her.'

'There, you see! You're better off without her.'

'No doubt of that.'

'Well, where's the sense in coming here like this and trying to take her back with you?'

'Well, she's Belinda, ain't she? I don't know what it is about her. She's as selfish as they come. She's no good to a chap like me. Yet I want her back. I do, really.'

'You could forget her.'

'I dunno about that.'

'You would, I'm sure. Suppose there was that nice person . . . loving, tender. Suppose you married and had a family . . . You'd look back on this and tell yourself what a lucky escape you had had, Mr Farrell.'

'Henry's more friendly.'

'Well, Henry, consider this. I ask you very sincerely to think about it. There's the child.'

'Yes,' he said pensively. 'There's the child.'

'Give her a chance. I really think she could be happy. I think she could make a fresh start. I expect she's told you about her childhood.'

'A few things.'

'It was a strange thing to happen to a child. And she really wasn't very happy with the man she thought was her father. He seemed to be against her from the first. That was not good for a child and it affected her. Here is a chance for her. Henry, do give it to her.'

He said nothing for a long time.

Then he remarked: 'She's treated me pretty bad. I don't see why I should go out of my way to please her.'

'You could do it because you'd be happier that way.'

'Without her, you mean?'

I nodded.

'I suppose you're right.'

'You could have your revenge, of course. But there's never much to that. If you would let her go . . . Will you? Will you think about it?'

He stretched out his hand suddenly and took mine. 'Yes, Lucie,' he said. 'To please you, I'll think about it.'

'Oh, I'm so pleased you agree to that. I'm sure you'll see it the right way. May I come and see you again when you have made up your mind?'

He nodded.

'When? Tomorrow?'

'You're not giving me much time, are you?'

'I should love to know this was settled before I went back to the country.'

'I can't promise. Just because you've been talking to me

so easy and friendly, well, that don't mean that I . . .'

'I know you will agree with me when you think about it.'

'Is there a saying – seem to remember my old Mum talking about –kissing the Blarney Stone?'

'Yes, there is.'

'Does it mean handing out the old flattery?'

'Yes, I suppose so.'

'I reckon you've given a good many kisses to that old stone.'

'No. It's just that I've brought you face to face with the logical truth.'

He laughed at me. 'How are you getting back, Lucie?' he asked.

'I'll call a cab.'

'I'll come and get you one.'

And that was what he did.

I rode back in a state of euphoria. I was certain we were going to win.

I went straight to Celeste's house where Belinda was impatiently waiting for me. She hurried me up to her bedroom.

'Well?'

'I think he might.'

'Might what?'

'Agree to the annulment . . . to be carried out quietly.'

'Really? Oh, Lucie, you're wonderful. I knew you'd do it. It's that solemn air of yours. Like a nanny or a schoolmistress.'

'He said I was like a lawyer.'

'Yes, that's it. What did he say?'

'He said you'd treated me badly, which you have, of course.'

She put out the tip of her tongue – that old habit I remembered so well from her childhood.

'Yes, yes,' she said impatiently.

'I told him about the child.' I looked at her suspiciously. 'There is a child, isn't there?'

'Oh yes, I'm sure of it. It's true. You don't think I would have said so if it wasn't, do you?'

'Yes,' I answered, 'I do.'

'Well, what else?'

'I pointed out to him that if you went back to him, it wouldn't be much of a life for him . . . and he agreed.'

'Oh, Lucie, you really are wonderful.'

'I've not finished yet. He's only agreed to think about it.'

'Oh, but he'll do it. He will. He must. What did you think of him?'

'A bit rough, but good underneath. A nice man. I thought he didn't deserve you.'

'No. He didn't really. Poor old Henry. Do you really think . . . ?'

'All I can say is he promised to think about it.'

'For how long?'

'I don't know. But I shall be seeing him tomorrow.'

'Oh good . . . *good*! And to think you might have been burned to death!'

'What a calamity – for then I shouldn't have been able to arrange your affairs!'

'I didn't mean it that way!'

'It was the first thought that occurred to you. However, I escaped and lived to see Mr Henry Farrell.'

She hugged me fiercely.

I thought: How different from Phillida! How different from Roland! They really care for me. But, as I had said many times before, this was Belinda.

I was amazed at my success. It was because at heart Henry Farrell was really a very good young man.

I think it was the matter of the child which finally swayed him. He was hurt and angry but he was shrewd enough to see that there could be no real happiness with Belinda.

When I met him the next day in the lounge of the Bayswater hotel, he was waiting for me and he looked quite pleased to see me.

He did not tell me immediately what he intended to do, but I think I knew it from the start. He wanted to tease me a little at first; and I think he wanted to listen to further advocacy on my part.

I pleaded as I had before, bringing out the same arguments. He listened patiently and after a while he said: 'How should we go about the divorce?'

I told him I did not know, but I would find out.

'Everything would be taken good care of,' I said.

'Then I suppose she'd marry this lordship again.'

'She will marry Sir Robert Denver.'

'Does he agree to this?'

'I don't think he knows about it yet.'

'What?'

'She has to tell him.'

'What if he says no?'

'I can't believe he will.'

'Mad about her, is he?'

'I think so.'

I had a moment of uneasiness then. I could see the memories in his eyes. Belinda had a powerful effect on men. There was Bobby who adored her and this young man had come from the other side of the world to pursue her.

I realized how fortunate I had been to be able to plead with him, for he was still hankering after her.

But he was no fool. He saw the point. The best way for

everyone concerned was to end the marriage so that they could get on with their own lives.

When we parted I had his promise that he would begin divorce proceedings against Belinda. The case would be undefended and with luck might not find its way into the newspapers.

Belinda was waiting for me when I returned triumphant.

'He's going to do it,' I told her.

'You're marvellous! I knew you could do it. Oh Lucie, you were always my best friend.'

'Don't forget this is only the beginning. The first thing you have to do is talk to Bobby.'

'I know,' she said gloomily.

'Then I think you should go back to him. If he lets you stay there that will make a blatant case of adultery. Let's hope it can be kept quiet. It could be rather awkward for you, but you have to be prepared for that. After all, it is a small price to pay for all your misdemeanours.'

'I'll do it, Lucie. I'll go back right away. I'll tell Bobby everything.'

'Let's hope he will be as forgiving and indulgent as you think he will be.'

'Of course he will be. He adores me.'

Her gloom had completely vanished. Once again she was on the point of manipulating the lives of others to suit her purpose.

She left that day; and I spent another day and night in Welling Gardens.

Then Roland and I went back to Manorleigh.

Phillida vociferously expressed her pleasure at seeing us.

'Anyone would think we had been away for at least a month,' said Roland.

'I missed you so much. Both away at the same time! It's wonderful to have you back. I want you to see your room. It looks quite different. Roland, Lucie has told you . . .' Her mood changed from joy to horror.

'Yes,' I said. 'I told him about the fire.'

She turned to him, anguish in her eyes. 'I think I should have died . . . if anything had happened . . .'

'But it didn't,' I said.

'It might have. Imagine it, Roland!'

'I am imagining it,' said Roland. 'It doesn't bear thinking of. But you must not be upset. It's over. It didn't happen. We were so lucky. Now let us have a look at the room.'

It did look different without the four-poster bed. It had been replaced by one in the Regency style which was plain in comparison with its predecessor; but it was very attractive and elegant.

'It makes the room look quite different,' I said.

'Less cluttered,' added Roland. 'Well done, Phillida, it was a good choice.'

'I never want to see another bed curtain,' announced Phillida. She shivered. 'They will always remind me.'

Roland put his arm through hers. 'Stop brooding,' he commanded.

'I'm trying to, Roland.'

It was good to be home, and I was rather proud of the manner in which I had managed Belinda's affairs.

I dismissed her from my mind. I need not think of her for a while and could devote myself to an existence which had become very pleasant to me.

The peaceful atmosphere was disturbed when, the following morning, Mrs Emery invited me to her room. I

294

guessed there was trouble ahead when she brought out the cannister of Darjeeling tea.

I soon heard what it was.

'The last thing I want to do, Miss Lucie, is speak out of turn,' she began, and proceeded immediately to do so. 'I know she is the sister . . . but that's a very different matter than being the mistress of the house, and it seems to me – and Emery is with me in this – that at times it would seem she thinks of herself as mistress of the house.'

'I am sure she does not, Mrs Emery.'

'Well, I'm pretty sure she does.'

'What is worrying you, then?'

'About this bed. She carries on for all the world as though this is her place. I said to Emery, I said, "Is it for her to choose the bed? Is it for her to decide to get rid of the old one?" That was a fine bed, that was. It's been here since the year dot. I reckon it was worth a pretty penny. Yet she had it taken away. Goodness knows where it is now.'

'It was ruined by the fire and all that water which was poured on it.'

'Ruined, me foot. I reckon it could have been put right.'

'She was so upset about the fire, Mrs Emery. She wanted to get rid of everything that would remind us. She had a point.'

'I should have thought it would be for the mistress of the house to decide, Miss Lucie. Neither Mr Emery nor I would say, "This has to go," or "That has to stay." That's for the mistress. That's what I don't like. "What next?" I say to Mr Emery, and he just looks at me and says, "Aye, what next?"'

'Well, there won't be any more beds to be got rid of, I hope. Mr Fitzgerald and I are very satisfied with the replacement.'

'Well, that's as may be. But it don't seem right to me. But if you say so. And there's something else.'

'Oh? What?'

'Well, prowling about. She's been in the attics looking at the trunks and things . . .'

'It's an ancient house and it fascinates her, Mrs Emery. She will be living here with us, you know, so it will be her home.'

'Well, frankly, that's what I'm afraid of, Miss Lucie. Two ladies as mistress . . . it don't seem to work somehow.'

'Oh, it will, because she's my sister-in-law and really a great friend of mine. I think she would be surprised if she thought she had given offence to you.'

'Well, all I wanted to say is that it wasn't only being in the attics. She's been prowling about the gardens, taking a rare interest in everything, talking to the servants . . . asking them questions about the ghost.'

'Did they mind?'

'Not them! They like that sort of thing. Makes them feel important. They seem to think something of her. But, of course, they're an empty-headed lot, most of them. No thought for the house. But if you say it's all right . . . What I don't like is to see someone quiet and gentle being taken advantage of.'

'It's kind of you, Mrs Emery, but I don't think that is what she intends. I am sure she would be very upset if she knew you were offended.'

Mrs Emery nodded in silence, but I could see by the vigorous manner in which she stirred her Darjeeling that she did not agree with me.

A few days passed. I was wondering how Belinda was getting on. I imagined all must be going smoothly, otherwise I should have heard, for if she were succeeding she would forget all about me. It was only if she needed help that she would remember.

I pictured her confessing to the complaisant Bobby. I was sure he would fall in with her wishes. They would employ the best lawyers and if Henry Farrell really would set the divorce in motion, there might not be too much delay.

I hoped it could be completed with speed and secrecy before the child was born.

It was difficult to imagine Belinda as a mother, but people often surprised one – particularly in this respect.

It had been a pleasant day. It was about a week after I had returned and we had slipped back into the old routine. I was always wondering when Roland would have to go back to London, for I supposed these visits would become a part of our daily lives. He had talked a little about the wool trade which was carried on in Yorkshire. I supposed I should accompany him when he went up North, which I realized he would have to do more frequently than he had been doing of late.

We had loitered at the table over dinner. We had been recalling our stay in France and Phillida enlivened the conversation with her versions of one or two incidents which had befallen her. She told them in a breezy manner and they were usually concerned with some gaffe of hers.

We laughed a good deal, remembering.

Afterwards we sat in the drawing-room, talking idly. Phillida left first and said she was going to bed. Roland and I went up soon afterwards.

It had been a rather chilly evening and Mrs Emery always ordered a fire to be lighted in the room when the temperature dropped a little. Now it gave a cosy aspect, throwing firelit shadows on the walls.

'I think Phillida is getting over the shock of the fire, don't you, Roland?' I said.

'Oh, I do. But she really was very upset. She is so fond of you. As a matter of fact, I have not seen her so disturbed since our parents died. I don't think she will ever really forget while she's here. She doesn't ever come into this room, does she?'

'I don't think she does.'

'How do *you* feel about it?'

'Well, I suppose I've forgotten for the most part. It was over so quickly. I just woke, saw the flames – and within half an hour the fire was out. Besides, it looks different here now.'

'I wish Phillida was not so . . . excitable.'

'It's part of her charm. She is always so full of enthusiasm and energy. Everything she does and says has to be with that exuberance. She enjoys life.'

'And for that reason she can sometimes be too deeply affected by it.'

Roland was in bed watching me. The last thing I did before joining him was draw back the curtains because we both liked to awake to daylight.

As I pulled them back I gazed down, as I always did, at the seat under the oak tree. As I did so, a great shock ran through me. Someone was on the seat. I saw him clearly in the light of the stars and that which came from our lighted room.

He rose from the seat. He was wearing an opera hat and cloak. I stood there, as though petrified . . . unable to speak . . . unable to move. And as I did so he took of his hat and bowed. He looked straight at me. I could see clearly the widow's peak on his forehead.

It was the same man whom I had seen from my window in the London house. It was my father's murderer whom I had helped to send to the gallows.

298

I heard Roland's voice. 'Lucie . . . Lucie . . . what's wrong?'

I turned away from the window, sank into a chair and covered my face with my hands.

Roland was beside me. 'What is it, Lucie? What's the matter?'

'It . . . it's down there.'

He went to the window.

'What? What is down there? What has frightened you?'

I got up and stood beside him. There was no one below.

'I saw him. I saw him clearly. He was . . . just as he had been outside the house in London. It was Fergus O'Neill.'

'Fergus O'Neill,' he repeated the name blankly.

'The man who killed my father.'

'Lucie, be calm. Tell me exactly what you saw. Who was it you thought you saw down there?'

'It was Fergus O'Neill,' I repeated. 'I gave evidence against him. I saw him before he killed my father. He was waiting outside the house for him . . . I looked down and saw him the night before . . . and when he killed my father I recognized him.'

'Lucie, let's try to see what this is all about. How could he be there? He was hanged, wasn't he?'

I nodded.

'You think it was . . . ?'

'I think he has come back to haunt me.'

'Oh no! You imagined it.'

'I didn't. I saw him clearly. I wasn't thinking of him. Why should I imagine him . . . now . . . here?'

'Come to bed. You're all right now. There's nothing to be afraid of here . . . with me.'

I lay in his arms while he talked to me, lovingly, soothingly. I poured out my fears to him, how I was afraid that I had condemned the wrong man. That was when I had

299

seen him almost immediately afterwards, standing in the street where I had seen him the night before he killed my father. It had worried me a great deal at the time, and then I had convinced myself that I was being foolish. Rebecca had said that I imagined I saw him and I had begun to believe her. But he was the man. There was no doubt of it. There was the distinctive way in which his hair grew . . .

'I think you imagined it.'

'Why should I . . . suddenly? I saw him clearly.'

'It's this old place. There are stories about the ghosts here. Wasn't there supposed to be someone who sat on that seat?'

I nodded.

'Well, that's just the place where you would expect to see a ghost and with that on your mind . . .'

'It wasn't on my mind. I hadn't thought of it for some time.'

'It couldn't possibly be anything but imagination.'

'You don't believe people can come back after death?'

'No,' he said emphatically.

'Even if that death was violent? Even if someone had helped to send them to the gallows?'

'No. I don't believe it, nor must you. You were tired and images from the past came into your mind. You say you saw him before . . . the murder. Well, that image must have been somewhere in your mind. You were sleepy, and there has been all that talk about the garden's being haunted. The picture came into your mind and you *thought* you saw it.'

'You make it all seem so reasonable . . . so logical.'

'There must be a logical reason for everything, Lucie, but sometimes it's hard to find.'

'You're making me feel so much better, Roland.'

'Then I am glad, my dearest.'

He had taken a lock of my hair and was twirling it in his fingers. He said gently: 'I'll take care of you. I'll protect you always from all the ghosts on Earth.'

I lay against him, drawing comfort. I supposed I had imagined it. But I could not think why, for I had not thought of the man for a long time.

Roland said suddenly: 'It's still on your mind, isn't it? This proves it. Do you know, I think we ought to get away from here.'

'Get away!'

'I have been thinking of this for some time. You see, this is *your* house. You are my wife now and I think we ought to have a home of our own . . . provided by me.'

'I couldn't give up Manor Grange.'

'You could come back to it, but you need not be here all the time. However, it is something we could think about. Naturally we don't want to rush into anything. You see, it's a little complicated. I should be nearer Bradford. I have not been up there much lately. Meeting you, and getting married – it's made a difference. But now we are settled, I ought to be there a little more for business reasons. It could mean long separations if I don't do something about it, and I wouldn't want that. I hope you wouldn't either.'

'Of course I shouldn't.'

'So I've been thinking . . . I ought to get a place, provide you with a home. It's what I want to do, Lucie.'

'You mean . . . we should live there . . . mostly?'

'Not necessary. We'd keep the *pied-à-terre* for when we were in London – which would be often, of course. And you'd have Manor Grange. I know that's essential. You feel sentimental about the servants. But this is what I've had in mind for some time. The fact is, Lucie, I don't think this place is good for you. There are too many associations . . . and tonight has made me feel the matter is urgent. Do think about it.'

'I can't say, Roland. Manor Grange has always been a home to me, much more than the London house.'

'But this ghost . . .'

'It's true I've always heard the place was haunted, but by benevolent ghosts . . . a loving mother come back to be with her daughter. It was very different from what I saw – or thought I saw – tonight.'

'I have wanted to talk to you about it all so much, Lucie. But I did know that you had suffered a terrible shock. That sort of thing has its effect. Even when you think it is behind you, it can leap out and confront you. You married me, and I thought a different way of life would make you forget. But here you are with a part of the old days. You can't forget here.'

'And you think if we went away . . . ?'

'I do. I don't want to rush it. We could rent a place while we looked round to find something just what you wanted, somewhere where you could get right away from everything that has happened. And as I shall have to be in Yorkshire . . . well, perhaps we could look for a place near Bradford. Give it a try, Lucie. I think it is the answer.'

I wondered if he were right. He could well be. I had so looked forward to being at Manor Grange, but it had not been quite what I had hoped for; and I could see that Mrs Emery had taken a dislike to Phillida. And after what I had seen – or imagined I saw – in the garden, perhaps we should find somewhere.

I was not really sure what I wanted.

I said: 'We'll talk about it later.'

'Of course,' he answered, kissing me. 'It was insensitive of me to bring it up now. It just came out, I'm afraid.'

'It was kind and thoughtful of you. You are always kind and thoughtful. I expect you're right. I expect it is this house and the talk of ghosts . . . and all the memories of my father, of course.'

'Yes,' he said. 'Just let's brood on this idea of the house.'

It was a long time before I slept and when I did I had a nightmare. I was going to look at a house with a prospect of buying it. I entered an old place. It was just like Manor Grange and as I stood in the hall a figure came down the stairs. He was dressed in an opera hat and black cloak and, as he bowed, taking off his hat, I saw how the hair grew to a peak on his forehead. I noticed the white scar on his cheek.

I awoke screaming. Roland held me tightly, comforting me.

I slept late next morning and was awakened by Phillida at my bedside.

'Lucie,' she said gently, 'you've had a bad night. Roland told me about it.'

I started up and my gaze went to the window. She followed it and I knew that when she said 'Roland told me,' she meant that he had told her everything about my hallucination, as he would call it.

'I think you should rest this morning,' she went on. 'I'm going to prop you up and you'll feel better when you've eaten. I've brought your breakfast. I prepared it myself . . . coffee, toast and marmalade and a lightly boiled egg.'

'Oh, Phillida, there's no need. I'm all right.'

'No, you're not.' She could be forceful. I could see what Mrs Emery objected to. And there would be trouble about her preparing my breakfast. Mrs Emery was probably at this moment stating that some people did not seem to know

303

that in a house like this it was the servants who prepared breakfasts.

Phillida insisted on propping me up with pillows and proudly she set the tray before me. Oddly enough, although I did not feel hungry, I found myself almost absent-mindedly eating what she had brought. But I did feel a little better. It was surprising what daylight does for fancies. Of course, I was telling myself, I had imagined it. It was an image lodged in the back of my mind and it came out from time to time. It was significant that I had thought I saw him on the haunted seat.

'That's better,' she said. 'I'm sorry, Lucie. Roland did tell me. I hope you didn't mind. He was so worried. He wanted advice.'

'I think I must have been overwrought – though I don't know why. I was tired, of course.'

'I think it is the talk about ghostly revenants in this house.'

'Is there such talk now?'

'Yes, among the servants. Lady Somebody, long since dead, is said to come back . . . and she still seems to be hanging around, according to them.'

'I hadn't been thinking of that. But I was here so much with Celeste and my father.'

'That's it, you see. It's all to do with this shocking business. Roland and I have been talking seriously about getting away.'

'He mentioned it last night.'

'Well, you see, he has neglected things in Yorkshire quite a bit lately. He really needs to have a place near Bradford.'

'He told me that.'

'This is a lovely house. Don't think we don't enjoy being here . . . immensely. But Roland says it's living on your

304

bounty. Well, you know what men are. They like to feel that they are the providers.'

'I understand all that.'

'I'm so glad you do. He knows how you feel about this house. You never want to let it go. Roland said something about its being in trust . . .'

'I'm not sure whether that applies to the house, but it does to everything else.'

'Well, I don't understand these matters. But I do know how you feel about this place. And you wouldn't want to upset the all-important Mrs Emery.' She grimaced. 'I've got on the wrong side of her somehow. I think that could be straightened out in time, though.'

'I'm sure it could.'

'In any case, at the moment she would be rather pleased to see me gone. I know what it is. She feels we are living at your expense. We understand it, in a way. Do you think we should be more comfortable . . . somewhere else? Roland's idea is for you to choose a house somewhere near Bradford. What do you think?'

'I should keep Manor Grange, whatever happened. You do realize that?'

'Of course. It will be a place to visit often. Then we shall be coming to London for short stays. I'm sure that would placate Mrs Emery.'

'She likes the house to be full of visitors. When my father was alive . . .'

Phillida put her fingers to her lips and shook her head at me. 'Well,' she said, 'what do you think? There'd be no harm in looking around.'

'I suppose not.'

'It's really rather exciting. I love looking at houses, don't you?'

'Yes, I do think it is rather fascinating.'

'Perhaps you would like a modern place, somewhere where nobody – or very few people – have lived before, so that no secrets or ghosts are left behind.'

'I don't know. I've always loved old houses.'

'Well, won't it be fun to look? Roland says he wants *you* to make the choice. He was so worried about you last night.'

'Where is he now?'

'He's downstairs. He's had a letter from Bradford. They want him to go up next week. He's rather upset about it. I think he'll want to take you with him. I shall go, of course. I'll have things to do there and he wouldn't want to leave you in this place without us.'

'He is kind and thoughtful . . . always.'

'Well, he's your husband, isn't he? And I love you too, Lucie. I keep thinking of that awful night and what might have happened. Why, of course! It's the shock of that.'

'What do you mean?'

'What happened that night.'

'You mean the fire? It has nothing to do with that.'

'But it happened in this house. It could have been . . . oh, I can't say it. It was the shock. Shock has strange effects. You did not seem so very upset on the surface. Your feelings have been driven inwards and have manifested themselves in this vision in the garden.'

'It sounds a little contrived to me,' I said, and found that I could laugh.

Phillida was laughing with me. 'You are laughing at me, really. You and Roland are a pair. Roland always laughs at me and my wild antics, as he calls them. But I do think that might be a good and reasonable explanation of your vision last night.' She was earnest suddenly. 'I am going to look after you, Lucie . . . just as I have looked after Roland. And the more I think of getting away from this place, the more I believe it to be the right answer.'

She surveyed the breakfast tray with pleasure, for I had eaten everything.

'I feel perfectly all right now,' I said. 'I am going to get up.'

She kissed me lightly on the forehead.

'Thank you, Phillida,' I went on.

'Don't you worry,' she said. 'Roland and I are here with you. We are the magnificent triumvirate. We'll stand together and beat all the hobgoblins in England if need be.'

She had certainly succeeded in banishing the horrors of the previous night, if not completely, which would have been impossible, to some extent.

Over the next few days there was a great deal of talk about looking for a house in Yorkshire. I felt a certain enthusiasm for the project. I could not cast off the memory of what I had seen. Every night before I went to bed, I would go to the window and look out, half-expecting to see the man or ghost – whatever it was – sitting there. There would be a rush of panic as I approached the window, and an intense relief when I saw that the seat was empty.

I would go to it by day and sit there, thinking. The past was back with me. I could not stop thinking of the night when I had waited for my father to come home from the House, when he had stayed the night with the Greenhams, so giving himself a few more hours of life. I thought of the following day, when I had looked straight at that man after he had fired the shot which killed my father.

I was back in the past. It would never be completely gone. Not until I knew the truth – whether there were two men with widow's peaks and scarred cheeks, whether the figure which haunted me was indeed a man or an image conjured up out of my tortured imagination.

But if I had condemned an innocent man and the real murderer still lived to taunt me, how could he have come to Manor Grange? How could he have sat there on the haunted seat?

The most likely explanation was, of course, that I had imagined what I saw. I had been far more shocked than I had realized at the time it happened; and the episode of the fire must have affected me more than I imagined.

These thoughts obsessed me during the next few days; and then another shock awaited me.

The local newspaper was always available during the mornings; and I took my copy and went into the garden to glance through it. Boldly I went to the haunted seat and, sitting down, began to read. There were the usual local matters . . . an account of a wedding and two funerals. People were more interested in their immediate circle than in the whole wide world.

Then a paragraph caught my eye, and my heart began to hammer as I read. It was brief and to the point:

> The two missing Members of Parliament, Mr James Hunter and Mr Joel Greenham, are on their way back to England. It will be remembered that they were taking part in a mission to Buganda. When returning to their hotel one night the two gentlemen disappeared and were thought to have been robbed and murdered by thieves. In fact, they were kidnapped and have spent several months in captivity. Their release has now been secured and they are on their way back to England to be reunited with their families.

I read the paragraph through several times. Was I dreaming? Was this another hallucination? Could Joel really be alive?

I went up to the bedroom. I was thankful that I did not meet anyone. I could only say to myself: Joel has come home. He is really alive.

Memories of him kept flashing into my mind. I had loved him for so long . . . all my life, it seemed. News of his death, following so close on that of my father, had completely stunned me. I had been lonely and lost.

I could not believe this. Joel alive! Coming home!

What would that mean to me? I was married now. I felt a terrible anguish; and it seemed as though a burden of sadness and despair was settling upon me.

Joel coming home . . . and I was married to Roland Fitzgerald!

I loved Roland, I told myself. He was a good husband to me. When had he ever been anything but kind and considerate?

But . . . Joel was coming home. We had promised that we would love each other for ever. And I had married Roland.

I was numbed by the shock. Roland and Phillida noticed. They noticed everything, I thought, a little resentfully. They believed that what they called my hallucination had shocked me more than they had first thought. Phillida was busy with her remedies. In addition to the nightcap she was bringing me some herbal drink.

She said: 'When we are next in London together, I'll take you to the health shop. They have just about everything to promote good health.'

They were talking a great deal about the house Roland was proposing to buy in Yorkshire. Phillida knew exactly how many rooms we should need. She chattered constantly about it. I let her run on. I did not wish her to guess at my indifference.

I was wondering where Joel was now. Coming home, they said. There would be more about it in the London papers. I wished that I were there.

What was he thinking? He would be remembering me, believing that I was waiting for him . . . as we had promised we would. That seemed years ago. So much had happened since.

The trip to Yorkshire dominated Roland's and Phillida's conversation. I was only half-listening to what they said.

I did hear Roland say: 'I thought we might rent a house for a month or so to give you a chance to look round. We don't want to commit ourselves until we're sure.'

'What an excellent idea!' cried Phillida.

'Does that appeal to you, Lucie?'

'Oh, yes . . . yes . . . I suppose it's a good idea.'

'You do think so?' pressed Roland.

'Of course she does,' Phillida answered for me.

'I think we should go next week. I really need to go, and it would be an excellent opportunity.'

'I'm so looking forward to it,' added Phillida. 'House-hunting is such fun, isn't it, Lucie?'

'Oh yes.'

'The moors are noted for their beauty,' said Phillida. 'I think somewhere close to the moors would be nice. Not too isolated, of course. Then there are those wonderful old abbeys . . . Fountains and Rievaulx. Ruins, of course. Henry VIII, wasn't it? What a dreadful thing to do! But the ruins are really fascinating. Next week, you said, Roland? I really can't wait.'

I wanted to shout at them: Stop talking about houses in Yorkshire! I wanted to tell them: Joel's coming home. I can't think about anything else.

*

There was a letter from Belinda next day.

> Dear Lucie,
>   Bobby and I are coming to London. We do want to see you. Everything is going to be all right now. I told him what you did. Bobby, the darling, does understand. He thinks you're wonderful. Both of us *do* want to see you. We shall be staying with Celeste, who is not very well. I think she is a little lonely.
>   So come up and be with us for a few days. You really must. Celeste would love to see you.
>   Love from
>   Belinda.

But next week I should be looking at houses . . . houses which didn't interest me, because Joel was coming home and I was beginning to wonder what I had done with my life.

Since I had read that paragraph about Joel, I had forgotten to look for the man on the haunted seat before I went to bed. The thought of Joel's return had closed my mind to everything else.

The idea came to me suddenly in the night. I would not go to Yorkshire with them. I had little interest in houses. I wanted to go to London. I must know what was happening about Joel. It was too frustrating to be without news.

I decided to be a little devious.

I said: 'I've heard from Belinda. She's coming to London and she thinks Celeste is not well.'

'Oh dear,' said Roland, all concern. He was always very sympathetic to others.

'Belinda thinks I should go to London to see Celeste.'

'You could go after we have got back from Yorkshire,' suggested Roland.

'I . . . I don't think I could really be happy if I thought she were ill and I wasn't on the spot.'

'What's wrong with her?'

'I don't know. But I feel I must go up to London and find out.'

'When?' asked Phillida.

'Well . . . now. I don't want to wait until she is really ill.'

'Is it as bad as that?'

'Belinda suggested . . .' I trailed off. I was thinking: Why should I have to make these explanations, tell them half-truths, just because I don't want to go with them, because I must find out all I can about Joel?

I went on firmly: 'I think it would be a good idea if you two went to Yorkshire. After all, it's your native county. You know a great deal about it. I know nothing.'

'But you were excited about looking for a house,' said Roland.

'Well, you are not going to find it in a day or so. Why don't you two go and if you find something I can come and look at it later. But it is going to take some time . . . and I shall be worrying about Celeste.'

'It will spoil everything,' said Phillida with a little pout.

Roland said gently: 'I understand how Lucie feels. She would be thinking of Celeste all the time.'

'That's exactly what I mean,' I said gratefully.

'Then, my dear Lucie, you must do as you wish. Phillida and I will go to Yorkshire. We'll look round, and then, if something seems possible, we'll get you to come and inspect it. We won't decide anything without you, rest assured.'

I smiled at him warmly. He really was very kind and always understanding.

I felt a sense of shame, but at the same time I was immensely relieved. I could not speak to them of Joel. I was

312

wondering whether I should see him; and had no idea what his reaction towards me would be . . . if I did.

Thus it was that I found myself on the train speeding to London. The cab took me to the house and there was Celeste waiting for me.

She rushed at me and hugged me.

'How lovely that you are here!'

'Belinda said that you were unwell so I had to come.'

'Belinda's exaggerating.'

'I'm so glad. When does she arrive?'

'Tomorrow. I'm glad you came a day ahead. It gives us a chance to chat a while. Where is Roland?'

'On his way to Yorkshire with Phillida. Celeste, I saw a piece in the paper . . . about Joel.'

'Oh yes, there has been quite a lot in the London papers. They didn't make it headline news, though. I suppose they'll wait until he gets home for that.'

'When is he coming home?'

'It must be soon now, I imagine.'

'Did you hear what happened?'

'No. I did think of calling on the Greenhams but I didn't. They were so odd at the time of his disappearance that I have seen very little of them since.'

'I thought there might be some news up here.'

'The press is being unusually secretive about it. I should have thought it would have made a good story. MPs kidnapped and held all this time . . .'

'Was a ransom paid?'

'I know nothing more than what I have read in the papers.'

'I wonder when he'll be home.'

'It can't be the same, can it? I mean, between you two. You're married now.'

'I was told he was dead, Celeste.'

She was looking at me in some alarm.

'But you are very happily married. Roland is so good, isn't he? Poor Joel. Perhaps you ought not to see him. Perhaps I should explain.'

'I want to see him, Celeste. *I* want to explain.'

'If you think it wise. Of course . . . he may have changed.'

'It's not really so long ago, Celeste.'

'But you are a married woman now.'

I nodded and turned away.

'How long will Roland and Phillida be in Yorkshire?' she asked.

'I don't know exactly. They're looking for a house.'

'A house? Right up there?'

'It's where Roland's main business is. It is more their home than the South is. Roland wants to buy a house. I think he feels that Manor Grange is mine and he wants to provide a home for us.'

She nodded. 'That's natural enough. But what about Manor Grange? Are you going to sell it?'

'I'm not sure that I could even if I wanted to. All that business about the trust. I don't know what it entails. I didn't listen much at the time.'

'We were too shocked, weren't we? I suppose the trustees would have to agree to the sale. I'm no more sure than you are.'

'I wouldn't sell in any case. Think of the Emerys.'

'I see. But if you are living in Yorkshire . . .'

'I shall come South quite a lot. I shall come to see you and Belinda. I couldn't be quite cut off.'

'Well, you can always come here when you want to be in London . . . and then you'll have Manor Grange if you want to stay there. Perhaps it's not such a bad idea. So they will be looking, and if they find something . . . ?'

'I shall go up and see what it's like, and if the three of us are agreed, well then, I suppose Roland will buy it.'

'Very exciting!' said Celeste. 'It's wonderful to have you here.'

She had put me in my old room; and that night, when I went to bed I could not resist going to the window. I stared at the railings of the garden square, half-expecting to see him there.

But the street was quite deserted.

Belinda came the following day. She was brimming over with excitement. Bobby was with her; he looked only slightly less jubilant than he had appeared on his wedding day. I imagined how shocked and horrified he must have been on hearing Belinda's confession; but she had managed to convince him that all would be well and it seemed he believed her.

She was soon in my room for a chat.

'It's working,' she said. 'Bobby's being an absolute pet and Henry is behaving almost like a gentleman, which I never believed he would.'

'Which means he is doing exactly what you want?'

She laughed. 'Same old Lucie!' Her tongue protruded in the old way. 'It's going to take a little time. Why do people always have to hang about so? Why can't they get on with things? *I* don't know why there has to be all this delay. But it *is* going to be done without fuss . . . and we're hoping very few people will hear about it. So soon Bobby and I will be well and truly married – and we'll never forget the part you played in this, Lucie.'

'I only did the obvious thing. There was, after all, only one solution for you.'

'But Henry could have turned nasty. He liked you a lot.

315

He thinks you're sensible. He hated doing it but he could see it was no use trying to make me go back with him. Besides, there's the baby.'

'You think that decided him?'

Belinda patted her stomach. 'Dear little baby,' she said. 'He'll be strong and powerful. Look what he is able to achieve merely by being here!'

I thought then that there was something rare in the way she was able to shift her troubles on to the shoulders of others and have an implicit belief that everything must come right for her – and in some miraculous way, it did.

Suddenly she said: 'Joel Greenham is coming home. I saw it in the paper.' She looked at me quizzically. 'He used to be a rather special friend of yours.'

'Fancy your remembering!' I said with faint sarcasm.

'Of course I remembered! It was quite exciting, and once you were going to marry him. And now he's coming home!' She was watching me, her eyes sparkling. 'He was kidnapped,' she went on. 'He'll soon be here.'

'Yes, I suppose he will.'

'Don't try to pretend to me that you're indifferent.'

'I wasn't trying to pretend anything. Of course I'm not indifferent. They thought he was dead. It's wonderful that he isn't . . . and is coming home.'

She nodded and I could see that she was contemplating all sorts of possibilities.

So, in fact, was I. My thoughts were in a turmoil as they had been ever since I had read that paragraph. I was longing to see Joel and I was more than a little afraid.

Another day passed. Celeste was certainly pleased to have us there. Her trouble was loneliness. Belinda was amazingly unperturbed about her affairs. She had clearly convinced herself that everything would soon be in order; as for Bobby, I think he was a little bewildered but he was clearly still deeply in love with Belinda and certainly thrilled at the prospect of the baby.

I admired Belinda in a way. I wished I could bring the same attitude to my affairs that she did to hers.

I constantly scanned the papers for news. There was none.

Belinda said she wanted to do some shopping while she was in Town. 'It's for the baby,' she explained. 'Lucie, I want you to come with me.'

So I went with her. She shopped as much for herself as the baby; and when we returned home, I thought Celeste looked a little excited.

When I was alone with her, she said: 'Joel has been here. He's very upset.'

'He came to see me?' I asked.

'Yes. His parents had told him that you were married but he thought he must have the news from you. When I told him that you were actually in London, he asked a lot of questions. He looks different, Lucie. Older.'

'I suppose we all do, and what happened is bound to have affected him.'

'He knew about your father, of course. He said he must get in touch with you.' She looked at me anxiously.

'I suppose he would want to talk,' I said.

'He left a note for you.'

'A note? Where is it?'

'I'll get it.'

She put her hand into the pocket of her dress and brought it out almost reluctantly. I seized on it.

'Thank you, Celeste.'

I had to get away to discover what he had written. I went up to my room, sat on the bed and slit the envelope.

Dear Lucie [I read],

I want to see you. I could not believe that you are married. My parents told me first. They explained so much. But I have to see you soon. Could we meet tomorrow? Shall we say by the Round Pond in Kensington Gardens at half past ten? Do come. I shall be there.

Joel.

I must go, of course. I had to see him. I had to explain.

It was hard to live through the rest of the day. Time passed with maddening slowness. I was thankful that Belinda was so self-absorbed that she did not notice my mood.

The night which followed was a restless one for me; but it passed, and then I was walking across the Gardens to the Round Pond where Joel and I had met so often during our childhood. That was why it must have occurred to him that we should meet there.

It was a bright day. Several children were sailing their little white boats on the Pond while vigilant nannies stood by.

And there was Joel. He had seen me and was striding towards me. He put his arms about me and held me close to him for a few seconds. Then he released me and looked into my face. I saw the anguish in his eyes and it matched my own.

He took me by the elbows and continued to gaze at me.

'Lucie . . .' he began.

'Oh, Joel,' I said. 'I never thought to see you again.'

I knew then what a mistake I had made. I knew that he was and always would be the only one I really loved. I knew that I would never be really happy again.

His eyes darkened as he muttered: 'How could you?'

'I have to explain.'

'Let's get away from here. Let's find somewhere quiet where we can talk.'

He took my arm and we walked rapidly away from the Pond towards the path where flowers grew on either side. We turned off to a patch of grass. There was a seat under one of the trees and he led me to it.

When we were seated he turned to me and said: 'How could it have happened?'

'They told me you were dead,' I answered. 'It was unbearable . . . after my father . . .'

'I know what happened to your father. And then they told you . . . what did they tell you?'

'That you had been set upon by thieves after you left a meeting and were on your way to your hotel. You were missing, they said. And after a time we heard that your body had been discovered. You had been murdered, they said, you and James Hunter.'

'They should have told you the truth,' he said. 'I would not have undertaken it if I had known they would not tell you.'

'The truth?' I cried.

He said: 'It is true that I went out on this mission with my fellow Members of Parliament. It was only when I was over there that the proposition was put to Hunter and me. We were younger than the others and more physically capable if the need arose. We had both done a little of this sort of work before and we were told that we had been selected to join the party because there was a need to carry out a little secret work . . . very secret. You know Buganda has recently become a British Protectorate, and in such cases there are always pockets of resistance to change in some quarters. There was a plot against the British brewing and Hunter and I were to discover the leaders of the proposed insurrection. It was necessary, of course, that they should

319

be unaware of our intentions, and because of that we had to cast off our identities as Members of Parliament. We had to work in the utmost secrecy. Because we were Members of Parliament we should immediately be objects of suspicion to those we were meant to track down. So . . . we were kidnapped; not by thieves, but by our own agents. Then we were made aware of what we had to do. It was given out that we were missing and later that we had been murdered. I did stipulate that my family and my fiancée must be told the truth. My father, as a well-known public man, could be trusted and this was conceded.'

'Your father did not tell me.'

'He decided you were too young to be trusted with such a secret. We were not officially engaged. He said that I had no fiancée; and a little word – even a look – could have betrayed the secret and perhaps cost us our lives. You must forgive him, Lucie. He was afraid for me.'

'He need not have been.'

'I know . . . but he was.'

'I went to see your parents. Your father was strange, aloof . . .'

He nodded.

'Oh, Joel, if only I had known!'

'It seems as though Fate was against us. And you, Lucie – you married that man.'

'I was bewildered, lonely. Rebecca – and everyone – advised me. I had to start a new life, they said. It was too much, losing my father and you. You see, I was there with my father when it happened. I actually saw the man who did it. I saw the gun. I saw him fall. I saw everything. Then there was the trial, and I was the one – I was the one whose evidence condemned that man. And then, I lost you, too. I went to France with Belinda and Jean Pascal Bourdon. He is her father, you know. They all thought it would be good for me to get away, and on the boat I met the Fitzgeralds – Phillida and Roland.'

'And you married Roland.'

'They were so good to me. *He* is good to me. He did a great deal to help. I felt I was becoming reconciled . . .'

'Where is he now?'

'In Yorkshire. We are going to have a house there . . . to be near Bradford where his business is. It's the wool trade.'

'And you stopped caring for me.'

'I tried to . . . but I didn't succeed. I would always have remembered. But I could have been happy in a way with Roland, because he has always been so kind and understanding. But I could never forget you and I can never forget what happened to my father. I have been tormented by a terrible fear.'

'Tell me about it.'

'It is this man who murdered my father.'

'This Fergus O'Neill.'

'You knew of him?'

'He was a terrorist, not unknown in this country. The authorities here were aware of him. He was under observation. That was why it was so easy to pick him up. He had been involved in other cases and had nearly been caught on several occasions.'

'So you knew of these things?'

'Well, I've done a little work . . . similar to that I was doing in Buganda. This Irish trouble has gone on for years. Who was it who said: "You can't solve the Irish question, because if you did they would only find another question."? It's been the case since before Cromwell's days. It looks as though it will always be there, no matter what happens. I don't think you need have any qualms about that man. In helping to convict him you have probably saved many lives.'

'There is one thing, Joel. Oh, it is so easy to talk to you. I haven't been able to talk to anyone like this – except Rebecca – since you went away.'

He pressed my hand and I went on: 'The night before my father was killed I saw a man waiting on the other side of the road, watching the house. I saw him from my window. His hat blew off and I saw that he had a decided peak where the hair grew low on his forehead and there was a white scar on his cheek.'

'That's Fergus O'Neill. That distinctive hairline was always against him. It made him so easily recognizable.'

'Joel, I saw that man standing on the same spot. It was *after* he had been executed.'

'How could that be?'

'That's what I wonder. Was there another just like him? Had I helped to convict the wrong man?'

'You were in an overwrought state. Do you think you imagined this?'

'That is what they say. Rebecca said that was the answer and I came to believe it. But it happened again.'

'At the same spot?'

'No. At Manor Grange.'

'Manor Grange?'

'Yes, only a few nights ago. You remember the Grange . . . the haunted seat?'

'Yes,' he said.

'I looked out of the window. The man was sitting there. As I looked he rose and bowed to me. I saw his hair . . . clearly. I saw the scar on his cheek.'

'No!'

'I swear I did.'

'You must have imagined it. Did anyone else see it?'

'No.'

'You were alone, then?'

322

'Roland was with me. He came to the window . . . and there was no one there.'

'It's very odd.'

'I know what you are going to say. It is what everyone says: I imagined it.'

'How could it have been otherwise? Just suppose it was Fergus O'Neill and he had a twin brother who looked exactly like him. Either the wrong brother had been hanged or, if there was no brother, Fergus himself had come back from the grave to haunt you. That's the only logical explanation. I could understand something like this if it were in London. But how would he come down to Manorleigh, change into his opera cloak and hat, walk from the station? It just doesn't make sense.'

'No. I think it was that which finally decided Roland that we must get away.'

'And you propose to go to Yorkshire?'

'They are looking for a house. I was going with them, but when I heard that you were back I had to come here.'

He took my hand and held it fast. 'Lucie,' he said, 'what are we going to do?'

'What can we do?'

'We could drop everything . . . and go away.'

I shook my head.

'You mean you are going to stay with him?'

'I married him.'

'Is that absolutely irrevocable?'

'I think so, Joel.'

'Then what is there for us?'

'For you a great career in politics. This affair of the kidnapping could turn out to be good for you in the long run. My father would have said so.'

'How can it be called good for me if it has lost me you?'

323

'You will recover from that. You will have a great career in Parliament.'

'I came back for you. I am not going to stand by and accept what has been dealt out to me.'

'We have to. I married Roland because it seemed the best thing for me at the time. It was selfish, perhaps. I didn't think I was using him because I thought I had lost the one I really cared for. But I suppose I was. I took that step and there isn't any turning back. Joel, you will have to forget me. I think we should not see each other again. You must go on with your career. It will be a brilliant one. My father always thought highly of you, and he knew. We wanted so much to be together . . . we planned to be together . . . but Fate decided otherwise. We have to accept what *is*, Joel.'

'I don't,' he said. 'I can never forget what we planned together . . . what should have been. You should have waited for me, Lucie.'

'If only I had known! How wonderful it would have been. I loved my father dearly, you know. I was staggering from that blow when I was dealt the other. I had lost you both . . . the two I cared most for . . . the two who cared the most about me. I was bereft. I had to make a new start. Everyone said so. I had to grow away from so much tragedy. And when Roland came along he seemed to offer a way out.'

'Now you tell me, I understand. And Roland, you are fond of him, are you?'

'I like him very much. He is a good man. He has always been kind and tender to me.'

He winced. 'I want to know more about him,' he said.

'He is devoted to his sister Phillida. She, too, has been a good friend to me. Yes, I am fond of them both. Roland has an office in London. He doesn't seem to work very much.

Now and then he has to go to Yorkshire, but he has been mainly in London.'

'And you were in France together?'

'Yes, for just over a month.'

'Where is his office?'

'I have never been to it. I think he mentioned Marcus Court . . . somewhere in the City.'

'I see. And does he have a place in Yorkshire?'

'No. They call the London house a *pied-à-terre*, but there isn't a house in Yorkshire now. That's why he and Phillida are there. They are looking for a suitable place to buy and then we are all going to live there.'

'I see. So you intend to abandon Manor Grange?'

'Oh no. I shall keep it. Roland did suggest selling it after the fire.'

'Fire?'

I told him what had happened and he looked very concerned.

'You might have been burned to death!'

'That's what they said at the time. But it woke me immediately. I was in no real danger.'

He was staring straight ahead.

I said: 'I suppose we should go. They'll be wondering where I am.'

'Not yet,' he said.

We were silent for a few moments. Then he said: 'We could leave everything. We could go away together.'

'I couldn't do it, Joel. I couldn't do that to Roland.'

'So you really do care for him.'

'It wouldn't be right. He has done so much for me. When I needed help he was there. I've got to accept what happened, Joel, and so have you. What you are suggesting is wrong. I have the temptation . . . just as you have. It's what I want . . . to be with you always . . . but it can't be.

325

You've got to go on and become a prominent politician. And I have to go on being Roland's wife.'

'All the time I have been away I have been thinking of coming home to you,' he said.

'It makes me happy to hear you say that, Joel, but at the same time I am desperately sad because it cannot be. You must continue with your career. I shall go to Yorkshire. It is the only thing we can do.'

'I won't accept that,' he said.

'You must.'

We sat for a few moments and then I rose.

'Joel, I must go now.'

He said nothing and we walked soberly back to the house.

No sooner was I in my room than Belinda was there.

'You've been out with Joel Greenham,' she accused.

'How did you know?'

'I saw you come along the street with him. I saw him take your hand and kiss it. Oh Lucie, you look so sad. Are you in love with him?'

'I don't want to talk about it.'

'How like you! It helps to talk, you know. I might be able to help.'

'You? How!'

'Don't sound so surprised. I would do anything to help you. So would Bobby. Think what you did for us. Are you going to leave Roland and go off with Joel?'

'Don't be absurd.'

'Is it absurd? You only married Roland because you thought Joel was dead. Now here he is, returned from the grave, and it is obvious how you feel about each other.'

'Is it?'

'The blind would be aware of it.'

'Belinda, leave me in peace.'

She came to me and kissed me. She was surprisingly tender. 'I know you think I'm a selfish beast, but I do love you, Lucie. I want to repay you all I owe you. I will one day, you'll see.'

'Thank you, Belinda. But the best thing you can do for me now is to leave me in peace.'

She went out ruefully, and I continued to brood. To go away with him? What would that mean? An end to his career for one thing, for there would be a great scandal, of course. Scandals had impaired my father's career and he was not the only one in the family who had suffered in that way. Joel's heart was in politics and, I supposed, in those secret missions which he undertook from time to time. And I? How could I hurt Roland who loved me? I knew he did. He was quiet and gentle, but with such people love went deep. How could I deal him such a blow?

And the alternative? To go on as we were. I must say goodbye to real happiness. All through my life I must be prepared to accept a compromise . . . a second best.

Temptation came. Go to Joel . . . forget everything else. We had been cheated of our life together. Joel wanted us to take it . . . and so did I. But whatever I did, there could not be unalloyed happiness.

If I went with Joel, I should always remember Roland. I would never be able to forget his kind, patient eyes. I could picture his misery when he learned of my defection. Yet on the other hand if I went back to Roland, I would always remember Joel. He would never be out of my thoughts. Whichever way I turned, I could never be truly happy.

I saw Joel again. He came to the house. He was determined to see me, to plead with me.

I met him once more in the Gardens and we sat on the same seat and talked.

He asked a lot of questions about Roland and his sister. I explained how close they were, how their parents had been killed in a railway accident and how they had looked after each other ever since. He asked about the wool business. There was so little I could tell him. When I was in Yorkshire I should surely learn more about it. I was not very interested. I could think of nothing but what I was missing; and I was telling myself that I must not meet Joel again lest I found the temptation, to let everything go and be with him irresistible.

I had been in London for a week and I was thinking that I must go back. Very soon now Bobby and Belinda would be leaving. Celeste wanted me to stay, but she knew that I was in some turmoil and she must have guessed it concerned Joel. Celeste had never intruded –unlike Belinda – and she had always been self-effacing. She was there . . . if one wanted her. Dear Celeste! Her life could not have been a happy one. Perhaps, I thought, few people's are; and it is only the Belindas of this world who are so determined to get what they want that they almost invariably do.

There was a letter from Roland.

My dearest Lucie [he wrote],

We are always saying how sorry we are that you are not with us. The search has not been very fruitful. It is amazing how difficult it is to find suitable property up here.

Something has come up, though. There is a reasonably suitable house here to let. Phillida and I thought we would take it as somewhere to live while we looked around until we find the right place to buy. Obviously that is something which

328

cannot be done in a few weeks . . . not if we are
going to find something we all really like.

We thought we'd stay in this house for a little
while and search. How does that strike you?

Let me tell you the house is called Grey Stone
House. It's a few miles out of Bradford. There are
stables and we could hire horses for a month or so.
So that problem is solved. It's in a sort of village –
Bracken. I thought we might take the house for,
say, three months and renew if necessary. I think it
might take that time to find our place and furnish
and do all that is necessary.

Do you think this is a good idea? We have taken
the house tentatively. Phillida is delighted with it
and she is sure you will be. It is furnished after a
fashion, and there are several rooms. It is by no
means grand, but adequate.

We thought you might join us here. It's not
worth our coming back. What about Wednesday
next? Would that give you time? That is, of course,
if all this is agreeable to you.

Phillida is very excited, but you know what she
is. She likes things to move. I am sure you and she
will throroughly enjoy house-hunting together.

I am so looking forward to Wednesday. It seems
such a long time without you.

I hope you are enjoying London, that Belinda
and Bobby are well, and Celeste better.

With all my love,

Your devoted husband,

Roland.

When I read that letter it seemed to put a seal on
everything. Of course I must go to Yorkshire. I must put an

end to my foolish dreaming of something which could never come to pass.

The night before Belinda and Bobby left she came to my room. I myself was leaving the following day. She looked at me with real concern in her eyes.

'I know what's happening,' she said. 'It's Joel, isn't it? You never really loved Roland. Well, he was nice and in love with you, and we all thought it would be good for you to marry. How were we to know Joel would come back? Oh, Lucie, I'm so sorry for you. It doesn't seem fair somehow. You've always been good to me and I've been awful at times . . . and now here I am with my wonderful old Bobby . . . and Henry doing what we want and it'll soon be through . . . and everything will be fine for us. I do think about you, though.'

'Thank you, Belinda.'

'You sound surprised.' She laughed. 'I do really wish there was something I could do. For you, I mean. I'd like to show you that I do care about other people sometimes – particularly you. Not often, I grant you, but I should so love to help you.'

'There isn't anything you can do, Belinda. It's all so clear. I shall have to go up to Yorkshire. It'll be all right. It has been so far.'

'Oh yes. It *seemed* all right because we thought Joel was dead and you got on well with Roland . . . and there were the three of you. It seemed cosy, but it was really the next best thing, wasn't it? It was because you thought Joel was gone for ever and you were making do with what was left. There's nothing you can do when people are dead, but when they're living – well, I think you should try everything.'

'I appreciate your concern, but you needn't worry. I shall go to Yorkshire and it will work out all right.'

'You're really going to get a house up there?'

'That's the idea.'

'When are you going?'

'Almost at once. They have found a house which they are renting. It's near Bradford, which I believe is the centre of the wool trade.'

'That's miles away.'

'Not so far, really. We shall get a house nearer Bradford, but just at first we shall be in – or near – a little village called Bracken. It sounds rather rural.'

'It will be lonely up there.'

'Oh, there are stables and we shall have horses. In any case, we shall be busy looking at houses and then, when we have found one, getting it ready to move into. We shall not, I suppose, be long in Grey Stone House.'

'That's the name of this house in this Bracken place, is it? Grey Stone House?'

'Yes, that is it.'

'Grey Stone sounds dreary.'

'Most stone is greyish and the country round about will be beautiful. But as I say, we shall only be there a short time.'

She came to me impulsively and put her arms round me.

'I'll be thinking of you, Lucie.'

'And I of you.'

'I do wish that you and Joel . . . I think that would be so wonderful. You're just right for each other.'

'Please, Belinda.'

She went on: 'Roland's a dear, but he is a little dull . . . isn't he? Not like a politician going on missions and getting kidnapped.'

'That's nothing to do with it, Belinda.'

'You're going to change your mind,' she said, her eyes lighting up. 'You're going to do something. You're going to be bold.'

'I am going to Yorkshire, Belinda. I shall be with my husband.'

'To old Grey Stone House . . . in that Bracken place.'

I nodded.

'Oh, Lucie, Lucie . . . !'

I was surprised, for there were genuine tears in her eyes.

I avoided Joel before I left. I dared not see him, for I felt the temptation to leave everything and go with him would be too great to resist.

Belinda and Bobby had gone. They were very tender towards me. I told them how happy I was that their affairs seemed to be working out to their satisfaction.

Belinda said: 'You must come and stay with us soon, mustn't she, Bobby?'

'The sooner the better,' added Bobby.

'It would be nice if you were there when the baby was born.'

'We must arrange that,' said Bobby.

How happy they were, in spite of their difficulties. Belinda had no doubt that they would soon be overcome and she carried Bobby along with her.

What would Belinda have done in my position? I asked myself. She would have gone with Joel. I had no doubt of that. Any trouble which ensued would be settled by others.

But I knew I had to go to Roland.

Celeste was sorry to see me leave. She wanted to come with me to the station, but I hated platform goodbyes and said it would be better for me to go alone.

When I arrived at the station I was surprised to see Joel

there. He had called at the house and Celeste had told him that I had already left.

He came on to the platform with me and saw me on to the train. He stood looking at me pleadingly.

'It's not too late, Lucie,' he said. 'Don't go.'

'I must, Joel.'

The guard was blowing his whistle and in seconds the train would begin to move. He took my hand and held it as though he would never let it go.

He said: 'Lucie, if you would change your mind . . . I'll be waiting.'

I saw him through a haze of tears as we began to move out of the station.

Grey Stone House

A fly had brought me from the station and as soon as I entered Grey Stone House a feeling of chill descended on me. I did not know why I should feel this, for it was much as I had expected. Built of grey stone, as its name indicated, rather ugly and somewhat isolated. It was that isolation which struck me at once.

The country was of the moorland type – flattish and craggy. I could see for miles around and there was only one sign of habitation on the horizon. It looked as though it might be a farmhouse.

Phillida was watching me anxiously.

'We're not very far from Bradford,' she told me. 'And we shan't be here long.'

'No, I suppose not.'

'Come and see the house.'

I stepped into a hall and my sense of despondency deepened. I told myself that it was because I was thinking of Joel, of never seeing him again, turning my back on true love and accepting that for which I had once been grateful, before I was absolutely sure of the depth of my feeling for Joel.

The hall was darkish, for the windows of Grey Stone House were small and leaded, but it was fairly large and there were several doors leading out of it.

'The first thing is for Lucie to inspect the property,'

declared Phillida, 'always remembering, Lucie dear, that it is not for long.'

Roland put his arm through mine. 'The house we shall have will be quite different,' he said. 'But it seemed a good idea to take this for a short period.'

'Other people's furniture never seems right,' commented Phillida. 'I suppose it is because it is not what one would have chosen oneself.'

She threw open one of the doors and disclosed what I supposed was a drawing-room. It was heavily curtained and again I was aware of the darkness. There was a fireplace with a mantelshelf on which were two vases, decorated with flowers, and an ormolu clock. The room was conventionally furnished with a couch and several chairs. The dining-room, laundry-room and kitchen were all close together. As soon as Phillida opened the kitchen door I saw Kitty.

'Hello, Kitty,' I said.

'Good afternoon, Mrs Fitzgerald,' said Kitty.

'Of course, we had to bring Kitty with us,' explained Phillida. 'She looks after us very well, don't you, Kitty?'

'I do my best,' mumbled Kitty. 'I expect you're ready for dinner.'

'How right you are!' cried Phillida.

She shut the door and cried: 'Oh, while you're here, I must show you. There's another room down here. It's quite small but it suits me. I hope you don't mind but I've claimed it as mine. It's my little herbery.'

'This will be where you keep your remedies,' I said.

'Exactly.'

There was a trunk in one corner and, seeing my eyes stray to it, Phillida went on: 'There was no room for that upstairs. It's rather weighty too. It's got some books and clothes in it. I said they needn't bother to take it up. After all, we're not going to be here long.'

335

'You know what Phillida is with her herbs,' said Roland.

'Oh yes. I've been missing the nightcap while I've been away.'

'And obviously you are in need of it. You don't look so good as when we last saw you – but you are going to be better now.'

'Of course . . . when she is with us, I hope,' said Roland, smiling fondly at me. And I thought: How could I ever hurt them? But what of Joel? Wasn't I hurting him?

'You are very pensive, Lucie dear,' said Phillida breezily. 'I don't think you are exactly enamoured of the house.'

'Well, as you say, it is only a starting-off point.'

'Exactly. That's just it. Come on. Let's show you upstairs. There are four rooms . . . a largish bedroom which has been designated to you and Roland. The next in size shall be mine. And there are two other smaller bedrooms.'

We inspected the bedrooms and I saw the short spiral staircase which led to the attics.

'Kitty's quarters,' said Phillida.

'Will she be able to manage the house?'

'Yes, for the time we are here. As we keep saying, it isn't going to be very long.'

'I'm sure it is not,' added Roland.

Phillida looked at him and laughed. 'It really is so exciting,' she said.

I wished I could agree with her.

Darkness fell. Kitty filled lamps with paraffin oil and lighted the wicks. The place looked dismal in the shrouded glow they gave. I felt an impulse to run out of the house.

In the dining-room we partook of the stew which Kitty had made. It was hot, quite appetizing, and I felt better. Roland was watching me anxiously.

'You'll get used to it,' he said quietly. 'Remember it isn't going to be for long. We'll soon find something, then you'll laugh at all this.'

'I think it's fun,' said Phillida.

Kitty had made an apple pie which she brought in proudly.

'The oven's quite good,' she said.

'You've done wonders, Kitty,' Phillida told her. 'Don't you think so, Lucie?'

'Oh yes, I do.'

When the meal was over I said I would finish my unpacking. Roland said he wanted to go out to look at the stables and see about horses for us. He had wanted to consult me and tomorrow would go and see what he could find.

I went up to the bedroom which had been allotted to Roland and me. There was a large walk-in cupboard which would be useful. I tried to lift my spirits by repeating what Roland and Phillida were constantly saying: it will not be for long.

Yes, it will, I thought, it will be for ever.

I toyed with the thought of telling Roland. I knew he would be sympathetic and understanding. It would be better than letting him think I had turned from him. I could not bear to contemplate his caresses. I knew now that I could not be happy with any man but Joel.

There was a knock on the door. It was Phillida, bright and breezy as ever.

'How are you getting on?' she asked.

'Oh, quite well.'

She came into the room. 'I'm afraid you are a little disappointed in this place.'

'Oh, it's all right. It is rather lonely.'

'You feel shut off from everything, do you? But there are the three of us. We'll be all right together. Roland and I are

337

getting used to it. It was just that we couldn't find anything else and we thought . . . just for a short time . . .'

'It will look a lot brighter when the sun shines.'

'We'll start in earnest tomorrow. I just love looking at houses, particularly with the prospect of buying one. Houses are fascinating, I always think. Ugh, it's a bit chilly in here, don't you think?'

'Yes, it is a little.'

'The window's open. Shall we shut it?'

'Yes,' I said and went over to it. I froze with horror. Standing below, looking up at the window, was a figure in a cloak and opera hat.

I gave a little cry.

'So chilly,' Phillida was saying. 'I think we shall need some fires in the bedrooms.'

I was not listening. I was just standing there, staring down. And as I did so, he lifted his hat. Clearly I saw the widow's peak.

I heard Phillida's voice: 'What is it, Lucie?'

She rose and came to stand beside me. I turned to her almost triumphantly because he was still there. Phillida was staring blankly out of the window.

'What is it?' she said. 'What are you looking at?'

'Look . . . look! He's there.'

'What? Where?'

'Down there.' I turned to her. 'Surely you can *see* . . .'

She was looking at me incredulously. I saw fear in her face. 'Oh . . . my God!' I heard her murmur. She sat down on the bed.

I went to her. 'You saw, Phillida. No one can say I imagined it now.'

She looked at me pityingly. 'Oh, Lucie, Lucie . . . I don't know what to say.'

I dragged her back to the window.

He was gone.

'You saw him . . . you can confirm . . .'

She shook her head and avoided looking at me.

'Lucie, I'm sorry. I saw nothing. There was nothing there.'

'You can't mean that. You're lying.'

'Oh Lucie, I wish I were.'

I was astounded and angry.

I cried: 'You *did* see him. You *must* have. He was standing there. He took off his hat and bowed. You must have seen his hair.'

'Lucie, my dear, dear Lucie, there was no one there.'

'I saw him, I tell you, I saw him!'

'Lucie dear, you have had a terrible shock . . . Sometimes it takes a long time to get over these things.'

'You are not telling the truth. Why do you lie?'

'How I wish I were! How I wish I could say I saw him. I'd give anything to say I did. But I didn't. I just didn't. Truly, there was no one there.'

I covered my face with my hands. She was lying, I was telling myself. She must be. But why?

Roland had come into the room. 'What on Earth is the matter?' he asked.

'Oh, Roland,' said Phillida. 'It was terrible . . .'

'What? What are you talking about?'

'Lucie saw – or thought she saw –'

'I *saw*! I *saw*!' I shouted.

'It was the ghost again.'

'Where?'

'Down there. Outside. The one Lucie thought she saw before.'

'Oh, Lucie,' said Roland. 'My dear Lucie.'

'I was there with her, Roland. There wasn't anybody there.'

'She saw him,' I said. 'She must have seen him. She's not telling the truth. Why? Why?'

'I think you should get to bed, Lucie. Phillida . . .' He looked towards the door. He was telling her to go. She disturbed me. 'Come, Lucie,' he went on. 'Tell me about it. Was it . . . the same?'

Phillida was at the door. 'I'll get something to drink,' she said. 'It will do her a lot of good.'

Roland sat beside me.'

'Tell me all about it,' he said soothingly.

'I went to the window and I saw him there. I called to Phillida. She came. She was right beside me. She said she couldn't see anything. She must have seen him. He was there . . . right there.'

He stroked my hair. 'Lucie,' he said, 'why don't you get to bed. You're tired out.'

'Please don't treat me like an imbecile, Roland,' I said sharply.

'It's the last thing I want to do. But you are tired out.'

'I don't like this place.'

'I'm sorry.'

'It's not for long, you're going to say. I don't like it for one night, let alone a month.'

'Look, Lucie. You're here with us. With me. I'll make everything all right. We'll find something soon. There'll be all the fun of getting it how we want it.'

I wanted to shout at him: I don't want a new house. I want to go to Joel.

'Look, why don't you get undressed and slip into bed? You'll find everything different in the morning.'

'Why did Phillida say she saw nothing when she so obviously did?'

'It could have been a trick of the light.'

'That's nonsense. He was down there. I saw the opera hat and his awful unmistakable hair.'

'Perhaps Phillida couldn't see as well. The light . . .'

It was no use. Mechanically, I undressed and lay down. I wanted to shut out everything. I longed to be back before that tragic day when my father was killed. I felt an overwhelming need to leave this house which I had begun to dread. I wanted to go back to Celeste tomorrow. I wanted to meet Joel at the Round Pond and talk and talk until we found some solution. I wanted to say: I am coming to you. I cannot live any other life.

There was a knock on the door. It was Phillida. She was carrying a tray on which were two mugs filled with a steaming beverage.

'One for each of you,' she said. 'It has been a tiring day.' She set the tray down. 'Sleep well,' she went on; and left us.

I did sleep well. I awoke to find myself alone. I saw that it was nine o'clock and I was amazed, for I usually awoke at seven.

I got out of bed and went to the leaded window. I looked down. I saw nothing but the moor stretching out before me. It undulated slightly. I saw the boulders and the sun glinted on little rivulets, making them shine like silver. It was beautiful in a wild way.

Kitty looked in. She asked if I wanted hot water now and I told her I did.

She brought it and I washed. I had slept so well that I felt a little better. I could not stop thinking of last night's apparition, but it was strange how different everything seemed by daylight.

I was sure I had seen him there, but Phillida had not. Could it really be that it was my imagination? He had seemed so clear. How could Phillida not have seen him, unless it was a ghost who appeared to me and not to others?

Why should she lie? There didn't seem to be any point in her doing so. On that other occasion when I had seen him, he had gone before I could get Roland to see him. I wondered if he would have been invisible to Roland as well as to Phillida. It did seem as though I might be suffering from hallucinations.

I was trying to look at this clearly. It had been a terrible strain. It was mainly my evidence which had sent that man to the gallows. Had that preyed on my mind?

I had hated Phillida last night. But that was not fair, for somehow I had felt that she had desperately wanted to say she had seen the man. But of course she had to tell the truth.

I must not blame her because I was becoming a little – what was it? – mentally disturbed through all that had happened.

I *was* mentally disturbed. Terrible things had happened to me. It is mentally disturbing to see someone whom you love dearly shot dead at your feet and then to be called on to identify his murderer. This man had died violently. It was said that people who died in such circumstances did sometimes return to this world.

Rebecca had thought the dead could return. She firmly believed that our mother had come back to beg her to take care of me. She referred to it now and then and always with conviction. If my mother returned, why not a man who had been hanged? And to whom should he return but to the one who had helped to bring about his end?

He was a murderer, I kept telling myself. He deserved to die. He had killed my father and, if he had lived, others might have died in the same way; no doubt others had. My father would not have been the first. He was a terrorist and an anarchist. He was no less a murderer because he had killed for a cause.

I must be reasonable. If I had seen him and Phillida had not, he must be a ghost. If that were so, there was a modicum of comfort for me, for I had had the fear that I had helped to convict the wrong man and it was the murderer himself who visited me in the flesh to mock me and disturb my conscience.

This was how I had felt in the days following my father's death. In the last year or so I had grown a little away from the nightmare and for long periods had ceased to think about it.

Now I wondered if I ever should.

Temporarily last night's events had taken my mind from the great problem of how I was going to continue my life with Roland when I wanted only to be with Joel.

I went downstairs. Phillida was in the dining-room.

'Oh hello, Lucie,' she said brightly, as though last night had not happened. 'Did you sleep well?'

'Yes, thank you,' I replied.

'It never fails. It's a herbal tea. Thoroughly recommended by that wonderful health shop in London. Remember? The one I promised to take you to?'

'Yes. I . . . I'm sorry about last night. I . . . said you were lying.'

'Oh!' She laughed. 'Forget it. You were overwrought. I quite understand it. I should have been the same. These things happen, you know. I'm sorry I had to say what I did. But you understand. I couldn't do anything else. You'll see. It's only a temporary thing. I've known it happen to people before. The best thing is to ignore it and it'll be forgotten in no time. Roland's gone off to see about horses. He said that is the first priority. We've got to be able to get about. And he is going to find out if there are any houses for sale at the same time. What do you want to do?'

'I thought I'd like to walk a little.'

'You don't mind if I don't come with you? There are one or two things I want to see to in the house. I can't leave it all to Kitty. Have some coffee and I'll get Kitty to make you some toast. We'll have to think about food, I suppose. Don't worry. You go alone . . . but don't go far. Don't get lost. It's pretty open here, isn't it? So you can see where you are.'

She went to the kitchen and I heard her talking to Kitty.

When she came back she said: 'Kitty's getting it right away. She won't be long. She's a treasure really . . . and I think she is rather glad to come here. She was very much aware of Mrs Emery's disapproval. It shouldn't have been directed against Kitty. It wasn't her fault I brought her in. It was mine, of course. But I will say that most of the disapproval came my way.'

'You mustn't take that too seriously. Mrs Emery's a good sort, but she is rather a stickler for conventions.'

'And I, alas, offended them.'

'It is very easy to do that.'

She laughed and I joined in. She looked very pleased.

'A nice little walk will do you good,' she said. 'I was thinking – if we had a little dogcart we'd be able to get into Bradford to shop comfortably.'

'That sounds as if we are going to be here for a long time.'

'Oh, good heavens no! I reckon we'll be out of here in a few weeks. The dogcart would be useful, though, wherever we were.'

'Yes, I suppose it would.'

'I'll talk to Roland about it. We both will.'

I was silent and Kitty brought in toast and coffee.

I came out into the fresh air. It was wonderfully invigorating. I stood outside the house and asked myself which way. I gazed towards the dwelling on the horizon and decided to make my way in that direction.

The keen air revived my spirits to some extent and I picked my way carefully over the springy turf. I was wondering whether I might tell Roland that I had met Joel again. He was so kind and understanding. I felt at moments that it might be helpful to talk to him; but at others I realized how difficult it would be.

I could see the farmhouse now. It appeared to be in a little hollow – to give it shelter, perhaps. I imagined how the wind would come sweeping across the open space.

The land was cultivated here. I could see sheep grazing and, as I came near to the house, some cowsheds. The people who lived here would be our closest neighbours. Not for long, I could hear Phillida saying.

Somewhere at the back of my mind I thought that it would be comforting to have neighbours – even though they must be almost a mile away.

I was close to the house now. I could see its grey stone clearly, similar to ours. I saw the courtyard with a few fowl roaming round, pecking at the earth. There was what appeared to be an orchard at the side of the house. I walked towards this and a childish voice called: 'Hello!'

A girl was seated on a swing fixed between two trees and a boy was pushing her. They looked about eight or nine years old.

'Hello,' I replied. 'Do you live here?'

They nodded and the boy pointed in the direction of the farmhouse. The girl stretched out her legs and moved them so that the swing rose higher. I stood for a moment, watching.

Then the boy said: 'You from Grey Stone?'

'Yes. And you must be our nearest neighbours.'

'Reckon.'

The girl scraped her feet along the ground and brought the swing to a standstill. 'Happen you won't stay long,' she said. 'People don't.'

I stood watching them for a second or so, and as I was preparing to walk away, I heard a voice calling: 'Daisy, you in that orchard?'

'Yes, Mam.'

A woman came into sight. She wore a print apron over a dark brown skirt and cotton blouse. Her hair was pulled into a knot at the nape of her neck and several strands had escaped from it.

'Oh,' she said, stopping short when she saw me. 'You must be one of them from Grey Stone.'

'Yes,' I told her. 'We've only just moved in.'

'How long will you be staying there? People don't stay long at Grey Stone.'

'No. I gather it is let out for short periods.'

'Well, seeing as we're neighbours – if only for a short while – come in and have a glass of cider.'

The invitation was given spontaneously and I felt it would be churlish to refuse. So I said I should be delighted to.

She took me through the orchard to the house. We crossed the yard where the chickens were rooting about for food, and she led the way into a large kitchen. It was warm, for there was a huge fire with an oven beside it. I could smell something savoury cooking.

'I'm Mrs Hellman,' she said, 'the farmer's wife. Them out there swinging is our two, Jim and Daisy.'

'It is nice to meet you and so kind of you to invite me in. I'm Mrs Fitzgerald.'

'Don't come from these parts, I see.'

'Oh no.'

'From the South, reckon.'

'Yes.'

'And you're at Grey Stone with your husband?'

'My husband and my sister-in-law.'

'Oh, the three of you. Got any help up there?'

'We brought a maid with us.'

'That's good for you. There's not much to be had round here, not unless you have them living in.'

'Yes. We are a little isolated here.'

She moved to a barrel. There was a tap at the side and she poured the cider into two pewter mugs.

She set them on the table and smiled at me.

'We like to be neighbourly up here, you know,' she explained. 'We're blunt. And honest. None of that waltzing around what you're trying to say to cover it up and make it sound nice. We say what we mean . . . and if them that hears it don't like it, well, they must take it as it comes.'

'Perhaps it's the best way.'

'So you're only staying for a short while?'

'We're looking for a house.'

'So you're settling up here?'

'If we can find the right house.'

'In Bradford, I suppose. That's a fine town.'

'I'm looking forward to seeing it.'

'What sort of house are you looking for?'

'Something not too new. I rather like old houses.'

'Plenty of them round here. I came here when I married and reckon I wouldn't want to move till they carry me out in my coffin. Hellman's family have farmed here for years. It's hard land to farm. Too much of the moor. Hellman often says we ought to sell up and go somewhere where the land's more fertile. But there's some good sheep country around here.'

'Yes, I know. My husband is in wool.'

'Oh, that explains it, you being here and all that. How's the cider?'

'Delicious.'

'See that old barrel? My husband's grandmother and her grandmother before her made cider in that. There's something about the flavour. It's all our own.'

'You must have a great deal to do.'

She laughed at me. 'On the go most of the time. That's why it's so nice to sit down and chat with a neighbour over a mug of cider. My husband knows a lot of what goes on round here. He would, of course, living here all his life. He rides into Bradford quite often. He knows most of the wool people there. Fitzgerald, you say? I can't say I've heard of him but I reckon Hellman will know him.'

'My husband has not been up here very often. He has an office in London, but he thinks he should be here more. That's why we are going to look for a house.'

'Well, I'm pleased. Grey Stone's been empty for over a year. I don't like houses to stand empty . . . and as I'm saying, it's nice to have neighbours. If you want anything at any time, you just pop over.'

'That's kind of you. Alas, it is rather far.'

'You're in the country now. We don't live on top of each other. You're from London, I reckon. You've got the look of it.'

She smiled, faintly amused, admiring me with a hint of contempt for one who was a stranger to the fresh winds of open spaces.

I said: 'I have lived a long time in London . . . and in the country, too.'

'The country! Not Yorkshire.'

'No. Quite near London. A place called Manorleigh.'

'Manorleigh. That rings a bell.'

I thought: I shouldn't have mentioned it. She will be remembering. Headlines flashed into my mind: '*The Member for Manorleigh was shot dead outside his house in London today*.'

And up to that moment from the time I had seen the children I had not thought of it and my dilemma.

'Yes,' she said. 'I seem to have heard of that place.'

I said quickly: 'So we are coming to Yorkshire – if we can find something.'

'You won't find a finer place to live in the whole of England.'

'It's certainly beautiful,' I said. The dangerous moment was past. She had forgotten Manorleigh.

'By the way,' she said, 'if you want fresh eggs at any time, one of the children would bring them to you . . . or I would myself. Hellman says the eggs are my affair. Well, it gives me a bit of pocket money and they're not much trouble really.'

'Perhaps I could take some back with me,' I said.

'Well, if you'd like to.' She went to the door and shouted: 'Patty!'

I heard an answering voice from some way off. She came back to the table. 'Patty's the dairy maid. I'll tell her to get some eggs for you. How many would you like? A dozen?'

'I should think that would be good.'

The door opened and Patty came in – plump like her mistress, with rosy cheeks and fair curly hair.

'This is Mrs Fitzgerald, Patty,' said Mrs Hellman. 'Just moved into Grey Stone.'

'Oh,' said Patty. 'That's nice.'

'She's taking a dozen eggs. Pick some of the big brown ones for her. Show her what a good country egg is like. She comes from London.'

Patty said: 'I'll get some of the nice big brown ones, Mrs Hellman.'

'You do that,' said my hostess.

While we finished our cider she told me about the difficulties of farming: the droughts, the high winds and the unpredictable weather generally. She said she hoped we'd be comfortable at Grey Stone. We were not far from Bracken.

'It's only a little village, but there are a few shops there. About a mile or so away. Hellman goes in every three or four days to pick up the post. Well, you can't expect them to deliver it out here. The only places are us and Grey Stone. You couldn't expect it, could you? So in he goes every day or so to collect it. There's a little post-office place in Bracken. It works all right. You'll be comfortable in Grey Stone, I reckon. It's a bit higher than the farm and the winds whistle round the place something shocking at times. Poeple say the place is haunted, but you don't want to listen to them. You don't look the sort who'd believe that kind of nonsense, coming from London. We don't hold with it much up here. But some people get silly ideas in their heads and when a place is empty . . . you know what it is.'

'I didn't know it had that reputation.'

'Well, it's no more than any old house gets, particularly if it is left standing empty.'

'Has it always been let out?'

'Since old Hargreaves died. That would be eight or nine years ago. He lived there with his old housekeeper. His family didn't bother much. They were after his bit of money. Then his son and son's wife came down to look after him. It wasn't long after that he was in his coffin. Of course, there were rumours. Did the old man die naturally or did they give him a little push? They got the house. We

350

all thought they'd sell, but they didn't. They did this letting and you get people there . . . for a while. Then they're off.'

The door opened and Patty came in with the eggs.

'There,' said Mrs Hellman. 'A dozen of the best.'

I paid her what she asked and she put the money in a box on a shelf with an air of satisfaction.

I was grateful for the cider and her friendliness. I felt remarkably pleased that we had a near and affable neighbour.

I said: 'I am sure we shall want more eggs. Although it's my sister-in-law who does the housekeeping. Could you send us another dozen in a week's time?'

She beamed her pleasure. 'Either I or one of the children will bring them over.'

Her eyes sparkled at the prospect. I could see that she was full of curiosity to see what the new neighbours were like; and as I rose to go she said how pleased she was that I had called.

'If there's one thing I like, it's being neighbourly,' she said. 'After all, we're only here once, aren't we? We might as well make the most of it. And here we are, out here, away from things, you might say. It's only good sense that we know each other.'

I agreed with her, said goodbye and carefully carried the eggs back to Grey Stone House.

Roland had returned and he and Phillida greeted me as I came in.

'How are you?' asked Roland anxiously.

'A lot better, thanks. I have been for a long walk and it has been quite interesting. I have met our nearest neighbours and I've brought back some eggs. I have ordered a dozen to be sent in a week's time. Is that all right?'

Phillida seized on the eggs. 'Marvellous. Oh, they're beauties. So we shall have eggs in constant supply.'

'We shan't need to bring them back from Bracken in the dogcart,' I said.

'What's this about a dogcart?' asked Roland.

We told him and he thought it was a good idea.

'I was invited in and given some cider,' I told them.

'My goodness,' said Roland with a smile. 'You do move fast.'

'The people are very friendly here. They may seem a bit gruff and they are impatient with our more diplomatic southern ways. Here a spade is called a spade, I gather. That's what was implied. However, beneath the rough exteriors . . .'

'I know,' put in Phillida, 'beat hearts of gold. It's wonderful about the eggs.'

'Their name is Hellman,' I said. 'There are two children, Jim and Daisy.'

'You have discovered a lot.'

'I did learn that Mr Hellman's grandfather and his father before him farmed on the same land. They've got sheep, too, so they know about wool. Mrs Hellman reckons her husband is on good terms with all the wool people in Bradford.'

'Oh?' said Roland rather quietly.

'Did you tell her we were concerned in the wool trade?' asked Phillida.

'Of course. It couldn't have been all one-sided. She said she had never heard of the Fitzgeralds.'

'I expect she enjoyed your visit,' said Phillida. 'It must be lonely for her out there. Visitors would be welcome.'

'I am sure that is so. I'm glad you are pleased about the eggs.'

'Now listen to Roland's news,' said Phillida.

'I've got the horses,' he said. 'They are being brought over this afternoon. There will be a nice little chestnut mare for you, Lucie.'

'That's lovely. And they are coming this afternoon?'

'I asked them to be quick. I want you and Phillida to be satisfied with what you are having.'

'Of course we shall be!' cried Phillida. 'Go on, Roland.'

'There is the possibility of a house. It's just outside the city. It sounds delightful.'

'How old?'

'This will please you. Eighteenth-century. It sounds elegant and is quite spacious. As far as I could gather, it has a lot of interesting features.'

'When can we go and see it?'

'The owners are living there. They haven't moved out yet.'

'That means that it would be a long time before we could move in.'

'No. They are ready to move out as soon as the sale is completed. They are away for a few days, but as soon as they come back we can view it.'

'Isn't that wonderful!' cried Phillida. 'I confess to feeling as impatient as you do.'

'So,' said Roland, 'we shall have to wait for a few days till they return, and then . . . well, let's hope it is all the agent says it is.'

'So it was a successful morning,' I said.

'Very,' replied Roland. 'And the best thing about it all is that you are feeling better.'

'Lunch will be served very soon,' said Phillida. 'What about an omelette with Mrs Hellman's eggs?'

'That sounds good,' I replied. 'I'll just go up to change my riding boots.'

'Don't be long. I'll take the eggs to Kitty.'

I went up to the room I shared with Roland. I don't want this house, I thought. I shall have to explain to Roland. It isn't fair to him not to. He's so kind and thoughtful, and he will notice the difference in me. I must tell him.

I took off my boots and put on a pair of shoes. There was water in the ewer so I washed my hands.

When I went down Phillida and Roland were in the dining-room. They were talking very quietly, but with some heat, which was unusual with them. I caught a few snatches of what Phillida was saying. 'It'll have to be soon. It should have been over by now. It's your fault. You were the one who wanted to wait.'

As I entered she stopped abruptly and I fancied she looked a little startled. Then she said lightly: 'I was scolding Roland. I was telling him that if he had gone to see about the horses earlier we should have had them by now.' She laughed. 'I was really cross with him, which was very wrong of me. Well, you can't keep an omelette waiting.'

Kitty brought in the food and we all agreed that it was delicious.

'The eggs are so fresh,' said Phillida. 'Possibly laid this morning. Good for you, Lucie, making such good use of exploring our local colour.'

A few days passed. Several times I had been on the point of telling Roland that I was in love with Joel and for that reason the relationship could not be the same as it had previously been between us. I reminded myself that I had thought I had loved him, that I had been very eager that we should have a normal and happy marriage. But now that I had seen Joel, talked with him, I realized what I had lost and I could never really be reconciled.

Roland knew that I was disturbed and thought it was due to the visions I had seen – or as he would say, 'thought I saw'. He knew I was in a disturbed state. I was indeed – both because of what I had seen and my loss of Joel.

He was not a passionate man. There had been no intensity in his love-making. Ignorant as I was of such matters, that thought had only just occurred to me. He was a kind, gentle, sensitive person. His great purpose really did seem to be to comfort me. Sometimes I felt he understood more than anyone else what I had suffered through the loss of my father. I could not have had a more gentle, more kindly husband. When we retired and I was alone with him he somehow made me understand that he would make no demands on me. I was upset, he implied. I was going through a bad time. I would get better soon, but in the meantime I needed to be quiet. I needed sleep.

I was grateful to him and at the same time I was grappling with myself as to whether or not I should tell him. The thought came to me that I could become free of him, dissolve my marriage as Belinda had done; and then marry Joel.

If Belinda had achieved it without too much trouble, why should not I?

I knew what Belinda's reaction would be. She would say I was a fool not to try. But it was different in her case. She and Henry Farrell had parted; they had quarrelled violently; whereas from Roland I had had nothing but love and understanding and I knew that he cared for me deeply.

How could I hurt him? And yet . . . what of Joel?

If I went to Joel I should never be able to forget Roland; and if I stayed with Roland I could not get Joel out of my thoughts; it seemed that I should be beset either by deep, disturbing regrets or a perpetual longing for what I had missed.

Each day I woke to this uncertainty. Should I? Could I? How could I go on like this?

So . . . how grateful I was to Roland for leaving me in peace.

We had our horses now. It was a relief to be able to ride.

355

The three of us went out together to explore; but mostly Roland and I were on our own. How many times, during those rides, was I on the verge of telling him everything; but I never managed it. I could not help being pleased that he had to spend a certain amount of time in Bradford on business. That left Phillida and me on our own.

Phillida was very kind and gentle. She was interested in maintaining good health and thought herself something of an authority on the subject. I remarked that she must miss her health shop in London.

'Oh, who knows?' she said blithely. 'I may find one in Bradford. They are springing up all over the country. They are such a boon. I'll guarantee I'll cure you, Lucie. It's taken a little time.'

'Cure me?'

'Well, all this nervousness.'

I was silent and she put her hand over mine. 'You must take more exercise. I'm so glad Roland had the horses sent. You looked in such good health when you came in from your gallop. I thought: This is the way. A healthy body means a healthy mind. I believe some sage said that once, and how right he is! All the same, you need these little pick-me-ups from time to time.'

'You and Roland have been so good to me.'

'Of course we have. We have good reason to be.'

'Just that meeting on the ferry . . . and all this. Life is strange, isn't it?'

'Very strange . . . and wonderful. I believe it is what we make it.'

'Oh, you believe in giving Fate a little jog, do you?'

She threw back her head and laughed. She had very hearty laughter. 'Well, why not? Who's going to help you if you don't help yourself? Aren't you thrilled because this afternoon we are going to see the house?'

'Oh yes. It will be interesting.'

'You don't sound wildly enthusiastic.'

'Well, Phillida, I'm not sure. We seem to be so far away . . .'

'Nonsense. Once we are settled you'll be able to go and stay at Manorleigh . . . and go to London. Don't forget Roland has business there, too.'

'Yes, of course.'

'So cheer up. I thought we'd have an early lunch. Then we'll go and see this wonderful house. Roland should be back soon. Listen . . . I think I can hear him.'

It was Roland. He looked anxiously at me as soon as he came in.

'Looking forward to seeing the house, Lucie?' he asked almost pleadingly.

'Yes, of course,' I lied.

We set out after lunch and rode in the direction of the big town –through the little village of Bracken, which seemed to consist of one long street and an inn and a church. I caught a glimpse of the shop which appeared to sell a variety of goods; it had a sign over it indicating that it was a post office. I remembered what Mrs Hellman had told me about collecting letters.

There would be none to collect. I had not given anyone the address. I must write to Celeste and Rebecca and to Belinda, perhaps. It would be comforting to hear from them and would make me feel less remote.

In due course we found the house. It stood back from the road in pleasant grounds. We rode up the drive and when we arrived at the house a groom came out to take our horses.

A man and woman came out; they were obviously expecting us.

'You are of course Mr and Mrs and Miss Fitzgerald,' said

the man. 'Do come in. We are delighted that you have come to see the house.'

'It is very charming,' said Phillida. 'What lovely gardens! I do like this type of architecture.'

'I always think it is one of the most interesting periods,' said the man. 'By the way, I am George Glenning and this is my wife.'

We shook hands and then went up the stone steps to the front door with its spiderweb fanlight and highly polished brass knocker. Then we were in the hall, which was lofty and spacious. There was a staircase at the end of the hall; it curved gracefully upwards.

'The main rooms are on the first floor,' said Mrs Glenning. 'There is a rather fine drawing-room. In fact, it can make a ballroom, can't it, George?'

He replied: 'Well, at times we have put it to that use. But let our visitors decide for themselves. Shall we start on the ground floor?'

We went through several rooms. I was thinking: I can't live here. I have to get away. Of course, it is a charming house, and of course Roland wants his own home. But I shall have to explain.

We went into the drawing-room. It was quite magnificent, but I could not concentrate.

Mrs Glenning was looking at me expectantly. Phillida was so enthusiastic, declaring her delight in the house.

'Mrs Fitzgerald,' began Mrs Glenning, 'are you feeling . . . ?'

I tried to pull myself together, to feign an interest in the house.

Phillida said in a soothing voice: 'My sister-in-law has not been very well lately.'

She was looking at Mrs Glenning as though trying to convey something to her.

Phillida went on: 'She is really loving it all, aren't you, Lucie?' She spoke to me almost chidingly, yet indulgently, as one might speak to a child.

'Yes, yes,' I said quickly. 'It's very charming.'

'Do you like this window?' asked Mrs Glenning. 'It's typical of the period, isn't it, George? George looked up a few details when we came here. He was very taken with everything.'

'I can imagine most people would be,' said Roland.

Phillida had put her arm round me protectively. 'It's lovely, isn't it, Lucie?'

And so on . . . through the house. It certainly was delightful and I thought that if Joel were with me and it was for us how thrilled I should be.

We reached the nursery – two light, airy rooms at the top of the house. There were bars across the windows.

'They were put up for the safety of the children,' Mrs Glenning explained. 'But they could easily be removed.'

Phillida said quickly: 'Oh no. They might become very useful.'

'You mean when the children come?' said Mrs Glenning almost archly.

'Well, I was thinking of that,' said Phillida with a faint air of embarrassment.

When we had seen everything we were invited to take tea in the drawing-room.

'How kind!' said Phillida. 'Oh, I do like this house. I hope it is going to be ours.'

Roland was looking at me anxiously. 'I . . . I think we shall have to talk it over together,' he said.

The Glennings were looking at me rather curiously.

'But of course,' said Mr Glenning. 'You cannot make a hasty decision. We have some more people coming to see it tomorrow, though. So remember, if you should

359

decide you want it you should get in touch with us immediately.'

'It's the sort of house that won't stay long on the market,' said Phillida. She looked at me almost pleadingly. 'You *do* like it, Lucie?'

'I think it is a very beautiful house,' I said.

'That's wonderful.' She was now looking expectantly at Roland.

'Lucie and I will want to consider a few things,' he said.

Phillida sighed and looked faintly but indulgently exasperated. It was typical of her that she would have liked Roland to have come to a decision right away.

'If you would like to look over it again . . .' said Mrs Glenning.

'That wouldn't be necessary for me,' said Phillida. 'Roland, you too. You love it, don't you? I can see you do. It's just what we had in mind. And it's in the right spot. It's even near the town, and of course there's the station nearby so that we could easily get the train to London.'

'It certainly seems to fulfil our requirements.' Roland was looking at me, too, but I said nothing.

We had had tea and were preparing to leave. I was in the hall with Roland and Phillida had gone back into the kitchen. There was something she wanted to look at again.

Roland was talking to Mr Glenning about the Adam doorway and I had moved a little apart. I heard Phillida's voice. 'I think it is almost certain. We love it, my brother and I. My sister-in-law . . . she has been rather unwell. We feel we have to be careful.' There was a pause. A whisper.

Then Mrs Glenning said: 'Poor lady, I do hope she will soon be well.'

'We are going to make sure that she is,' said Phillida. 'It is just a matter of a little care, I am sure.'

They came out and joined us, smiling brightly.

I thought Mrs Glenning looked at me oddly, almost pityingly. We said goodbye and Roland promised them that he would be in touch very soon.

When we reached Grey Stone House, it looked more grim than ever in comparison with the house we had just seen.

'What a difference!' said Phillida. 'I do hope we don't have to stay here much longer. I thought the house was lovely. Just what we wanted. What didn't you like about it, Lucie?'

'I . . . I thought it was a fine house, too,' I said. 'It's just that I am uncertain about being here.'

'Still hankering after London and Manorleigh? Oh well, that's understandable, isn't it, Roland? You've always been there. Naturally you feel a little strange at first. But it will pass. When you are feeling better, you'll see what a wonderful place it is.'

'Phillida,' I said firmly, 'I am not ill.'

'Oh, no, of course not. You're just a little upset. You're going to be perfectly well. You're going to love it here. Roland and I are going to look after you.'

I smiled faintly at her. It was ungrateful of me but I felt irritated.

That night I did talk to Roland.

We were alone in our room. Phillida had brought our nightcap and said goodnight.

I burst out suddenly: 'Roland, I've got to talk to you. I've got to explain.'

'Yes?' he said. 'Tell me what it is. I know something is on your mind. It's not only the . . .' He hesitated. He knew I hated it to be referred to as the vision or the ghost.

'It's Joel Greenham.'

He looked at me in astonishment and I went on quickly:

'Joel and I were engaged to be married. It was not official but it was understood between us. Then he went away and was reported dead. You see, that was why . . . Everything seemed hopeless. My father dead. Joel, too. I shouldn't have done it, Roland. I should never have married you.'

'Lucie!'

'Wait,' I went on. 'Listen to what I have to say. You see, Roland, I love Joel. I always have, ever since I was a little girl. It was only because I was so young that we were not already married. But we were going to announce our engagement on his return.'

'And now he has come back,' Roland said sadly. 'I think I understand. You were convinced that you would never see him again and you were very unhappy. And you liked us, you liked Phillida . . . and me. We got on so well together. We were happy together, weren't we?'

I nodded.

'And,' he went on, 'You would have been happier . . . if he had not come back.'

It was true, I supposed. I had begun to be reconciled. I could picture quite a happy life ahead with Roland. I thought we should have children and they would have made up for a good deal. Phillida was my good friend.

'Perhaps,' I said. 'But he has come back.'

'You have seen him?'

'Yes. When I was in London.'

'And he has talked to you . . . about us?'

'Yes.'

'What does he want?'

I did not answer and Roland went on: 'I know what he wants. He wants you to leave me and go to him.'

There was silence. I looked at him miserably and felt I could never be happy, whatever happened.

'And you?' he went on.

'I . . . I . . .' I stammered.

He smiled rather wanly. 'What do you want, Lucie? Don't be afraid to tell me.'

I could not bear to answer.

'I love you very much,' he said.

'Yes. I know.'

'I can't imagine my life without you.'

'You have always been so good to me. I can never forget that.'

'But you love him.'

'I am fond of you, Roland . . . and I should hate to hurt you.'

'The time we have been together has been wonderful for me. I don't know whether I could let you go. But it is what you want. It is what you are asking me.'

For a few seconds there was silence.

Then he went on: 'I knew there was something. Ever since you have been back from London – before that, even – I thought everything was not well.'

He stood up and went to the window and looked out. It was as though he could not bear to look at me.

I went and stood beside him. I looked down, half expecting to see that dreaded figure. There was nothing . . . only the empty moorland. The wind had risen and it moaned like someone in pain as it ruffled the grass.

He turned to me and gripped my hand. 'Lucie, don't do anything rash, please.'

'Rash?' I repeated.

'Wait awhile. Think about this. Promise me you won't do anything without telling me first. I do deserve that, don't I?'

'Oh Roland, you deserve the best – the best of everything. I wish . . .'

'You wish things were different. Oh, so do I, Lucie. So do I. I think you could be happy here . . . with me. You couldn't just walk out and leave me.'

'Not like that, Roland,' I said. 'And I should always remember you . . . whatever happened.'

'It may not be the right thing for you, Lucie. I want you to be happy. That's what I want most of all. But you must be sure that it is right for you.'

'Do you mean that if you thought it was right for me you would agree?'

'I don't know. I can't think clearly. It has been too much of a shock. It's not your fault, of course. It's circumstances. I want time – time to think. That's it, Lucie. Give ourselves time. Let's think about it, talk about it. I don't know whether I could give you up. I know that it would be the good and noble thing to do and that I should – because it is what you want. I don't know whether I am strong enough. I like to think that if I were sure it was the right thing for you, I would do it. But I am not sure, Lucie. I'm terribly unsure.'

'I know, I know.'

'And, Lucie, I believe you are unsure, too.'

He took my face in his hands and kissed my forehead gently.

'Let's think about it,' he said. 'Let's not make hasty decisions.'

I nodded. 'Oh, Roland,' I cried. 'I'm so glad I told you.'

'Yes,' he said. 'So am I. Even in something like this it is better to know the truth.'

Roland went off next morning before I was up. I felt a certain relief because I had spoken to him. He himself had said it was better to know, and he was right. I wondered what he would do. He was a very unselfish man and I was

364

sure that he meant it when he said that if he could convince himself that it was best for me, he would let me go. He would release me; he would give me the sort of divorce which Henry Farrell was giving Belinda – and that would leave me free to marry Joel.

The thought did not fill me with the joy it might have done if it had not been that to go to Joel would mean hurting Roland. I had grown to care for him and he dearly loved me. But perhaps he would find someone in due course, marry and have children. Phillida would make an excellent aunt. Perhaps she herself would marry. I wondered why she had not. She was attractive with her vivacity and her moderately good looks; she was always graceful and elegant. I had never seen her otherwise.

She was a year or so younger than Roland and that was not very old.

I went down to breakfast. Phillida looked at me with some anxiety. 'How are you feeling?'

'I'm all right, thanks. And you?'

'Very well,' she replied. 'Roland didn't look so good this morning. I made a special porridge for him. It's full of goodness. Poor lamb, he didn't want to eat it, but I made him. If I didn't know he was as strong as a horse I'd be worried and think he was sickening for something. He said he didn't sleep so well. That was all.'

'Did he say when he would be back?'

'No. He wasn't sure. It's going to be a busy day. He's neglected business up here so much in the past months.'

After lunch I rode into the village of Bracken. I saw the post-office-cum-store again and reminded myself that I must write to Rebecca. There was so much that I could have said to her if I had been with her. It would not be so easy to write it. I wished she were at hand to advise me.

I arrived back in the late afternoon. Phillida was in the drawing-room, reading. She asked if I had had a good ride.

'Yes,' I said. 'I went as far as Bracken. I saw that post office Mrs Hellman told me about. You have to collect your letters there, you know.'

'Well, nobody knows our address, do they?'

'No. They should, though. I've been meaning to write to Celeste and to my sister. But I've put it off so far.'

'Plenty of time. Have you thought any more about the house?'

I had completely forgotten the house. How could I be interested in the purchase while such a decision hung over me? And that would apply to Roland, too.

'We ought to decide soon,' Phillida was saying. 'There seemed to be others going to look at it.'

'They might have said that to urge us on,' I pointed out.

'Possibly. But it is a beautiful house. I loved it.'

I said I was going up to change.

I did so and sat down to write a letter to Rebecca.

Dear Rebecca,

I am very unhappy. I wish you were here so that I could tell you about it. Joel is back. I should never have married Roland. Joel wants me to leave Roland and go to him. I want it too, Rebecca. I know there can never be anyone else for me but Joel. Yet what can I do? I have married Roland. It seems as though I used him when I needed some-one . . . and that is really the truth. It seemed right at the time. He has been so good to me. I have told him about Joel. He is very sad but he wants to do what is best for me. I don't know whether it means that he will let me go. He wants time to think. But just suppose he did let me go. Suppose he divorced

366

me. It is the only possible way. I suppose a divorced woman would not be too good for a rising politician. What can I do, Rebecca? It seems that whichever way I turn someone is going to be badly hurt . . .

I tore up the letter.

I could not possibly write to her in that way. It sounded almost incoherent. If only I could talk to her. Suppose I went down to Cornwall? I could explain to Roland how close we had always been, how she had always helped me over my difficulties.

Ideas whirled round and round in my head.

No, I must write to her.

Dear Rebecca,

I am at the above address. It is a house we have rented while we look round. Roland wants to buy a house in this neighbourhood. There is so much I want to tell you. I do wish you were here. Perhaps I could come down and see you. It must be soon.

Belinda is having a little difficulty, too, but her affairs are sorting themselves out. I'll tell you all about it when we meet. It may be that she will have everything settled by then.

Dear Rebecca, I *must* see you. It is difficult to write and explain. I shall be arriving at High Tor very soon. You said it would be all right for me to come at any time.

So please expect me. I need to talk to you.

Love to Pedrek and the children and to you as ever, dear sister,

Lucie.

I read it through. It was a strange letter. It sounded mysterious, so she would know something was very wrong.

I would tell Roland that I must go as soon as possible. Rebecca was level-headed and wise. Moreover, she had my interests at heart. I must go to her.

I sealed the letter and put it into a drawer. Tomorrow I would ride into Bracken and post it. I would talk to Roland tonight and tell him I was going to Cornwall.

Roland did not return until it was almost time for dinner, and there was no time for conversation until after we had retired for the night.

He looked pale and very unhappy. He regarded me sadly when I said: 'Roland, I want to go and see Rebecca.'

'To Cornwall!' he cried.

'Yes. You know she and I mean a lot to each other, as well as being half-sisters. I want to talk to her.'

He nodded.

'You do understand,' I went on. 'I feel if I talked to her . . . someone sympathetic . . . someone who understands me . . . it would help a lot.'

'Can't you talk to me? Can't we sort out our own affairs?'

'We become . . . too emotional. I feel so wretched. I hate to hurt you . . . and I can't hurt Joel. Rebecca is calm and understanding.'

'If you go away,' he said, 'you will never come back. Wait a little, Lucie. Don't make hasty decisions.'

There was a knock on the door. Phillida stood there with a tray, beaming at us.

'This will give you a good night's sleep,' she said. 'You look as if you need it, Roland.'

She set the tray down on the table, and as she did so I heard a sound below . . . as though someone was walking under the window.

I went over and looked out. I cried out in horror. He was there. He took off his hat and lifted his face to me, smiling that evil smile.

I cried out and Roland was at my side. Phillida had come to the other side of me. The figure below stood there, hat in hand, revealing his hair. Once again he gave that ironic bow. I watched, the familiar terror gripping me.

Roland had put an arm round me.

I cried out: 'There! Down there! You've seen it. You've both seen it now . . .'

Roland was shaking his head.

'Dear Lucie,' said Phillida. 'There's no one there.'

'What?' I cried. 'Look! Look! How can you say . . . ?'

Roland drew me forcibly from the window. He took my head in his hands and held it against his chest. I wriggled free.

'I am going down there to meet him,' I said.

'Lucie . . . Lucie . . .' Roland was talking soothingly. 'There is no one there.'

'I'm going down to see. I don't believe you didn't see him. *I* saw him. You must have seen him.'

'Oh dear,' said Phillida. She was looking at Roland. 'What are we going to do . . . about her?'

I felt a sudden rush of anger against them. 'There is something down there,' I said. 'I am going to see.'

'There is no one there.' Roland drew me to the window. The figure had disappeared.

'Who is it?' I cried.

'It's nothing, Lucie. It's just something you've got on your mind.'

'I wasn't thinking of it then.'

'But it was on your *mind*,' cried Phillida. 'It's not uncommon for this sort of thing to happen. People have hallucinations. You have suffered a terrible shock.'

I made an impatient gesture. I had heard all this before.

'You saw it,' I reiterated. '*I* saw it clearly. You must have seen it. You were looking straight at it, both of you.'

369

'There was nothing there,' repeated Phillida firmly. 'If there had been we should have seen it. You must believe us, Lucie.'

I sat on the bed helplessly. Roland sat beside me and, putting his arm round me, stroked my hair.

'I think the best thing is a good night's sleep,' he said.

'Just the thing,' said Phillida. 'Here, drink your night-caps before they are cold.'

Obediently we did so.

'You both need a good night's sleep,' said Phillida. 'You'll feel better when you've had that.' She laid a hand on my arm. 'Don't worry, Lucie. These things happen sometimes. The thing is to forget them. We'll have all the fun and excitement of getting into the new house. That'll take your mind off it. It's what you need. You've been brooding. It isn't unusual, you know. It happens to people after terrible shocks. Sometimes it takes quite a long time to recover. I'll leave you now. Good night. Sleep well.'

She kissed me lightly and then did the same to Roland.

'See you in the morning.'

And then she went out.

When she had gone, Roland said: 'We won't talk any more tonight. You must get straight to bed and to sleep. Phillida's right. Sleep is what you need. You'll feel better in the morning.'

To sleep? To rest? Phillida's nightcap was not exactly efficacious. I lay still through the night. What did it mean? I asked myself. Why was I haunted by this vision? And both Roland and Phillida had been unable to see it. If it had been a real person they must have seen him. So he must be a ghost . . . the ghost of Fergus O'Neill, the man I had sent to the gallows.

I saw the dawn come and only then did I sleep.

I was awakened by the sound of wheels. I was startled.

It was very late. I saw by the clock that it was ten o'clock.

Roland had gone and I guessed that Phillida had given instructions that I should not be disturbed.

I wondered who was below. I went to the window. I could never approach it without a shudder, wondering what I should see below.

It was a dogcart and Mrs Hellman was alighting. The little girl Daisy was with her.

I heard Mrs Hellman's penetrating voice: 'Good morning, Miss Fitzgerald. Your sister-in-law said you would like some eggs.'

Phillida, charming and gracious as ever, was standing there.

'How good of you! The eggs were delicious. We'd love some more.'

'Is young Mrs Fitzgerald around?' asked Mrs Hellman.

'She's sleeping. She's not very well.'

'Oh dear. I hope it's nothing serious.'

'Well, we're worried, my brother and I. Yes, very worried.'

'Oh deary me!'

'Well,' said Phillida. 'She's – er – a little strange.'

'Oh?'

'She sees things. Visions. It's rather frightening, but we're hoping she'll get better.'

I felt sick. How dared she tell this – to a woman whom she had never met before!

Mrs Hellman had come closer to Phillida. 'Well, I would have said she was just a nice, normal young woman, just like everyone else.'

'It's only at times,' said Phillida.

'A little . . .' Mrs Hellman tapped her forehead.

'Would you like to come in?' asked Phillida.

'Well, that'll be nice. Daisy, come on.'

'I'm just on my way to Bracken.' Mrs Hellman was saying as they went in. 'I just thought I'd drop the eggs in on my way.'

I sat down. So that was what they thought of me! And Phillida had told Mrs Hellman, almost as though she were warning her. I was horrified.

I must be reasonable, I told myself. I had been hysterical last night. I had seen him so clearly, and they had been standing beside me and had not . . . both of them.

I stayed in my room all the morning.

At midday Phillida came in. She smiled at me tenderly.

'That's right,' she said. 'Roland and I both agreed that you needed a rest. How are you feeling now?'

'Better, thank you.'

'Good. I'll send Kitty up with a little light lunch on a tray. How's that?'

'Thank you. Then I think I'll get up.'

'Why not? If you feel like it. Kitty can bring up hot water.'

'Yes, I'll wash and then have the food.'

'That's a good idea. Have it quietly in your room and then, if you feel like it, perhaps a little walk would do you good.'

'Thank you, Phillida,' I said.

'It's our pleasure to look after you. To get you well.'

She stood smiling at me and I thought: How could you have said what you did about me – and to a stranger? But what had she said? Nothing but the truth. It was what she had implied. But then, I *had* seen visions . . .

'How would you fancy an omelette? I have some very fresh eggs. Your Mrs Hellman called this morning to bring some. A pity you weren't up. She asked after you.

What a talker she is! I suppose she doesn't get much opportunity to talk in that farmhouse.'

'I heard her,' I said.

'Oh? So you were awake. Well, I'll see about things. Hot water first. Kitty will bring it up at once.'

She smiled at me benignly and went out.

I was glad to be in my room for a time. I did not want to talk to Phillida. I might mention that I had heard what she said to Mrs Hellman.

I wanted desperately to see Rebecca, and had an impulse to ride into Bradford and get a train to London. I could go to Celeste for a night and then on to Cornwall.

But how could I do anything so melodramatic? I must talk to Roland tonight. I could tell him that I had made up my mind that I must go at once to see Rebecca. He would understand. He always did.

I thought then of the letter I had written to Rebecca. I went to the drawer. There it was. I could at least send it off. I would ride into Bracken this afternoon to the little post office.

I felt better now that I had decided to take some action.

The hot water came. I washed and Kitty arrived with the omelette. I was surprised that I felt hungry and was able to eat with relish.

I put on my riding habit and went downstairs.

Phillida was in her herbery. She came out, looking surprised when she saw me dressed for riding.

'Do you feel well enough?' she asked anxiously.

'Yes. I think it will do me good.'

'Not too far, then. Just a little amble round.'

I nodded as though in agreement. She came to the door and waved as I rode away.

I felt better. Why did I see these visions? It was because

others could stand beside me and see nothing that I was alarmed.

I longed to see Joel. Suppose I went to him? No, that was not the way. He would persuade me to stay and I could not hurt Roland that way. It was Rebecca I needed to see first. I needed my half-sister's cool common sense. I touched the letter in my pocket and wondered how long it would take to reach her. But I did not have to wait for a reply. I only had to appear at High Tor. They had always made me feel as though it were my home. If only she were near now!

But I was feeling better because I was taking some action. I would speak to Roland tonight and tell him I would leave tomorrow because I must see Rebecca.

I arrived in Bracken and went straight to the post office. I tethered my horse outside while I went in.

The shop was a typical village store. It sold most things necessary to ordinary household requirements. It catered for a small community but it had to be able to supply all necessities. There were cakes, biscuits, sugar, tea – all that a grocer would sell; there were clothes, boots, shoes, fruit, cough mixture and such remedies. And in a corner of the shop – the post office.

A thin, middle-aged woman was seated behind a kind of wire grille with a gap at the bottom. I bought a stamp for my letter. The shop was deserted and it was clear to me that she was inquisitive and wondering who I was. I supposed she was fully acquainted with most of the people who came in, and here was someone whom she had never seen before.

She said it was a fine day and asked if I had come far.

'Well, from Grey Stone House,' I said. 'Do you know it?'

'Reckon,' she said brightly.

I was not sure what that meant, but it soon became clear that she was not only aware of it, but knew that there were new people there and that they were looking round hoping to buy a house in the neighbourhood.

My thoughts immediately went to Mrs Hellman who, having the news, would have quickly imparted it to anyone she encountered. In a community like this where very little happened, newcomers were of the greatest interest.

'Well,' she said, 'it's a mercy you've come this morning. You're Mrs Fitzgerald – or are you Miss?'

'I'm Mrs Fitzgerald.'

'Well then, I was just on sending a message out to you. We don't deliver. Letters come here to the post office for people in outlying districts and they call in and collect.'

'I heard that from a neighbour. You have something for me?'

'That would be Mrs Hellman from Hellman's Farm. I was going to give it to her but she hasn't been in this morning.'

'What is it?' I asked urgently.

'Half a minute.' She opened a drawer. 'Here it is. Came yesterday. A letter for you.'

'Oh, thank you.' I glanced at the envelope. It was Belinda's handwriting. 'I . . . I'm so pleased.'

'Come in once or twice a week. We keep the mail for you. Happen you ought to have a number. Box they call it. Box 22. That could be yours. Tell them to send to Box 22, Post Office, Bracken, near Bradford. Got it? Then you come in as often as you like to collect.'

'I am so pleased I called.'

She smiled. I was longing to read Belinda's letter, but she went on: 'You see that one's sent to Mrs Fitzgerald, Grey Stone House, Bracken, Bradford. Well, that's all right because we know who you are. I knew you had come to

375

Grey Stone. But if you remember Box 22 it's best – though it wouldn't matter all that much.'

'You've been very helpful.'

'How are you getting on at Grey Stone?'

'Very well.'

'That's the ticket. It's a bit lonely up there.'

'Well, we don't expect to be there long. Thank you so much. I am so glad I called in.'

She was reluctant to let me go and I am sure she would have made a greater attempt to detain me if someone else had not come in at that moment.

Oh, Mrs Copland,' she cried. 'There you are – and how's that daughter-in-law of yours getting on?'

I did not stay to hear the condition of Mrs Copland's daughter-in-law, but came out on to the street clutching Belinda's letter.

Desperately I wanted to read it, but I could not do so there. I mounted my horse and rode out of Bracken. I found a field bordered by a few trees, so I alighted, tethered my horse to a fence and sat down under one of the trees to read.

Dear Lucie,

I am sending this in the hope that it will reach you. I hope I've got the address right. You did mention Grey Stone was the name of the house – remember? And I'm sure it was near a place called Bracken. So here goes.

Things are working out very well here. All is going smoothly, and as Henry is not raising any objection and it is a clear case of my being the sinner, we're hoping all will go well.

We are a bit afraid of the press, but Bobby's family have influence and they are working hard for us. It is this dear little infant who is making them all so eager – Bobby's family, I mean. They are all desperately anxious that he shall be born in wedlock. Though of course if we do just miss, it will all be suitably covered up, and Bobby and I will go through the ceremony – very quietly – as soon as it is over. So I am not worrying. I wish you could come here and stay. It would be great fun. It's really rather pleasant. I quite like being the lady of the manor. None of the people on the estate know that I have no right to the title and we are hoping to keep that little matter dark.

However, it is all rather thrilling and quite amusing – or it will be when it is all over.

Why do these people have to take so long?

Well, that's all about me. What of you? How are you getting on in Grey Stone? It sounds dreary. And how is dear Roland and his sister?

By the way, Joel came down to see us. He stayed a night. He wanted to talk to me – about you, of course. He asked if I knew where you were. I gave him the address I'm putting on this letter. He asked if I was writing to you and he wanted me to tell you something specially. That's why I'm writing to you now.

He said, 'Could you write and tell Lucie that I'm working on things?' He said something about its being wrapped up in mystery and he was going to get to the bottom of it. One thing I have to make sure to tell you is this: here is the message: Fergus O'Neill had a brother . . .

I stopped reading. A brother! Did that mean that the brother was pretending to be him? Were they alike? Did they both have that widow's peak? Then could it possibly

377

be that the brother had decided to haunt me? How could that be? Both Roland and Phillida had been standing beside me and had not seen him.

And Joel had discovered this. I felt suddenly much happier. He was working for me. It was a wonderful feeling of relief.

If I could only see Joel!

I turned back to the letter.

Joel said that the brother was as deeply involved as Fergus. He said they were all working for what they called 'the cause'. Joel is delving into things and there are one or two points he can't be quite clear about as yet. As soon as he has found what he wants he is coming to you. In the meantime he said – and he stressed this – you must take the utmost care. He would like you to get back to London. He was very serious. He is a most attractive man. If I weren't so devoted to Bobby . . .

Well, enough of that.

Dear Lucie, do come and see me. I don't like to think of you all those miles away.

I do hope this reaches you. Anyway, why haven't you written to me? Then you could give me the proper address. When you do, I shall pass it on to Joel! I can't understand why you haven't written.

Love from Belinda – and Bobby, and that one who will soon be making his august entry into the world.

I smiled and read the letter again. Joel was thinking of me. Probing, he said. How I longed to be with him!

I was glad I had posted my letter. I was feeling considerably better. What a good impulse it was that had led me into Bracken this afternoon. The letter would of course have come into my hands eventually; but it was just what I needed this day.

Back to Reality

I settled my horse in the stable and went into the house. I called to tell Phillida that I was back, but there was no answer. Apparently she had gone out, and I thought I would ask Kitty to make me a cup of tea.

I went into the kitchen. Kitty was sitting on a chair dozing. I did not wake her.

I was not sure that I wanted to tell Roland and Phillida that I had received a letter from Belinda and discovered that Fergus O'Neill had a brother. It would bring up the subject of the vision. Nor did I want to mention that the information had come through Joel by way of Belinda. But I usually had a cup of tea with Phillida at this time, and the thought suddenly occurred to me that she might be in the herbery, for she spent a lot of time there preparing her herbs.

I went to it and knocked at the door. There was no answer so I opened it and looked in.

I had been in this room very rarely. Roland referred to it as Phillida's sanctum.

I was immediately aware of the overpowering aroma of herbs. I advanced a few paces. Bunches of herbs were hanging from a hook on the wall. She was dedicated to the study of them. I suppose it was an interesting subject. There was a desk with a blotter on it and lying close to the blotter was a bunch of what looked like dried sunflowers.

My attention was immediately caught by the markings on the blotter because they reminded me of my own name, but looking rather odd because it was backwards. I looked closer. Of course that was how it would come out if blotted. It was as though someone had written my name and blotted it while it was very wet.

Could Phillida have been writing something about me?

My curiosity was aroused. I examined the blotter more closely. There was other writing which I could not decipher, and my own name was below this as it would be had I signed a letter. I was amazed really because what I was looking at was remarkably like my own handwriting.

I felt an urgency to discover what this meant. My senses were suddenly alert. Was it due to the fact that I had heard this afternoon that Fergus O'Neill had a brother and there was a possibility that he might look rather like him and it was he who was playing tricks on me? I had had to abandon that theory because neither Roland nor Phillida had seen him when I had thought he stood below.

But what was Phillida writing about me? I had felt afraid since I had heard her speaking to Mrs Hellman about me. It had shocked me deeply. I knew that she and Roland thought I was hysterical and I understood why, but I had been disagreeably surprised that she should betray this to Mrs Hellman who was a stranger.

I had an irresistible curiosity to discover more and that forced me to act in a way which I should previously have hesitated to do.

I opened a drawer and looked in it. There were some papers, a pen and a bottle of ink. I looked at the papers on top. They were all blank. I opened another drawer and saw a book about good health and the cultivation of herbs.

Underneath the book were other papers with some wording on them. They were written in that handwriting rather similar to my own. The dreadful thought occurred to me that Phillida had copied my handwriting. There it was . . . the manner in which I made a sort of curly start to a capital letter and left the tails of my 'g's unfinished.

I seized on one piece of paper. Horrified I read:

> Dear Roland,
> Forgive me. I know I am going mad. I have tried to fight against it, but it is no use. Thank you for everything. You have been a good husband to me and Phillida a good friend. But I cannot bear it any more. You know, as I do, that it is getting worse. I am sure this is the best way out for us all.
>
> Lucie.

It was the note of someone contemplating suicide. It was growing alarmingly clear what was happening. Phillida was planning to kill me and make it appear that I had taken my own life.

Terrible suspicions were crowding into my mind. I looked about me. What other secrets were in this room?

I went to the door and locked it from the inside. I was going to find out. It was imperative that I did.

Feverishly I opened all the drawers. There was nothing. There was a chest in one corner of the room. It was locked. I hunted for a key and found one in a drawer of the desk. I had noticed it when I was searching for the papers.

It fitted. I opened the chest and looked inside. There were clothes in there, Phillida's clothes. I turned them over and then I saw what I had been subconsciously looking for: it was an opera hat and a cloak and with it a dark wig, the hair of which came to a widow's peak.

Phillida! I thought. Phillida!

And Roland? What did he know of this? It was mysterious and very frightening.

There had been times when Phillida had been with me when I saw the vision. Could Roland have done this? There had been another time when they were both with me . . . together. Who, then?

I could not believe this of Roland, who had always been so loving and tender.

While I stood there I heard someone arriving at the house. Phillida was coming back. She must not find me in this room. I took the garments, the wig and the suicide note, unlocked the door and ran up the stairs. I reached the top just as Phillida, with Roland, was coming into the house.

I had to get away . . . at once. I would take the horse and ride into Bradford and get the next train to London.

I must tell neither of them. It was imperative that I get out of this house immediately. I hid the incriminating garments with the wig in the walk-in cupboard. The suicide note I put into my pocket.

I listened for sounds from below, but I could only hear the beating of my heart.

How was I going to get away? If only they would go out again.

Then I heard their voices. I must try to behave as though nothing had happened and be ready at the earliest moment to get away.

I could not believe that Roland knew of this. Yet he had stood beside me and looked down at whoever was wearing those clothes and he had said he could see nothing.

The only other person in the house was Kitty.

Could it possibly be that Kitty was the one? It must be Kitty. Could it be that Roland and Phillida did not know? Would Kitty have written that note? Would she have put it in Phillida's drawer? Perhaps she had been disturbed suddenly.

But the fact remained that both Roland and Phillida had declared they had seen nothing of the figure in cloak and wig. Both had treated me as though I were a little deranged.

It was all too mysterious. Whatever I thought, one thing was clear. I must leave this place without delay.

Roland and Phillida were still downstairs. I could hear their voices.

Then Roland came into the room.

'Lucie . . . my dearest . . . what is it?'

'I'm going to see Rebecca,' I told him.

'Not today, surely?'

'I think it best.'

'What's happened? You look shaken.'

I said: 'I am shaken. Something has happened.'

'What is it? Lucie dear, please tell me.'

'I have heard from Belinda.'

'How did she know where to reach you?'

'I had mentioned the place. The letter was at the post office. It was given to me when I went in there.'

'From Belinda . . .' he said.

'Yes.' I blurted out: 'Fergus O'Neill has a brother.'

I could not interpret the expression on his face. He said quietly: 'How did you find out?'

'Joel discovered it. He would be able to, you know. In his position he would have special means of doing so. There is something else . . .' I could not stop once I had started, and try as I might, I could not believe evil of Roland. I went to the cupboard and brought out the hat, cloak and wig. I laid them on the bed.

'There,' I said. 'What do you think of that?'

He stared at them in horror and for some seconds was speechless. Then he stammered: 'Where?'

'In Phillida's herbery. In a chest. And I found this too. It

384

is a note to you supposed to have been written by me. It tells why I killed myself.'

'Oh my God!' he said. Then he turned to me: 'Lucie, we've got to get out of this house. There's not a moment to lose. We must go at once – quietly. We'll take the horses, go to the station, take the first train. Let's hope it's to London. But we must get away – quickly.'

I have never seen such misery in any face as I saw then in his. I thought: It is Phillida . . . and he knows.

'Come,' he said. 'Don't waste time. Oh my God, what can I do?'

He was looking for money. He found some in a drawer and stuffed it into his pocket. 'There's not a minute to lose,' he murmured.

He opened the door and looked out. Then he turned to me.

'Come,' he said urgently, and quietly we went down the stairs. We reached the door which he opened quietly and we were speeding to the stables.

We were breathless as we saddled the horses, but as we did so I heard a sound. The stable door opened and Phillida stood there. She glanced towards us; I saw the venom in her face. She was a different person from the Phillida I had hitherto known. A fleeting image of the black swan which I had encountered on Jean Pascal's estate flashed into my mind. So elegant . . . so graceful . . . and then the sudden change to hatred.

Jean Pascal had said: 'There are people like that. You must beware of them.'

I saw with horror that she held a gun. Roland had seen it too. I heard his gasp of fear and horror.

She was looking at him. 'You coward!' she cried. 'You traitor! You should have done it months ago.' The invective flowed from her; she could not contain her contempt. I listened in dismay. 'Your fancy ideas. They were going to be the best way. It is just because you wanted to keep her alive. Roland, how could you! You have betrayed us all.'

Roland did not speak. He put an arm round me . . . protectively.

'Well, the plans have changed, brother,' went on Phillida. 'We'll do it differently. We have to think of another solution. She did it here – in the stables. That'll do. In the stables. Why not?'

She came closer.

I knew she was going to kill me. She was going to leave the note in my bedroom. I had it in the pocket of my coat. Perhaps she would not think to look there. She would think it was still in the drawer in her room. That would not matter. She would write another. The note would explain my growing fear of insanity. I had had visions. I had told Rebecca of this. Joel, Rebecca . . . you will believe it. It sounds so plausible. They will destroy the wig and the clothes; they will produce the note. The people in that house and Mrs Hellman, they will say they were warned of my obsessions. Phillida had planned every detail. I wondered why. And Roland . . . He was my husband whatever else he was.

I would never know because I was going to die.

She was coming closer, holding the gun. It had to be near, as my death must pass as suicide. I believed there were means of testing these things.

Now . . . at any moment. Her hand was on the trigger. Then Roland made a sudden movement and thrust himself in front of me. I heard the two shots. Roland and I fell to the ground. I was aware of warm blood on my face . . . and then of nothing more.

*

386

I seemed to be emerging from waves of mist. I heard a voice say: 'The lady's not seriously hurt. It's in the shoulder, I think.'

I was in the stable. I saw the light from lanterns.

'Better get them to the hospital, both of them.'

'I heard the shots and came straight over, me and my cowman,' said a man's voice. 'Hellman's Farm, that's me. Thought it was thieves or something.'

I did not remember any more until I woke up in the hospital and learned that it was next morning.

A nurse came into my room. I said: 'Roland . . . Mr Fitzgerald?'

'He's here. He's having attention.'

'He's not . . . ?'

She hesitated. 'He's having great care.'

What did it all mean? Why did Phillida want to kill him? I was beginning to realize that I had been in the centre of a conspiracy, completely unaware of all the dangers around me. And Roland had been involved.

During the morning a doctor came to see me.

'You were lucky,' he said, looking at me benignly. 'The bullet glanced off. It's just grazed you, really. You'll be all right in a week or so.'

I said: 'And Mr Fitzgerald?'

He said: 'We're looking after him.'

'You think . . . ?'

'We'll do our best,' he added vaguely yet meaningfully. Then I knew that Roland was very badly hurt. He had taken the bullet which had been meant for me.

They came in later and asked me whom they could notify.

I gave them Celeste's address, Rebecca's and Belinda's . . . then I added Joel's.

I thought: They will come to me. And I felt a certain peace.

In the late afternoon the sister came and sat by my bedside.

She said: 'It's your husband. He's asking for you.'

I tried to get out of bed, but she restrained me. 'No, no. Don't try to stand. We'll take you to him. He—er—is very ill.'

'Is he dying?' I asked.

'He's not really in a state to see you. But he is very agitated and Doctor thinks that in the circumstances it might be best.'

'Then please take me to him at once.'

They wheeled me into the small room where he lay. He looked quite unlike himself.

'Roland . . .' I said.

He opened his eyes and I saw the joy in them.

I looked appealingly at the nurse and she said: 'I'll leave you. Only a few minutes, mind.'

'Thank you,' I said.

'Lucie . . .' Roland was smiling at me. 'Dear Lucie . . . you came.'

'Of course I came.'

'There's not long for me,' he murmured.

I did not answer. I took his hand which was lying limply on the coverlet and pressed it.

He smiled. 'You see, I love you,' he said. 'I . . . I couldn't do it.'

'Don't talk if it's painful, Roland.'

'I have to. You must know. I'm the brother of Fergus O'Neill.'

'You! Then Phillida is his sister.'

'It was for the cause . . . freedom for our country. We all believed it was right. We'd all worked for it . . . my father . . . the whole family.'

'Your father was dead. You told me so. He and your mother died together in the railway accident.'

'No . . . no. He is one of the leaders of our cause. We, his

388

children, have always been brought up to work for it. We intended to kill you when Fergus was hanged. Revenge, you see, and to show the world that our heroes are not to be treated as common criminals. They are martyrs and must be avenged. Then we thought of this other plan. You were rich. I would marry you and then stage your suicide. The money which I would inherit would come to us . . . to the cause. It seemed amusing to them that the money of our enemies should be used to support our cause. It would be used to bring about the extermination of other enemies.'

'It can't be . . .'

'You don't understand, Lucie. We are dedicated, all of us. And I was until . . . It will not be the last time . . . except for me. We wanted the money.' He smiled wryly. 'It's an expensive operation to run. Trips to France, houses in the country. When we found that the money could not come to us because it was tied up in some trust we had to change the plan. We were going to kill you at once. You remember the fire. Phillida was good with her herbs. Her nightcaps were used so that, if she wanted to send you into a deep sleep at any time, she could do so and it would all seem quite natural. At other times they were quite harmless.'

My thoughts went back to that night when Belinda had drunk the draught prepared for me. If she had not, of course, I should not have awakened in time to save myself. I murmured: 'Belinda saved my life.'

'Yes. If she had not taken the nightcap you would have been in a deep sleep and would not have awakened until it was too late to save yourself. I was not to be in the house. We had arranged that. I think it was then that I began to realize how much I loved you. When I saw you in London, expecting you to be dead, I was so happy, so overjoyed. I realized then what you meant to me.'

I was living it all again, seeing Belinda sleeping deeply throughout that night.

I said slowly: 'So there was never any connection with the wool trade in Bradford?'

'It was the background we had set up. I was to marry you, make sure that I would be in possession of your fortune, and then we were going to kill you. It could not be a straightforward execution. That would have been too dangerous for us. We had to stage a suicide. With a victim so close it was taking a great risk. We had to plan very carefully. We knew you were going to France through the maid with whom one of our workers had become friendly. It was easy to get the information out of her.'

I remembered then. Amy, I believe was her name. And there was the man Jack who had 'delivered documents'. How meticulously they had laid their plans!

Roland went on, his voice becoming a little slurred: 'The police in England are aware of our family . . . the O'Neills, not the Fitzgeralds. Phillida did most of the ghosting. She was very good at it. I did it once, Lucie. I am ashamed to tell you. Kitty did the last one. She is one of us, of course. I hated doing it, Lucie. But I had to do it. It was the plan.'

'It is all becoming clear to me now,' I said.

'We could not have done it that way if it had not been for Joel Greenham's disappearance and reported death. If you had refused to marry me we should have had to make other plans . . . but the thought of getting our hands on all the money seemed an opportunity not to be missed.'

'It seems incredible.'

'If you knew more of our organization you would realize that things which seem incredible are a matter of course. Phillida has always been more dedicated than I, and she was very close to Fergus. He was our father's favourite, too. He was the adventurous one. He loved what he was doing for its own sake as well as the cause. He brought a touch of melodrama into it. Phillida is like that, too. I was different. In a way they despised me. They will more than ever now.'

'You did this,' I said. 'You made all these plans . . . and yet at the end you saved my life.'

He said simply: 'Yes . . . but you see, I grew to love you, and that was more important to me than anything else.'

I sat very still. My throat was constricted so that for a moment I could not speak. At length I said: 'Roland . . . what will happen now?'

'To me?' he said. 'I am going to die.'

'They are caring for you here, doing everything they can to save you.'

He shook his head. 'What could they save me for? It is better so.'

He lay back. His eyes were closed and there was a blue tinge about his mouth. I realized then what a great effort he had made to talk to me.

I sat watching him, thinking: He has given his life for me. He, the terrorist, who had planned to murder me in a most devious way, has saved me . . . with his own life. And all for love.

His lips were moving. His speech was slurred. It had been such a strain for him to talk but he had wanted to explain to me. He had not wanted me to discover through other means. And . . . he had wanted me to know how much he had cared for me.

What a strange life he must have had! He had given me a glimpse of his forceful family. His father, the stern revolutionary . . . and Phillida who was made in the same mould.

She was a complex creature. She had appeared to be so kind to me, so friendly, always merry, a little insouciant,

391

loving life. But how different she was in truth: setting herself a purpose, never diverging from it. I was to be her victim, and all the time she was professing affection she was planning to murder me.

When I thought of her now I remembered the black swan on the peaceful lake, and the sudden realization that he was waiting for me to come near to the lake before he attacked me. I had come too close to Phillida and she had marked me down for destruction.

The nurse had come in. She took one look at Roland and I understood that she was aware at once that talking to me had been too much for him.

I was hurriedly wheeled away and the doctors were coming in.

Roland died that night.

I spent only a week in the hospital in Bradford and a great deal happened during that time.

My whole life had changed.

It is a sobering experience to come close to death and to know that you owe your life to another person who had lost his own in saving yours.

For some time that thought was uppermost in my mind and I knew that there would be incidents in my life with Roland which I should never forget.

I had been fond of him; I had been fond of Phillida. She was a magnificent actress. I was thinking of her now as The Black Swan.

And Roland? It was hard to believe that in those early days he had been in the plot to murder me. How easily deceived I had been!

I lay in my hospital bed and conjured up images of what must have happened that night. Later I was able to verify that much of what I thought had taken place actually had. Perhaps it was logical that, being so close to it, I could see clearly what was inevitable.

When Phillida had seen Roland and me lying on the floor of the stable, covered in blood, her story must be that I, verging on insanity, had shot my husband and then myself. She must have been very shaken because she had killed her brother. I do not know if she ever really cared for any person. People who serve causes with such dedication rarely bestow great affection on individuals. This was, however, her brother. They had worked closely together. Perhaps she had some regard for him. But in her eyes he would have seemed a traitor. He had brought their scheme to an ignoble end. He had failed the cause – and all because he had fallen in love with me. I understood how a person such as she was would feel. Roland had failed her, himself and the cause. He had allowed his personal feelings to get the better of his duty.

But to see him lying there dead, or on the point of death, must have shocked her considerably. Otherwise she would not have been so careless. She put the gun in my hand but did not make sure that I was dead. I must have looked as though I were, with the blood all over me. It would have been unnerving because events had gone so differently from what had been planned.

A new suicide note was needed and that would have been her first concern – for how was she to know that it was in my pocket? It was not easy for her to produce the writing exactly like mine and she would obviously have to make several attempts.

It must have been while she was doing this that Mr Hellman and his cowman arrived.

The cowman was immediately sent off to get help. Thus a policeman and a doctor arrived from Bracken before

Phillida had a chance to set the stage. They discovered Phillida's notes – several of them, because she had not found it easy to imitate my handwriting. They also found the opera cloak and hat with the wig in my bedroom.

Then she learned that I was not dead as she had carelessly thought. In a short time I should be able to give my version; and it would not take long for it to be discovered that Phillida Fitzgerald was in fact Deirdre O'Neill, who in her own name was not unknown to the authorities; and there was the damning link with Fergus, the murderer of my father.

She had failed – after all the elaborate planning of months. She had killed her brother instead of me; and it could only be a matter of hours before she was arrested.

Her next action was typical of her. It may well have been that she had always known that in the kind of life she led it might have been necessary at some time to take such an action.

She did the only thing that would have seemed possible to her. She took the gun and shot herself.

There followed the headlines. Everything was revived and we had to live through it all again. But it was a small price to pay for release. I was not seeing visions. I was not going mad. I was safe and this was the end of the nightmare which had begun when I had sat waiting for my father, and had looked out of the window and seen Fergus O'Neill waiting for the opportunity to kill him.

A week after Roland's death I came out of the Bradford hospital and was taken to London with Joel, Rebecca and Celeste.

Rebecca said: 'As soon as you are well enough, I am going to take you to Cornwall. The quiet and peace of High Tor is what you need.'

I wanted to be with her. I wanted to tell her about

Roland who had started by planning to murder me and had ended by saving my life.

I thought of him often . . . of the many kindnesses, the loving care he had given me. I believed he had truly loved me. Poor Roland, he had not been a strong man. He had been born into a family which lived by the gun. He had been brought up to hate; and such a man had made the supreme sacrifice for love.

It was wonderful to be in Cornwall. Rebecca took me back with her, and there was a very warm welcome for me from Pedrek and the children.

I loved the peace of the place which struck me afresh every morning when I awakened. There were, of course, times when I took a fearful look out of the window; then I would remind myself of the hat, the cloak and the wig as I had seen them lying on the bed in that room at Grey Stone House. The dreams came too . . . now and then; although even in those dreams the knowledge that that phase of my life was over was becoming more frequent.

Joel came down to Cornwall. We rode together. We went to Branok Pool and there I would think of Jenny Stubbs who – as Roland had – gave her life for mine. How strange that there should have been two people in my life who cared for me enough to do that.

Joel knew this spot and of its special significance for me.

He said to me as we stood there, looking over that eerie pool: 'When I came back from Buganda we were to announce our engagement. Do you remember?'

Of course I remembered.

'Hasn't there been too much delay?'

And I agreed that there had been.

*

395

A year after that terrible experience in the stables, Joel and I were married. It was a quiet wedding which was what we both wanted.

Belinda was present – safely married to Bobby now – and both immensely proud of their son and heir, young Robert.

I am deeply happy. I am putting the past right behind me, though there are still times when I dream of the black swan gliding so gracefully across the lake. Then he comes towards me and steps ashore, changed into a figure in an opera cloak and hat – and he takes off the hat and bows.

I awake in fear. But Joel is beside me. He takes me into his arms and says: 'It's all right, my love. I'm here, Lucie. There is nothing to fear any more.'

And I can laugh at my folly, for I know, as time passes, the reality of the present will overcome the nightmare of the past and I shall cease to dream of the Black Swan.

Web of Dreams
Virginia Andrews

GHOSTS FROM THE SHADOWS OF THE PAST

On their return to Farthinggale Manor, the mystery-shrouded luxury home of the Tatterton family, Annie and Luke believe that they will be putting the past finally to rest, and bringing peace to the spirit of Annie's mother, Heaven.

But Annie discovers a diary at Farthinggale – 'Leigh's Book'. There she finds the story of her grandmother Leigh, and of her great-grandparents. Born into the privileged life of Boston's wealthy classes, Leigh hopes for happiness in her life. Her dreams are shattered, however, when, at the age of twelve, her adored parents divorce, and her mother Jillian marries Tony Tatterton. The awful shadow cast by the Tatterton family over the lives of the next three generations begins to spread.

Virginia Andrews' bestselling Casteel Family saga
**HEAVEN ● DARK ANGEL ● FALLEN HEARTS
GATES OF PARADISE ● WEB OF DREAMS**
All available in Fontana

FONTANA

Fontana Fiction

Fontana is a leading paperback publisher of fiction.
Below are some recent titles.

- ☐ KRYSALIS John Trenhaile £3.99
- ☐ PRINCES OF SANDASTRE Antony Swithin £2.99
- ☐ NIGHT WATCH Alastair MacNeill £3.50
- ☐ THE MINOTAUR Stephen Coonts £4.50
- ☐ THE QUEEN'S SECRET Jean Plaidy £3.99
- ☐ THE LEMON TREE Helen Forrester £3.99
- ☐ THE THIRTEEN-GUN SALUTE Patrick O'Brian £3.50
- ☐ STONE CITY Mitchell Smith £4.50
- ☐ ONLY YESTERDAY Syrell Leahy £2.99
- ☐ SHARPE'S WATERLOO Bernard Cornwell £3.50
- ☐ BLOOD BROTHER Brian Morrison £3.50
- ☐ THE BROW OF THE GALLOWGATE Doris Davidson £3.50

You can buy Fontana paperbacks at your local bookshop or newsagent. Or you can order them from Fontana, Cash Sales Department, Box 29, Douglas, Isle of Man. Please send a cheque, postal or money order (not currency) worth the purchase price plus 22p per book for postage (maximum postage required is £3.00 for orders within the UK).

NAME (Block letters)_____

ADDRESS_____

_____